Conscription- Carnival Series Book One

by C.J. Milnes

This story is dedicated to my daughter and my dad.

Copyright 2024 C.J. Milnes

Chapter 1 - A routine is a routine for a reason

System initialising...

"People of Earth, your planet has been scheduled for assimilation by the Void Imperium in the near future. The Illuminated Alliance has chosen to intervene and provide you with a fighting chance. We are not able to intervene directly at this time and wouldn't even if we could. You must earn your place in the worlds to come. However we will help you help yourselves. This will not be easy on you, without struggle, without sacrifice nothing worthwhile can be achieved.

The time is now 06:00 local time. Your movements will be restricted initially, each village, town and city is encapsulated in an impregnable barrier and you cannot leave your starting area until the end of the recruitment process. Communications technology has been limited. All citizen soldier recruits of sufficient age will receive one Essence as a gift and have an ability unlocked automatically. Learn to use your new powers swiftly and learn to use them well. They are all that now stands between you and oblivion.

The recruitment process will involve a winnowing of your species. There will be three attacks on each settlement, chosen by lottery, your task is to adopt, adapt and survive. Those of you who emerge from the crucible will be reforged and ready to remake your world into a valuable member of the Alliance. The first wave will begin at 09:00. At 08:45 the details of the wave will be announced.

Good luck.

The Light shines

Well, that's a first, thought John. He had been woken up in some fairly strange ways over the course of his life. The dog deciding to try and confirm if she prefers the taste of his earwax over her own and taking advantage of his sleep-slowed reactions to get a suitable sample was ill advised.

Then there are nicer ways to wake up. Waking up gently as the autumn sunlight falls through the curtains on a weekend safe in the knowledge you don't have to get up yet, a lover's embrace or a small child bouncing up and down because it's Christmas and you *will* get out of bed and open presents at half past five in the morning *whether you like it or not*.

John rolled over, dislodging the dog who had been using his legs as a pillow as usual and reached for his phone. He glanced around his room as his arm stretched out. *Still a mess,* he thought. His dumb bells were mostly covered with dirty laundry, it had been a few days since he'd felt the urge to pretend to exercise.

The phone showed 06:01 but had no wifi or data service available. He clicked on messenger and whatsapp, trying to send messages to family members, he tried to make a call but nothing connected or went through. He felt like this should worry him more but found he was strangely unmoved by the situation. He put the phone down and laid back on the pillows.

He felt a sort of numb contentment, not the rising panic you would think a man with glowing golden letters in his face telling him his world was about to be invaded should feel. He clicked on the browser... "Unable to access the network" - the net was down. He reached for his tobacco and laid back. He began rolling a cigarette. *A routine is a routine for a reason.*

"Kid, are you awake? Are you seeing this as well" he called out to his daughter, Evie.
"Dad it's the holidays, I'm not getting up for..." she began groggily. "What the hell! Wow! Are you seeing this?" she finished with the panic of a preteen being cut off from the internet. The thumps and bangs of her hurriedly climbing down from her bed echoed through the house. It seemed it took glowing letters and the promise of magic powers to make Evie even vaguely a morning person.
"Yes I am, that's why I asked you if you could see it," he called back. "Clear", "Delete", "Minimise", "Get Rid", "Sod off!". He muttered trying to remove the notification from his vision as he swiped at the writing with one hand. He was wondering how he would manage with a wall of text floating in front of his eyes for the rest of his life when it vanished and a new screen appeared.

"You have received one Essence and automatically advanced to level 1. Say or think status to review your information"

"It says I'm too young to receive an Essence! This is crap dad, I am *not* an NPC!" a now enraged eleven year old yelled. She stumbled into John's room putting on the oversized hoodie she used in place of a dressing gown and glowering at the world like it owed her money.
"Language child! Uh, status?" said John.

Level: 1
Name: John Borrows
Ability: Teleportation
Constitution: 100%
Reserves: 100

Ability: Teleportation: A shut in who hates to travel. You've barely left your house for years and now you can go wherever you like with a thought. Have fun with that.
Guidelines:
Maximum weight: 100kg
Maximum Distance: 1km
Line of sight required
Modifications: none

John sat dumbfounded. If this worked it was going to make putting the bins out a doddle. *Well, at least it's a useful power* he thought to himself. A grin slowly spread across his face as he stared at the text before him. He dismissed the notification. As usual their dog, Zeeg, immediately crawled out from under the duvet as Evie sat down on the edge of the bed, the dog stretched like she should have been born a cat and moved to Evie.

Her tail was wagging like a whip and she wanted her morning scratches. Evie's heart was clearly not in it, more concerned at being robbed out of becoming a superhero. Or losing access to the internet. *Could have been both*, John supposed. Evie patted Zeeg twice on the head and immediately broke into an angry tirade.

"I haven't got an ability! I can see the message but when I think "status" all I get is "You are underage, try again when you are sixteen," she threw her hands in the air, "what the hell is all this Dad!"

She is not taking this well, thought John with his usual deep incisiveness, and it's a shame because I could use a gamers mind to help make sense of all this.

"I'm sorry but I don't understand what's happening kiddo," he said with a gentle smile as Evie tried to settle the pup down. John concentrated on his dressing gown hanging on the door and felt his mind catch on to it and *twist* in a very unsettling way, then his dressing gown fell onto his head.

"What did you just do?" asked Evie in an awed voice continuing her half hearted attempts to give Zeeg the necessary attention required before she would calm down.

"Teleportation kiddo! I got teleportation for my "ability". I'm not sure this system has been very well thought out," he finished in a more thoughtful voice,

"Because you dropped it on your head?" she asked, giving him the look daughters reserve for their fathers when they know the father in question has made a mistake and is faking infallibility.

"It wasn't bad for a first try, thank you very much! But no that isn't what I meant, Youngling." he mumbled scratching his head after removing his new head wear. He checked his status, just bringing up his Constitution and Reserves and found his reserves were showing at 98.

"Does it give you any other information? Ability, constitution and reserves?" John asked her.

"It just says You Are Underage. Lamest system apocalypse ever dude." she sat down in what promised to grow into an epic huff and crossed her arms with a frown.

The dog was now getting more and more excitable, Evie had stopped fussing with her, weighed down by her disappointment at not getting a power. When Zeeg started getting worked up she kept going until something settled her down so John called her over and began giving her a fuss to try and let Evie have some space for a minute.

"C'mon puppy, who's a good girl? Tummy rubs?" The dog jumped next to him on the bed and rolled over for the tummy rubs, tail still wagging frantically.

"You'd like super powers too wouldn't you? Yes you would," John said in the soppy voice humans insist on using when talking to animals and spoiled children, "you'd get super powers and then I'd invite you to my team and you'd be the super dog in the group. Would you like to join my team, Zeeg?"

For discovering the Team function before the start of the first wave you are rewarded one Essence. Would you like to use one Essence on Dog: Zeeg Borrows to awaken her ability and invite her to your team? Y/N

"Oh , OK!" John thought about it for a moment, concluded Evie would literally kill him if he gave the dog magic before her, then said "No"
"Invite Evie to Team" he declared with a hint of smugness in his voice.
"What are you doing dad? I'm a bloody NPC you can't..." she replied grumpily.

Would you like to use one Essence on Human: Evie Borrows to awaken her ability and invite her to your team? Y/N
Donating Essence to juveniles is not recommended.

"Yes"

You have gifted one Essence to Evie Borrows and she has joined your team. Initialising advancement to level 1 for Evie Borrows. Calculating...
Complete.
Level 1

Name: Evie Borrows
Ability: Electrogenesis
Constitution: 100%
Reserves: 100
Ability: Electrogenesis: You hate physics and maths so here's a power that will be more useful the better your understanding of physics and maths. You can create and control electricity. Good luck!
Guidelines:
Maximum Discharge: 240V
Line of sight required.

An almost ultrasonic scream of joy erupted from Evie. She jumped up and down on John's bed, launching the dog to the floor in the process and yelling extremely unladylike things. After about thirty seconds she calmed down enough to throw herself at John in a cross between a flying rugby tackle and a hug.

"Thank you, thank you, thank you! No more NPC Evie! This is going to be so cool. So I can Zap stuff now?" she asked smiling like a lunatic. John was knocked off balance and had to spin around to bleed off the momentum.

"No worries Ginger; as to the zapping we'll have to find out. but not in the house!" he chuckled, "the phones aren't working and the net is down but the power is still up... I'm going to have a smoke and get us some breakfast. Then we can see what we can do to prepare for this first wave".

"It'll be a cake walk dude, now that I'm Electro Girl! Nah that's terrible. I'm the Great Zap! Lightning Bolt? Also bad, sounds too much like an animated sled dog. Picking a character name is always the hardest part isn't it?"

"How about Spark Plug? " She scowled and shook her head in response. "Let's eat while we figure it out." John said firmly with a grin. Picking a character name in a game was always the longest part of character creation for anyone with any class.

They went downstairs into the kitchen/dining room. The dining part of this room was largely occupied with a two tier planter by the window to take advantage of the south facing aspect and the room had ended up cluttered with random bits and bobs. They never ate there. They were very much an "eat on your knees in front of the tele" kind of family.

John went into the kitchen and moved some rubbish and unwashed pots out of the way, thinking to himself that cleaning up will be a lot easier now he could teleport stuff with his mighty brain powers... He looked at the chopping board, still greasy from the garlic bread he had cut on it yesterday to go with their dinner and *twisted* space and time. It appeared in the sink with a blip and a splash. *Neat but need to work on the landing*, he thought. Evie had gone through into the living room and judging from the intermittent pops and crackles was probably going to start a house fire, blow all the fuses or both.

Once the bacon was cooking he had a thought. Why not see what his ability could do? He teleported four slices of bread onto a fresh chopping board, opened the cutlery drawer and teleported a knife to the board then opened the fridge and teleported the butter to the board. He checked his reserves and saw he was down to 94. Two reserves per use. So fifty uses from a full charge? How fast does it recover? He looked out the window and saw the two large thirty litre bags of compost he hadn't put on the vegetable patch yet, checked his reserves, *still at 94*, then teleported them to the end of the garden, about five metres.

His reserves dropped to 84. "Interesting, so the rate is variable depending on the weight maybe?" he muttered before turning his attention back to making bacon sandwiches. He got out his phone and started a timer, keeping an eye on his reserves while putting breakfast together. He put the kettle on for a coffee and grabbed an orange juice for Evie.

"Here you go, Sausage," he said handing the plate with the sandwich to her. He then went back to the door so he could see the glass of OJ he left on the side and teleported it next to her plate. John moved to his seat and sat down with a smirk. He started eating while waiting for the kettle to boil.

"Show off" she mumbled around a mouthful. "Check this out" she proceeded to make sparks flash between the outstretched fingers of one hand. "I guess I'm not going to see Mum today then? It was meant to be a girly day as well!" Evie had lived with John since she was four due to what might be called "some unpleasantness" so these days she saw her mum for visits every other Sunday and on Thursday during school holidays, making today a "mumday" that wasn't destined to happen.

"I'm sorry sweetheart, I'm guessing this is happening everywhere and she won't be able to travel to see you."

"And it was going to be a Greg-free-day as well. Sucks." Greg was her half brother who was a few years younger than her and had a "challenging personality". She continued rolling sparks around her hand with a grimace of disappointment.

"How much of your reserves are you using?" John asked to try and change the subject, "I got mine down to 84 by blipping the sarnie components around the kitchen and moving the compost. After three minutes or so they were back at 100. So that's a regen rate of five per minute I guess? 5% per minute isn't' too bad? Is it a percentage based rate or a flat 5 per minute? Could be other factors I guess, those books you read always have ambient levels of magic in the air that affect regen rates and stuff right? Moving the compost took a lot more Reserves than moving the butter. I'm not sure why though."

"Check your log," she replied casually, chewing into the bacon buttie.

"My what?"

"Your combat log. Think or say "Log"".

"Log"

Combat log:
Previous entry:
Teleport Glass of Orange Juice
Successful
Reserve cost: 20
Cost mitigated by the following factors:
Less than 10% of Weight Limit – cost reduced by half
Less than 10% of Distance Limit – cost reduced by half
Minimum cost cannot be reduced by more than 90% of base cost.
Final Cost: 2 Reserves

"You, child of mine, are a god-damn genius."

Chapter 2 - So are you going to magic up the dog then or what?

"I got an Essence for it as well," Evie said happily. "Still not sure what to do with them." John finished his sandwich with a contented sigh and went to make his coffee.
"I got the option to give one to Zeeg that I rejected to give it to you. We could invite her to the party?" he called from the kitchen.
"Or I could figure out how to level up... Oh, of course it's that simple... Yes"

Team member Evie Borrows has chosen to spend one Essence and advance to Level 2.
Levelling in process...

"This is weird Dad, I've got three choices to pick from: Ability, Efficiency and Utility. What do you think." she looked at him questioningly..
John came back with his coffee, slightly miffed to have to wait and see what Zeeg became with an Essence but glad Evie had once again figured something out. He was starting to feel being a little left behind was going to become a motif in his new life. Going from constant provider and protector to "How are you this dumb, Dad?" or something equally caustic in such a short time would take some getting used to.
"Any explanation or description?" he asked, sitting down and waiting for his drink to cool.
"Nothing else at all. I'm going to pick efficiency I think." she looked at him questioningly.
"Fill your boots, test subject number one. Be the guinea pig. Live the guinea pig!" He said, taking a slurp of his coffee.

Evie Borrows has chosen to modify Efficiency.
New status for team member Evie Borrows:
Level 2
Name: Evie Borrows
Ability: Electrogenesis
Constitution: 100%
Reserves: 200
Guidelines:
Maximum Discharge: 240V
Line of sight required.
Modifications:
Level 2: Reserve capacity X2

"Woah. That felt very weird!" said Evie, glancing around the room. "Like a part of me I didn't know existed and can't normally feel, somehow got bigger".

"What did you get?" he asked curiously.

"Reserves times two so I've got 200 now."

"You doubled your reserves with one level?" he asked, amazed, "that has the potential for exponential growth! No way the levelling system is that broken. Right?" He asked hesitantly and Evie shrugged, "if you can get maximum efficiency, now when you use your power now you can use it 100 times instead of 50 without needing a break. I'm guessing it's less than 10% of your voltage?".

"Yeah? I think? I've just been using max strength."

"If you double your voltage for a few levels you'll end up doing a lot of damage, you probably zap someone like they stuck a fork in a plug socket already. How about you get dressed and we go into the garden to really test out these powers?" John asked, consumed by curiosity about their new abilities.

Five minutes later Evie was dressed and John was still rocking his post covid business attire: PJs, a dressing gown and crocs ensemble. Working from home was not good for his fashion sense. Evie sported black jeans and a Nirvana t-shirt that had John contemplating a lecture about putting things in the laundry basket more regularly.

After a brief argument Evie was ordered to wear her trainers because there was no way John was giving up his croc/dressing gown combo at this time of day. They let Zeeg out first, who immediately went to sniff around her domain and do what dogs do when you let them out on a morning.

"Hang fire a second, I need to gather the dog eggs," John used his preferred euphemism for bagging up dog poop. Then an evil grin appeared on his lips, his voice dropped to a whisper.

"Do you remember the trouble we had with the lady over the fence at the end throwing stuff into our garden last year? And what I told her I'd do if she didn't stop?"

"Dad, I'm pretty sure she stopped... don't..." but she grinned anyway.

John began teleporting "dog eggs" into the gutter of the unpleasant lady's conservatory while Evie giggled quietly into her hands.

"Whatever else, whatever the hell this apocalypse brings... that made it all worth it!" grinned John at his daughter, "now don't tell grandma I did that under any circumstances! Or your mates at school. Or anyone at all in fact. So, what can you do, Little Miss Sparky? Give me a second to set up some targets for you."

John fished some bamboo canes from the garage, carefully ignoring the mess in there he had been planning on clearing out for nearly a year now, and planted a dozen poles spread across the garden. Evie pointed at the first and a fat spark leapt from her finger to the middle cane on the first row. A baby lightning bolt.

Evie Borrows:
Reserves: 190

The bamboo cane exploded throwing burning splinters across the garden.
"I used Maximum voltage for ten reserves. I'm not sure how I knew how to control it but I just understood it. Like... it's like how I know how to walk or breathe. Pretty sure that would have hurt if it hit a baddie!" she grinned
"I don't think a Hello Kitty bandaid would be enough to make it feel better, for sure. My guidelines are weight and distance so the reduction is based on what I try to move and how far. I can control how far much like you said about how much voltage you use, I just know how. Unfortunately the weight is just whatever the thing weighs. Hopefully we end up being attacked by things weighing less than 10kg but I'm not wildly optimistic about that. Take another shot?"
The second bamboo cane on the front row exploded and sizzled. Evie went through eight more, doing quick draw finger guns to take out the last couple.
"I've got an idea. Can I try something on you?" she asked.
"Um, as long as it isn't a Zap... ok?"
It felt like John's entire body went weak and then everything went black. He came to, flat on his back, a bump growing on the back of his head from collapsing with a semi-hysterical Evie slapping his cheeks.

"Ok kid, I don't keep my awake-ness in my cheeks! What the hell happened?" He said groggily, and silently cursed for jinxing himself by joking that she could play guinea pig.

"I thought I'd killed you! I'm so sorry Dad! Are you sure you're OK? How many fingers am I holding up?" she said calming now John was awake again but still distraught.

"I'm alright Sausage, bit of a headache though. I can see… twenty seven fingers." One of the twenty seven was deployed to poke him in the beer gut.

"Ouch! You can see my constitution in the team status thing. I only took… 2%." John grabbed his phone and started a stopwatch. "Now we have a chance to figure out how fast that regenerates as well, if it does. Good job Sausage!"

"That was not a good job," she said with guilt clear in her voice, "are you sure you're OK?"

John slowly got up, rubbing the back of his head and checking for blood. "All ship shape and Bristol fashion here kiddo, despite the pigeon egg on the back of my noggin. What was it you, um, did?"

She hesitated a moment then said "I was thinking about how electricity is in our nerves right?"

"Well kind of but it's not really electricity per se I think?

"Well, whatever, I figured living things, things with nerves anyway used electricity so I kind of, um, stole some of yours. I'm so sorry dad," she hung her head.

"Did it work and did it take any reserves?" her dad asked with a hint of excitement in his voice, for the moment completely unconcerned about the potential danger he had just been in.

"Yeah I got a bit but it knocked you out like a light. Cost me one reserve. Can we just call it Mana Dad? This reserve thing is lame."

"Well please don't do that to me again and you can call it Unicorn Poop Units for all I care. I might feel a bit strange asking you how many UPU you used though. Thinking about it... I'm going to stick to the words this stupid system uses for now. Wait right there a sec kiddo, I've got an idea."

John opened the garage door again, continued to ignore the mess and boxes he'd been putting off sorting out, he had a years worth of practice at ignoring it so he was fairly competent in that regard by now. He found what he was looking for and re-emerged into the light. "The battery for the mower/strimmer thing we got from Grandad," he said, presenting it with a flourish. He pressed the button to check the charge level, "Fully charged. Can you pull power from this?"

Evie frowned and raised a hand. "Woah there! Gimme a sec!" John put the battery down and backed away a metre or so. Then went back, picked it up and moved the battery to the end of the garden, about ten metres away, and then went to stand safely *behind* Evie.

"Righto. Do your thing."

"Scared?" Evie laughed.

"Not going to lie. Whatever you did really sucked to be on the receiving end of. Let's hope whatever the first wave is has nerves. Fire away kiddo" A blue light shot from the battery to Evie's hand.

"Johnny Five is alive! I've got a 100% boost on the next zap now!" John went and picked up the battery, hit the power level button and saw she had completely drained all of the power from it. "Empty. I'm going to stick it back on to charge, see how long it takes to show full again. How much reserves did that take?"

Evie checked and responded "10 reserves. Ouch"

ZAAAAPPPP

ZAP

More bamboo exploded. "This boost to damage when I drain stuff is great! Did you see that first shot? How long does it take to charge the battery dad?"

John Borrows is back to 100% constitution.

John grabbed his phone and saw it had been just under two minutes since he started the timer and he now felt absolutely fine again. The lump on the back of his head was gone. Fifteen seconds unconscious give or take...
"1% health per minute I think? So I can be almost dead and then be completely healthy in an hour and a half or so? This is ridiculous. Anything less than instagibbed and you are fine in a couple of hours" he mumbled.
"Uh, five or six hours on the battery, I think? You'll need another option to stay topped off than draining me. It seriously messes me up, maybe treat the Zaps as your "special" attack and drain as your bread and butter move? If you pull less power you'll use a lot fewer reserves."
As Evie resumed creating every panda's worst nightmare, a panorama of shattered, burning bamboo, John took stock. He was trying to understand how to weaponize his ability as the first system message made it clear a fight was coming. He had been giving it some thought and concluded gravity would be his best friend. He didn't feel overly worried about this situation and with his daughter's and his own lives apparently on the line this struck him as very odd. He also didn't seem to be terribly worried about not being worried so he focused on what was at hand.

He began teleporting the ornamental rocks at the end of the garden around. A few centimetres either way at first before graduating to dropping them from three metres up. Then ten. Then twenty metres up. They were digging themselves in quite deeply and throwing mud all over from the impacts at that point. Two reserves each time. Less than 10% weight and less than 10% distance keeping the costs low. Dropping a few kilos of rock on something's head was undoubtedly going to be effective but rocks could be surprisingly sneaky beggars. Two rocks that looked the same size could weigh significantly different amounts due to their density and composition.

An additional problem would no doubt be that things he wanted to be able to drop rocks on might not want rocks dropped on their heads. For some reason. They would be extremely unsporting and move out of the way or cheat in some other underhanded fashion. A pickle to be sure. He sent a rock ninety nine metres straight up and waited a moment, eyes fixed to it. He watched it fall, drifting over towards landing in the neighbours garden due to the wind, building speed and momentum then teleported it again to right above another rock. Both rocks shattered with a resounding crash, sending shards of stone flying, some of which were left embedded in the fence.

"Well that works" He grinned at Evie.

We have a status screen, levels and upgrades. All very video game-y... John considered everything he had learned from the video games he had played and silly stories he had read in his life and decided to chant random words to see what happened. As all sane people naturally would in this situation.

"Inventory" he muttered. Nothing. No infinite pocket dimension to make logistics a doddle for Johnny boy. Bugger. That would have been handy. Having worked in logistics for the last few years he knew moving things in bulk was not a simple process and being a

pathological fan of survivalist blogs and videos he knew how difficult it was to keep people warm and fed without modern supply chains. Supply chains they were apparently now completely cut off from. The power being on was nice but they couldn't pay electronically for anything now with the internet taking a break and he didn't keep much cash in the house. Just in time delivery systems suddenly didn't seem like such a great idea as John considered the ramifications.
Thousands of people in town and most of them only have a few days food on hand... This will get ugly fast.
"Active effects?" Nothing. "Status Effects". Zip. "Buffs". Nada. "How does this thing start?" Nothing, no infinite ammo Dodge corvette for him. "God Mode, uh, Infinite Essence..." Double nothing. Long odds for sure but they had been worth a shot. "Identify" he whispered as he was getting an increasingly funny look from Evie.

You have discovered the Identify function. +1 Essence.
Small rock
Approximate weight 2kg

"Booyah!" He looked at Evie and thought *Identify*.

Level 2
Name: Evie Borrows
Ability: Electrogenesis
Constitution: 100%
Reserves: 44
Weight: 57kg

"Kid, look at me and think IDENTIFY!" John said with a distinct tone of smug in his voice.

"Oh cool. A level one noob and you're good for 25% of a power boost to my next zap but it would kill you. Let me try it on something less weak." *Hurtful!*

Evie looked at the the house, began waving her arms over her head and said in what someone who watched too many Japanese cartoons might think sounded like a magical chant "IdEnTIFyyYY!!!!" John assumed she was being snarky about his overly optimistic "god mode". In all fairness he probably deserved it.

"That is going to be really handy!" she continued in a less melodramatic voice, "The house is plugged into the grid so I can pull a lot of power from it. As in a really large lot. Nearly infinite in fact. That's going to be useful. Did you get an Essence for it?"

"Yes, I got an Essence."

"So are you going to magic up the dog then or what?"

Chapter 3 - Let's go find some flying stuff to fight

John stood up straight and raised his right hand, cupped upwards and declared in his best Patrick Stewart voice "Alas poor Yorik I knew him well. Zeeg, a puppy of infinite jests but poor socialisation and recall yet of most excellent fancy... yadda yadda... something about slings and arrows... to magic up the dog or not to magic up the dog. That is the question," he finished in a more normal voice as he failed to recall the Shakespeare he was forced to read all those years ago.

"Well?" asked Evie in the unimpressed voice of someone who had become immune to non sequiturs from her dad.

"Not sure kid. Not sure. The dog is mental. Imagine her with superpowers. What will she do next time we're out for a walk and she sees a random SFD and decides to go for it?" John was silent for a few moments. "I think I'll take the level. We can magic Zeeg up when we have a better idea of what's coming and a better chance of stopping her from using flying powers, or whatever she gets, to go and hunt down all the Small Fluffy Dogs or whatever madness takes her fancy. Level up!"

Would you like to use one Essence and advance to Level 2? Y/N

"Yes"

Please select from the following options
Ability
Efficiency
Utility
You have selected Efficiency.

New Status:
Level: 2
Name: John Borrows
Ability: Teleportation
Constitution: 100%
Reserves: 76
Guidelines:
Maximum weight: 100kg
Maximum Distance: 1km
Line of sight required
Modifications:
Level 2: How about we split the difference?
You always were a cheapskate. Maximum cost reduction due to efficiency bonus' increased to 99%

"Ok, this is nuts," John said before making rocks bounce back and forth across the garden. "That took 1.6 reserves for eight teleports. As long as I keep the objects small I can do... um... what 500 teleports from a full tank?" he looked up at the sky and declared, "you know this is mental right?"

Evie ignored her father ranting at the sky. This wasn't the first time it had happened after all. Usually it was on an evening and he'd had a few glasses of wine though, so this was a bit out of character. "Sooo when are you going to take the plunge?"

"What plunge?"

"You know the 'why don't you stop being a baby and become the Nightcrawler you were always meant to be' plunge?"

"I find your lack of respect… disturbing," said John in a Darth Vader voice, "but par for the course. Fair point... I guess it's one thing to blip rocks about the garden but to blip me about, what if something goes wrong? What if it isn't 'folding space' or whatever and I actually create a duplicate in the new location and something goes wrong and the original isn't destroyed and then he decides to hunt me down because of something stupid I did twenty years ago that ruined his life??? What if..."

"Dad, stop, she held up both hands and made 'chill' gestures, "as usual you're overthinking this. I think there is a limiter or override that stops us hurting ourselves with the powers. There is only one way to find out, so man up!" She poked him in a kidney.

John became very serious. "Please promise me you'll be careful experimenting with your ability? 'I think' doesn't mean it is."

"Ok Dad, sheesh fine but like I said, I don't think we can hurt ourselves with our own powers. Other people? Stuff? Sure we can hurt them but not ourselves."

"Nevertheless, Sausage, be careful. There's a pinnacle to climb or whatever the crazy system means, and no one will be climbing anything if they fry their own brain or teleport themselves into a wall. Speaking of not doing the latter... Right. Here we go. Maximum effort. No fear. Fear is the mindkiller, the little death that brings total obliteration..."

"Stop reciting the Litany Against Fear and just do it already Dad."

And for the first time in his life John did something that would eventually become humdrum and routine but this first time was somehow magical and special. This moment in time, crystalised in his memory, would never be forgotten.

Blip.

John appeared two metres up the garden, slipped on a muddy patch and promptly fell on his ass. Truly a memory to cherish.

Combat log:
Previous entry:
Teleport: Self
Successful
Reserve cost: 20
Cost mitigated by the following factors:
More than 50% of Weight Limit – No reduction
Less than 10% of Distance Limit – cost reduced by half
Final Cost: 10 Reserves

John leapt to his feet and unleashed a rather undignified whoop before realising his dressing gown was now covered in mud at the back.
"Crap. Now I have to go get dressed and it isn't even 7 o'clock. This is not what working from home was meant to be like." He smirked despite the setback as Evie chortled quietly at his expense.
"Real smooth dad! Looks like you crapped yourself"
Returning to the garden after putting his PJs and dressing gown in the washing machine and now attired in jeans, an old t shirt emblazoned with "Summer of 88" and a hoodie, John briefly thanked the gods that the water and power grids hadn't been affected so far. In minutes he was back in the garden blipping from one end to the other occasionally while making it rain rocks at the far end.
ZAP. Another bamboo pole shattered.
"You know Dad, I think we need to test how effective drain is on a living thing. ZAP of DOOM is brutal but I think you are right about it being a special rather than the usual attack." Evie had a calculating expression on her face.
John disappeared from her left and reappeared on her right.
"Awesome," he said to himself. He was revelling in the power he had

been given and becoming increasingly comfortable at moving without moving.

"Hmm? ZAP of DOOM? You might want to work on that. What else have you got? In terms of powers, not terrible names for powers. Maybe you should call it The Frank? After Frank Zappa? Geddit?"

Evie scowled briefly at her Dad. "Boomer music," she scoffed, "you went down like a tower of cards in a gale when I drew on you so stop tempting me to try again. And it cost a lot less reserves. I need something else to try it on."

"Leave the dog alone! You are not experimenting with possibly harmful magic powers on the puppy," said John sternly.

"As if I would. I've got a much better target in mind," she said as her eyes roved across the nearby rooftops. She fixed her gaze on two pigeons and a faint blue light shot from them to Evie. "Take that sky rats!" The pigeons twitched as they dropped off the roof.

2 Harmless Pigeons Killed
Harmless Pigeons yield 0.05 essence
Total Essence gained: 0.1

"Did you really just murder a pair of pigeons in cold blood to test out your power?"

"Hang on... log says yes, they are dead as a parrot what is nailed to the perch, pining for the fjords, etc. etc. I will purge all the sky rats to gain ultimate powah!!! Bwahahaha!" she cackled.

"Dude, I don't know what pigeons ever did to you but I'm not sure this is healthy."

"Mum calls them sky rats, I'm really not a pigeon-ist. Much. Anyway they deserve it. Flying flea bags. We both got 0.05 essence from each of them and I got their charge. Not much charge in them though.

Maybe a bit of a boost to my next Zap and cost was 2 reserves. I bet it gets higher the further away I drain something from. So I've got 100 shots at anything that gets close. I hope we get slow monsters or whatever in the waves," she said with a worried expression on her face.

"You moved us both towards a new level by murdering pigeons?" he asked, slightly horrified and somehow unsurprised at the same time. A very strange form of ambivalence.

"Seems so. Maybe we should take a trip to the abandoned club and farm some essence from baddies whose only way to attack us is giving us fleas or pooping on us? Whatever happens with the wave the stronger we are at the start the better."

Evie's enthusiasm was starting to take John aback. Evie had played violent games and watched violent films for a couple of years now, probably starting younger than was strictly acceptable but had always seemed like a calm, easy-going sort of kid. She did prefer it when he killed spiders rather than threw them out the window but that was spiders and she was eleven. Perfectly normal? This bloodthirstiness was very unlike her in John's mind. The problem was that he largely agreed with her plan for a local pigeon genocide.

"I think whatever this is, it's messing with our heads. We need to take a breath. Let's go grab a drink and spend a few minutes thinking and getting our reserves back before we make a decision, OK?" John rested one hand on her shoulder.

"You're no fun! But fine, just remember tick tock the clock is ticking," Evie grumped but went inside and got herself a glass of squash, moving to the living room and making sparks jump around her fingers.

"No powers!" John said seriously, coming through having put the kettle on again.

"I think we are missing a trick here kiddo. It's... ten to seven, we have until quarter to nine. If we stop using powers at 08:45 we will have full tanks when whatever will happen, happens, leaving us fifteen minutes knowing what we are facing to fine tune a plan. So we've got an hour and fifty five minutes. Let's take ten to come up with a plan to take us through till we get the notification. Sounds good?"

"Sure Dad. I've been messing about with "Identify" by the way." Evie mentioned as she gestured to the computer sat on the coffee table., adding, "your laptop is worth two full empowered Zaps to me."

John was not impressed and shook his head, replying, "do not use my laptop battery as a battery. For you I mean, it works as a battery for the laptop *only!* I don't want to lose my save games, thanks very much. Some of them have hundreds of hours behind them."

"Nerd, but fine whatever," Evie rolled her eyes. "I don't know what you see in those 4X games. Give me a shooter any day of the week. Can I drain the house instead?" she asked hopefully.

"Maybe try to pull power from a plug?" John said, pointing to the wall. "Gladys is a nice landlady and I don't want to upset her by letting you melt all the wires in the walls or something," he said with a gentle smile.

Teamchat:
Evie Borrows: So this is what I got :)
John Borrows: Oh great now you can project emojis into my brain. This will end well.
Evie Borrows: Shut up and look.
Evie Borrows: Combat Log: Evie Borrows used Identify on 3 Bedroom End Terrace. 3 Bedroom End Terrace: a modest 3 bed house in the small market town of Normanby. Market valuation:

£286000, connected to - National Grid, making near infinite power available for someone at your level.

"Called it!" said John, once again smug, "as long as the grid's up, you're demigod tier. The S Class Kiddo. The Stumpy Lightning Slinger, Zeus' More Annoying Ginger Half Pint Female Clone-"
"Shut up Baldy and don't ever say the names I come up with suck again." she interrupted, "No idea why it felt the need to include the value of the house, but I am beginning to agree that the system is weird. The point *I was trying to make*, if I could just get a word in edgewise, Dad." She gave him "The Look" before continuing, "is that I can overcharge Zaps no worries as long as I'm a hundred metres from a house but Zap is expensive in reserves at max strength. Even switching between drain and Zap I'm still very glass cannon-ey and won't have much staying power."
"The ZAP did a number on the bamboo but unless the first wave is bamboo monsters or very vulnerable to electricity, maybe robots or something." John shrugged. "We don't know how much damage you'll be doing. I think drain is your best bet until we know more. It worked on me and the sky rats. Focus on efficiency for the first few levels until you've got more reserves?"
"Yeah I can see that. And you are basically a controller aren't you? Something gets too close you can blip it a kilometre away if you have to. I kill, you keep them off us? You can blip stuff into the sky and hope the fall kills it I suppose. Which means flying stuff is your worst match up... Sooo let's go find some flying stuff to fight?"

Chapter 4 - The Great Sky Rat War of 2024

"One sec Sweetie" John grinned malevolently and teleported her across the room.

"What the actual... Dad - why?" Evie stumbled and put out a hand to the door frame in order to right herself.

"To see how many reserves it takes to move you obviously. It might be handy to know how many reserves I need to keep in "reserve" to give us an escape option?" John replied, scanning his log. It definitely hadn't been revenge for her earlier snarky comments. Definitely not.

"And... you my dear are no longer allowed chocolate!"

"Get stuffed old man. Chocolate is life! That felt really weird. Let me guess no reduction due to weight?"

"Good guess Short Stuff. It's ten reserves to move either of us. It says you are 53% of my weight limit, tubby, so no reduction other than the distance one. I can jump us both a hundred metres out of a pickle as long as I have a fifth of my reserves."

"Are you happy now?" She said, giving her old man a stern look.

"Weirdly yes, and me from yesterday would be freaking out. Which is kind of making me freak out but not as much as I think it should. Something funky is going on in my noggin, Sausage."

"Just like normal for you then." She smirked at him, "let's go launch the Great Sky Rat War of 2024. Death to the feathered pests! The scouring will commence now!" she declared grandly with a fist in the air.

"You know the Australians launched a war on Emu's? They didn't win."

"Emu's are massive, Dad. I'm not surprised."

"Yeah but they had guns."

"They gave the emus guns?" she asked incredulously, "now that's mental!"

"No dopey, the Aussies had the guns!"

"Well that's pretty embarrassing then. Any other random wars humans have waged on birds that failed? Perhaps a broader historical perspective will allow us to not die to air strikes of poop."

"Uh, I think the Chinese had a war on sparrows once? Not sure."

"Fascinating," she drawled sarcastically. "Let's go murder some pigeons. We can call it a special military operation if it makes you feel safer?"

"When this is over you and I are going to sit down and have a talk, kid."

The abandoned club was at the corner of Back Lane before it turned to go into the marketplace, just down the way from the medical centre and a couple of minutes west from their house. John and Evie had moved to Normanby six years ago and the club had been derelict long before then according to things locals had told John.

They left through the backdoor and the gate next to the garage. John's drive was more moss than concrete, getting it power washed hadn't been a priority for a long time. They stepped into the street and it was just as it always was. Terraced houses facing off against each other with scraps of grass in front. The autumn sun shone down gently, warm for this time of day.

They moved off west, heading towards the library. As they got to the snicket they heard a startled shout from ahead of them and they both flinched. The streets were eerily silent. It was early but you would expect more people about. Some dog walkers or people bustling off to work but they had seen no one yet.

"What the hell! Fucking wall!" came a stressed out voice. John and Evie moved forward to the bend in the snicket so they could see ahead.

They got to the corner and saw a young woman dressed in joggers and a t-shirt scowling at the wall at the end of the snicket.

"Are you ok?" called John uncertainly.

Her head whipped round. She was young and pretty with long blond hair tied back in a ponytail.

"Did you see that shit too? I'm too fast now! This is too fucking strange!" she scowled, looking down at her feet that seemed to have betrayed her.

"We got the message as well, we were going to try and get some Essence!" called Evie. She leant in towards John and murmured "she's cray cray!"

"Do you want-" John began.

"Screw this! I'm going back to bed and calling in sick!" The woman stormed past John and Evie heading out onto their street and disappearing from view. They could hear her cursing and muttering to herself for some time after she passed out of sight.

"Not handling it well?" asked John, pointing a hand after the woman.

"What is it you always tell me? 'People are weird, Evie,'" she adopted a gruff voice, "I'm guessing she isn't a gamer. Or normal. Who goes running at this time in the morning for fun? What a weirdo."

"At least we know we aren't the only ones left, I suppose. The quiet was starting to freak me out."

They moved on. Their destination wasn't far and they didn't see anyone else on the way. The old club sat on the corner with a straggly overgrown patch of ground that may once have been a gravel parking area but was now essentially scrubland. The windows were all boarded up as were the main doors at the front but enough of the boards on the upstairs windows had been knocked out by kids throwing stones or simply by time and the weather causing them to sag.

Ever the opportunists, a substantial part of Normanby's population of pigeons had set up shop inside, the boards on the upstairs windows beneath the gap they used to get in and out were streaked with the evidence of their passing. The place hadn't been the site of drinking and dancing into the wee hours for twenty odd years and the husk of the structure was starting to show its age and lack of repair.

"So what's the plan? To get inside I mean," Evie asked.

"Good question... should have brought an axe or a crowbar I guess."

"Even if it's dead quiet, wandering around town with a splitting axe over your shoulder and hacking through a door would raise some eyebrows Dad. Even at this time of day. In fact that would raise some eyebrows at any time of day. Do you think they all just went back to sleep except for the crazy lady? For once I'm actually grateful you disturbed me, normally it's just nagging me to get my breakfast cos 'It's half eleven child, you're not a teenager yet so stop acting like one, get out of bed now.'" She finished in the gruff voice which was an undeniably accurate impression of John's "Dad" voice.

"Well you aren't a teenager yet however much you think you are," he sighed, "I honestly don't know, kid. Maybe they are hiding under the covers freaking out? Maybe they figured it was a weird dream and rolled over to go back to sleep? Maybe one or both of us has had some sort of psychotic break and we're actually just drooling and rocking back and forth in a corner of the living room. I have to assume this is real though and not a dream. When I banged my head it hurt like the blazes and should have snapped me out of a dream. I think? Is that how dreams work?"

"Who knows? Or cares dad? You always go off topic! Focus! How are we getting in there?"

John and Evie began examining the main doors and found that despite the age and lack of care they were solidly locked and boarded. They were not going to be brushed aside easily or quietly. They went down the side of the building and stopped by a window. None of the boards were loose but one had not been set in place correctly and left a narrow gap that John could see through.

"I'm going to blip you in"

"Through that gap? Are you sure abo... ut this? Eep!" She finished from the other side of the window.

John appeared next to her a moment later and said "Yes." Evie punched him in the arm.

Looking around they found the first floor was a large open area, the remains of a bar at one end and everything was covered in dust and the filth that accumulated with long periods of neglect. Bits of wood and plastic lay strewn here and there and the stairs up to the second floor rose from the far side of the room, curling up from behind where it looked as though the bar had once been. The floor was marked where tables had been fixed down around the dance floor, said dance floor having been ripped up so only the rough floorboards beneath remained. A constant cooing echoed down the stairs confirming their quarry was at hand.

"I'll go first and start draining, if they freak out can you blip them away from the exits to stop them escaping? Any getting away you send them over to me and I'll fry them," Evie whispered.

"OK kid, let's try and keep it quiet, we don't want to draw any attention. This is technically breaking and entering. Although it's more "breaking the laws of physics in order to enter", I still don't think the Police will be A-OK with it."

They moved as quietly as they could up to the stairs and began to creep slowly upwards. Aged wood tends to shift and warp if it is left unattended for long periods and the staircase was no different. A series of quiet creaks and groans emerged with every step they took, each noise making them both wince and pause to check the noise from above. The birds didn't seem to notice judging by the constant cooing remaining unchanged as they both moved slowly and carefully on to the last step and crouched down by the banister.

Several of the pigeons noticed them and fluffed themselves up but they didn't seem to feel any sense of danger and quickly went back to ignoring the Father and Daughter Extermination Squad.

"Can you move whatever that is to block the window with the board missing? In case they freak out," Evie whispered, pointing at what appeared to be an old door that had been removed from its frame and left lying on the floor.

John nodded and with a blip the door appeared almost completely blocking the gap in the window and plunging the room into darkness. There was a slight thunk as the door settled into place that made John wince. The pigeons, being ineffably stupid birds, were briefly startled but quickly settled back down. At this moment John realised he was little more intelligent than the winged rats. He had switched the orientation of the door from horizontal on the floor to almost vertical against the window *while blipping it*. A new trick that should have been obvious to him from the start. It also occurred to John that humans need light in order to see and this might be a problem.

"Damn, can you still see them?" he asked.

"Not with my eyes anymore. I can sort of sense their, um, energy though. Maybe it's like with blind people getting super hearing but I can kind of "see" the electricity in them. I think I could do this all along but I'm just used to seeing stuff with light and didn't notice. It's really weird."

The unsanctioned extermination quest was already paying out rewards in innovation and hidden secrets it seemed.

"Alright then, start with the ones on the ground. The ones on the rafters will drop and scare the flock," John murmured.

As previously mentioned pigeons are not terribly bright and the gentle chorus of coo's gradually diminished as each pigeon settled on the floor fell into unconsciousness and was unceremoniously shoved into the final slumber from which no feathered thing can return. John sat in the dark and did literally nothing, listening to the gradually reducing volume of the pigeon chorus as the members died and watching the Log entries tick in.

Team member Evie Borrows has killed x28 Harmless Pigeons. Each team member has gained 1.4 essence.

John nudged Evie gently and gestured that they should creep back down stairs. Once they got to the bottom they moved away from the stairs.

"I am become death! Destroyer of sky rats!" Evie whispered.

"Chill your beans kid. Lets level and see what we get in mods?" John suggested quietly. "After you child" he said with a gentle smile. Evie grinned and nodded.

"What the hell?" she exclaimed quietly. "It says I need two Essence to get to level three!"

John tried and got the same result. "We should have thought of that shouldn't we really? We play enough games to know that you need more xp for higher levels. Still, we needed one essence for level two, two for level three. Do you think it will be three for level four? That seems like they want us to power level really fast. Coupled with the mods being multiplicative when they aren't plain weird and rude, we'll get very powerful very quickly. Let's go bag another dozen of the feathery bastards and then come back."

Three minutes later and having sent twelve more unfortunate pigeons to the great nest in the sky, they were back where they began just inside the main door downstairs.

Team member Evie Borrows has chosen to spend two Essence and advance to Level 3.
Levelling in process...
Evie Borrows has chosen to modify Ability.
New status for team member Evie Borrows:
Level 3
Name: Evie Borrows
Ability: Electrogenesis
Constitution: 100%
Reserves: 200
Guidelines:
Maximum Discharge: 240V
Line of sight required.
Modifications:
Level 2: Reserve capacity X2
Level 3: Waste not Want Not. When you drain energy beyond 100% overcharging your next Zap rather than going to waste, the excess energy is used to invigorate yourself and your team members, providing a temporary buff that boosts reflexes and reserve regeneration. Buff duration is refreshed when reapplied. You're kind of a vampire but with electricity instead of blood. Rather than science you fall back on horror tropes? Emo Kid!

"Cool but I am not a bloody Emo Kid!" Evie said. "Remember to check the log when we go back upstairs and see what it actually does." "I thought you were going to go with efficiency to begin with? Meh, it's your build sweetheart. What are our reflex scores, do you think? I don't like hidden stats. Let me level up and we can go finish the pidgies off."

John Borrows has chosen to spend two Essence advance to Level 3
John Borrows has chosen to modify Ability.
New Status:
Level: 3
Name: John Borrows
Ability: Teleportation
Constitution: 100%
Reserves: 100
Guidelines:
Maximum weight: 500kg
Maximum Distance: 1km
Line of sight required
Modifications:
Level 2: How about we split the difference? You always were a cheapskate. Maximum cost reduction due to efficiency bonus' increased to 99%
Level 3: Weight limit x5

Chapter 5 - "Doris?" she asked sceptically

"Hang on a mo" whispered John before blipping himself and then Evie a short distance. "Down to five reserves to move either of us now. 10-50% of weight limit is a 25% cost reduction. Now I need a couple of reserve multipliers and we are golden."

"Let's finish the rest of them off. We might get enough for another level," Evie replied quietly. Once again they crept upstairs and resumed playing he 'gainst whom no door nor portal barred can keep out. But for pigeons.

By the time they had done their somewhat morally questionable deed they had killed a further nineteen pigeons and accrued another 0.95 Essence. They also confirmed the waste not want not buff provided 1% reserve regen rate per minute and 5% to reflexes that lasted for five minutes but neither of them could figure out what difference the reflex bonus made. It looked good though, John supposed.

Evie was getting more than twice as much benefit as John from the extra reserve regen due to her doubled reserve pool, twelve reserves per minute to his five and a half per minute. Those multipliers on modifications would be a massive deal as they progressed and highlighted just how truly stupid this system was.

"Well that's disappointing," declared Evie in a normal voice, no need to whisper now all the pigeons had been reduced to potential pie and pillow stuffing. "Shall we head home?"

John checked his phone to get the time. 07:35. Seventy minutes until fifteen minutes to 'go time'... "Let's head back through town. See if anyone else is about? We might find another sky rat to get us up to a full Essence so one of us can supe up the dog." He walked over to the door he had moved to block the window and pushed it over. As it fell it kicked up a cloud of dust that he wafted away from his face with a hand.

Blip.

Blip.

"A little warning next time Dad!" John had moved them both down to the path he could see outside the window.

"Pigeon!" said John pointing up into a tree. Evie pivoted on her heel and thrust out a hand. A brief flash of blue light and they both had one Essence in the bank.

"Homeward bound the long way, Old Man?"

"I'm not that old, child. It's age-ist of you to speak to your elders like that" John grinned, rehashing an old joke they shared. "Let's at least visit the marketplace. Even if most folks ignored the notification and turned over to go back to sleep, a lot of people need to be at work by now, delivery people, bakers and whatnot. Might be worth seeing if we can speak to someone without braying on their door at this ungodly hour" John suggested.

"You're normally up at this time Dude so it can't be that ungodly."

"That does not mean I like it. It just means I need to bring forward teaching you how to make and pack your own lunch for school," Evie winced at the implied threat of yet more responsibility, as though emptying the dishwasher wasn't enough! "C'mon, I'm going to try something."

Blip blip. Blip blip.

Nothing in Normanby was very far apart. You could walk from one end of the scenic Georgian town to the other in under an hour if you walked quickly. Normally a walk from the derelict building back to the marketplace was about ninety seconds, give or take. It wasn't far. They covered it in two seconds and four blips.

The marketplace was mostly a car park in reality, it got filled up with stalls on Saturday and Tuesday each week as local traders came in to sell their wares. It was Thursday today, so it was reserved for parking instead of stalls. Some of the buildings that lined the north end were listed and hadn't been modernised in decades as a result. Old fashioned, drafty windows set in ancient brick walls made up the terraced houses at this end of town. The manor house and the big posh houses were all to the south on the other side of the river. They walked from the north end of the market down towards the main market area and the imaginatively named Main Street that ran through the middle of it, looking around for anyone else who was out and about. They saw no one on the streets whereas normally there would be cars and lorries passing through as well as people arriving for work. "Even stranger, let's head towards the shop and have a look," said John as they turned west onto Main Street and started towards the mini supermarket that was more or less right in the centre of town. As they were nearing the town hall, a large three storey rectangle built of stone in the late 1800s and lined with multi-pane windows on every side and floor, they heard a cry from around the far corner of the building. Maybe not a cry, maybe more of a super villain cackle and some ranting?

The cry was followed by a much clearer "Finally, it lives! hahaha". Definitely verging on super villain if not actually already there. They then heard a series of crunching sounds as if something was grinding up the cobbles that lined the path. John was not entirely confident this was a good sign.

John gestured for Evie to stay back with one hand and whispered "Stay here and watch my back, I'll blip back to you and then move us both away if it's trouble". He moved forward and called out "Good morning!" A grunted reply came from around the corner. "Lovely weather today isn't it? Not many people out and... about... today… for some… reason..." as John turned the corner he stopped, his greeting grinding to halt before ending in a shocked exclamation: "What the hell is this!?"

He stood and stared, slack jawed in amazement. Evie shook her head. Her dad's very English approach to meeting someone new: talk about the weather cheerfully despite the fact the weather usually sucked, was well known to her, as was his total lack of social grace, which was why he fell back on verbal cliches and film quotes so often, but his sudden stop and open mouthed stare had put her on edge.

"So now we just need to join these bits together with the last of my reserves and she's sorted! … Now I climb in and… If only the lads in the tank shed could see me now!" came a reply followed by further crunching sounds "Ah, hello to you! Now this is a war machine don't ya agree? Watch this!"

John continued to stare but blipped Evie to his side who joined him in open mouthed wonder. As she appeared in a position to see what was going on she saw what looked like a scrap yard version of an up-armoured lifter from Aliens with a barrel shaped body, the metal work was in various shades of blue and orange instead of yellow. Nothing was smooth or well connected, it frankly looked as though it would fall apart at any moment with wires hanging out of joints and strange, unhealthy sounding hissing noises being made as it moved. Despite all this it stubbornly remained in one piece and functional. And mobile. Albeit the thing wouldn't be winning any sprints any time soon. Behind the, for want of a better word, "robot", were the remains of two cars, one with scraps of blue metal strewn around it, the other with orange scraps, both reduced to little more than seats connected by some strips of steel and plastic, surrounded by debris.

Behind a repurposed windscreen from one of the cars in the upper part of the machines chest was the grinning face of a man in his early fifties, his face framed by neat, well trimmed hair and an impressive moustache. He was smiling like a maniac as his hands flashed over a control console mostly consisting of windscreen wiper levers, car radio controls, AC switches and a steering wheel.

The mecha was more than four metres tall and two wide. It was big and intimidating but as it took a lumbering step forward towards the raised planter the council kept populated with flowers even in winter, it was clear it wasn't an agile machine. An arm that was bigger than Evie swung up and back before coming down on the planter with explosive force, shattering it, throwing soil and soon to be dead plants across a wide area

Blip blip. John moved himself and Evie back to the other side of the road to avoid a rain of petunias that the weather forecast had somehow failed to predict.

Evie used Identify... sharing in team chat
Level 1
Name: Robert Gillybrook
Ability: Mechanaut

"Woah, how did you get over there?" came the voice from within the mechanical beast.

"Look at us and think Identify, Mr. Robert Gillybrook" Evie replied, brushing off some soil she hadn't managed to dodge.

"It's Sergeant Gillybrook to you young lady! Late of Her, well now, His Britannic Majesty's Army. Identify! Ah, very useful! You can teleport and, Identify, you can... zap things or something? Give birth to electricity? How odd!" John snorted and got an elbow in the ribs for his trouble. "How on earth did you get to level up?... oh. Seems obvious really. Says I need more Essence.

How do I get Essence? Do you know what Essence is by any chance please? Do you know what happened to kick this FUBAR situation off? I've tried to reach out to my old battalion but the blasted phones aren't working. Technology that doesn't involve solid mechanical parts and tons of steel isn't worth the trouble as a rule in my view. Eventually this beauty will be able to dance with dozens of T-72s like they aren't worth a damn!

Have you received any kind of sitrep about what's going on? If an invasion is coming we need to dig in, get the old girl belly down in a fighting position and let them come at us! Have you seen the barrier or tried to leave town? I was planning on reporting down to Fulford barracks as soon as this thing was up and running. I've seen no one except for yourselves which is rather strange. Nice to meet you by the way."

Team Chat:
Evie Borrows: He's got worse social skills than you.
John Borrows: Shut it short arse :-) he seems alright and he might be useful? Ex military could be handy.
Evie Borrows: He's an old tank nerd who apparently hates the council's flower choices. Seems like a good fit lol
John Borrows: ... I'll invite him.

"Hi Robert, As you now know my name is John and this is my daughter Evie," he waved, unable and unwilling to shake hands with the mecha directly, "nice to meet you too. We'd be happy to go through all your questions but I don't think we know much more than you. I'm going to send you a team invite, no pressure though: if you want to go solo and say no that's fine but I think those of us who are being proactive about this situation might want to stick together?" John racked his brain for a military aphorism. "Quantity has a quality all of its own?"

John Borrows has invited Robert Gillybrook to join Unnamed Team. Robert Gillybrook has accepted.
Team chat:
Robert Gillybrook: Ah that's the commo situation resolved then. Over.
John Borrows: Glad you can see the positives. Hello!

"We can just talk normally," said Evie. "We can answer some of your questions. Essence comes from figuring something out about the system as a one-off or from killing stuff. We got one essence for figuring out Identify and one for figuring out the team thing. We've been taking out pigeons to get essence. No idea what Essence is, it seems to work like a crap version of XP though."
"Killing pigeons? How did you figure that out? And mind your language young lady! It is most unbecoming to hear a young woman swear so." The mecha raised an arm, extended one of its three fingers and wagged it in Evie's direction.
"Umm the pigeon thing was definitely an accident and you'll get used to the language, although you should be on Mess Rules with new people Madam, outside the house you behave properly!" said John, pointedly not looking at his daughter who apparently considered pigeons to be worse than head lice for some reason. "We haven't looked at the barrier yet. We could take a walk down to where they do the Country Fair in September, that should be close enough to the edge of town to check out the barrier. Want to join us?"

The machine raised an arm again and gave them what was either a thumbs up or a middle finger. There were three fingers on each hand and they were spaced equidistant around the wrist. It wasn't entirely clear what the gesture meant.

"Is that a yes?" asked John.

"It is. Next upgrade... thumbs I think," said the mechanaut.

"Have you considered ranged weapons?" asked John as they headed East towards the edge of town.

"I'm afraid I'm limited to the parts I have around me and the number of upgrade slots on the chassis. It takes parts and focus and a bit of time and then poof. Walking tank. I've got no guns, stupid leftie gun laws, so it will be fisticuffs for me when the time comes."

"So you need ranged weapons to use as parts to create add ons? I might be able to help out there if you head back to my place with us before the wave starts. What about power? Evie might be your new best friend in that regard."

Evie looked at John and raised her cupped right hand to her mouth then gave a thumbs up with her right hand and brought her left fist down over the thumb.

"Be nice kid, Mess Rules for now," John said gently.

"What was that? And why are civvies talking about Mess Rules?" asked Robert.

"She… said something rude in American Sign Language. The Mess Rules… well my old man was in the RAF and it's a tradition I've passed on to her. Regarding the sign language… I am going to have words with my Dad about age appropriate Christmas presents going forward. Assuming we survive. And he does. Do you have any family in town?"

"Son of a fly boy eh? You have my sympathies. No, my son moved to London after his degree, History of Science! I was so ashamed. He and his family are doing well though and we keep in touch. I'm ex Army, worked as a mechanic attached to the Queens, eh, King's Royal Hussars for thirty odd years. Just retired and I've been renting in town waiting for my house to sell. Bloody solicitors dragging their feet."

"And the cars you turned into knock off Optimus Prime? Were they yours or are we going to have angry no-longer-motorists after us?" John asked.

"Ah. Indeed. Not mine I'm afraid. I just got caught up in the moment. Suddenly I knew how to make a giant fighting machine and I just didn't think it through. Could we fudge things a little so the insurance companies will pay out or am I off to the Glasshouse when the MPs catch up with me?" He sounded a little ashamed of how he had acted, and was obviously worried about the potential consequences.

"We've been murdering pigeons with magic for a good part of the last hour... I think traditional ethical concerns and law enforcement may have largely gone out of the window. Stay in the bot and I doubt anyone will make too much of a stink anyway, just don't say anything and loom harder than usual if anyone complains," laughed John.

"Sky rats, twelve o'clock," said Evie. John and Robert looked straight ahead and said "Where?" in unison.

Evie raised a hand and started draining the pigeons on the roof of the old smithy which was very much at nine o'clock not twelve.

"Twelve o'clock is straight ahead, six is behind you... you know what, never mind, just go ham kid," said John as Evie continued to cull the local pigeon population mercilessly.

"What are you doing Evie? You're pulling something out of them? And I'm getting Essence! We must find more pigeons urgently!" said Robert.

"All their juice. Electrical juice I mean. Pulling the actual juices out of them would be gross. I bet someone's got a power that does that though. Nasty. I have, like, a battery thing that I can charge up by sucking the electrical power out of living things. And robots... you see the buff?" she unleashed a Zap on the last visible pigeon which exploded into a cloud of feathers, "and that is what I can use my battery for".

"Righto," said Robert, sounding somewhat impressed. "Objective "remain in Evie's good books" just went up a few places! That buff is nice, I must say. It works on Doris as well but buffs her power regen instead of reserves. Do you think you can recharge Doris manually?"

Evie gave him a look. "Doris?" she asked sceptically.

Chapter 6 - Limited Chronomancy

"Yeah... Doris," began Robert confidently, "Uhh... Destroyer Originator Robot... um Issue Supreme. D.O.R.I.S." he finished in a far less assertive tone.

"Robert, did you just make that up and it really stands for something else?" asked Evie suspiciously.

"Certainly not! And call me Bob, young lady. Please would you be so kind as to kill a few more pigeons? Three more then I'll have one Essence so I can level up and then I can make this machine really special!" Doris clanged her orange arm against her chest.

They continued the walk towards the barrier they could now see faintly falling from the sky over the field where the country faire takes place in September. The rest of the year it was used for grazing sheep. It was a wide open space lined with old trees that towered over the buildings in town. As they walked John and Bob talked quietly, the hulking Doris plodding slowly down the middle of the road which was devoid of traffic. They discussed their concerns and theories as Evie continued to one-shot pigeons.

John explained the three options for modifications he had seen when levelling up and what they knew about them. As they reached the roundabout approaching the country fair site Evie got the 20th sky rat and Robert declared he could get a level.

"Shall I level here?" Bob asked panning the chassis of his bot back and forth across the empty streets.

"There's no traffic," said John, "and it doesn't take long. Well it didn't for us. Our powers don't involve building bots though."

"Right then." he took a deep breath that whistled around his windscreen. John wondered if he had a microphone system in there. "Level up," said Bob.

Team member Robert Gillybrook has chosen to spend one Essence and advance to Level 2.
Levelling in process...
Robert Gillybrook has chosen to modify Ability.
New status for team member Robert Gillybrook:
Level 2
Name: Robert Gillybrook
Ability: Mechanaut
Constitution: 100%
Reserves: 100
Ability: Mechanaut: A lifetime in the army fixing tanks has left you with a powerful obsession with armoured fighting vehicles. Now you can build them with magic! You will still have to maintain them though.
Guidelines:
Maximum Equipment slots: 7
Maximum Weight: 2000kg
Modifications:
Level 2: Equipment Slots available on primary Mech +5

"That is rather good if I do say so myself. Now I need to find things to make into 'equipment'," said Bob.
"As I mentioned, I might be able to help you out there-" began John.
"You know those crazy doomsday prepper guys on TV? Dad is like a budget English version of them. With worse teeth as well," another pigeon died in a faint blue glow, "the amount of random survivalist

crap he has in the garage for "just in case, SHTF, TEOTWAWKI" or whatever is frankly worrying, and that doesn't count the mediaeval stuff he's collected. Dad is it normal to have all that stuff?" Evie chimed in, finishing in an overly sweet voice.

"What were those abbreviations? I'm used to a lot of abbreviations but those are new to me?" asked Bob.

"SHTF and TEOTWAWKI? They mean… Well, don't worry about it too much. They both kind of mean the collapse of civilization. Zombie apocalypse kind of stuff," said John a little sheepishly.

Doris pivoted at the waist so the cockpit was aimed at John. From within, Bob's tanned face was peering over his moustache and giving John a look that kept switching between the joy of a kid in a toy shop with a pocket full of cash and deep concern about John's mental wellbeing. Ambivalence seemed to be the theme of the day for everyone. "I don't suppose there would be any firearms perhaps? Maybe a 155mm cannon in this stash of yours?"

"No, sorry Bob, but I have to respect your borderline insane optimism. I'm a prepper not a member of a militia!"

John turned his head to face Evie,. "And thank you for the brutally honest description, kid. Seeing as this is a literal apocalypse I think you are wrong to use the adjective "crazy" quite so liberally. If this whole thing doesn't completely vindicate me I don't know what would," John turned back to Doris/Bob and continued, "I'm not sure how much of it will be any good for you but within reason I'm happy to let you have some stuff. Let's go check out the barrier and then we can head back to my place, have a cuppa and see if there is anything you can use."

The fair ground was enclosed by a five bar wooden gate and a wire fence. The fence faced onto the roundabout at the end of Main Street and as they crossed it they could see the barrier, a waterfall of light coming down vertically from the sky halfway across the field. The barrier ran left and right, maintaining a fifty metre distance from the supermarket on the left. It followed the road down past the 17th century catholic church to the right; at the top of Station Road by the church they could just see it through the trees and hedges running parallel to the roadside. The barrier seemed to continue on and was inclusive of the industrial estate and high school that lay south and west of the church.

Evie climbed up and jumped down from the fence, scattering the nearest sheep. John blipped over to stand next to her. As they turned back to check on Doris and Bob they heard a crunch and saw Bob attempting to get Doris to step over the gate but misjudging as Doris' foot came down directly on the gate, which was promptly reduced to kindling. The centre of the gate was crushed and the extremities were yanked from the hinges and lock, falling down with a soft clatter onto the gravelled road.

"Oops."

"At this point I think we don't need to worry too much. We've got monsters coming after all." John picked up a length of wood from the now defunct gate and started walking towards the barrier. "You two stay back, I'm going to see what happens when you poke this thing." He set off towards the barrier.

"I wouldn't do that if I were you," came a female voice from up in a tree to their right.

John's natural level of paranoia, a legacy of a misspent youth, had been gradually building into a full blown tinfoil hat fest throughout the morning. He hoped he had managed to keep the worst of it from being obvious to Evie. With the unnatural quiet that prevailed in a town that should have been quietly bustling before business hours on a week day, he had grown gradually more freaked out. As a result, as soon as he heard the voice he turned and blipped Evie seventy metres back, just behind the wall separating the field from the supermarket car park. He couldn't do anything about Bob and Doris, too heavy, but he trusted the mech could handle itself as it was essentially an ambulatory tank.

Then he blipped himself into the branches of the tree where he had heard the voice, pointing the shard of wood at roughly where the voice had come from but falling slightly and struggling to catch the trunk as his feet landed badly on the branch he had aimed for. The woman before him vanished and reappeared a few metres away from the tree. *Another teleporter?*

Before he could blip again to land behind her he got a team notification:

Evie Borrows has used Identify and shared in team chat:
Level 2
Name: Katie Johnson
Ability: Limited Chronomancy
Constitution: 100%
Reserves: 500

As John appeared behind her once again, reaching for her shoulder to throw her to the ground or deploy his wooden spit, Katie once more vanished, reappearing on the other side of the trunk of the tree she had been hiding in. A blue glow crept out of her and moved towards Evie.

"Pax! Please, peace ok? Fuck that hurts! I'm not an enemy, I swear!" She called before John could teleport again. The blue glow faded as Evie stopped draining her.

"Why shouldn't we test the barrier, Katie?" asked John, moving back to Bob and Doris who hadn't done more than twitch his cockpit left and right in the interim.

"The last 'dudes' who tried it ended up like that," she said, pointing to what could be mistaken for a day-old campfire twenty metres from the barrier but which smelled slightly of roast pork now his nose caught up with his adrenaline. "Seriously... oh Identify, that's how you got my name. Makes sense. Why didn't I figure that out on my own?"

John's mind, normally fairly relaxed, had leapt into overdrive. "Identify is how we knew your name, you didn't know about it?"

"Dude, bloody op sec!" chimed in Evie, shooting a glare at John.

"I'm so glad you both decided to say that, the backlash from accessing non viable timelines is a proper pain. Makes the ability more trouble than it's worth to be honest."

"You're a precog? And you can teleport...?" asked John.

"Correct, well half right anyway! Yes to the precog but limited to glimpses, ten minutes at most into the future or past, it's not as useful as you think. I'm as likely to know in advance that a bird will fly past a window as I am to learn anything useful and if whatever I see doesn't happen I get the mother of all headaches. Apparently fate is flexible but doesn't like to be seen being flexible. I'm really not a fan of the skill to be honest. I can also freeze time for everyone else for short bursts and move about. Then I have to wait the same amount of time before I can use it again. I've shown you mine, what are you capable of? Turn around is fair play and if we want to begin a mutually beneficial relationship, honesty from all parties from the start usually yields the greatest gains for everyone involved."

"I'm a Mechanaut, my ability let me make this beauty. She's called Doris. A time stopper eh? It would be very useful to have you guard my dugout with me! Care to join this ragtag militia?" boomed Bob, stomping up and performing a very impressive bow considering he was in a 1.5 ton, badly articulated mech.

Evie arrived back with the group now gathered beneath the beech tree Katie had hidden in.

"I can suck your energy away or hit you with lightning, and I am not ok with just throwing out invites," she said with a scowl at Doris' back, reluctantly accepting that some of the team seemed to be inclined to trust this woman who she had taken a dislike to, possibly because when John blipped her out of harm's way she had landed in a puddle and her trainers were now wet through.

"I'm a teleporter. I can move myself, other people and... stuff. What turned the last lot to mess with the barrier into charcoal?" asked John curiously.

"The barrier did, of course. They threw a rock at it and then they burned." she closed her eyes shuddered, "it wasn't quick but it was thorough. Never made a peep either, must have been too hot for their lungs to work or something. Reduced them to ashy puddles in a couple of minutes." She took a deep breath. "Look, I'm kind of running on a ragged edge here, I was visiting town for work, I had a face to face with potential clients, my partner and kids are down in Devon. I could use some friends to get through the whatever-the-hell it is that's coming in an hour or so. You lot seem to be handling this better than most and aren't psychos like the piles over there. The things they were saying..." She grimaced and scrubbed a hand through her hair. "Everyone who isn't up and about is going to have to stop hiding soon but those of us out now can get a head start. Any chance of a team up? Me and you guys?" she finished with a winning smile at them all and a hand thrust into the air waiting for a high five.

Doris delicately raised a hand and gently tapped a massive three fingered fist against her palm. She then saluted with a clang.

"How did you get your Essence?" asked John, they had had to massacre pigeons, he wanted to know how Katie had managed it. "Rats. When it's quiet the little buggers come out to play, especially in the edges of the fields. When I got the notification I had just set off for a run so I bolted for the trees and hid. I was staying in an air BnB at the end of Main Street. I've always hated rats since I was young. I saw one, stopped time, stomped on its head," She raised up a blood stained right running shoe so they could see the red, "and got 0.1 Essence. I moved over to the field and nine later, I was trying to figure out how to level up. Is this system created by an idiot or what? It takes twenty reserves to stop time for ten seconds or catch a glimpse of the future, with one level I went from five uses to twenty five uses. It's been a while since I played WoW but that is a steep power climb for my first level."

She sighed. "Look, are we good? Can I join up with you guys? Please?" She seemed quite forlorn as she said please.

John and Evie's family were scattered here and there but being apart from them was normal. He could only imagine how he'd feel if Evie had been away at her Mum's when this started. Both trapped in barriers, thirty miles apart. It would have driven him crazy.

Teamchat:
Evie Borrows: I'm not sure pops.
Robert Gillybrook: I LIKE HER! SHE'S GOT SPUNK!
Evie Borrows: Stop the all caps Bob! And gross, spunk has a different meaning these days. Of course you like her, you perv.
John Borrows: She seems OK. Someone who can see the future... she could let us know ten minutes early what the wave will be! More time to plan. I don't get a bad vibe from her and she must be feeling rough being stuck away from home. Shall we vote?

Robert Gillybrook: I vote Aye.
John Borrows: Kiddo?
Evie Borrows: I'm not sure but she's not hiding in her house. And she kills rats for fun... maybe she'll feel the same about sky rats? Fine, whatever: yes.
John Borrows has sent an invitation to Katie Johnson to join Unnamed team... Katie Johnson has accepted.

Level 2
Name: Katie Johnson
Ability: Limited Chronomancy
Constitution: 100%
Reserves: 500
Ability: Limited Chronomancy
Always watching the clock for yourself and others you have developed an obsession with time. Catching glimpses of the future and controlling the flow of time are now within your grasp. This is taking your work home with you to an extreme.
Guidelines:
Time control: Pause time for up to 10 seconds. You can still act as normal. The abilities cool down is the same as the time as you paused for.
Past and future sight: Up to 10 minutes.
Modifications:
Level 2: Increase reserves X5

Chapter 7 - Putting the loot inside Doris'... "dimension"

In a rare display of common sense they decided that not messing with the barrier was probably the best course of action. The newly expanded team turned and headed back to Main Street, crossing the northern part of the car park to get to the ginnel that lead from town itself to Northfield Drive. As they walked the adults talked about their worries and possible plans for the wave while Evie murdered any small bird she saw. John and Evie got up to three Essence so they could level once more and both Bob and Katie had the two they needed to get level three. At that point John convinced Evie to end her slaughter of feathered fiends to which she reluctantly agreed, albeit while continuing to complain noisily about flying pests.

At the north end of Northfield Drive was a transformer, turning the high voltage grid power supply into 240v suitable for the homes in the neighbourhood to use. John had Evie Identify it just to be sure it was essentially infinite overcharge Zap refills for her. It was. Keeping it in line of sight would be vital for the upcoming wave he decided. She could draw on it without damaging anyone's home.

They rounded the corner to the left and John and Evie stopped. The others noticed after a moment and came to a halt themselves.

"Well this is it," said John gesturing to his home, "Casa de Borrows, my home is your home etc"

Katie suddenly burst into laughter, snorting like a pig looking for truffles.

"I know it's not much but that's just rude…" said John.

"It's not that! I just got a glimpse... it's a doozy... bwahahaha!" Katie said, "ah I'm sorry!" she wiped her eyes with her wrists.

"Go on, sorry again... hrrmph hrmmph" she buried her face in her sleeve to muffle her continuing laughter.

"OK. When someone who can see the future starts laughing hysterically... On the plus side it made you laugh, not scream or panic, so... that's good I guess?" muttered Evie.

John and Evie's house was an end terrace property built in the late eighties. Two storey red brick construction with a scratch of grass at the front that John never kept neatly trimmed. When asked he always replied he liked things to be a little wild. In reality he just hadn't cared about the aesthetics of the street.

"Where should I park?" asked Bob, shuffling Doris from side to side on the road.

"On the drive, just don't wreck the elderflower tree that's trying to take it over." The tree in question was not much of a tree, barely five feet tall and was growing from a crack between the wall marking the edge of the drive and the drive itself. "I make elderflower tincture from the fruit in autumn. Oh, also don't turn anyone's cars into parts please? Most of my neighbours are pretty much strangers to me but I still don't want to piss them off."

"By tincture, he means elderflower vodka by the way," offered Evie innocently.

"Yup, that's a tincture," John grinned, "booze and medicine rolled into one. A double shot in a tall glass topped up with lemonade and ice with a twist of lime: sweet vitamins and alcohol. The best of both worlds."

Bob carefully waddled Doris over and sidestepped into the driveway. Once he was happy there was a hiss and a crunch as the front of Doris' chest opened up and he carefully clambered down to the ground. Bob stepped forward offering his hand to the rest of the group. "Bob, nice to meet you, in the flesh so to speak" he smiled at them all.

Bob was heavily tanned and his hair had silvered at the sides. He looked as though he had once been in excellent condition but age was starting to catch up with him. About 5 and half feet tall he stood a few inches shorter than John and the same height as Katie. Burnished skin suggesting a Mediterranean heritage with a full head of carefully trimmed hair that John, as a possible avatar of male pattern baldness, was certainly not jealous of. He was everything you'd expect in an ex tanker who could now make fighting robots.

Evie in comparison was short, pale and ginger. At just over five feet tall she was slim with her hair running down her back like a waterfall of copper fire. John took his turn to shake the old man's hand, standing 5 inches or so taller and just beginning to set into middle age himself, he was still about the same weight he was in his early twenties, but it had moved from muscles on his limbs to a slight beer belly. His cropped, greying hair was fighting a valiant but hopeless defensive action against his ever rising forehead. His scruffy beard was wild and untrimmed earning a reproving look from Bob. Katie stepped up and greeted Bob, she was a slender woman in her thirties, hair dyed blond and clearly a lady who exercised regularly. Out of all of them, she looked the healthiest, although that wasn't saying much to be fair.

"Let's head round the back, the time is... 08:00 so we have forty five minutes to figure out a plan and level up," said John, "...and just a heads up but the dog is going to be insanely happy to meet you. I don't have many visitors so she gets very excited when she meets new people."

Katie burst out into further inexplicable giggling which John chose to politely ignore.

They went into the garden and John unlocked the patio door, moving in first and pushing Zeeg back so the others could get in. Evie entered last and closed the door. As soon as it was evident no one else was coming Zeeg lost interest in John and immediately mobbed Bob and Katie. Jumping up, tail wagging like a piston, ignoring all instructions to calm down, she insisted on sniffing them from top to tail as they fought their way through the canine affection to the living room.

"I'll put the kettle on. How do you take your tea?" called John, leaving Evie to wrangle the overexcited puppy and give their guests a chance to sit down. As soon as they were on the settee Zeeg broke free from Evie and immediately jumped into the middle of the settee, resting her head on Katie's leg and her backside on Bob as she rolled over, fishing for tummy rubs, tail still wagging like a machine but now it was thwacking Bob in the arm. Katie and Bob called out their preferences while wrestling the dog as John brought a glass of cordial through for Evie.

"How about you guys level while I sort the tea, do you want biscuits or anything? Then I'll magic up the dog and we can figure out the best way to survive and prosper in what's coming" John called as he returned to the kitchen.

"No biccies for me thanks, I'm watching my weight," called Bob, "I've got to ask, why do you have replica set of Roman armour but with a Greek helm on top of your bookshelf? Why not a matching set? And there are a lot of swords in this house. A worryingly large number of swords."

"Evie, go grab the crossbow out of my wardrobe please," John asked, "well most of the swords are just toys, movie replicas, that kind of thing. Not much more than lumps of metal shaped to look like swords. No tangs, no edges, scratch the shiny surface and it's pig iron underneath if you're lucky. I did get a few pieces before the laws got all temperamental about mediaeval weapons back in the late nineties. The armour was for a Halloween costume, not sure why I got the helm. I kind of collect this stuff I guess? If you can use them I'm fine for you to have most of them to equip Doris."

"You sir, are a scholar and a gentleman... oh wow!" Bob exclaimed as Evie returned with the "semi-automatic" crossbow and three packs of bolts. "Now this I can use for sure! It's hardly a howitzer but it's better than nothing. How much would I owe you for the armour and helm, a couple of the prop swords and the crossbow?" Bob enquired.

"I'll just put it on your tab," chuckled John, "I can teleport, Katie can freeze time and Evie isn't strong enough to use the armour. Just promise if you get the ability to make gadgets or robo-suits or whatever for the rest of us it will be at cost! Share and share alike?"

"Not a problem John. Scouts honour! I'm going to level and then go equip Doris with this gear? Ah thanks" he finished as John handed cups of tea to Bob and Katie.

"Couple of things," said John, "based on what we got when we levelled: Ability and Efficiency will give you boosts or changes to your guidelines or resource pools. The named ones seem to be weird and kind of good but we don't know how often they'll come up, so we don't really know enough to have a solid understanding. The rest are all multipliers, times two to whatever which are also really strong so I don't think you can go wrong. No idea what utility will give but best guess is it will follow a similar pattern."

Bob looked thoughtful for a moment, "I am going to roll the dice and see what Utility looks like I guess. I can recharge the old bird with reserves and I'm not going to lie, I can move her about easily but constant rapid actions take it out of her quickly, cost reduction and recharge rate are sorely needed now I have some parts to equip her with, but I'll take one for the squad and explore new worlds where no man has gone before! Level up!"

Team member Robert Gillybrook has chosen to spend Two Essence and advance to Level 3.
Levelling in process...
Robert Gillybrook has chosen to modify Utility.
New status for team member Robert Gillybrook:
Level 3
Name: Robert Gillybrook
Ability: Mechanaut
Constitution: 100%
Reserves: 100
Guidelines:
Maximum Equipment slots: 7
Maximum Weight: 2000kg
Modifications:
Level 2: Equipment Slots available on primary Mech +5
Level 3: Pocket dimension. A private mini universe. Store your stuff, store your friends, grow plants or raise animals, build a town. It's kind of up to you. 1km x 1km. Accessed through Doris' derrière.

"I am sorry Bob, but I am not walking through your robot's arse," declared Katie immediately.
"That is absolutely insane," continued John, "we could just hide in there throughout the wave if we need to! We need to check it out and set up some kind of base. I've got food and water, cooking and camping gear. If someone gets hurt we can hide them away in Doris'

behind. Reminds me of a joke from when I was a kid: yo momma's asshole is so big when King Kong and Godzilla got into a fight they..."
"Shut up Dad. So Doris' butt is now a pocket dimension. That solves any loot issues we may have in the future but dibs on not being responsible for putting the loot inside Doris'... "dimension". Actually we should discuss loot rules sometime soon. I will not have my stuff ninja'd by noobs." Evie declared.
"How bizarre. Can I get that crossbow please? And a couple of the fake swords? Once I've geared her up we can have a shufty up her back passage. Politely and in a gentlemanly fashion of course," offered Bob.
"I don't know how there is even a rule for gentlemen in that kind of situation. Fill your boots but we really need to find a better way of referring to this storage space. I vote for storage space. Any takers?" replied John.
"I think I prefer The Shed, or maybe The Ultimate Man Cave. I'll think about it and get back to you!" Bob stood and snapped to attention.
He took the crossbow as well as a fake oversized gladius and a longsword with a word of thanks to Evie. As he struggled out the door he asked John to blip the armour and helm over to Doris. John stood by the front window and did as he was asked. A faint feeling of loss troubling him for a moment. The swords were junk but the other stuff was good gear and had been quite expensive. With a sigh he decided he didn't need them anymore and to trust that it would be worth it. He turned back to Katie, Evie and a still frantically excited dog.
"So which of you is going next?"
"I will, if you are still OK about magicking up Muttley?" John nodded and Evie declared "Level up and make it a good one this time!"

Team member Evie Borrows has chosen to spend three Essence and advance to Level 4.
Levelling in process...
Evie Borrows has chosen to modify Ability.
New status for team member Evie Borrows:
Level 4
Name: Evie Borrows
Ability: Electrogenesis
Constitution: 100%
Reserves: 200
Guidelines:
Maximum Discharge: 240V
Line of sight required.
Modifications:
Level 2: Reserve capacity X2
Level 3: Waste not Want Not.
Level 4: Elemental Body: Briefly transform your physical being into one of pure electricity, becoming immune to physical damage. Costs no reserves and all reserves recharge to full while in this state. Lasts for 10 seconds, cool down period 10 minutes.

Evie immediately flashed into a glowing, crackling jagged silhouette of herself and zipped in and out of the front window several times, leaving smouldering footprints in John's fireplace rug and smudged, smokey marks on the window. She also caused Bob, out in the drive, to jump and swear in a way that most sailors would be ashamed of as he tried to work on Doris.

She returned to her normal form standing amid faint curls of smoke rising from the singed rug wearing an extremely self satisfied smile.

Chapter 8 - This will get messy won't it?

"Kid, that rug was a gift from Grandma..." grumbled John.
"Who cares? I'm electric now! Let's see Smith try and mess with me at school, that little turd!" yelled Evie, sparks crackling around the finger guns she was waving in the air.
"Child..."
This word was followed by the sternest of looks John could muster which while very stern indeed wasn't on a par with, say, the look someone might give having been clipped round the head by a waiter for no reason. It wasn't that far off though.
"Sorry dad. You know you go a bit cross-eyed when you give me The Dad Glare™?"
"No I don't and that won't fix the rug... Maybe next time check your clothes will go with you *before* you zip into the street? Lucky break there for you *and* the rest of us. I've got to say though, that mod is amazing. Almost teleportation, phase through glass, maybe other stuff? Can you travel through metal or conductive material? Fully restores reserves, do you think that might include your constitution? Even if it's just your reserves, that is broken as hell. Immune to physical damage? So you'll want to dodge enemies with elemental powers or whatever but otherwise it's a temporary invulnerability! If it's a heal to full health as well... that will be a massive weight off my mind. Regarding Smith, who the hell calls their kid Smith as a first name... I'm pretty sure none of your friends and frenemies from school will have been gifted powers yet so he will just be a baseline human. I don't think you need to worry about any of them for now," said John.

"Can we go give Max and George powers? Maybe Millie too, she's pretty cool? She lives just up the road." Evie asked hopefully.

"Nope, we've got less than an hour till kick off now. They will have to look out for themselves I'm afraid."

"As amusing as watching a man-child try to parent and it being strangely effective, I'm going to level up now if that's OK with you two? It is? I'm so glad. Level up!" said Katie.

Team member Katie Johnson has chosen to spend two Essence and advance to Level 3.
Levelling in process...
Katie Johnson has chosen to modify Ability.
New status for team member Katie Johnson:
Level 3
Name: Katie Johnson
Ability: Limited Chronomancy
Constitution: 100%
Reserves: 500
Guidelines:
Time control: Pause time for 30 seconds. You can still act as normal. The abilities cool down is the same as the time as you paused for.
Past and future sight: 10 minutes.
Modifications:
Level 2: Increase reserves X5
Level 3: Increase maximum time control X3

"I am not a man-child... So is that thirty seconds pause for twenty reserves? That would mean fourteen seconds for ten reserves with the cost reduction for using less than fifty percent? And three seconds for two reserves?" asked John, sipping his tea in between sharing a Dad Glare™ between both Evie and Katie. He was feeling generous this morning but they didn't deserve a full Glare each.

"One sec, or rather fourteen of them- and now I'm stuck for fourteen seconds with it on cooldown," Katie didn't move and nothing happened except her reserves ticked down by ten in the Team display. "Yeah, this system is insane. At this rate the whole world will have god-like powers in a few hours. I'm guessing the shorter stops used judiciously will be my best bet."

"You can do a surprising amount in three seconds," said John thoughtfully.

"Is that what your ex wife said?" chortled Katie.

"How did you know I'm divorced?"

"No ring, single dad, this house does not have anything even close to a woman's touch, you've got a mounted goat skull on your mantelpiece for god's sake. But it's clear Evie lives here full time from all her bits and pieces lying around. No regular dusting either. I work with people, reading them is kind of my thing."

"Oh great, the HR edition of Sherlock Holmes in my house judging me." John mock-glared at Katie.

"In order to become a demi-god they need to A) survive and B) fight. Most people are just hiding under the covers it seems," he finished. From the driveway there came the sounds of clanging and an extremely excited whoop. "Sounds like Bob is making progress at least," he smiled. "Sweetheart, can you try to level up again? I know you don't have the essence but I want to see how much it says you'll need."

"It says I need five for level five."

"Damn. It's a Fibonacci sequence. Early levels will be quick and then... levels will be few and far between."

"You know I hate maths dad, care to spell it out for someone who prefers English?"

"Each number is the sum of the last two numbers in the sequence. One for first level, one for second level, two for third level, three for fourth, five for fifth, *eight* for sixth, *thirteen* for the seventh and it will just keep getting worse. By the time we get to level ten we'll need a lot of essence per level. Now the power curve doesn't seem quite so broken. We will stop levelling unless we hit a lot, and I mean a *lot,* of essence before very long. we'll need hundreds of thousands to get into the twenties."

"If the challenge keeps ramping up we might be OK? Still, best to make the most of the early upgrades. I could really do with a spreadsheet to work it all out," said Katie.

"Not to change the subject but it's about now you decide to "magic up the mutt" and if you don't I'm going to have a crippling headache." she stifled a giggle.

"Do you know something I should be aware of before I do this? Either you're on the laughing gas or this is going to be a very funny experience for you. On a totally unrelated note, would anyone like something to eat? Maybe we could spend a few minutes talking about our feelings or discussing philosophy?"

"Bastard" laughed Katie "Just make a super dog already, you know you want to."

Would you like to use one Essence on Dog: Zeeg Borrows to awaken her ability and invite her to your team? Y/N

"Yes"

Are you sure? Elevating non sentient species can have unexpected consequences. Y/N

"Christ, I know she's not the best behaved dog but she's got a heart of… whatever, Yes."

You have gifted one Essence to Zeeg Borrows and she has joined your team. Initialising advancement to level 1 for Zeeg Borrows. Calculating...
Complete.
Level 1
Name: Zeeg Borrows, AKA Get down you stupid dog; yes I know they are walking their dog on your street but be quiet; why don't you understand fetch; why do you always go mental when I'm in a Teams meeting; this is not your half of the bed.
Ability: Ghostly Sight Hound
Constitution: 100%
Reserves: 100
Ability: Ghostly Sight Hound
What have you done? She's a natural thief and spy, always watching and listening and now she has superpowers. In line with her nature she has become stronger and faster and harder to catch. We told you this was a bad idea.
Guidelines:
Ghost Form: Become incorporeal for 10 seconds
Physical Enhancement: Constitution and speed increased 100%

Katie fell off the sofa laughing as Zeeg raised her head.

Team chat:
Zeeg Borrows: JOHNDAD, I WANT A CHEWY TREAT, the nice one with the chicken wrap not the ridgy ones you call Dentachew. CAN I HAVE THE CHICKEN WRAP TREAT NOW?

"Um, Hi Zeeg and I guess so and you can just call me John if that's OK?" began John then he had a thought. A big and important thought. "You can only have a treat on one condition though. You need to start following what I say. Not ignoring me until I use the angry voice, not running off whenever you smell or see or hear something interesting. You need to be a good girl OK?" Now that she was The Dog Who Could Walk Through Walls, John was suddenly very concerned about the kind of trouble she could cause.
A loud crash followed by swearing so explicit it cannot be recorded sounded from outside. Something had distracted Bob at a bad time. The words "The fucking dog???" in an incredulous voice echoed down the chimney and into the living room.

A bark and what looked suspiciously like a dog's version of a disingenuous grin was the response but he went and fetched her the treat she wanted.

Congratulations, for unlocking team buffs ahead of schedule all team members receive One essence.
Calculating team buffs...
Evie Borrows: 1% improved reserve recovery rate
Katie Johnson: 5% improved reflexes.
Robert Gillybrook: 1% damage reduction
Zeeg Borrows: Seeing Eye Dog

John Borrows: Hide and Seek Champion 2024

Full buffs are unlocked when you have a complete team of 10 members and allow you to name the team. These buffs are permanent and require no upkeep.
Seeing Eye Dog:
Team mates can close their eyes and use Zeeg's senses as long as both parties are willing.
Hide and Seek Champion 2024:
All team members are aware of the location and distance of all other team members. Both parties must be willing. Removes line of sight requirement for using abilities on friendlies.

"Haha! now do you see why I was laughing? This is not your half of the bed hahahah! You soft bastard!" guffawed Katie.
"To be fair dad, you do treat the dog more like a badly behaved human than a dog," said Evie.

Team chat:
Zeeg Borrows: Zeeg bad?

Her eyes rose from the chew she was demolishing on the singed rug in front of the fireplace to flick between Evie and John. Big and brown eyes possessing a sadness that was heart wrenching to behold.
"No Zeeg, you're a good girl. When you listen," said John gently.

Team chat:
Zeeg Borrows: Zeeg will be better. Zeeg will listen.

She immediately lost interest and focused on finishing off the treat.

"Hey dog, think or say: Level up" said Katie.

Team chat:
Zeeg Borrows: Nope, you are not my human.

"You can level and get stronger. Faster, tougher, better able to steal food," said Katie.

Team chat:
Zeeg Borrows: LEVEL UP!

Team member Zeeg Borrows has chosen to spend one Essence and advance to Level 2.
Levelling in process...
Zeeg Borrows has chosen to modify Ability.
New Status for team member Zeeg Borrows:
Level 2
Name: Zeeg Borrows, AKA Get down you stupid dog; yes I know they are walking their dog on your street but be quiet; why don't you understand fetch; why do you always go mental when I'm in a meeting; this is not your half of the bed.
Ability: Ghostly Sight Hound
Constitution: 100%
Reserves: 100
Guidelines:
Ghost Form: Become incorporeal for 10 seconds. Immune to physical damage and can pass through solid objects.
Physical enhancement: Constitution and speed increased 100%
Modifications:
Level 2: Barghest

The black dog of myth. You are more of a tan colour but you can now shapeshift into a very large tan dog, increasing physical characteristics and damage. Lasts 60 seconds, cool down 10 minutes.

Team chat:
Zeeg Borrows: I am the best doggo. Going to hunt.

Zeeg promptly became incorporeal and walked through the wall. Sniffing at Bob who was frantically doing something that defied the laws of physics to John's crossbow and muttering to himself. He absently reached out a hand to pat her on the head but it passed right through as she was functionally not there.
"Weird dog." he muttered before going back to attempting to clamp a heavily modified semi automatic crossbow to a strange gimbal system he had just finished mounting to Doris' left shoulder.

Team chat:
John Borrows: Zeeg don't go far ok? It's not long till we get attacked. And don't go through the walls into other people's houses PLEASE!
Zeeg Borrows: Will I get a treat?
John Borrows: If you stay close and don't walk through peoples walls you will get a treat.
Zeeg Borrows: Ok, needs to be a good treat though...

"Right" said John with a long suffering sigh, "Thirty minutes to the notification. I can get a level and then I think we need to come up with a rough outline of a vague idea of a plan for how we are going to do this and not die. Katie do you think you can spam your Glimpse skill when it's the ten minute countdown please? If you get a look at the notification early it could be a game changer."

"Sure thing champ, now do your level"

Team member John Borrows has chosen to spend three Essence and advance to Level 4.
Levelling in process...
John Borrows has chosen to modify Utility.
New status for team member John Borrows:
Level: 4
Name: John Borrows
Ability: Teleportation
Constitution: 100%
Reserves: 100
Guidelines:
Maximum weight: 500kg
Maximum Distance: 1km
Line of sight required
Modifications:
Level 2: How about we split the difference? You always were a cheapskate. Maximum cost reduction due to efficiency bonus' increased to 99%
Level 3: Weight limit x5
Level 4: Portion control. Sometimes you don't want to teleport the whole cake, just a slice. You don't want to get fat do you? Well now you can teleport parts of things instead of the whole thing. This will get messy won't it?

Chapter 9 - Is it a suppository kind of thing?

"This will get messy... what the hell are they turning me into?" wondered John in growing horror.

"If you teleport me, please make sure you move the whole cake," said Evie.

"OK, twenty five minutes to the notification. Let's get organised," said Katie.

Teamchat:
John Borrows: Bob, are you about done mate? About to get a fresh brew on and we need a plan of action.
Robert Gillybrook: I'll be two minutes, just fixing the crossbow on, do you have any optics? Sights, binoculars, a telescope. Anything like that would be great.
Evie Borrows: I'll go get my telescope. Not like I use it anyway.
Robert Gillybrook: Thanks Evie!
John Borrows: Zeeg, can you come back as well please? We want to all stick together from now until it begins.
Zeeg Borrows: OK. Coming back now. Getting big is great. Angry man shouted at me, then I got big and he ran away. It was good.
John Borrows: I did ask that you not cause any trouble. Come back now and I'll let you have a treat anyway.

John briefly closed his eyes and connected to Zeeg through Seeing Eye Dog. He could see the ground blurring past beneath her. She was on the other side of town and at her current pace she'd be home in a couple of minutes. She had always been fast, the lean build and musculature of a greyhound coupled with her larger size had made her very strong and very fast when she was a regular dog. Now she was clearly much faster. Deciding to try out an experiment John looked through her eyes and searched around for a suitable target. *Time to try out portion control and see if using Seeing Eye Dog gets around the line of sight requirement.*

It was still eerily quiet on the streets. Through Zeeg's eyes John couldn't see any other people moving about. *That will do,* thought John. The top third of a lamppost blipped sideways one foot and crashed to the ground, startling Zeeg who leapt onto a six foot tall wall by reflex and sped up.

Teamchat:
John Borrows: I can use teleport on things Zeeg can see. It counts as line of sight! Come on home girl. Tummy rubs have been earned!
Zeeg Borrows: Woof!
Evie Borrows: Zeeg, you don't need to type woof into the chat. Just say OK or yes boss or to hear is to obey!

John got the kettle on once more and returned to the living room to wait for it to boil. How many cups of tea was that this morning? Too many. Or not enough.

They discussed their options, waiting for the others to return. Evie was adamant they stay within sight of the transformer so she could constantly top off her Zap and her buff. Katie wasn't particularly bothered where they fought as long as they had good sight ranges so they couldn't get snuck up on. Bob wandered in through the back door and took a seat as the kettle started whistling. John went and made a final round of tea and fished a pack of digestives out of the cupboard to dunk.

"We'll need to keep our strength up and I doubt there will be a paid hour-long lunch break once the wave starts so top yourselves off with the biccies. I'll make some flasks of tea. And some sandwiches. Evie, can you go get a couple of the big bottles of water out of the garage please? Just pop them in the kitchen for now."

Evie left to go about her task as Zeeg walked in through the wall of the living room.

Teamchat:
Zeeg Borrows: Treat? Nice treat?

"Sure thing pup, how about some cheese?" asked John.

Zeeg's tail briefly went nearly hypersonic; it wagged so fast. John left and came back with a thick slice of cheese he broke pieces off and threw to Zeeg who caught them with a 'clomp' sound as her jaws snatched them out of the air. Then he began to share his thoughts.

"We can't be everywhere so most of the town is going to have to take care of itself. I'm sure there are others out there who have been messing about with their abilities who can hopefully help themselves and anyone else nearby," said John.

Teamchat:
Zeeg Borrows: Saw some people. Scary, tried to catch me but too slow. Hurting people. But not my people so I didn't fight and ran away.

"So not everyone is going to be a maximal altruist, that's sad but unsurprising. It will complicate things," added Katie. "So where are you thinking about setting up shop, JohnDad?"

"Just John... You know what, don't worry about it. I was thinking Northfield drive would be good. It's the road leading to the path into town and it is all retirees. They are in old folks' bungalows, I don't think the coffin dodgers will be early adopters and someone will need to try and keep them safe. We don't need to go running around trying to keep everyone safe but if we set up somewhere good for us and we can help some people as well? That seems pretty reasonable. If we stay towards the north end of the road we can keep the transformer in sight, maybe set Evie up on a roof as she's all ranged damage. She can get a bit of oversight as the situation develops. Zeeg can scout and bait the baddies back to us. whatever they actually are, assuming we get this area under control. Bob will be on the ground tanking, I can't port Doris so we'll need to keep him covered and not let him get swamped. Katie, do you want to be on the ground as well?"

Katie considered it for a moment. "Where will you be?"

"I figured I'd stop on a roof and use Zeeg as a mobile sensor array but blip about as needed when not using Seeing Eye Dog. I can port anything she can see so I can protect her as she scouts, that way I'll be hitting targets before they get near us, which is an aspect of it I *really* like. So I'll aim to thin the herd a bit if we are lucky? Anything goes wrong I can port you out of danger if you are on the ground supporting Bob? I'd think it would mostly involve not getting in the way of Bob and Doris for you."

"That's fine but I will hold you to the emergency rescue thing. I'm going to need some sort of weapon if I'm going to fight. I doubt I'll just be able to stomp on the monsters' heads."

Evie returned carrying the telescope John had bought her for her fifth birthday, shortly after she had come to live with him full time. Bob's eyes went wide and he did an excellent re-enactment of the mad scientist cackle he had been doing when John and Evie first ran into him.

"Perfect! Thank you so much, Private! I'll need a couple of minutes to fit this before we start... and I haven't shown you how strong Doris is now!"

"No worries dude" said Evie, "Katie, Dad probably has us covered in terms of weapons, he didn't give Bob the good stuff, except the crossbow. Do you think we can use Doris' butt to bring food and drinks and things? Maybe blankets in case it is still going tonight and we get a chance to rest?"

"Both good points kiddo" John stood up and went upstairs. He came back a few moments later with an armful of things that clattered and clanged as he put them down, then went back out to get a few more from the kitchen and garage. "Knives, hatchets, a machete, a Kukri, a short spear and two bows with... thirty six arrows. Oh and the katana. Who wants what?"

Katie looked at John, "You're not normal are you?" Pretty sure most of this is illegal these days," Katie reached and took the katana, "mind if I take this one?"

"No problem and it's all perfectly legal as long as it never leaves the house. Which we are about to do but I think the police will have other things to worry about. Bob, you have to fit in the cockpit so I suggest this knife for you and Evie you *are not taking that spear!* You can have a knife for emergencies or whittling, understood?"

"Didn't want the stupid spear anyway," she grumbled moving her hand away from it. "Does it become my knife? Not yours, no take backs allowed? Mine forever?"

"Fine, but it's not a toy!" Evie snagged the survival knife from the pile. It was nothing fancy, a six inch blade razor sharp on one edge. She clipped the sheath to the top of her jeans and swaggered about a bit looking very pleased with herself.

John took the spear, just over a metre long and tipped with a long double edged blade. The handle was some sort of composite material that was marketed as "unbreakable". John figured that might be put to the test soon if things went sideways. As an afterthought he undid his belt and threaded the Kukri's sheath through it so the curved knife sat on his left hip. And then he stuck a sheath containing three throwing knives into his pocket. He reached out again... but figured that was probably enough so dropped his hand.

"Bob, can you incorporate this into Doris as well?" John passed Bob a Bluetooth speaker.

"She isn't a walking stereo system, John. She doesn't even have a CD player at the moment. Next, uh, *unwanted* car we find I will fit a radio to her though. Had to use the parts from the first two for bits of the actuators in her limbs and the control panel. What do you want it on her for?"

"A taunt!" Evie exclaimed, realising John's plan. "Basic video game setup: Bob, well Doris, is the tank, literally in her case and keeps the mobs focused on him slash her so we can burn them down. Katie and Dad are control/DPS and I'm DPS. Zeeg serves as scout. We could really use a healer and then we'd be pretty well balanced. Bob gets the attention, Dad and Katie control, killing where possible to stop Bob getting swamped, all while I blaze away from the back lines. I like this plan."

Bob took the speaker and put it next to the telescope. "It's not standard protocol to have your armour out front these days. Usually a tank crew digs in, makes a fighting pit with an easy exit to escape return fire. But I guess this isn't the army anymore. So, I'm big, noisy and attention grabbing while you keep them off me?"

"Sounds good," said Katie, "now Mr Doom Prepper, how much food and water have you got in this rat's nest of a home?"

"Hah, um, seventy litres of water in five litre bottles in the garage, camping stove with half a dozen gas refills for boiling water plus pots and pans. a couple of thousand water purification tablets, cleans one litre per tablet. A couple of life straws good for two thousand litres each. About forty kg of spaghetti, twenty kilos of rice, loads of tinned tomatoes and fruit, loads of tinned meat and fish out in the garage, a bunch of legumes, lentils, pearl barley and beans and whatnot in big jars in the cupboard under the microwave..." he paused briefly to draw in a deep breath before continuing, "uh we don't know we'll be able to come back or if this place will be destroyed, might as well load up Doris' caboose with everything we might need. Evie, please could you show Katie and Bob the stuff in the kitchen, oh don't forget the fifty kg of flour in Harry's bedroom... I'll go start moving stuff out of the garage. Medkit! Grab the medicine bag from on top of the cupboard as well! Probably pretty useless, no antibiotics but there are bandages, closure strips, disinfectant, plasters, loads of things that might be handy. Oh and the solar power station thing, big battery with a three pin socket so we can run a microwave or a light or a laptop and watch movies... if we get time. The solar panel is next to it under my desk!"

"Harry's bedroom? Who's Harry?" wondered Katie watching in mild amusement as John bustled off ranting to himself about preps, gear, calories per person per day, litres of water per person per day... *The guy seemed to know his stuff, at least a little* she thought.

"Harry isn't a real person, it's a joke. His bedroom is the cupboard under the stairs... From the book..." Evie grinned seeing the look of incomprehension on Katie's face. "Your poor children. Anyway, Dad always said it was better to have something and not need it than to need something and not have it. He's going to be insufferable now, seeing as there is an actual apocalypse. Good job he was wrong about the grid going down though."

"Seeds! Don't let me forget the heirloom seeds! We might need them come spring. Tools! Shovels and the garden forks! And grab the can opener! Finest invention mankind ever came up with! Bring the whole cutlery drawer actually! And the booze cabinet! Or just the booze I guess..." echoed John's voice from the garden, fading away as he disappeared into his garage.

John immediately teleported all the crap he had been meaning to clear out of the garage into the middle of his garden and felt a sense of great pleasure knowing how much time teleporting was going to save him when it came to chores, should chores ever become a concern again in the future. He rapidly blipped the cans of meat, the water, the camping equipment, tents, sleeping bags, an array of hand tools he didn't really know how to use but which would make most pre-modern carpenters green with envy, all of it was rapidly piled next to a very different looking Doris.

"Bloody hell Bob!" The sight of the new and improved Doris was enough to snap John out of his prepper fever dream.

Doris was far less clunky now. She was more streamlined with slender armoured limbs and the addition of articulated armour covering her torso with large pauldrons on each shoulder clearly showing the design of the lorica segmentata Bob had received from John. The torso gleamed in burnished steel, replacing the mismatched colour scheme from merging the cars. The arms were sleeker, each with a sword blade resting along the outside of the forearm and atop the left shoulder was a crossbow that was clearly a primitive cousin to the shoulder mounted weapon preferred by the Predator. John really hoped it had a laser sight. All the loose wires and bits dangling from joints earlier had vanished.

"Nice, very nice," John said in admiration.

"I know right? Two ticks" Bob put down the speaker and telescope and picked up the helm he hadn't attached earlier. Katie and Evie had walked with him and now stood open mouthed by the gate, dropping the bags loaded with food and trinkets they were carrying. Zeeg once more walked through the wall and chimney to emerge next to John but remained unimpressed, sniffing at Doris' feet uninterestedly. Bob closed his eyes and his reserves dropped sharply as grey mist poured out of him and surrounded the items in his hands that blurred together and moved up to meld onto the chassis. Finally turning Doris from an ambulatory lump with arms to something that was starting to look like a proper mecha. The helm had one large reflective eye set on the right side of the vision slit and within the cheek guards the grill of the speaker could be seen. She now stood nearly five metres tall and was extremely menacing.

"Can we swap powers?" Evie asked Bob, "that looks pretty sweet."

"You got what you were given kiddo, come with me and let's grab some more stuff," said John, resuming his frenetic effort to fill Doris' butt space with a survivalist's hoard.

Evie fetched things from cupboards and dropped them in front of the patio doors while John stood in the garden and blipped them to the gate. He then moved over to the gate and blipped them over to Doris' side. In less than two minutes they had cleaned out everything useful in the kitchen including seasoning, herbs and spices (no reason roughing it had to include bland food after all) and deposited it next to Doris.

"So how do we get into the pocket dimension?" asked Evie. "Is it a suppository kind of thing or is there a door we can use?"

"Not sure..." Bob moved round to Doris' side and suddenly a rectangle of light appeared by the robot's leg. "Well that worked."
"Zeeg can you go stand inside please? Then I'll blip everything in." asked John.
The dog, for once obedient, walked through the door of light and vanished. They all closed their eyes and looked out through Zeeg's. Inside was a flat white expanse, totally featureless, that seemed to extend forever but this was probably due to a lack of reference points.
"I like big butts and I cannot lie, all you other brothers can't deny, when a girl walks in with an itty bitty thing I get... crap, can't remember the rest. Anyway, let's put some junk in the trunk!" sang John as the items outside began to rapidly blip into Doris' trunk.
Katie checked her watch as the last of the food and gadgets vanished. "Twelve minutes to notification. I'll start trying to get a glimpse as soon as we are under ten minutes. Then we revise the plan if needed and rest up so we have full tanks when it starts."
"I'll go put the kettle on then," John looked between them, "I would suggest we all use the loo before it starts as well, apparently finding a safe place to have a dump is one of the worst parts about being in an active combat zone. Besides the risk of dying I suppose."
Zeeg wandered into the garden, phasing through the gate that had swung shut behind them and set about relieving herself next to the discarded junk from the garage.

Chapter 10 - Maybe looting laws would be relaxed

As the kettle boiled once more John rolled himself a cigarette and looked at his pouch. Half full. Good for a few days, maybe more if he cut back a bit. He had a sneaky feeling whatever was coming would make him want to smoke a lot more but not have the time to. Maybe looting laws would be relaxed and he could "borrow" a few pouches next time he passed a shop and stock up? He tucked the pouch into his pocket, blipped over to the patio door, slid it open and lit up. No point worrying about Zeeg getting out now that she can walk through walls, he ruminated, but that is going to pose a challenge. She goes nuts when another dog walks past the window and now she can phase through the glass, and the wall... It will come as a surprise to the fat bloke with the three rat-dog things that yip back at her! John smiled at the thought.

Deep drags and the cool air settled him down after the rush of loading up Doris. The others were talking quietly in the lounge when he heard Katie announce she would start using her future sight. John continued smoking peacefully, surprised at how calm he felt. He should be panicking. God only knew what was about to attack them. Sure they had weird super powers now but the system must design the waves to still be dangerous to them. He was growing more and more convinced they weren't in their right minds.

Not that this was some psychotic break or a fever dream but that the system had changed them all somehow, while leaving most of their personalities the same. Altered their emotional responses, made them calmer, more accepting of this dramatic shift in their lives and able to cope with the strange change of circumstance. None of the others seemed to be noticing it but Bob should have been more worried about his son and Katie had barely mentioned her kids. John was man enough to admit that he had sometimes reacted poorly to sudden shocks, emotional or otherwise, and had in the past not dealt with things like that very well; taking this situation in stride was somewhat out of character and he knew it.

"Got something, get your arse in here!" called Katie.

John put his smoke into the jar he used for butts and called out, "I'll bring the tea, I can hear you from here!"

"OK so I didn't get to see the notification but I saw that we stuck to the plan. I saw us getting set up round the corner, pulling food and drink out of Doris, Evie up on the roof. Evie was teasing John, something about "at least they can't fly so you can be useful". Katie sighed. It took me nine tries to get even that much. Mostly I saw Zeeg sniffing things. Or... cleaning herself. Oh and one time... John, you really shouldn't pick your nose."

"Ah, um, old habits and all that.... Can you keep trying please? So we know it's ground based and we stick to the plan. That sounds like we are approaching this the right way at least," John looked sheepish and desperately tried to divert the conversation away from his nasal hygiene routine.

"Maybe, it's just a glimpse, I don't get context, I don't know how relevant a glimpse will turn out to be even if it actually happens!"

"How about someone just reads out the text of the notification over and over again for a few minutes after it comes out? If you catch a glimpse of one of us going over it we can know in advance right?" suggested Evie.

"Maybe but I really think the system is limiting me, which is why I'm getting so many close ups of Zeegs behind being... washed. I think it is mad at me for trying to cheat?"

"Are we saying it's sentient now? Or reactive at least? I don't think it likes me much judging from some of the descriptions of my mods. It's possible it's reacting I suppose. Please can you keep trying anyway?" asked John.

"Will do. I'm quite sure that your dog has the cleanest bum on Earth though," Katie returned to using her ability as Bob dipped biscuits in his tea and shovelled them away. John was fairly sure that he'd have had a quick nap as well if he could. The old army rule of sleeping and eating whenever you get a chance.

Evie had created a small ball of crackling energy she was rolling from hand to hand, in her own world as she explored her ability. Zeeg flopped out next to Katie on the sofa and rolled over, one front foot thrust forward the other curled back, the classic " more tummy rubs please" pose. Katie absent-mindedly began stroking Zeeg's chest.

John sipped his tea and considered rolling another smoke. He started rolling two, one for before the wave and one handy for if he got a break at any point. Always be prepared. Dyb dyb dob dob or whatever the Boy Scouts say.

"If we know where we will fight, why don't we head over now and start setting up? We might be able to improve our chances, build some barricades or something? It can't hurt right?

Bob looked at John, slowly dipped his biscuit once more before stuffing in his mouth. "I'll go suit up" he grinned then slurped down his tea.

"Alright Iron Man... Katie can you walk and see the world of tomorrow at the same time?" asked Evie.

"Sure," said Katie, finishing her tea, grabbing her sword then heading for the back door. John picked up his spear, weighing it in his right hand and wishing he had stuck to his numerous resolutions to start exercising again over the last few years. He was fairly sure desk jobs being so common nowadays was responsible for a lot of illness as unused bodies just wasted away.

As they walked out onto the drive Bob was clambering up into Doris whose chest then closed, the lower armour clam shelling shut and the windscreen coming down to seal with a hiss.

"You good dude?" John stepped back as Doris stepped to the side and moved out into the road.

"Better than good. She's a lot more nimble now." Doris began clomping along the road towards the site they had chosen to fight, and possibly die in. The others tagged along, Zeeg zipping ahead and back again tail wagging. As they rounded the corner they had a brief discussion and chose to set up right as the road curved and the bungalows sprang up on either side.

"Put me up there please dad?" Evie pointed at the garage roof. Blip. "Woah." Evie wobbled for a moment before sitting down, perched at the peak of the garage roof and clinging on with both hands.

"Bob, where do you want to be? We've got a good line of sight down towards town and Evie and Zeeg can watch that side, shall I make some barricades on this side of the transformer?"

Doris suddenly surged forward, and pivoted at the hip with arms outstretched. The swords shot out so they extended a couple of feet from her fists. As the mecha pivoted at the waist she just kept going, blurring around creating a whistling circle as the blades flashed round and round.

"And now I'm dizzy. I need... however much room that was but a safe line of retreat is vital," came Bob's woozy voice from within Doris. A white rectangle of light appeared behind the mecha. "Grab what you want from the stash while my head stops spinning?"

"Calling it the stash is much more palatable. I'm getting nothing useful from the future. I'll get the stuff, you do your barricades" Katie began going in and out of the door. Bringing out some food, water, the medkit, the bows that John paused to string and set up rows of arrows pierced into the turf. They built a modest pile of essentials at the foot of the garage Evie was perched on while she tossed a ball of lightning from hand to hand. Clearly she had been experimenting with her ability, John was worried but trusted her not to fry herself. Mostly. John took a quick look at a street he had walked down everyday for years going to and from the shops with a fresh set of eyes.

He began by scooping chunks of road out to create a trench and piling the mass up behind on the side closest to them. He could go one metre deep, sixty centimetres across and one metre long or variations thereof for ten reserves. The weight of the concrete and soil was the limiting factor. Half a ton of dense material isn't as much as you might think. The houses were close to the road here. The road was just shy of four metres wide. A one metre path on the left side... Bushes and trees in front of the six foot spiked iron fence that ran around the school to the right. He began scooping out a trench two metres deep and two metres across in chunks. He had built a barricade and trench from the house to a quarter of the way across the road from the left for eighty reserves. He had four minutes till the notification, five reserves per minute... plus 2% from buffs so seven per minute… maybe six more scoops before the notification.

As the clock ticked down John got to the point where the trench and barricade extended into the middle of the road, forcing anything coming round the corner to pass through a much narrower space. He'd get five minutes to work on the other side after the notification but the time to discover their fate had finally arrived.

Initialising the first wave...
Normanby, population 4327. Classified as a small town.

First wave is a survival event. Survive or hide are your only options. Fight hard and get stronger or hide and stay weak.
Rolling for Wave type...
Normanby has selected Swarm Wave.
Rolling for creatures...
In fifteen minutes Normanby will be attacked by 12981 R.O.V.S.S.
R.O.V.S.S.
Rodents Of Various Shapes and Sizes. Rat-like monsters varying in level and abilities. Due to early advancement by some of the population level range is set to: 1-14.
You have nine hours until the wave ends. Any surviving R.O.V.S.S at the end of this period will flee through the barrier and begin setting up nests in the nearby countryside. They will breed rapidly and become an indigenous threat in a short amount of time.
Good Luck.

Evie cackled from above "At least they can't fly so you can be useful Dad, flying things are your kryptonite!"
"I'm not so sure now, I can just blip their wings off I think?"
"Gross Dad, just keep that kind of thing away from me. I like these jeans and washing magic rat blood out... What am I saying? You do my laundry! Go crazy with it."
"You know how the washing machine works young lady. Maybe it's time you took up a few more chores around the house?" John glanced up and saw his daughter grinning down at him. Evie blew a raspberry at him and resumed bouncing a ball of lightning from hand to hand. John went back to building a trench and barricade to the north. He had five minutes before he needed to stop to recharge for the start so

three more scoops. He began working on the other side of the road, leaving a narrow gap between the trench and barricades to hopefully funnel the beasties into a choke point. When he was done they all returned to the garage and passed around sandwiches and mugs of tea, John blipping a cheese and ham up to Evie. Bob cracked his windscreen and accepted a flask to keep inside with him.

"Does she have cup holders?" asked Katie

"She's a fighting machine not a family saloon! Although next time I level or find a car I can "borrow", cup holders will be on my list, after thumbs and a radio."

"Should I try and catch a glimpse?"

"Probably best you're at full reserves when we start. We know enough I reckon" replied Bob.

"Bob, back up Katie and Katie can you guard the pass between the defences? Three second pauses and a few swings of ole reliable then take cover behind Doris to recharge" John pointed at the katana in her hand as he said reliable.

"Evie is on overwatch keeping the south checked out and I'm floating and available wherever I'm needed. Zeeg, can you scout the north first then head down to the marketplace, as sneakily as possible? Be very careful puppy! Please don't put yourself at risk."

Zeeg snorted but nodded her understanding.

"A couple of possible rules I'd like to suggest if that's OK?"

"Sure, Katie" said John.

Katie pushed her hair back behind her ears and began. "Firstly, hair bobbles for us girls. Don't want hair getting in our faces or getting grabbed so some kind of ponytail or bun is in order. Evie, do you have some spares?"

"In Doris' prison wallet," replied Evie.

"Charming, I believe we just agreed to call it the stash but thank you. I'll grab them in a moment. Secondly, communication and teamwork. Evie, John and I guess Zeeg needs to be keeping an eye on Bob and I. This is going to be intense so we need to be looking out for each other."

Katie looked around the group and everyone nodded, Zeeg wagged her tail and yipped. "Finally reserves. Twelve thousand rats, it had to be rats didn't it? Anyway it's a lot. We'll need to make the most out of every point we spend so we need to be smart about it. Evie, no lightning bombs if that is what you've been working on, unless it's desperate! Stick to draining as much as possible. John, little ports, portion control is your best friend. Just port ratty heads a few inches to one side. Sounds icky but it's 0.2 essence and seeing as you only have 100 total you need to make the most of it. And keep enough to pull me or Evie out of trouble so twenty reserves minimum held back. Can you use those bows?"

John nodded, "Not very well but I can usually hit a barn door on the third try".

"So keep them in reach." Katie continued, "it's better than nothing if you need to recharge for a while. "Bob, don't push yourself, realistically how long can Doris fight for?

"She's a lot better now that I, um, borrowed the battery from John's lawn mower."

"Dude, that was a gift! Are you a klepto?"

"Is everything you own a gift? Anyway now I should be good for up to fifteen minutes of fighting but then she'll need to do not very much at all for a good ten minutes. She can walk but it will slow down the recharge. Maybe we can figure out a recharge option from Evie?" Bob turned the mech to look up at her on the roof.

"I can try but everything I push power into goes zap... it would be pretty bad if it happened in the middle of a fight."

"Let's rule that out until we have a chance to experiment when we aren't about to be eaten by giant rats. We can provide cover if Doris needs to recharge. Any other business?"

"Did you work in HR by any chance?" asked Bob.

"Management but yes. Why?"

"No reason," Bob replied.

"I've got something to add," Evie pulled back her hair and tied it up into a ponytail before continuing. "Remember your roles. Katie you're a killer, stone cold, heart made of ice, murder machine! You don't fight fair or play nice, you stop time, move in and slash then move out as quick as you can. Bob, you're our juggernaut, unstoppable and in your case a *literal* murder machine. However killing rats is not your primary objective here, big guy! Be big and scary and hold the attention of anything we can't kill quickly. Doris is tough and they are going to be rats. How strong can they be against that much steel? Dad, you're a killer and support. Blip stuff's heads off or whatever and blip rats away if they are going to get one of us. I will be the prime murder machine" she declared proudly, "culling the herd with drain and lightning grenades. Any questions?

"Not a question but we *are* going to have words about how much time you spend playing online games after this," grumbled John.

Chapter 11 - No more GTA for you Bob

As the clock ticked down to 09:00 the tension rose but not as much as you might expect. John blipped a can of coke up to Evie who cracked it open and took a gulp as he lit up his pre-wave smoke. Katie was doing stretches and faint sounds of singing were coming from Bob within Doris' chest.

"Whatever will be, will be, the future's not ours to see..." grated a rough singing voice that sounded more used to bawdy rugby songs than anything else.

"Is that Que Sera Sera you're singing Bob? I love that song! Who sung it again?" asked Katie, moving onto arm swings.

"I have no idea what you are talking about," said Bob quickly, cutting off the singing.

5...
4...
3...
2...
1...
And they're finally off!
Survivors: 4327
R.O.V.S.S.: 12981

John threw his cigarette butt into a grate, consigning it to the sewers forever, and straightened up, rolling his round shoulders. *Really should have started working out more when I hit forty. Desk jobs really aren't good for people.*

"The die is cast as they say. Stay frosty people"

"Dad, don't quote Caesar and Aliens at the same time, you're going to jinx us and we'll get Xenomorph Rat Lords who are military geniuses or something." He waved dismissively at her, perched on the apex of the garage roof.

"Freddy foreshadowing! Can you see anything up there, Short Stuff? John replied.

"Other than your bald spot? The glare is really interfering with my vision... Nothing really. Wait a sec... Actually yeah, looks like a cloud or something? It's moving in from the barrier out past The Acres. Bits keep swooping down at houses I think?"

"Pooper, I'm going move you up there and borrow your eyes OK?" Zeeg yipped and crouched. John then blipped her up next to Evie who reached out with one hand to steady her.

As John blipped Zeeg up they began to hear distant reports, crashes, explosions and faint screams echoing from all across town. It seemed they weren't the only ones fighting. Three R.O.V.S.S per human didn't sound that bad but the humans were separated, a lot of them confused and scared. Many were simply hiding it seemed, and would be little help today.

Seeing Eye Dog gave the team a much clearer picture than Evie could provide verbally. Zeeg's eyesight was clearly enhanced by her ability and she could see fine details all the way to the barrier. John used Identify and confirmed what Zeeg's eyes were telling him.

Sky Rat.
Level 2
Weight 5kg

Evie groaned, "We already won the sky rat war! This is crap! No do-overs system, you cheating git! There's hundreds of them! Can I maybe get down from up here please?" she asked plaintively.

The cloud of sky rats was swooping down and flooding into chimneys. If the houses had log burners or sealed fireplaces they should be OK as the rats wouldn't get loose in the house but if it was an open fireplace anyone in there would be forced to defend themselves as swarms of winged rodents with a mean disposition poured out of their chimneys. As they watched minor swarms flew back out of some of the chimneys while more sky rats bolted down into others, clearly having found victims. It was like a ravenously hungry swarm of evil Rat-Santas had been unleashed to the north of them.

Through Zeeg's excellent vision John felt he had a good chance to start doing some damage. As long as he could see the target, it weighed less than 50kg and whatever he moved was sent less than 100 metres he could use his ability very efficiently.

The sky rats didn't respond initially as the southernmost rats' heads started blipping one foot to the side of their bodies. Sprays of blood flew from the necks as the now dead rodents lost momentum and began to spiral and plunge down to the roofs and streets beneath. They were spattering the quiet streets of Normanby in shocking sprays of brilliant ruby blood.

John checked his reserves. Four reserves spent for twenty of the swarm. He went back to it, heads and bodies beginning to fall in ever increasing numbers transforming the world beneath them into a scene from hell. Gore and twitching bodies quickly covered the rooftops and presumably the streets below as well. The council street cleaners were going to make his life hell if they survived. As he found his stride it began to look like a crimson waterfall from a serial killer's worst dreams. The swarm became agitated, finally starting to duck and dive as they spread out but if he could see them he could hit them. Dodging didn't work against his ability.

As John worked through Zeeg to thin the swarm the sky rats moved close enough to spot Evie and Zeeg on the roof. Almost as one they shot forward sensing easy prey, foolishly exposed in the open. By now the flock had been substantially reduced but there were still a hundred or so literal sky rats hurtling towards them. The tiny rat bodies hung between flapping, furry bat wings, chittering and screeching, jagged rotten teeth snapping on the air. Having finally found the killers of their kin they closed in with vengeance in mind. John worked frantically to whittle them down before they closed with the team. Now they had a target it became clear their earlier movements were aimless scouting and once they could see victims the remaining beasts flew fast and true towards them.

At forty metres, as they passed above the transformer, Evie yelled something incomprehensible and probably very rude. Her right hand pulled back, a ball of crackling energy taking form in her palm and she threw. The ball sailed through the air and hit a sky rat a few back into the swarm. The ball detonated. Arcs of lightning flickering through the swarm, setting fur alight in places and shocking the whole group. A blast of power came from the transformer itself in response to the surge, bolts shooting up to hit the rats missed by Evie's ball made sure all the rats got zapped to some degree.

The survivors of John's attacks broke into spasms as Evie's power washed over them and they fell from the sky, some dead, some smouldering, unable to fly but feebly still trying to reach them, dragging their bleeding, smoking bodies across the ground, leaving thin trails of red in their wake. The survivors' vicious crimson eyes glared at their killers as they crept forward despite being half dead.

"Got 'em!" called Katie. She ran forward. Watching someone stop time to move and attack was like watching an old movie, one recorded on physical film but with only one frame every three seconds left in. Katie appeared over some of the survivors and then the next moment the rats were all slashed open and Katie was off to one side to let the cool down elapse. She flickered back and forth half a dozen times before walking slowly back to the barricade, clearly tired and shaking blood off her sword.

John checked through Seeing Eye Dog to confirm no more were currently coming for them. With a clear sky he felt confident enough to query for an update:

Survivors: 3951
R.O.V.S.S.: 12420
Team report: 365 Literal Sky Rats killed. 0.2 essence per kill. Essence gained 73 for each team member.

"Ha, 420, that takes me back..." said John, feeling giddy and slightly crazed. He worried that online dictionaries that included the phrase 'to paint the town red' would in future just have a picture of his face. He was out of sorts, to say the least. He sat down sharply and pulled out a smoke, lighting it up as he fell back against the grass staring at the sky.

"That was awesome!" called Evie from above, "did you see me nuke them? Boom! So cool!"

Katie sat down next to the barricade and put her blade across her knees. "Zeeg, Any sign of more enemies nearby?" Zeeg cocked her head for a moment to listen and scanned around. She woofed in a way that was somehow clearly negative. "Evie, get your levels... 73 essence! How many levels even is that?"

"Most of the way to nine I think. You level up, Sausage, I'm just going to have a smoke and chill for a bit." John stared glassy eyed into the sky as he puffed away on his cigarette.

"You ok dad? You seem a bit..."

"I'll be right in a few minutes kiddo. I just... I didn't expect it to look like that, you know? Like a black cloud raining blood and body parts... and I was causing it... Give me a minute and I'll be OK." he began rolling another cigarette while still drawing on the current one. Evie looked at her dad, worry clear on her face. *He used to be a gamer too, this shouldn't be such a big deal to him* she thought.

Team member Evie Borrows has chosen to spend 47 essence and advance to Level 8.
Levelling in process...
Evie Borrows has chosen to modify Ability, Efficiency, Efficiency and Utility.
New Status for Evie Borrows:
Level 8
Name: Evie Borrows
Ability: Electrogenesis
Constitution: 100%
Reserves: 1000
Guidelines:
Maximum Discharge: 720V
Line of sight required.
Modifications:
Level 2: Reserve capacity X2
Level 3: Waste Not Want Not.
Level 4: Elemental Body
Level 5: Increase Maximum Voltage X3

Level 6: Reserve Capacity X5
Level 7: Reserve Regeneration X2 (base level now 10% per minute)
Level 8: The Flesh Is Weak. Reduce the cooldown for Elemental body to 5 minutes.

"Wow Evie. Just... Wow. How strong was that ball lightning you threw?" asked Bob.

"It was the max and had a full overcharge. I know, I should have been more careful but I panicked and I'd just figured out how to shape the lightning into the ball which lets me manually overcharge it. Now I can do one three times as strong and have so many reserves I don't need to be stingy though so it's OK, right?" A blue glow shot from the transformer as she topped herself up and refreshed her waste not, want not buff on the team. "Who's next? Gotta be quick, there's still a lot of the little buggers running around somewhere."

"Language! Young ladies shouldn't swear. Katie you go next?" suggested Bob as Evie made the hand gestures for a very obscene phrase in ASL at him, which he did not understand and chose to ignore. "Give John a bit longer. First time in combat can hit some people hard," he added gently. John raised one hand and waved lazily at the mecha from his prone position on the grass, regular clouds of smoke floating up above him. "I'll need parts to make the most of my level gains I think... Do you reckon those cars down the road are... important to anyone?"

"No more GTA for you Bob!" called Evie.

"What on God's green earth is GTA?"

Team member Katie Johnson has chosen to spend 50 essence and advance to Level 8.

Levelling in process...
Katie Johnson has chosen to modify Ability, Efficiency, Efficiency, Utility and Utility.
New status for Katie Johnson:
Level 8
Name: Katie Johnson
Ability: Limited Chronomancy
Constitution: 100%
Reserves: 1000
Guidelines:
Time control: Pause time for 60 seconds. You can still act as normal. The abilities cool down is the same as the time as you paused for.
Past and future sight: 10 minutes.
Modifications:
Level 2: Increase reserves X5
Level 3: Increase maximum time control X3
Level 4: Increase maximum time control X2
Level 5: Reserve Regeneration X3 (base level now 15% per minute)
Level 6: Maximum Reserves X2
Level 7: Isolated Temporal Flow
Level 8: Rewind

Isolated Temporal Flow:
You can speed up or slow down a target's relative time frame. Enhance your allies and hinder your foes.
Rewind:
Undo the last second of time across the entire universe, returning the pieces to where they started. You retain the knowledge of

what would have happened. Requires reserves to be above 80% and will reduce you to one reserve.

There was a woof. An ominous woof.

Team member Zeeg Borrows has chosen to spend 52 essence and advance to Level 8.
Levelling in process...
Zeeg Borrows has chosen to modify Ability, Ability, Efficiency, Utility, Utility, Ability.
New status for Zeeg Borrows:
Level 8
Name: Zeeg Borrows
Ability: Ghostly Sight Hound
Constitution: 100%
Reserves: 400
Ability: Ghostly Sight Hound
Guidelines:
Ghost Form: Become incorporeal for 60 seconds
Physical enhancement: Constitution and speed increased 300%
Modifications:
Level 2: Barghest
Level 3: Increase incorporeal time X2
Level 4: Increase Physical enhancement X3
Level 5: Maximum Reserves X4
Level 6: True Shapeshifting
Level 7: Enhanced Senses
Level 8: Increase incorporeal time X3

Teamchat:

Zeeg Borrows: I continue to be the best!

Zeeg had grown physically. She was a couple of inches taller at the shoulder and she had filled out. In the same sense that a steroid abuser fills out, she had been mostly bone and muscle due to her breed before John had given her an Essence but now she was taking the look to a whole new level. Now she looked like a dog with a serious addiction to the gym. She did a dog grin and wagged her tail, knocking a tile off the roof behind her.
"OK, Bob, do your thing," said Katie.
"Sure, go check on John will you? He needs to snap out of it, can't have a loose link in the platoon while we are in harm's way. Level up!"

Team member Robert Gillybrook has chosen to spend 50 essence and advance to Level 8.
Levelling in process...
Robert Gillybrook has chosen to modify Utility, Ability, Efficiency, Ability, Utility.
New status for Robert Gillybrook:
Level 8
Name: Robert Gillybrook
Ability: Mechanaut
Constitution: 100%
Reserves: 400
Ability: Mechanaut
Guidelines:
Maximum Equipment slots: 7 (available 4)
Maximum Weight: 6000kg
Modifications:
Level 2: Equipment Slots available on primary Mech +5

Level 3: Pocket Dimension
Level 4: Neural Interface
Level 5: Increase Maximum weight X3
Level 6: Maximum reserves X4
Level 7: Overdrive
Level 8: Gadgeteer

Neural Interface
Once you have the parts you will be able to create a mind/machine interface. This will significantly reduce the command-response delay associated with manual control.
Overdrive
Spend 100 reserves to dramatically increase the speed and strength of Doris for 60 seconds.
Gadgeteer
No self respecting tinker is unable to make weapons, armour and gadgets for his friends to help them kill their enemies. Now you can be slightly less ashamed.

"John, come on mate you need to sort yourself out please" Katie said softly, crouching down next to him.
"It was... awful. What the fuck am I? It rained bits of them... all over... Jesus Christ..."
Katie looked him over. They didn't have time for this. Desperate times call for desperate measures. She stood, grabbed him by the front of his collar and lifted him slightly. Her hand pulled back until it pointed straight at the sky and it swung through 180 degrees to slam into John's cheek with all the force she could throw behind it.

Chapter 12 - Fire in the hole

As the slap landed Katie saw John's gaze snap into focus and lock onto her. She stopped time. His eyes had burned with rage and Katie knew in her bones it wasn't just the slap that caused the anger. The anger was just there, the slap had simply broken through the masks this man wore while he was in a state of shock. The easy going attitude, the dad jokes, the doom prepping, swift adaption to this system... the doting father... Who or what was this man really? She moved back to stand behind Bob, out of John's line of sight, before she unfroze time.

John's eyes snapped back and forth and when he couldn't see the target of his ire his eyes softened and he raised his right hand to rub his jaw.

"Relax, Evie," Evie had brought back an arm to throw a lightning ball at Katie and was using most unladylike language regarding Katie's ancestors and progeny that surprised even John, who was used to the foul mouthed child's verbal explosions. The things they learn on the playground these days. As well as from gifts from crotchety grandads...

"It was the right thing to do. Although it could have been a little gentler," He rubbed a smear of blood from his lip where the slap had split it. 99% constitution. 100 of those and I'd be dead. *Maybe we don't just need to worry about being instantly killed.* Death by a thousand cuts was still an option.

The fugue state from the horror of what he'd done was still there but he had been yanked out from wallowing in it and was no longer overwhelmed. He hadn't been hit by anyone for years and while it stirred up unpleasant memories best left buried, he had to admit that it had worked. He was still shaky and horrified but he was thinking and functioning again. He began to roll yet another cigarette.

"Zeeg anything coming?" he asked as he licked the paper and rolled the tobacco into a cylinder and put it to his lips.

Teamchat:
Zeeg Borrows: Nothing in sight. Lots of noises though, bad noises. All around. Screaming, tiny feet scurrying, bangs and crashes and something scratching underneath.

"Thanks girl, can you go scout up to the north?" he raised arm and pointed away from town, "don't go far and be careful! Come back if there are any enemies." Katie emerged from behind Bob and asked if he was ok. He nodded curtly, avoiding her eyes. Zeeg jumped down from the roof and in moments was disappearing around the corner 200 metres up the road.

John lit up and said "Update"

Teamchat:.
Survivors: 3204
R.O.V.S.S.: 11403

A thousand of us died in exchange for two thousand of them. One thousand people, that was more people than John would see, let alone speak to, in a month.

This, John decided, was neither acceptable nor sustainable. Some people must have gotten some levels, the first levels were easy to get Essence for, so with luck the ratio would start swinging back in humanities favour soon. John knew he would have to get his shit together and start evening the odds. Fuck this system. His anger turned outward and focussed on the system. He would not fail and he would keep his daughter and new friends alive come what may.

"Level up"

Team member John Borrows has chosen to spend 47 essence and advance to Level 8.
Levelling in process...
John Borrows has chosen to modify Ability, Ability, Efficiency and Utility.
New Status for John Borrows:
Level: 8
Name: John Borrows
Ability: Unlimited Teleportation
Constitution: 100%
Reserves: 100
Ability: Unlimited Teleportation.
Guidelines:
Maximum weight: 2500kg
Maximum Distance: 3km
Modifications:
Level 2 (Rare): How about we split the difference?
Level 3: Weight limit x5
Level 4: Portion control.
Level 5: Maximum Weight X5
Level 6: Maximum Distance X3
Level 7: Reserve Regeneration rate X5 (base regen 25% per minute)
Level 8: Where did I leave my keys?

Where did I leave my keys?

A question you will never ask again. Think of an object or person. Your system enhanced memory will let you know exactly where they were the last time you saw them. If they are within your range and weight limits you can then teleport them. The desired object must be within ten metres of where you remember it being for this ability to work. Removes all Line of Sight limitations.

"Ok. So 250 kg and 300 metres for 0.2 essence. Really need to get a boost to my essence reserves. Or do I? 25% regen is 25 per minute, plus the team buffs is 27 per minute. So one point after just over two seconds which is five ports. Only problems will be outside of the efficiency reductions..." he muttered to himself.
"Dad, are you off with the fairies again?" Evie called.
"No sweetheart, I'm fine. I just got a major power boost and I'm trying to wrap my head around it.
"Good because it looks like Zeeg is coming back and bringing a lot of new friends with her!"

Teamchat:
Evie Borrows is sharing Identify results:
Level 1:
Chittering Scavenger

"How many?" called Bob.
John blipped up to stand next to his daughter on the roof. "I think the technical term is 'a metric fuck-ton'," he said slowly.
A sea of claws and fangs snapped and scratched as it rounded the corner behind Zeeg, many simply rushing past the turn and tumbling as they tried to change direction but were moving too fast. As John

stared they just kept coming. Zeeg was dodging back and snatching a couple of scavengers at a time then leaping away to worry them and break their backs before repeating the process, leading them towards the barricade.

"Evie, nuke em when they get into range, don't hit Zeeg. Bob, I think you're up mate. Doris should be alright just stomping these things. We'll watch your back." Heads of rodents began to blip away from their bodies releasing sprays of gore.

Doris stepped through the choke point they had made earlier and strode towards the tidal wave of flesh and teeth surging after Zeeg. As she saw Bob move towards her, Zeeg used her Barghest ability and rounded on the swarm. She grew to nearly two metres at the shoulder, her fur thickening and darkening. Her fangs extended and her claws threw bits of tarmac into the air as she launched her greatly increased bulk into the swarm. Evie yelled out in concern but it soon became clear the dog was in no danger as rats and parts of rats began flying into the air. She thrashed and kicked, stamped and bit as the swarm broke around her like a wave on the bow of a boat.

The outer edges of the swarm moved away from the murderous hound and towards the houses lining the road. They quickly began scratching at the doors, climbing up the walls and throwing themselves head first against the glass of the windows. Soon, doors began to splinter and crack as the relentless razor lined maws of the 50cm long monsters found purchase and they worked to widen the damage. Screams and shouts began to come from inside as the people hiding realised what was happening.

"John, we have to help them," said Katie urgently.

John took half a second to assess the situation. Bob would shortly join Zeeg to serve as a distraction, his amplified yells already drawing some of the horde towards him as Doris ran towards the fray. Zeeg would

have to disengage when her Barghest ability ran out. There were a dozen or so houses down each side of the street although only three or four were under serious assault by the swarm at the moment.
"Evie, Katie, I'm going to move us all closer. Evie, you bomb near a door, I blip the door away and then Katie to the doorway. Katie, stop time and drag out the survivors then I'll move you all to safety. We let you reset your ability then we go again. Sounds good?" they both nodded so John moved them to twenty or so metres behind where Bob was beginning to squish rats. Being well over four metres tall, Doris' helm was on a level with first floor windows now. The scavengers quickly took notice of her and began to scramble at her armoured legs despite the massive size difference. The rats rarely found any purchase and either flew off if they were lucky, or beneath her feet if they were not.
"Go easy Evie, they're level ones and we don't need too much space to work here. We do not want to fry anyone bracing the other side of their door!"
Evie nodded, toned down her power and lofted a weak ball of lightning towards the doorway of the nearest house being invaded. It landed and fried all the rats in a two metre area. Just after it landed John blipped the door away and Katie in.
With no time seeming to have passed Katie was standing holding a middle aged man and women, both looking shocked, and John blipped them in sequence to just behind the trio of fighters.
"How long is the cooldown?" he demanded.
"Fifteen seconds," Katie replied, panting. John began blipping the heads off of rats attacking houses and Evie drained them while they waited for Katie to be able to use her ability again.
"Next one Evie!" Evie hauled back her arm and lofted another ball of electrical death.

The couple they had rescued had regained their senses in the meantime and approached the trio.

"What the hell is happening here? Who the hell are you? What the fuck were those things?" yelled the man they had rescued. He was late middle aged and long since gone to fat.

With her part of this attack done Evie turned to the man and said "Language! There are children present!" which earned a snort from Katie that was cut off as John removed the door and blipped her into position. Katie immediately appeared holding a young woman clutching a toddler. John blipped them back to join the growing group.

"What are those things?" asked the woman they had rescued.

"Did you see the system message?" asked Katie, "This is what it was talking about. Please rest and take a moment, you're safe for now. John, can you get them some water, maybe a little food?"

John focused on sandwiches and water, in the pile on the other side of the garage. He could see perfectly in his mind's eye where they had been. Blip, blip, blip. A five litre bottle of water and the remaining sarnies appeared at his side. "That is going to be insanely useful. We should have a moment or two I think. Bob and Zeeg are keeping most of the little shits attention and they don't look to be about to break in anywhere else."

"Please, have something to eat and drink. I'm sorry it isn't more but this is a very difficult situation for all of us." said Katie in a gentle voice.

The young mother burst into tears and her little boy began trying to comfort her, not understanding what had caused the distress.

"Sweetheart it's alright now, what are your names please? What a lovely little boy you have!" Katie reached out and guided her to sit on the curb, wrapping the pale blue blanket back around the child where it had fallen away. She had used Identify but didn't want to disturb the woman any further by magically knowing her name.

"Helen," she sobbed, "Fred," she gestured at the kid with her chin and her eyes caught Fred staring up at her, confused and frightened. Helen pulled herself together and tried to smile at the boy.

"Just hang in there you two OK? We need to help some other people but you're safe and we'll explain everything as soon as we can alright?" Helen nodded, Fred looked at Katie and gave her an uncertain thumbs up. Katie smiled at them and stood back up.

"Young lady, you had best explain what is happening right now." blustered the man they had rescued. His wife was pulling him back and whispering to be quiet.

"Please sir, this isn't the time. We are still in a dangerous situation until the swarm is dealt with."

"Fire in the hole" called Evie, having seen another door begin to give way. They repeated the process and in a matter of moments another couple were safe behind the lines and Katie was checking if they had been hurt.

The new couple immediately started speaking to the man and woman they had rescued earlier, demanding explanations.

"This bitch won't tell us anything" exclaimed the first 'gentleman', failing to listen to his wife's increasingly urgent demands that he be quiet. Evie pivoted and drained him into unconsciousness. He fell back into his wife's arms who began fretting and talking about his heart condition.

"Please tell me you didn't kill him or give him a heart attack?" whispered John. Evie briefly looked panicked then her eyes lost focus for a moment.

"Nah, no kill notification. Just drained him a bit. He'll be alright and we'll be better off with him quiet."

"When did my little girl become such a savage?" asked John quietly.
"I'm only eleven, I still get to blame my parents!" she replied with a smirk.

Then a door at the end of the street flew open and a young woman emerged waving her hands in front of her. Wherever she pointed, rats burst into flames and screamed, curling up like bugs under a magnifying glass on a sunny day. After a few seconds she swayed and collapsed to the ground, the swarm gathered itself and closed in on her prone form.

Chapter 13 - Not any more

John reacted fast, a couple of rats had just begun to chew on her leg when he blipped her behind them. He looked at Katie and said "check the house" before blipping her to the door the woman had emerged from. Katie was suddenly running down the road half way back to them, the rats behind her slashed open and the sword she carried coated in red. John managed to catch her with a blip as she paused after clearing the immediate area of the swarm and brought her back to the group. She was panting heavily and dropped to rest her hands on her knees as she recovered.
"Empty" she gasped, "must have been home alone".
"What on earth did you do to my husband?" demanded the lady they had rescued first.

Identify...
Level 1
Name: Audrey Gardener
Ability: Lesser Telepathy

Huh, now that is a scary ability. Not much use against the rats I expect but put her in a board meeting or a court and she'd be terrifying. John stepped forward and began in his most diplomatic voice which wasn't terribly diplomatic at all. "I'm sorry, Audrey, but do you remember the notification that woke you up this morning?"
"That was just a dream, now explain what happened to Phil right this instant! We are both in the chamber of commerce, I don't know what you do for a living," she looked him up and down and sneered, "if you are even employed but there will be *professional* consequences for you if

you don't explain yourself right this instant! I can promise you that!" her conciliatory attitude had vanished the moment her husband passed out. John tried really hard to be nice to people most of the time. It didn't come naturally to him. He didn't like most people but he understood that it was mostly him and it was really not their fault. He had had a rough morning so far to say the least and it only promised to get worse as the day progressed. He was running very short on patience.

"Listen lady, it wasn't a dream, you're now some sort of telepath and are those rats out there trying to eat my dog and that MASSIVE ROBOT A DREAM?"

"This isn't productive," said Katie quickly stepping between John and Audrey, touching his shoulder as she passed to try to calm him. He flinched away from her hand and turned back to watch Bob and Zeeg killing the swarm. Zeeg's Barghest ability ran out and she leapt away from the fight, returning to her normal size and running back towards John and Evie. A dozen or so rats followed after her, causing Audrey to yell and point but John dealt with them quickly, heads vanishing from necks as fast as his eyes could move between them.

"Perhaps we should move you all away from the fighting, yes? This must have been extremely difficult for you and a break, a chance to catch your breath, perhaps something to drink or some food might help? While we sort that I can explain as much as I know. Is there more tea left John?"

John grunted and nodded, focussed on Bob turning rats into paste. "I'll port you over if they break into any more houses."

Zeeg arrived, pressed her head into Evie's legs then went to sniff and lick at Fred who started giggling and pushed her snout away. His hand came back covered in rodent blood which caused his mum to gasp and swat at Zeeg who gave her a very dirty look before moving off to sniff at the unconscious man. She growled, low and quiet, before moving over to John and jumping up to rest her paws on his chest and push her head into his neck. She dropped down after a moment, leaving long red streaks across his chest and shoulders. John didn't notice, patting her head absent-mindedly then wiping the blood on his jeans without thinking. He continued watching Bob as the swarm thinned and finally started to break apart, the furthest creatures starting to bolt away from the metal giant killing their kin.

"That's fine, thank you John, without you we couldn't have saved these people," said Katie as she began to shepherd their new found compatriots away.

Teamchat:
John Borrows: I'm not made of glass Katie, don't try to handle me. Go help these idiots. We'll need you when the swarm is dead or breaks to deal with the other survivors. I'm clearly not a good choice for that kind of thing.
Katie Johnson: It was for their benefit not yours John. Most of them are traumatised and are retreating into themselves. but some people react badly and try to bluster their way through situations they don't understand like Phil and Audrey. They're scared and need a gentle touch but it will go better in the future if we reinforce that we helped save them. That you helped save them. Once they have a chance to settle they'll understand.
Evie Borrows: They ARE idiots! They should have got out and teamed up and trained, then we wouldn't be stuck carrying them for the rest of the wave!
Katie Johnson: A chip off the old block. Evie, do you think your dad would let these people get hurt? It was his plan that saved them. Give them time. They're in shock. It may take me a while

to "handle" them so it might be best if you try to get the other survivors to join us.
Evie Borrows: I'll bloody shock them if they don't sort themselves out.

Katie decided not to point out that she had had to "shock" John into sorting himself out when he had been traumatised by using his ability to kill the sky rats less than ten minutes ago. Discretion is the better part of valour.

Robert Gillybrook: Sorry to interrupt this summit of the minds but the little bastards, pardon my French ladies, are running. I think we are clear for now.

"You go with Katie kid, I'll go start knocking on doors and *being tolerant,*" John said.
Doris was surrounded by a ring of rat corpses almost ten metres across. The bodies were piled up like snow drifts in places that almost came up to the mecha's knees, where they hadn't been turned into outright paste. They had taken a terrible toll on the monsters but John found himself much more at peace with what he had personally done. Despite not being terribly fond of other people he didn't want to see them hurt. While he had done a fair share of head-blipping again he wasn't as upset by it as he had been before. The little shits had it coming after all. Doris waded through the pile of corpses and stopped in front of John who had teleported to the edge of the killing field.
"You OK mate?" asked Bob.
"I'll be right dude. I will be right." Was he talking to Bob or to himself? "Can you guard the top of the road please? If the rats regroup and come back or the civvies that come out panic, having you

to herd both groups in the right, and opposite, directions would be a god send."

"Sure thing John. Any chance we get, I could use half an hour and some unwanted cars to boost up ole Doris if you know what I mean? You're going to rouse these folks out of their hidey-holes?"

"If they stay they aren't safe and I think we may need to start moving around soon. We can only bait so many of them to us. It's not a big town but it's big enough. Once we get them out and back to the stash you can go play GTA again," he finished with a faint smile.

John used his ability to clear out the corpses that littered the street in a series of blips. He considered dropping them in the open space that gave "The Acres" its name. It was about one acre rather than multiple acres but English street names are often interpretatively whimsical when not boring and literal like the Back Lane or Main Street in almost every village and town.

He decided that any survivors emerging and seeing a pile of hundreds of rat corpses would turn right back inside and bar the door so he began moving the bodies to the middle of the primary school playing fields. He very much doubted any of the kids would be at school today and it was away from anyone's home. The street in front of John still looked like the set of a slasher flick with blood draining into the gutters but he couldn't do much about that. Hopefully it would help those still in their homes not having piles of super-rat corpses scattered about at least.

Bob moved away to stand guard as John began to knock on doors and tell people it was safe, they could come out and they had a safe area to move to. How much of that was true he honestly didn't know but anyone who stayed locked up was unlikely to survive if the team had to move away. Of all the houses on the street they had only rescued the inhabitants of three so far, so he worked his way up the road.

The first few he knocked on and spoke to told him to go away with varying levels of civility. John held his cool and said it wasn't safe to stay and to please reconsider. He then moved on to the next house and sometimes people began to emerge and ask questions. John told them to head to the growing gathering behind the barricade and that his friend Katie would explain everything.
He also asked if they knew the reluctant ones well enough to knock and let them know they were OK, moving to safety and to ask the hiders to join them. When he got to the end of the road he saw what the swarm had left in its wake. Almost all the doors on the adjoining street were chewed through. He slowly walked into the first house and looked around. This had been Evie's classmate Millie's house. Millie had been at home with her parents and two siblings when the rats came, judging from the scattered remains.

Robert Gillybrook: Anyone in there?
John Borrows: Not any more.

John emerged from the house and looked down the street. He could see nearly one hundred houses. Most with doors destroyed. Family homes. He fought to shut down his emotions and rising gorge at the... leftovers he had seen. No way to know if they had all been at home this morning from what was left but at least one of them had taken a few rats with them. It just hadn't been enough.
"I'll knock on the ones who haven't come out yet on the way back to the others. You OK to hang here for a bit and then follow? A blood coated mecha will freak out anyone who hasn't accepted what's happening." John said in an arctic voice as he struggled with what he had seen.

"Sure John. Go easy on anyone who won't come out OK? They're scared."

"They'll be dead if another swarm comes through and we aren't here... but I'll try."

John began going back down the street, knocking on the doors of the recalcitrant, doing his best to cajole and reassure them the street was safe. Most came out and moved down the barricades. But some didn't. *They get to make their decision and live with the consequences, or not,* he thought sadly. As the survivors moved off towards the barricade Bob came stomping up in Doris.

"You know you've got red on you?" asked John.

"Very funny," Doris put a leg out and the torso craned down so Bob could see. Doris was painted in rat blood almost up to her waist. "Did you happen to stick a lot of cleaning solvents in the pocket dimension that you just happened to have lying around in your garage because you're a totally normal guy and not some weird hybrid of prepper and hoarder by any chance?"

"Sorry mate, a few bottles of bleach and a lot of hand soap was all I had, I've got a few bottles of shampoo if you think it will help? Head and Shoulders so her legs won't get dandruff?" Bob barked a laugh at the bad joke and set off back to the rest of the team.

"Update" John said softly.

Teamchat:.
Survivors: 2347
R.O.V.S.S.: 6982
Team report: 2197 Chittering Scavengers killed. 0.02 essence per kill. Essence earned 43.94.

"Level up"

Team member John Borrows has chosen to spend 34 essence and advance to level 9.

Levelling in process...

John Borrows has chosen to modify Ability.

New Status for John Borrows:

Level: 9

Name: John Borrows

Ability: Teleportation

Constitution: 100%

Reserves: 100

Ability: Teleportation.

Guidelines:

Maximum weight: 2500kg

Maximum Distance: 9km

Modifications:

Level 2 (Rare): How about we split the difference?

Level 3: Weight limit x5

Level 4: Portion control.

Level 5: Maximum Weight X5

Level 6: Maximum Distance X3

Level 7: Reserve Regeneration rate X5 (base regen 50% per minute)

Level 8: Where did I leave my keys?

Level 9: Maximum Distance X3

Chapter 14 - Chuck the bloody spear Dad

The woman who burned the rats was being looked after by another lady who had the Night Nurse ability and while her injuries seemed to be minor the brave but foolish fire starter still hadn't woken up. John and Bob rounded the corner and walked into what was for John almost more of a nightmare than ravenous swarms of rat monsters trying to eat people. A social situation. Various people were clustered together shouting at other groups or individuals. Fists were being raised and insults exchanged. *They all lived on the same street for years for god's sake,* thought John, *why are they so angry with each other?*

"EVERYBODY SHUT UP AND STAND TO!" blared Bob through the speaker in his helm causing John to flinch and twist a finger in his left ear. The sheer volume stifled most of the complaints and when they turned to look at who had shouted, that silenced the rest. A mecha as tall as a house and half covered in blood has an amazing ability to quell discord. "Please listen to what my friend Katie has to say and when *she has finished* you can ask questions! Not before! Go ahead please Katie," Bob finished at a less damaging volume.

"Thank you Bob," Katie ran through a short version of how we had all met, what we had done since the notification and what we knew about the system.

"This is rubbish" declared Phil, "the ramblings of lunatics! I admit that the robot thing is impressive but this is just not possible. I'm supposed to believe I can suddenly make plants grow or whatever by magic? Madness. What the hell is really going on?"

"Excuse me" Evie said in a loud voice. She stood just behind Katie facing the semi circle of confused and scared people but stepped forward as she spoke out. "This may be hard to believe without further proof, you know, beyond the ravenous rat swarm you saw us destroy to save you I mean," *perhaps a little too much sarcasm there kiddo*, thought John. "So maybe I should do a demonstration? I got the electrogenesis ability," she raised a hand and pointed it at the top of a nearby tree. A bolt of lightning shot from her finger and hit the tree, blowing branches and leaves into the sky and shredding a foot wide hole into the trunk. Her levels had been kind, it seemed. John hoped she didn't have the same hatred of trees that she had for pigeons. "Does anyone still doubt the abilities or have anything else crappy to say about my team that just saved you ungrateful assholes from being eaten alive by giant rats? No-one?" The trunk of the tree, above where she had hit it, sagged to one side and began to fall towards the people below. They flinched and raised their hands as if to ward it off, an instinctive and ineffective approach. Blip. The branch crashed down on the other side of the tree. "My dad got teleportation as you just saw. Katie got time magic which is how she grabbed some of you out of your homes so Dad could teleport you to safety and finally Bob made this awesome mecha," she waved a hand at Doris, "that turned most of the puny level one rat bastards you lot were hiding from into a gooey red paste!" Her voice rose half an octave, "and in case-" "Thank you Evie, I think that's enough. I'll take over from here." interrupted Katie.

Teamchat:
Evie Borrows: Fucking normies.
John Borrows: Language!
Robert Gillybrook: Language!
Katie Johnson: What's a normie? You know what, never mind.

Evie walked back to Bob and John. Katie continued her Ted Talk about their new magic powers to the confused and scared people who gradually began to calm down. She identified a few and asked them to

describe their ability and then to use it for everyone to see. She
explained Identify and what they knew of the team system. Soon there
were random powers going off, plants growing in seconds, flashes of
fire, icy patches appearing, people yelling at other people to get out of
their minds. It was sort of wholesome in a way John didn't think he
would have appreciated a few hours ago.

Then Katie asked for volunteers to go knocking on the nearby houses
and trying to get people to come join them. Most were reluctant to go
out of sight of the group but over the next ten minutes or so, they
gathered together the old folks living on Northfield Drive and brought
them into the growing band of survivors.

John and Evie took a few of the braver ones round onto Northfield
Close which had escaped attack thus far and watched out for trouble
while the level ones brought people out and directed them back to
what passed for their base. Nothing attacked them so they escorted
the latest group round the corner telling them Katie would explain
what was happening. Most of the older folks had gone into the houses
but the middle aged and the younger people were all in the street,
playing with their abilities.

Teamchat:
Zeeg Borrows: Scratching underneath getting closer. All around Dad, not good.

John looked down and frowned. The survivors remaining outside
were mostly standing around the stash they had put down earlier but
some were scattered down the street experimenting with their powers.
The group had run out of tea and sandwiches (an unforgivable sin) but
one of the ladies who lived a little down the road called Elizabeth had

got her kettle on and was churning out hot drinks as fast as it could boil.
"What do you mean pup, scratching underneath?"
Zeeg moved to the verge and began digging.

Zeeg Borrows: Scratching underneath sounds like this.

"Ah crap. How far away?"

Zeeg Borrows: Very close. Getting closer. Soon.

"WE ARE ABOUT TO BE ATTACKED!" blared Bob at maximum volume, "come out of the houses' quickly!"
One of the ladies who had opened up her kitchen for the survivors bustled out demanding to know what was happening. She had a lovely gravel garden planted with easy to maintain perennials which gave an almost alpine feel to her "bit" of the street. As she came out raising her voice, the gravel to her side erupted into a tangle of writhing snakes. Not snakes, John realised. A nest of tentacles snapping out in all directions, snatching at the people carrying drinks back and forth. John began porting the closest to the middle of the road fifty metres away where they immediately began running for cover, trying to force their way into houses before running for the ones with open doors. Some of them made it inside but not all. As they ran more Lovecraftian nightmares rose from beneath the turf and began snatching at people. Half a dozen humans were caught and dragged into the octopus-like beak that hid at the heart of the tentacles beneath the creature's milky eyes. As they reached the beak it bit down, cutting them into pieces that the tentacles flung away or shredded with the tiny hooks that lined their undersides.

Teamchat:
Robert Gillybrook used identify:
Level 10
Name: Star-nosed Mole-Rat

Katie appeared next to the first one that had emerged, two severed tentacles falling next to her and the horrified man she had freed scrambled back. A blast of lightning from Evie hit the thing next to its dull, creamy white eyes that sat just back from the squid-like mouthparts and within the ring of tentacles. It lurched to the side and emitted a keening wail as its tentacles shot out like a halo and fell twitching to the ground. Unfortunately it was only stunned and not seriously harmed as after a moment of uncoordinated writhing the arms soon began snatching at other people too close or too slow to escape it's range.
Screams and yells echoed from the people they had rescued. Katie would move from one location to another in an instant, chopped off tentacles falling from the nearest beast before she would pause to catch her breath and recharge her power.
Bob lurched forward in Doris, taking long strides and moving far more quickly than usual as he went to intercept the beasts that had emerged further away. The crossbow on his shoulder whirred as bolts flew from it into any of the monster's eyes he could see. John moved people out of the way as quickly as he could, having discovered he was unable to make portion control work on the beasts and they were too heavy to move in one go.
Evie drained the nearest one which slowed it down but it was too powerful with its level and physique. She yelled at Katie to get clear

and as soon as the blond woman appeared further away Evie hurled her largest lightning ball yet into the abomination's face.

"Bob, they're blind, save the bolts! It will be vibrations that draw them and Doris is the heaviest thing moving!" shouted Katie. The blades on Doris' forearms snapped out into position.

John snatched the civilian stragglers out of the way with his ability, depositing them in the middle of the road twenty metres away as the creatures didn't seem to be able to dig through the concrete and tarmac of the paths and roads.

The ball from Evie hit it right in the beak and it emitted an eldritch scream, flopping and spasming as the power of Evie's attack shorted out its nerves. "I'll drain this one out, go help the rest!" she called, blue light flowing from the beast into her palm.

John looked up the road to see that things were not going well. The creatures were emerging from the grass lining the paths on either side of the road and while they couldn't immediately reach the survivors they could slowly drag their massive bodies out of their tunnels, showing the two foot claws on the end of their stubby forelimbs that they must have used for pushing themselves through their tunnels as they crawled closer to their prey.

 As soon as they humped themselves far enough into the road their tentacle began snatching people up and dragging them towards those hellish beaks. One man got lucky and his elbow was presented to the beak instead of his head or chest as was happening to some of the others. The beak bit down, severing his arm with a spray of blood. He screamed as John ported him out of the reach of further harm and the healer they had rescued rushed over to help him.

Realising his earlier mistake was costing lives and resulting in gruesome injuries, John began moving the people who hadn't made it inside a house up onto the roofs of the nearby buildings, as soon as he cleared an area Evie lobbed in her lightning bomb and a moment later Katie would flicker through the area, leaving tentacles and monster blood scattered behind her. Evie would then drain the stunned beast to death, in order to charge up another bomb.

Doris was wrapped up to her chest in the grasping limbs of four of the creatures, swords extended from her wrists as she hacked and slashed at the monstrosities. Ominous creaks that you might expect to hear in a submarine movie came from the armoured body. She was encased in what could have been a tangle of mating eels, if eels were ten feet long and lined with vicious barbed hooks. Even with four of them they couldn't completely hold her as she was dragging them slowly away from the civilians and trying to slash at them with the blades on her arms.

The non combatants were all out of harm's way for now so John turned to the monsters. He couldn't port them. Or even bits of them. All his abilities were voided. Evie could still hurt them with her abilities but none of his would work. He stood momentarily transfixed by his powerlessness. What the hell was wrong with him?

"Chuck the bloody spear Dad!" yelled Evie in a terrible Michael Caine voice. She lofted another bomb into half a dozen of the beasts, causing them all to shriek and thrash.

John looked down at the spear he had been carrying around for the last however long. He looked up at the nearest beast and drew back his arm to throw but he aimed as high as he could and threw it almost vertically. His eyes followed as it arced up, peaked and began to descend. It wasn't going to land anywhere near the beast but that didn't matter. As it reached its maximum falling speed he blipped it to directly above the thick neck of the nearest surviving monster. The blade of the spear sank all the way in, only stopping when the cross guard at the top of the staff met the rubbery flesh of the mole-rat. It jerked and the spear slipped sideways before John blipped it high into the sky. The creature wailed as everything behind its face tentacles went limp.

Teamchat:
John Borrows: I think I can cripple them. Katie, Evie focus on the ones I paralyse. Watch out for the tentacles though, they'll still work. Bob, I'll try to take out the ones on you next. Evie can't bomb them while they are so close to you. Once they can't hang on to their holes with their legs it should be easier for you.
Robert Gillybrook: Not going to lie, Doris is a tough old bird but some assistance would be very much appreciated chaps!

The spear began to fall and once it was moving at deadly speed John again ported it point down just above the neck of the nearest beast that was attacking Doris. The body went slack but the tentacles continued to squirm and pull at Doris. The spear flashed into the sky and into the neck of a beast again and again. Once they were all finally paralysed Bob was able to sever enough of the tentacles to be able to free his machine. Doris then began cautiously moving back in to finish them off.
John moved on to the rest of the beasts that had come out to attack the civilians. The spear did its work and soon the road was lined with thrashing tentacles and angry, unearthly screeching from the nightmares that couldn't retreat or attack. Katie was moving from one to the next in flickers, tentacles falling behind her as she reappeared.
"Give me a second Katie! I have an idea, the power cables are under the paths on this street! Get out of the way!" Katie flickered back, appearing well off to the side and Evie raised her hands assuming the traditional "mage about to unleash hell" pose. Walls of lightning shot

along the paths, rising from beneath and dancing with actinic blue light. The arcs cut through the face-tentacles and heads of some of the beasts. A handful survived but even they had had their brains partially boiled in their skulls.

The spear was now appearing in front of the rats faces, the momentum spun so it moved horizontally into the open beaks of the wailing monsters. The spear would sink over a foot into the creature's maw before flashing back into the sky to begin again. Even this didn't kill the beasts outright but it was definitely not appreciated, judging by the thrashing and screaming that resulted.

Soon the road was lined by dead or dying mole-rats. Katie appeared next to Doris and began cutting and pulling at the few tentacles still wrapped around the mechas legs.

John looked over the battlefield and felt his heart sink. There were too many people, and parts of people, scattered across the road, never to move again but that wasn't what worried him most. Evie had collapsed.

Chapter 15 - I ain't gonna do my own hoovering up

John blipped to his daughter with his heart in his throat and leant down to check her over. No visible injuries. "What happened? Why did you collapse?" he asked with a note of panic in his voice.
"Used all my mana, reserves, whatever. God this sucks! Is this like a hangover? Throbbing headache, feeling sick and weak?" she grumbled.
"Sounds about right kid, I'm going to port you up to the roof while you recover OK? You did great in that one, the walls of lightning made a huge difference. Well played on sussing out more of your powerset, youngling." He ruffled her hair and she tried to swat his hand away weakly.
"Ger'off! Thanks I guess... Using outside sources of juice takes a lot of reserves it turns out. I thought I had pretty much infinite reserves after the last couple of levels."
"Let yourself have a minute to recover and get your levels. I'll go see what I can do to help the others." Blip. Evie appeared back in her former roost on the garage roof.
Zeeg was suddenly walking next to John as he made his way over to Katie who stood panting and trying to catch her breath. He petted Zeeg for a moment, checking she was OK and reassuring her. Clearly the mole rat things had scared her, she had vanished at the start of the attack and only now skulked out from wherever she had been hiding.
"Good girl, not really your kind of fight pup." he said softly to her and her tail wagged briefly.
"You OK Katie?"
"I will be in a minute! Yesterday... I thought I was really fit... All the running... Now I'm not so sure. This sword gets heavy after a couple of dozen swings. Is Evie OK? I saw her fall." Katie gasped out.

"She's fine I think, says she used up all her reserves with the lightning wall thing. Apparently hitting zero reserves feels really unpleasant. As in 'kill me now so i can escape this hangover' not nice from the sounds of it."

He looked around and continued "What do we do with this lot?" he gestured at the dead monsters. "And the survivors?" He refused to look at the scattered human remains.

Katie glanced around. No one who had made it into a house had come back out yet and the ones on the roofs were shivering and clutching each other. Now they could see the danger had passed, at least temporarily, they were pulling themselves together slowly. "You'll need to get the ones on the roof down but give them a minute, I'll go talk to the ones inside and *then* try to talk to the ones up top. Can you use portion control to move these... things now?" John blipped a tentacle off the face of one of the corpses. "Good, take a beat and then start clearing the bodies." Katie set off into the first of the houses people had taken refuge in.

Doris waved a hand at John and lowered herself, one leg back with it's knee on the ground, kneeling like a mediaeval knight before a king. John walked over as her chest split open and Bob climbed down carefully, dripping with sweat.

"Gets hot in there, that it does. AC just went on the upgrade list. I've got my levels, got an inventory list that shows what is in the storage and what I can make with it. You stored some weird shit in there you know, boy? Taking one of dozens of possibilities at random: robot hoover... Why? In an apocalypse you thought to save a robot hoover! Anyway, I'm going to borrow a bunch of it for the big girl if you don't mind, please and thank you." Bob gave him a grin that made it clear John didn't have much say in the matter. "I'm going to, uh, 'feed' some cars to her as well, she is going to get a lot bigger over the next hour or so assuming we don't get hit again. I'll see if I can sort some armour out for Katie, you and Evie aren't the wet work types so I'll focus on protecting her first in case she misses a time-stop at some point. Good work with the spears by the way. I thought I was SOL and going to buy the farm there for a minute." he clapped John on the back. "Wherever this thing takes us I can tell you one thing for damn sure: I ain't gonna do my own hoovering up. Remind me to grab the dishwasher as well when we get a minute." he smiled before the expression dropped for a moment. "And I'm not a boy, old man... I'll level and start tidying up while we wait for Katie to get back. Help yourself to any stuff we stashed in Doris. Except for the board games," he thought for a moment as Bob turned away then called, "and not my bloody laptop either!" Bob paused and glanced back. John looked briefly at the traumatised people clinging to the roof peaks of the bungalows. "My "charisma score" is much too low to deal with people who just watched some of their neighbours get ripped apart and eaten." He kicked out at a tentacle draped across the road near his foot. It twitched after the kick, curling around and making him teleport himself back a metre by reflex but it was just the muscles figuring out they were dead. He looked around to see if anyone had noticed him flinch and saw Bob smirking back at him. The older man then nodded amicably and headed off to look at the cars on the other side of his machine.

"Update"

Survivors: 1257

R.O.V.S.S.: 4398

Team report: 27 Star-nosed Mole-rats killed. 4 essence per kill. Essence gained 108.

"Oy, what the hell do you think you are doing to my car? Get the fuck away from it you..." The voice came down from a nearby roof, understandably irate as most of his car was evaporating and flowing into Doris, who shone with light as she grew.

John ignored the man and smiled sadly, "Puppy, can you scout around nearby, let us know if anything is coming?" Zeeg yipped and shot away, moving incredibly fast. "Level up."

John Borrows has chosen to spend 144 essence and advance to Level 11.

Levelling in process...

John Borrows has chosen to modify Ability and Ability.

New Status for John Borrows:

Level: 11

Name: John Borrows

Ability: Teleportation

Constitution: 100%

Reserves: 100

Guidelines:

Maximum weight: 7500kg

Maximum Distance: 45km

Modifications:

Level 2 (Rare): How about we split the difference?

Level 3: Weight limit x5

Level 4: Portion control.

Level 5: Maximum Weight X5

Level 6: Maximum Distance X3

Level 7: Reserve Regeneration rate X5 (base regen 50% per minute)

Level 8: Where did I leave my keys?

Level 9: Maximum Distance X3

Level 10: Maximum Distance X5

Level 11: Maximum Weight X3

Right, thought John, 750kg up to 4.5km for 0.2 reserves. Broken. Assuming my power works on whatever the hell we meet next unlike these Cthulhu looking pricks. Going to have to start getting creative, like with the spear. Was it because they were immune or a higher level than me or what? The increase in Essence per level is already starting to bite. I've got just under one and I need... 144 for level twelve? Damn.

He sighed and began blipping parts of the mole-rats beyond the trees into the primary school sports field, building what he assumed would eventually be a very large and disgusting barbeque. *I'm sure it will get cleared up properly before the kids go back to school...*

Evie called out to John and he blipped her down to him, giving her a quick hug and double checking she had recovered.

"I'm fine Dad, got some good stuff from my levels, more max voltage and a passive recharge from ambient and enemy sources for the overcharge and... I can now summon "a barrage of lightning from the sky" which sounds sweet but it's *super* expensive. 80% of my reserves and leaves me with one. knowing what hitting zero reserves feels like it will have to be a last resort power."

"That's great sweetheart! You are really coming into the title of being Zeus' half pint ginger clone!"

She punched him on the arm.

"Oof!" another chunk of monster vanished from the street.

"Where are you putting the bits?"

"Um, well you remember the playing fields at your old primary school?"

"You aren't?" she started cackling "bet the groundskeeper will shit a brick when he next gets in to work!"

"Language... Not sure when that might be, kiddo," John said thoughtfully, "I don't think anyone is going back to work anytime soon." John thought about his colleagues at work. Most of them were nice people, he wondered briefly how many of them were still alive. They mostly didn't live in Normanby but they had lost nearly three quarters of the people living here in the last couple of hours and they weren't done yet. He had to assume it would be the same everywhere else. Worst case, 75% of the human species had just disappeared in a few hours. The more Malthusian environmentalists might be the only ones happy about this whole thing. He began to seize up and forced himself to push the emotions to the side. He had to remain functional. "We need to power level these noobs Dad. We should organise hunting parties or something, go find the scavenger types, the level ones and let these guys farm them. If it gets any tougher in the next wave this lot are walking corpses."

"True, I suppose. Go find Katie please and put the idea to her? She went into that one," He pointed to the house where Katie had gone to talk to the ones who were once again hiding inside. "We could have Zeeg bait the little buggers back to us. Let this lot have the first crack at them after they've formed teams while we babysit, making sure none of them get eaten."

"On it!" she grinned and ran off to find Katie. She was definitely far too calm for what was happening, just like Bob and Katie. He couldn't really assess Zeeg, she would have simply chased anything that moved this morning but now she had shown the good sense to hide away when faced with opponents she couldn't match. John looked down at Zeeg who had come back from the marketplace and said "Get your level's pupper," with a smile.

Teamchat:
Zeeg Borrows: Got stronger and faster. Claws, teeth and fur got better. I got proper shape shifting as well but what's the point? I am perfect already. Nothing moving nearby. A few tunnellers

are to the south somewhere. Lots of dead little rats. Saw a swarm of sky rats as well but over that way.

She gestured to the east with her head where she had seen the sky rats as she visibly grew and not by a small amount. When John had woken up this morning her shoulder height was just over his knee. It was now just over his waist. She mimed savaging her favourite toy for him and briefly turned red with white trim all across her fur. She also grew a fluffy white beard.

"Is that a hint you want me to get your chew toy? What a way to try out a shapeshifting skill! Never change Dog." A happy woof was the reply.

He summoned her favourite toy with a 'Blip'. Zeeg was immediately the same mad, badly behaved dog she always had been, tail wagging as she began worrying at the Santa themed dog toy, spraying foam filler from the head she had long since chewed a hole into around the road. A greyhound can get up to 45 mph in a flat sprint. Zeeg was a lurcher cross so heavier and slower but she could still move when she wanted to... John tried to run the numbers in his head... His dog could probably now run at close to 150 mph for short distances and maintain 100 mph for a couple of kilometres. *If she ever sees a rabbit again that poor fucker is toast* he thought.

Katie emerged from the house she had gone into and moved to the next. Evie walked next to her and talked excitedly. A moment later Evie came back out and ran back over to John.

"Katie thinks it's a good idea but we need to get everyone down and discuss it with them, some of them won't go for it. She suggested maybe getting some food on? It's nearly lunchtime and everyone has had a rough morning. Bob's busy making a Gundam which leaves me and thee, old man. Think we can feed this lot?" she finished with a grin/

"Yeah probably." A series of blips followed, a ring of stones was made in the middle of the road well clear to the north of the blood from the giant tentacle rats and the people who didn't make it.

Next a bag of firewood John had stashed in Doris' pocket universe appeared and he began laying out logs in the circle of stones. A ball of cotton wool appeared and then a tub of Vaseline blipped into place as well. The cotton wool was rolled in Vaseline and then placed just under the top most logs. John's lighter appeared in his hand and he lit the cotton wool which burned brightly, the heat evaporating the Vaseline like a candle melting wax to fuel the flame. Father and daughter sat next to each other in silence, watching as the wood caught and quickly burned to settle into a bed of coals, each reassured by the other's presence.

He sat back, wiped his hands on his trousers leaving greasy strings of cotton wool on top of the blood on his legs and promptly rolled a cigarette. He lit it while waiting for the bed of coals to form.

Next a chopping board and two onions appeared. "Have at them kid, finely chopped please and *use the bridge method*" Evie grinned and drew her survival knife.

"No way short stuff." Blip. A two inch paring knife now sat next to the onions. "Use the right tool for the job!" Evie scowled but put away her knife and began chopping onions. John used his *where did I leave my keys* ability and packs of mushrooms, bags of potatoes and bags of carrots, beef stock cubes and a bottle of red wine appeared next to the chopping board. He grinned and a can of coke appeared next to Evie who nodded her thanks and promptly cracked it open. She had a long drink before she resumed badly chopping onions and complaining about her eyes watering.

By this time most of the people on the roofs had waved at John and been brought down to the ground.

John summoned his Dutch oven from Doris, which caused Bob to call out that he had wanted that for parts. John politely but forcefully told him not to use survival gear for parts unless he could make more and began loading up the onions into the pot.

Within a few minutes the onions and mushrooms were sizzling and John blipped in a half dozen packs of chopped beef, tipping them straight into the pot and giving them a stir. Some water, a little red wine, some beef stock, some herbs and some stirring and they were well on their way to John's signature beef stew. The smell coming off was pretty good and some of the folks who had emerged from the houses began to drift closer and chat amicably with the pair which made John's neck itch. He forced his attention to the food and began adding the vegetables to try and escape the conversations.

Katie drifted through the gathering, exchanging words and smiles with people as she passed, having somehow united the disparate, scared and angry people into something approaching a united group.

"Smells good. You know the power is still on and you could have just used an oven right?" John and Evie looked at each other for a moment before Evie facepalmed and began muttering unkind things about her father.

"Anyway. You're on cooking detail from now on! Where did you get the ingredients?"

"I, um, borrowed them from the shop? The 'where did I leave my keys' ability turned me into the single greatest thief on planet Earth I think," John said quietly, slightly embarrassed. "Another fifteen minutes for the veggies to cook through and we should be good to go." John frowned and multiple packs of plastic bowls and cutlery appeared.

"And those?" She gestured at the plastic bowls.

"Party shop. They won't need them and I am not washing up after this lot!"

Katie laughed, "Your surname was weirdly prophetic wasn't it? Chefs don't wash up," she smiled. "I'm glad you're feeling better. Evie told me the plan the pair of you came up with. I've been pitching it to the others. Some are not going for it at all, they just want to bunker up and hide but there are a few who are willing to try," she shrugged, "we rescued nearly forty people earlier, now there's just over twenty of them left after those tunnelling fu-," she glanced at Evie for some reason, "uh things got done with us. Most are scared but I think there will be a team of six or seven who want to gather some Essence, including that brave pyromaniac. She might be a good choice to join our team if she's willing. Once they have eaten and sorted themselves out we can send Zeeg to bring back some of the scavengers and feed them to the new team. Would that be Ok please, Zeeg?" Katie looked down at Zeeg and Zeeg looked up from her mangled chew toy, those new fangs were lethal, and woofed happily.

Blip, blip blip. Two loaves of bread and a tub of butter appeared next to Katie.

"Start buttering, the stew won't go far without something on the side," said John giving Katie a slight smile.

Chapter 16 - No, the other golden rule

The survivors moved past the impromptu kitchen and filled tiny plastic party bowls with stew and got slices of bread for dipping. Everyone seemed to perk up a bit with hot food in front of them but they still seemed distraught from the attack.

John headed over to Bob who was still focused on Doris and brought him a bowl.

"Gotta keep your strength up, old man," he said with a smile, handing the food over to a distracted Bob.

"Thanks John. This is getting really complicated for me."

"What's up?"

"Everything that goes into the storage unlocks more designs for Gadgeteer. I'll have body armour and helmets for the humans in our team in the next day or so but Doris is the primary focus and she is going to be an absolute terror in about five minutes. I've been producing simple crossbows and bolts as well for the others, those are easy. If they can't fight up close they can at least have some kind of ranged attack," he sighed.

"The thing is when I unlock a blueprint by getting one ingredient for it, it shows me the stuff I need to get to complete it. Some of it is amazing. I unlocked a blueprint for a fusion reactor from optic cables but I need a bunch of focusing lasers, a lot of titanium and steel and an insane amount of hydrogen. Where the hell am I going to get that lot? And don't even get me started on the magitech stuff I can make now! Way beyond what we thought was possible before but the materials are totally alien."

"I may have just become the greatest gentleman thief to walk the earth so maybe I can help with some of it?" John explained about his 'where did I leave my keys' modification.

"I don't think you can just steal fifty cubic metres of hydrogen John, and that's just to start the initial reaction, I need tons of the stuff as fuel but some of the materials for a few other projects might be a lot easier to source. We will have to 'requisition' some stuff from around town when we get a chance," he cackled greedily.

"Requisition is a polite term for 'looting' I take it? Have you thought about setting up a house in the pocket dimension? With plugs and maybe running water and stuff? Would be nice to stash the chest freezer somewhere safe. We could hide the civvies in there as well," John suggested.

"I'll look into it but not sure how feasible it is, it would take a lot of reserves," he stood up and moved back, spooning stew into his mouth. "This isn't half bad you know lad? You could have been a chef."

"I worked as one for a while a decade or so back. Sous chef anyway. The advantage of never knowing what you want to do with your life is that you end up with a broad base of experience in various fields," John replied ruefully.

Bob nodded, "Well you've found your calling now. Teleporting things heads off their bodies is very niche but wildly effective."

He finished his stew, possibly by somehow teleporting the food directly to his stomach as far as John could tell. He clapped John on the shoulder. "Back up a bit and give me a moment please."

John backed away as requested and Bob reached out to touch the upgraded mecha. The chest clam shelled open and a ramp descended to the ground. It was now too far for Bob to easily climb up the limbs to get in.

"Back in two mins" Bob said with a grin before scurrying up into the bot. The ramp retracting behind him and the chest closing to seal him in. Within a minute the chest opened again and Bob walked back down the ramp and waved John forward. Bob now had a large silver electrode, an inch across, melded to each of his temples, with fine wires running back into his annoyingly thick hair. The wires met at some kind of small control box with a couple of stubby aerials poking out that looked melted into the back of his skull. The change was quite stunning, giving him the look of a true mad scientist.

"Upgraded your hairdo, I see? Very Buck Rogers."

"Jealous, are you Baldy? It's the neural link to Doris. Just you wait lad, this should be something special. Up and at 'em girl!" he called.

The robot rose to her feet and the changes Bob had made since the mole rats became apparent. She was now nearly six metres tall, similar in height to a three storey building and had become even more streamlined in appearance. Her armoured limbs were smooth and all her joints were sealed with flexible coverings. The bot turned to look down at John and Bob then reached to her back and grasped the hilt of a sword.

"You are going to get soooo sued Bob."

There was a roar as an engine somewhere in Doris' spine fired up, presumably stolen from one of the many cars Bob had "borrowed". A cable running from her spine to the blade vibrated and faint clouds of smoke began sputtering out behind her. "Just do me a favour and always, always and I do mean always, refer to that thing as a "chainsaw-sword". Do not shorten the name. Ever. The Black Library guys are always watching."

The blade revved and the teeth lining it's edge spun at terrifying speed. Bob grinned as Doris stowed her two metre long Chainsaw-Sword on her back. "Her right hand has a thumb and four fingers now so thumbs up are on the table," Doris obligingly demonstrated her vital new ability. John applauded politely. "But this is what I've gone for on the left." Doris lowered her left hand that was still a flat, circular palm with three fingers spread equidistant around it.

The fingers folded back and the centre of the palm stretched forward. The face of her palm slid to the side and somehow folded into her wrist as the rotary faces of two angle grinders, enlarged to fill the foot wide palm, were extended as a circular saw blade pushed through the gap between them. They all buzzed to life and whirred at terrifying speeds before snapping back into the palm of her hand as the fingers bent back into the right positions. Anything the circular blade cut into, the edges of the wound would then be forced back over the angled faces of the grinders. It was pretty horrifying to imagine what it would do to anything made of flesh and somehow Bob had taken the parts and changed their shape and size. His ability defied logic as well as the laws of reality.

"OK. I don't think you need to worry about people getting pissy about what you did to their cars. So you have remote control now?"

"Agreed," he smirked, "and yes I do, young man. Lets see what happens to those tentacle bastards in the second round eh?"

Teamchat:
Katie Johnson: Are you two done playing with the new toy? Nice work by the way Bob, Doris is bloody terrifying.
Robert Gillybrook: Aye, she's remote control now as well but it all works better if I pilot her directly. Heading over now.

Doris pivoted to face towards the centre of town as John and Bob walked back to where Katie was holding a meeting with the survivors. The ones who wanted to fight stood to one side and the rest were understandably complaining loudly. Why bring more monsters here? Who will protect them while the team is away? Who was going to pay for the damage to the lawn, for 25 years that lawn has been perfect and I won't be the one to put it right! Where are the police and the council and the army etc etc.

John winced listening to them and felt deeply grateful they had found Katie at the start. He would currently be blipping the complainers to six feet above the rat corpse pile he had built in the school grounds and playing "let the twat splat and see if it adjusts their attitude". Probably not the most productive approach but it would have been cathartic.

The team who wanted to fight had joined up and John Identified them.

Level 4
Name: Victoria Smith
Ability: Pyrogenesis

She was the woman who made the mad dash out of her house and collapsed. Brave but perhaps not very smart. She was in her late 20's with black hair cut into a bob and green eyes.

Level 1
Name: Phil Gardener
Ability: Biomancer (plants)

Level 1
Name Audrey Gardener
Ability: Lesser Telepathy

The obnoxious couple from before. They seemed to be a lot more calm and focussed now but he caught Phil shooting angry looks at Evie, likely still mad about her draining him unconscious. He no doubt checked his log after it was explained to him and discovered what she had done. Might be trouble there in the future but they needed everyone who was willing to get some levels to fight together.

Level 2
Name: James Pooley
Ability: Aeromancy

He was one of the younger ones, early 30s maybe? Brown hair in a ponytail and slightly overweight, not that John had much room to comment, what with his beer gut.

Level 1
Name: Jennifer Bruce
Ability: Athletic Prodigy

She was a young lady, John estimated late teens or early 20s. Thin as a whip and clearly someone who spent a lot of time running or at the gym before today.

Level 1
Name: Geraldine Mulroney
Ability: Night Nurse

John smiled to himself. He was glad the healer would be trying to get some levels.

"OK everyone, listen up! Quiet please!" called Katie. "We will be leaving Doris, that's the giant robot and her pilot Bob, to keep an eye on everyone who doesn't want to fight. I will ask that you stay in one house and don't come out until the teams return, this makes it easier for Bob to make sure you are safe. Anything that attacks will be dealt with by Doris or we will teleport back if she is in trouble. Please stay inside and listen to Bob while we are gone. My team and the ones choosing to fight will move back up to where we fought the swarm of little ones before.

"Our scout will find and bait small groups back for them to kill and take Essence from. Everyone in the team gets the same Essence per kill so there is no need to compete with each other! You need to work as a team and support each other as you've seen us do. I will stay close by so I can rescue anyone in immediate danger and John and Evie will stay back and deal with any monsters that get past you. Is this all clear? You will do the killing and we will provide assistance and protection in case you need it."

Katie smiled at the braver ones. The healer and the fire girl looked back confidently while the others shuffled about, clearly unsure but with looks of determination on their faces. "We've checked over your abilities and I know we've gone over this twice now but I just wanted to reiterate it all again to be sure we are all on the same page: Victoria has some levels and will be your main damage dealer. She will stay well back from the fighting and burn things down. Jennifer will work as what Evie calls a "dodge tank", distracting monsters that get close but focussing more on keeping them off the others than dealing damage. James you'll support Victoria as a ranged damage dealer with your air blades. Phil you will use plants to trip and tangle the rats wherever possible and Audrey, you will be attacking them mentally to hopefully confuse and slow them. Finally Geraldine will stay to the rear and heal anyone who gets bitten. Are we all clear?"

A chorus of nods and grunts of acknowledgement came back. "This will be as safe as we can make it for you but there is still a lot of danger so please, please stay focused and be careful. Zeeg, could you go and find a small group of the little ones and bring them back to where we fought before?"

"The dog is the scout? You never mentioned this!" said Phil, preparing for what looked like another bitching session in John's estimation. Zeeg gave him a look just as John blipped in next to her. "Use Identify on her, Phil," John said quietly.

"Oh uh well, level ten is quite impressive I suppose but... Is she intelligent enough to follow the instructions? Can we trust our lives to a stupid dog?"

"She is," said Katie cheerfully, ignoring Zeegs growl at the word stupid. "Her mind was raised to be something like a human when John gave her an Essence according to the system and she can use the team chat as well as any of us. She is fast and strong and she has earned our, and your, respect and trust, please Phil." The final phrase sounded part question, part instruction and part threat. Zeeg decided she'd had enough of the *stupid* human and set off to find some rat monsters.

"Very well but this is very unorthodox."

"Not sure what the "orthodoxy" is for this whole situation dude," said John with a patented cheeky grin he hadn't used in twenty years, "Maybe we should all put aside preconceived ideas about how things ought to be and focus on how they are. Identify me." Phil must have done so as he took a half step back.

"As of now I can teleport," John used Identify on Phil, "83 kilos of... whatever, 45 kilometres straight up and unless that 83kg of whatever can fly and doesn't need to breathe it might behove the 83kg thing to be more polite? I'm using Identify on everything and everyone as a matter of course. Anyone with a much higher level is automatically going to get a lot of cautious respect from me, the tyranny of rank as they say. To be perfectly fair though, a level one who can turn blood into ice with their mind or whatever is equally as worthy of respect as any level thirty. Kid! What's the golden rule?"

"Uh, do unto others as you'd have them do unto you?" replied Evie hesitantly.

"No, the other golden rule."

"Oh, right. Don't be a dick!" she glared at Phil who had become even paler than before.

"That's the one. Good advice under any circumstance. Now, Zeeg is bringing you some victims, about fifty of the little ones, so get your heads in the game. You may be revolted by what happens to the monsters, all the blood and body parts are pretty shocking. I was horrified the first time I used my ability on living things, but these little shits have it coming. They have been *eating people* so show them no mercy and **kill them all**!"

James gave a quiet cheer before realising no one else was and stuttering to a stop. John gave him a thumbs up. "Thanks for that John. I think. Very inspiring... They'll be here shortly so get yourselves ready," said Katie. "Evie, John, keep an eye out and keep everyone safe."

"Did you try to go full on Razak Roughnecks at the end there?" Evie asked quietly as the rest moved into position.

"Too much?"

"Nah, I think you got away with it."

Chapter 17 - I am not going anywhere near this thing

It went surprisingly well overall.

There was a rough patch at the start. Jennifer locked up and didn't step forward when Zeeg brought the first group round the corner but Victoria started burning the rats as soon as she saw them. John got the feeling she was holding a serious grudge against them all because of the ones that took a bite out of her earlier. Katie appeared next to Jennifer and had a quiet word, a hand resting on her shoulder. John kept blipping back anything that got too close and James began chopping them into pieces with near invisible blades of empowered air.

Zeeg used her ghost mode with the first pack to cover for Jennifer's shock, dancing around and distracting the rats who became more and more frustrated as every attack passed straight through the dog. She bought the rest enough time to get themselves together and begin to burn the monsters down. In Victoria's case: literally. From the inside out on occasion. She really didn't like the rats it seemed.

By the time the third pack of rodents were brought back they were working smoothly as a team. Audrey baffled the frontrunners causing them to slip and stumble, slowing and tripping those behind them and disrupting the swarm. James brought slicing waves of air in from the sides to chop up the fringes, Jennifer danced and twirled, her feet hardly touching the ground as she led the monsters round in circles while Phil kept tangling any that moved away from the kill zone in grass that leapt up and bound the rats to the ground until James or Victoria finished them.

The next hour passed relatively uneventfully. John occasionally had to blip back a monster and he periodically cleared out the bodies, adding them to the corpse pile he was building in the primary schools fields. *Hope that doesn't become an issue,* he thought. *It must be more like a mound or barrow than a pile by now.*

They had brought back six swarms and the last couple had been destroyed almost casually. The team was working together like a well oiled machine. Victoria was up to level five and everyone else was up to four. James was not far off joining Victoria at level five as well. They had discussed what modifications to take between themselves and with John and Katie but Evie turned out to be a font of wisdom and advice on the subject. Some of it was actually useful as well. Katie once again demonstrated her aptitude for handling people and breaking down the complex possibilities that Evie created in their minds by waffling about RPGs and manga so that they were clear and understandable.

"I think we should head back now. It's not far off three PM, we only have to hold out a little longer and we will be safe." said Katie.

They walked back to re-join Bob and the now enormous Doris, exchanging greetings. Bob congratulated the new team on their growth and asked for a quiet word with his own team.

John, Evie and Katie moved to the side, away from their proteges who were mingling with the folks cautiously stepping out of the house they had been hiding in.

"There's something big going down by the river. Doris can't see the details but she can see clouds of dust and explosions kicking up into the air. It looks *significant*. I've seen a couple of humans get booted into the air and go flying as well. God knows if they survived but something is going out of its way to destroy buildings and it's working its way into town. If it started in the south east corner of the industrial estate I bet most of that area is rubble now."

"No idea what it is? No glimpses?" John looked between Bob and Katie.

"I couldn't see it. There are too many houses in the way," said Bob. "It's got to be big and mean though. Way I see it, we can run or we can fight. Not many of the little bastards left now and I reckon they're mostly looking for easy kills so there's plenty of places we could run to."

"The little ones are crap for essence and we are all starting to need a lot of it to progress." chimed in Evie, "maybe we should scout it and if we think we can take it we nuke whatever the hell it is and get another level or two if we are lucky," she looked around at the adults hopefully.

"Glimpse isn't giving me anything useful. Mostly clouds and me standing trying to calm down people John has pissed off somehow," Katie scowled prettily. "Can you take a look please Zeeg? Don't go anywhere near it, just find somewhere as far away as possible and take a look?"

Zeeg looked up, whined slightly but nodded and began moving off, heading down the east end of the river so she could cross the bridge and work her way up to the source of the commotion, under the cover of the trees that lined the river.

Teamchat:
John Borrows: Update.
Survivors: 757
R.O.V.S.S.: 2561

"Something has changed. We were improving the ratio before, but now it's getting worse. I think?"

"Not by much and it might be that most of the lower levelled on both sides have been taken out?" said Katie, "Only the real monsters are left." John ignored the side look she gave him as she said the last part.

"Let's take a minute. I'll deal with the survivors while Zeeg tries to get us some info".

Katie left and began talking quietly with the older folks, the lady with her son who'd stayed inside and the new team. John made a beeline for Jennifer, hoping to pick up some info having seen how her ability seemed to be related to movement, like his own. Jennifer saw him coming and moved towards him with a warm smile. "Hi John, I wanted to say thanks for your help. I missed a few dodges and would have taken a hit or five if you hadn't been on the ball."

"My pleasure, I was hoping to ask you about your ability if you don't mind? While our powers are very different, you're the first person I've seen with something even vaguely similar to mine."

"No problem, not sure how similar they are though! But we all owe you and your team a favour or two so what do you want to know?"

"Can you tell me what your ability description is please? I want to know if there are any similarities or inconsistencies, especially with the mods. The more you know, you know?"

"I'll share mine if you share yours?" John nodded, "I'll go first: my ability description is really weird: Athletic Prodigy: You have dedicated your short life to getting as close to perfection as possible in athletic endeavours. You are more agile, stronger and tougher than you look."

She frowned, "it's like it's kind of insulting me? I didn't just work out and play sports. I mean I did do a lot of sports but it wasn't the main "me thing" you know? I drew comics and painted as well!"

"The system wasn't very kind to me either. It pretty much called me a tight-fisted git in one of my mods. Mine say's I'm a shut in so it gave me the power to go anywhere at a thought. What are your guidelines?"

"Enhanced Physique which is now up to 400% but I don't feel four times faster and stronger and then Untouchable, it's an active ability that lets me dodge perfectly for ten seconds. At the start it did anyway, I've got a mod now that has boosted it to thirty seconds."

John explained his own ability and limits.

"So my limits are to do with my body, or conditioning or whatever and yours are to do with what your power will work on? There's no connection I can see."

"Zeeg has a similar ability to your enhanced physique. She got bigger and stronger as she improved it. She also got some pretty good mods from utility, a war-form kind of thing, enhanced claws, fangs and armoured fur, true shapeshifting… I think those are the main ones. You might want to have a chat with her and compare notes about that part of your ability?"

"You want me to discuss my magic powers with your dog because she has something similar? You're a weird bloke John."

John laughed, "I know how it sounds! She can shift into something that can talk but I think she's a bit of a dog supremacist now, all other forms are lesser than her natural perfection or something. If she won't change to speak to you we can add you into our team for a bit so you can have a chat with her that way."

"Any chance I could swing a permanent invite to the team?" She smiled.

"Best to speak to Katie about that kind of thing Jennifer, she's the people person," He said quickly.

"Please call me Jen, and I'll find the time to talk to her," she grinned at him and turned to go back to the rest of her team.

John was relieved to dodge the team invite conversation bullet and went back over to Bob and Evie who were having what appeared to be a fairly heated debate about what defines a robot. Evie was running through various anime featuring giant robots and explaining the possibilities to Bob who was looking confused and slightly scared.

"And that is why Shinji should stop being a bitch and get in the bloody Mecha!" Evie exclaimed. "Am I right?" she spread her arms as if expecting applause.

Bob looked up at John as he approached with a pleading expression. "I think that is a question your Dad would be able to answer better than me, young lady. I just make robots. I'm impressed by your broad knowledge of fictional mechanical fighting machines though." His eyes lit up as he had an idea to escape the strangely knowledgeable child. "John, good, any joy? Shame, don't be down though, I have something for you two that should cheer you both right up!" A door made of light opened next to Doris' leg and he ducked in, returning after a few moments, with his hands behind his back..

He handed over a couple of bars of chocolate.

"There had better be more of this left! If you've started turning *my* chocolate into robot fuel I will file a formal complaint with your commanding officer!" Evie declared angrily.

"I haven't and you can complain to whoever you like on one condition: no more explaining how the mechs in Lalouche work ever again, whatever the hell that is."

"Alright, fine. I was trying to help though! You really do need to build some retractable wheels into Doris' feet so she can scoot about on roads and stuff."

"Noted," replied Bob tersely.

"Cheers Bob, any news on the armour?"

"First lot will be done by tomorrow. Should be pretty good but it will just be ballistic, stabbing and slashing protection. No force fields or reactive charges or anti-grav."

"Those are on the cards? For later I mean?" Bob nodded at John, "Awesome!" John smiled broadly and when Evie offered a hand for a high five he obliged.

Bob caught Katie's attention and waved. She took a moment to settle her conversation, apparently imparting some instructions to the newly levelled team and the non combatants before heading over to join them. Bob proudly handed her the body armour he had made for her.

"Thanks Bob! It's a bit heavy but if I make a mistake it should stop me from getting gored. Do you have more for the others?"

"It's not so easy I'm afraid. Compared to what Gadgeteer is capable of, I'm making stone age tools at this point but it all costs reserves, time and materials. I've made a dozen crossbows to give to the non combat folks. John, can you go in and port them out please?"

John nodded and walked into the light. He emerged a minute later. "You know you're going to owe me for all my stuff you've used right?"

Bob chuckled, "It's for a good cause, boy. Can you put the bows down over there?" he gestured to an undisturbed patch of grass.

"I'm not a bloody boy Bob, but fine," John grumbled with a scowl. A rack of crossbows hanging from wooden brackets appeared and short barrels of bolts followed.

"I don't know if any of the more venerable ones will be willing to arm up but I think the younger ones might find it reassuring. A lot of them don't trust their abilities is what I'm getting from them. Hopefully real, physical things they can protect themselves with might help," said Katie. Then she sighed. "Maybe not though. Some of them are not handling this whole thing well. They think it's a prank or a mass hallucination or something"

Teamchat:

Zeeg Borrows: In position. I am not going anywhere near this thing. Take a look. I think we are in big trouble.

Chapter 18 - It had the potential to go far

The team all used Seeing Eye Dog.
Identify:
Level 14
Name: Dracorat Queen
The Queen was at least ten metres long if you included its tails. It was hard to tell as the three tails were flashing back and forth trying to swat the people fighting her, never staying still and stretched out to let John gauge the true size of it. She had a long sleek body with iridescent green-brown fur that almost gave the impression of scales. Her neck was far longer than a rat-like-creatures should be, ending in a head that was nearly half a metre long. Her distended face had a mouth that split the head almost in half when she opened her maw to snap at the human pests trying to fight her. She was a true monster in every sense.

Her wings periodically flapped frantically as she repositioned. She could fly in the same way a chicken could it seemed, surprisingly impressive jumps enhanced by mostly ineffective flapping. At least she wouldn't take to the skies and rain fire down on the whole town. *Please god don't let it have a breath attack. And if it does please don't let it be a poison cloud breath attack,* John thought.

Facing off against her were four people. Three men and a woman who were trading blows with the Queen and not immediately dying, which was very impressive. The first John identified was the woman. It took John a while to find the real one as there were multiple images of her attacking from all sides.

Once he spotted her real body hiding by a tree twenty metres behind the creature and Identified her he learned she was a Greater

Photomancer, level seven. Her illusory selves were launching eye beams at the giant rat as the ghostly bodies leapt and twirled to dodge the counter attacks. She maintained half a dozen images of herself, keeping them mostly in front of the Queen, bouncing back and forth, unleashing the eye beams on the beast. She replaced the illusions whenever a jaw or claw or tail destroyed one. Her eye beams did little more than leave a charred line on the Queen's flesh which healed quickly as they watched through Zeegs eyes, the monster fully recovered in seconds after each attack.

One of the men had a Lesser Titan Born ability. He was lurking to one side out of danger and then growing to three metres tall with a steroid addict's physique to rush in and pound on the Queen before retreating as he returned to normal size. His attacks seemed to do little more than annoy the queen, whenever his blows created the satisfying crunching sound of bones breaking, a tail would lash out and force him back. After thirty seconds or so he would fall back as he shrank back to his human norm. He was level six so his efforts against a much higher levelled monster were impressive despite the lack of serious damage done. Even when he broke bones it barely slowed the monster down, dents in her flesh popping back out as her vitality pulled her bones back into position with nightmare inducing cracks. He could knock her over and push her around a little. That was about the limit of his achievements unfortunately.

Next was a skinny young man dressed in black. He had the weird sounding Necrolocutor ability, John had no idea how it might work. Shambling hordes? Talk to dead birds? Hopefully not the latter as there were a couple of hundred recently created pigeon ghosts that might hold a bit of a grudge against Evie and himself. The man was carrying a small knife and dashing in and out leaving little more than faint lines on the beasts flesh.

As John watched he realised the man had truly uncanny timing. He was never where the monsters blows would land, usually escaping only by a hair's breadth and while his attacks did nothing to really hurt the Queen he somehow was always in the right place to cut at a limb or a tail or shove the body just enough to redirect an attack from a blow that would have smashed one of his companions into a miss or grazing hit. It was bizarre to watch, like a child successfully fending off an MMA champion. Despite his allies' efforts this man seemed to be the reason the Queen hadn't killed them all with ease as far as John could tell.

The last was an old man who stood well back leaning on a walking stick and frowning. John used Identify and saw he was a level four. His ability was listed as Gravitic Symbiote. *Gravity magic? Is he stopping it from flying? Boosting his allies?*

The Necrolocutor, who looked like a skeleton in black jeans and a hoodie, twitched to the side to avoid a heavy blow from a tail that shattered the path next to him and called out in a deep basso voice "Keep going, help will come soon!"

"You've been saying that for ten minutes, Greg," boomed the Titan Born, growing to his full size and charging forward once more. "**I'm starting to doubt the reliability of your 'friends'.**"

***

"Where's Ripley when you need her? We need to help them. They're just slowing it down, they can't hurt it," declared Evie, snapping them all back to their own bodies with her outburst.

"I don't think even the new and improved Doris would do much against that monster. It's level fourteen! You saw it healing right? How are we supposed to deal with the damn thing?" said Bob, shaking his head.

"Hate to be the one to say it but... running is still an option guys. They aren't part of our team. We don't know any of them and there is zero need to risk our lives pissing that thing off. We can move around for a few hours, lead it through the dead parts of town that weren't defended if we have to, where there's no one left alive so we can run out the timer until it buggers off," said John quietly.

"No, John. We need to help those people. They might be holding it back for now but if they fail... God knows what it could do. They are lower level than us and are keeping it busy. What if it heads over here? Vic's team won't hold it and the other survivors are just fodder for something like that."

"I don't like to point it out but your kid isn't on the line here Katie. So what is your magic plan to beat that thing, Boss Lady?" John asked with a growl.

"Fuck you John," Katie snapped. "That was a shitty thing to say. Evie said she wants to help them so wind your neck in. Give me a minute to get the others to bunker down. Then we move out. Can you port us over?"

John looked angry at the rebuke but when he glanced at Evie he saw he was getting "The Look" again and chose to indeed wind his neck in. "Us, yes. Doris no and Doris is our big hitter. My abilities don't work so well on higher level baddies it seems. We can't leave her behind," he muttered.

"Then we let Doris lead and move as a team to come at it from the east. We take the pressure off the illusion woman by giving her Doris to chew on," said Katie thoughtfully.

"Not sure I like how you phrased that but I think it's a good idea overall," said Bob. "I'll get into the cockpit while you talk to the others."

Bob ran over as Doris knelt down and a ramp extended from her chest. He ran up it and settled himself in what was starting to look like an armoured womb of cables and steel from the glimpse John caught before the outer armour sealed shut. All the clunky steering wheels and car radio switches that had comprised the control panel before had been replaced. The windscreen was gone, replaced by smooth armour.

Evie was still giving John disapproving looks between bouncing a ball of lightning around. "We're going to have words later, Dad. The golden rule is 'Don't be a dick' and you were just now being a dick."

"My job is to keep you safe, Evie. I have to keep that as my main priority. You're eleven for god's sake!" He threw his hands into the air. "When you're all grown up you can go get killed for stupid reasons and it will be on you. Right now, whatever happens to you is my fault and that was an *easy problem to solve* yesterday. Today it's a lot more complicated so cut me some slack."

"Don't use me as an excuse for your cowardice, old man." Evie turned on her heel and walked over to Doris leaving John pole-axed.

Katie ran back to Bob and Evie as John walked behind his daughter in stunned silence. He was responsible for her. He had personally slaughtered the monsters they'd been attacked by so far in job lots. Thousands of the little ones had had their vital bits teleported off their bodies. He'd helped with the mole rat things and then kept the other team safe while they levelled. He hadn't been a coward.

As his thoughts turned over in his mind he realised that he hadn't been at risk and neither had Evie or his new friends. Not really at risk anyway. He would have teleported Evie and himself out of harm's way at any time he was truly afraid for their lives and he finally admitted this to himself. The others as well, but he would start with Evie.

None of what had happened thus far had been much of a direct threat to him, outside of his inability to control his emotional responses to what he saw, heard and smelled. He had the option to flee whenever he liked and take anyone he cared about with him. The look in Evie's eyes as she had turned away hit him like a truck and he realised it wasn't as simple as he had been telling himself. He swore to himself that if nothing else was true, he would not be a coward in his daughter's eyes.

"Going to join us then?" asked Katie with a raised eyebrow.

"Yes. I'm... sorry. If we can help we should at least try but... we shouldn't take unnecessary risks. I'll leave it at that."

"Thank you, John. Doris will lead the way, you and I will follow with Evie bringing up the rear. Grab a quick drink and we'll head out."

Evie looked at John and crossed her hands in front of her chest with the first two fingers out in a V on each of them, one facing towards her and one away. She then raised two crossed fingers on her right hand to her lips and moved them up in front of her face. *Bit rude,* he thought. John decided he kind of deserved that and once again resolved to have a very serious discussion with his dad about future Christmas presents being age appropriate. And normal.

Teamchat:

Zeeg Borrows: Coming back now. Giga-rat is winning but slowly. Be there shortly.

Katie slipped her armour over her head and took a long drink of water from a bottle John blipped from Doris' storage. They all checked each other over, making sure they didn't have any unnoticed injuries and knew what the plan was. Doris began to lead the way into town. John took a breath and fell into position, Katie next to him with Evie following behind.

They moved into the snicket cutting through to the North end of the marketplace. Evie was joking with Bob about how lacking Doris was compared to "real" mechas from anime she had watched and Bob was politely ignoring the precocious brat. Katie was glancing around and jumped as Zeeg appeared at Doris' feet. Smiling, she tried to distract John who seemed to be falling into some kind of emotional fugue state again.

She turned her head towards him and asked "So what did you do for work, before all this I mean?"

A flash of light reflecting on metal flew down and suddenly a foot long blade at the end of a prehensile tail was deeply wedged into John's skull.

You have died.

John opened his eyes and looked around. He was in a world of mirrors and doors that all led to nowhere and reflected nothing. He reached up a hand to touch his brow and found his skull wasn't split in two down the middle. He stood in shock for what could have been a fraction of a second or an aeon.

"Shit. Evie!" he leapt to his feet and began running, jumping through mirrors and doors that all brought him back to the same place. He was desperate to find a way back to the real world not whatever this joke version was.

WHAT DO WE HAVE HERE? AH, A SHAME, IT HAD THE POTENTIAL TO GO FAR. QYINSJDNKFLANDJIHD, COME SEE THIS ONE MY LOVE

A cloud of golden fireflies was suddenly next to him. It had also always been next to him but this temporal contradiction didn't seem to bother whatever it was even as John's mind spun. He recoiled and jumped through a door but it remained next to him, moving without moving. Or perhaps he wasn't moving and the world seemed to move around him?

A cloud of black spots was suddenly next to the golden fireflies and it had always been there as well. The two had always been merged together, black and gold specks orbiting each other within the space the first one had always occupied.

HKDGUJJUILND, WHAT DO YOU WANT? I AM BUSY WITH THE NEW... OH, WELL THAT IS A SHAME. IT HAD CLASS FIVE POTENTIAL. THEY ALMOST ALWAYS SURVIVE THE CULL. WHATEVER HAPPENED?

I CANNOT SEE PRECISELY WHAT... A LOCAL TEMPORAL DISTORTION IS INTERFERING... AH AN UNFORTUNATE AMBUSH BEFORE FULLY REALISING ITS POTENTIAL IT SEEMS. IT IS GOOD TO REMOVE THE UNLUCKY ONES.

CONCUR, IT IS GOOD. THIS ONE CANNOT BE SALVAGED, FATE WAS AGAINST IT. WOULD YOU LIKE TO HARVEST IT OR MAY I? WAIT, WHAT IS HAPPENING ??? AH PERHAPS HE IS NOT AS UNLUCKY AS WE THOUGHT MY LOVE! GOOD LUCK LITTLE SPATIAL MAGE. WE'LL BE SEEING YOU IN THE FUTURE, ONE WAY OR ANOTHER.

Katie Johnson has activated REWIND

Chapter 19 - My favourite arm

Katie saw the blade cut into John's head and for a fraction of a second was too horrified to react. Then she reflexively activated Rewind and the universe unspooled, the blade at the end of the monster's tail flowing back to where it had been laid invisibly along the roof by this ambush predator as everything went back a second.

She tried to stop time but her single point of reserves was instantly consumed and a crippling headache hit her, knocking her thoughts from her mind. The attack only she knew was coming began to descend and only she could do anything to change what was about to happen. She latched onto John's left shoulder with both hands as she began to collapse, pulling him back and away from the attack as she fell towards the soft grass lining the path.

John's right arm shot out to balance him as the blade flashed past, missing his head by mere inches. His eyes tracked back along the tail to see the main body but it was blended into the background, only a vague outline could be made out. He tried to teleport the beast but his power failed to activate on it. He immediately teleported the wall and the edge of the roof it was hiding under up into the sky.

The monster appeared, a two metre long rat, skinny, with the arms and legs growing out from its sides, it was built more like a lizard than a mammal. Its three metre tail flailed, the leaf shaped blade at its tip flashing and reflecting the colours, a coruscating rainbow coursing over its skin in its surprise, as it suddenly found itself without support and began to fall to the ground.

A blaze of crackling energy shot past John and Katie as Evie became lightning and ran along its side, dragging a hand down its body, leaving a burnt and stinking line in its flesh. Doris had pivoted and quick as a snake her left hand shot out to grip the things head. The three fingers locked into place around its skull and the cutting faces of the grinders and circular saw extended, chewing through the things head and killing it.

"Evie," croaked Katie, "touch the stump while you're in your elemental body."

Katie, despite her agony, had crawled round to John's side and clamped her hands around his upper arm. John looked down, feeling suddenly lightheaded, to see his right arm ended halfway down his bicep and, despite Katies vicelike grip, blood pumped furiously from the terrible wound.

"That was my favourite arm. And I really liked this hoody. It was a gift," He muttered, trying to wave his stump around as Evie appeared next to him.

"I can't Katie, it'll kill him" her voice was distorted and crackled while she was in her elemental form but the fear and concern were clear in her tone, "Anything I zap dies!"

"Blood loss… kill him anyway… only hope… trust me" Katie finally succumbed to the pain of depleting her reserves and fell away from John who had mercifully passed out, she was left rolling on the ground in agony, clutching at her head with both hands and moaning. The blood flow from John's wound increased dramatically.

Evie hesitated for a half a second before flashing over and clutching the end of the stump in both hands. She cried out as her dad's flesh popped and sizzled, the lightning rising away from the stump in arcs and leaving angry burns up John's shoulder, across his chest and carving jagged lines on his neck and right cheek to just below his eye before Evie leapt away weeping.

Bob was suddenly there, snatching off his shirt and binding the now cauterised wound untidily. Evie returned to normal and fell to her knees, tears streaming down her face.

"Well done little one," he said gently.

"I killed him," she whispered quietly. Burying her face in her hands she emitted a low, keening wail full of grief and regret.

"Use your eyes, child. He is down to 32% health but it isn't falling anymore. You saved your dad's life Evie. He'll live, I promise you."

Evie checked the team display and saw Bob was telling the truth. Her tears gradually slowed and after a minute she stood, taking a position just away from the group and shooting hateful looks at every shadowy corner and branch moving in the breeze. Zeeg curled up next to John on his left side, laying her head gently on his chest as though to listen to his breathing and heartbeat.

After a couple more minutes Katie picked herself up groggily, still clutching her head with one hand and moved over to check on John.

"Christ that hurt! But not as much as this did I expect. I need to fix the bandage but good work Bob and well done Evie. He's back up to 35% so he's on the mend, albeit minus an arm. What the fuck was that thing?" She began to retie the bandage, looping part of the shirt around his neck and cinching it in gently to hold the stump across his chest.

Team report: 1 Assassin Rat killed. 12 essence per kill. Essence gained 12.

"Looks like it isn't just the tunnelers that are high level. It must have been level twelve or thirteen." said Bob. "Should we press on or wait for John to come round?"

"No idea how long it will take for him to wake up. Can Doris carry him? In her right hand I mean, the one without all the whirling blades built into it that is currently covered in rat brain."

"Aye lass."

"No way, we need to get Dad somewhere safe!" Evie objected.

"We need to help the ones fighting the Queen, Evie. Nowhere is safe until that thing is dead. Bob can carry your dad until he wakes up, if he isn't up by the time we get near we can leave him with Zeeg out of sight while we help them."

"We should take him back to the other team and the old folks. They can guard him. They've got a healer!"

"We may need him sweetheart. It's better to have something or someone and not need them than need them and not have them right? Isn't that what he told you? Nothing is going to regrow his arm darling. He'd want to be near you, to keep you safe as soon as he wakes up, wouldn't he?" Katie said softly, tears in her eyes. While Evie was precocious and more than a little rude sometimes her pain at seeing her dad injured stirred something in Katie.

Evie scowled and clearly wasn't happy but acquiesced reluctantly. Doris stooped down and laid her hand out, Katie and Evie carefully moved John so he was cradled in her palm, legs dangling between her fingers and his head resting by her wrist.

"We need to stay clear of buildings, no idea how many more of those invisible shits there are. Let's go, Doris leads, the rest of us move in a triangle, me first, you and Zeeg watching my back, ok?" Katie said firmly. Evie nodded and Zeeg woofed quietly. They set out and once clear of the snicket carefully avoided getting close to any other building.

As they entered the marketplace proper there was a colossal crash and an explosion of dirt and brickwork flew up into the sky half a kilometre behind them, creating a cloud of debris that rained down on the surrounding area..

"I guess that's where the chunk of building Dad teleported went. Good job he didn't blip it straight up. That looks like a bomb went off."

"He mustn't have teleported it to his max distance, I'll run the numbers... maybe 15km up, according to Doris? That should be about 300 seconds to hit the ground and it's been about five minutes-ish. That would be an amazing offensive use of his power. Much better than the spear."

The sound of the fight against the Queen gradually drew closer. They moved carefully, having Evie Zap any areas they had to pass by that would be good spots for the Assassin Rats to hide. No more of the chameleonic monsters attacked them.

"You two should get your levels if you have any to take." whispered Evie, "this won't be easy."

They had crept up on the fight and stood well back shocked at the violence and the fact the humans were still standing. Evie watched the ongoing battle between the Queen and the fighters who had been keeping her busy with wide eyes. The tide was inexorably turning in the Queen's favour now.

The titan was battered and bleeding from a dozen serious wounds but despite that he kept rushing in every time his ability was available. The illusionist was slumped against the tree she had been hiding behind before and was only maintaining two illusions, neither of which were attacking with their beams anymore. They were focused solely on dodging and distracting the monster. The old man with gravity powers had collapsed to the ground. The only one still in good shape was the skeletal man in black who continued to harass and divert the giant creatures attacks but who didn't seem able to do any damage.

The Queen was clearly winning but it hadn't had it all its own way. One wing was broken at the joint connecting to its torso, it must have been pulverised by the titan and it wasn't healing as quickly as it had been before. Minor cuts and gashes covered its body and its black blood leaked out, the injuries only healing gradually now.

Doris lowered her hand and John was carefully removed and laid on the ground.

Katie and Bob both used all the Essence they could. Bob got one level and three more equipment slots on Doris. Katie got a longer time stop, raising it to 120 seconds, a Stop ability to freeze one enemy in time and a boost to the relevance of her glimpses into the future.

Evie moved forward slowly and began charging a maximum strength lightning ball. Doris lurched into action as Bob activated Overdrive, drawing her chainsaw-sword and charging towards the nightmare.

"Stop doesn't work on it... Shit, slow doesn't either!" Katie must have cast her haste ability on everyone else involved though, as the titan and the skeleton suddenly moved more quickly, dodging with ease where before they had barely escaped unharmed. It didn't seem to affect the illusions the light manipulator was casting but the woman drew herself up and summoned a third illusion to join the pair dancing before the draconic rat monster.

"So you weren't bullshitting us," called the titan, retreating as he returned to normal size. "Welcome to the jungle new friends! Could you *please* be a bunch of dears and kill this fucking thing?"

Evie launched her lightning ball and it flashed across, striking the beast in its flank and causing it to scream, lightning arcing across its body. It was still thrashing as Doris arrived and brought down her buzzing blade to slice at the things neck. With a scream of sparks the blade bounced off at first but began to slowly dig into the skin behind its skull as the mech applied her weight to the blade.

Doris' other hand swept out and latched on the wing joint that had been damaged, three fingers flipping forward to lock on as a horrific grinding noise issued out. Blood and flesh and lumps of metal spewed out of Doris' grip causing the beast to scream again and throw its weight to the side, knocking Doris back into the river some ten metres away, her left hand a smoking wreck.

Her chainsaw sailed away, the blade slowing to a stop and pivoting around the cable connecting it to her back, causing it to splash into the water behind the mech and sputter out. In her damaged left hand dangled the savaged remains of the creature's right wing. The beast wailed as blood sprayed from the severed appendage. Doris dropped the gory trophy into the water and prepared to charge back in.

Evie began draining it and casting Zap every time she had a full overcharge. The bolts caused the beast to writhe and twist but didn't seem to be doing a great deal of damage. The smell of burnt fur began to permeate the air.

Katie was everywhere and nowhere. Appearing for a moment right under the beast's chin to slash up at its neck then reappearing to hack at one of its tails. Her sword work wasn't doing much damage but the creature was becoming frantic as it dove about to handle this seemingly untouchable threat. Doris surged out of the river and crossed the distance to slam into it once again and knocked the beast onto its side, swinging her sword down to cut at a leg joint just as the titan returned to the fight and began hammering at the gruesome wound left by the wing the mecha had pulled off. A tail flicked out and the titan was thrown backwards, slamming into a tree that cracked as his boosted weight slammed into it.

Team invites sent by Evie Borrows.
New members have joined the team:
Level 7
Name: Greg Smith
Ability: Necrolocutor

Level 6
Name: Raoul Forrester
Ability: Lesser Titan Born

Level 7
Name: Samantha Jones
Ability: Greater Photomancer

The Queen spun and a tail thrust out at the titan charging in to attack once more. He raised an arm to block and the tail cut a gash on his forearm as his other fist came down with a crack on the beast's spine. Whether it was his hand bones that broke, the creature's ribs or spine or some combination of all three was impossible to tell. He drew his fist up again uncaring, preparing to hammer at the same spot as he heard a snarling growl flash past behind him. One of the other tails had curled around and had been poised to plunge into his exposed back but a mass of fur, disrespect for authority and a penchant for the treats with the chicken wrap had snatched the tail from the air as she sailed past.

In her Barghest form Zeeg now stood three metres at the shoulder, towering half a metre over the Queen. Her snatching the tail from the air had spun the Queen around with a pained squeal, scattering the humans cutting and pummelling her as it spun and leaving her prone on the grass. Zeeg bit down hard and with a gush of blood the tail was severed halfway down its length. She spat out the chunks in her mouth and snarled, leaping onto the Queen's flank, biting and snapping at the remaining wing as her claws tried to dig into its stomach and disembowel the monster. The remaining tails flailed and tried to stab at her but they slid and sparked off her now armoured fur.

"Zeeg NO! You need to guard Dad!" screamed Evie.
Teamchat:
John Borrows: I'm awake. Keep it busy for sixty more seconds for me.

Chapter 20 - Time to finish it

Katie appeared behind Evie and collapsed to the ground as John walked up to his daughter, left arm wrapped across his chest to cradle what remained of his right.

"Hey kiddo. Sorry about the scare," he said weakly.

Katie struggled for breath, dropping a now broken sword and gasping "I'm done, power isn't the problem, body is the problem, I'm still only human," she fell to her knees and curled her arms around her chest.

A spurt of milky fluid splattered across the Queen's face, the other half of Katies sword sticking out of its ruined left eye. She must have made the attack and fled with the last of her strength, leaving half her sword buried in one of the Queens eyes, a jagged length of metal wedged into its skull and sticking out of its face.

Evie clutched her dad around the waist and began to cry, burying her face into his chest, accidentally jostling the remains of his right arm, making him wince. He patted her gently on top of her head with his one good hand. "Hey Sausage, it's ok, I'm fine," he murmured.

"It's great that you're up now sleeping beauty but how exactly are we supposed to keep this thing entertained for another minute? We were running on fumes before you even got here," the titan called to John as he retreated, shrinking back to normal size, "Oh shit!"

A tail swiped out and launched him back into the river where he staggered to his feet, spluttering, with a new gash across his chest.

Doris leapt. When nearly eight tons of mecha leaps everyone nearby feels it as the force reverberates through the ground. She came down next to Zeeg, landing astride the things shoulders and pinning its chest beneath her weight. There was a sickening crunch and this time there was no doubt that it was the monster whose bones had yielded.

It screamed in pain and its head spun to snap at the mech. Before its jaws could latch on, the chainsaw came down again, across the beast's ruined face this time. The weapon screamed mechanically as the teeth bit and broke, sending flesh and fragments of metal once again flying into the air. Doris' ruined left hand scrabbled and latched onto the things' jaws, pushing its head back down and letting the chainsaw wreak further gory havoc.

Zeeg continued to attack, claws flashing and ripping thin lines through the monster's armoured fur and flesh, desperately trying to get at the guts and spill them across the ground. Her jaws snapped at the exposed foreleg of the Queen, preventing it from swinging the limb to help right itself. The two remaining clones of the illusionist both appeared by the beasts head and unleashed their gaussian beams into its remaining eye.

The Queen thrashed again far more violently, tossing the mecha and giant dog off with its pained spasm. It drew itself to its feet slowly, trembling from head to tails and snarled, spewing spittle and black blood in front of it. It began to sniff then cocked its head to the side. The beams might not have destroyed its remaining eye but it was blind, at least for now.

The dog leapt once more and tackled it in the gut, knocking it back and again lunged to try and disembowel the thing. Doris regained her feet slowly, off to one side. The jolt from being hurled a dozen metres had knocked Bob into a woozy confusion this time, the robot lurched awkwardly and moved aimlessly.

The rat kicked Zeeg once more, sending her spinning with a yelp just as the titan again charged in, fist slamming into the Queen's face, snapping it back as the neck flexed and curled to absorb the damage. Zeeg spun in midair and landed on her feet. She launched herself again at this impossibly strong enemy.

Teamchat:
John Borrows: Everyone except Zeeg get back NOW. Puppy, go ghost mode in
3...
2...
1... now

Everyone except for Doris threw themselves away from the beast, leaving Zeeg alone, pinning the Queen on her back. The monster brought its back legs up to use the claws and the immense strength of its limbs to rip into and cast off the annoying dog. As her legs moved to attack the dog became transparent, the Queen's feet passed straight through her. The force of the Queen's movement left her sprawled out, stretched on her back across the ground. Momentarily vulnerable. A three metre obelisk of stone appeared an inch above the stomach of the Queen travelling at 65m/s. It passed straight through the intangible dog and into the Queen. John had teleported it into the sky as soon as he had regained consciousness and seen the situation.

The tip of the cenotaph, for that was the only thing he could think of to use that had all the characteristics he needed, stabbed down and pierced straight through the creature. The Queen wasn't killed outright thanks to her monstrous vitality but her spine was severed. Her lower body went limp and her upper body thrashed uselessly, her still blind head twisting on its prehensile neck to snap and bite at the length of granite pinning her to the ground like a butterfly to a cork board.

"Hell yeah! Time to finish it!" shouted the titan, growing in size far beyond what John and his friends had seen before, towering six metres tall and rivalling Doris. He was once more preparing to charge in.

"Wait," called John in a wintry voice that brooked no dissent as a ghostly, giant dog trotted up to his side to sniff at him. He raised a hand that passed through her massive snout as he tried to pet her. Six cars appeared above the obelisk in sequence, separated by two seconds each. Each having been falling for at least a minute judging from the speed they hit the beast. Each impact drove the stone stake deeper through the beast before the cars exploded as the petrol in the fuel tanks detonated, flinging shrapnel and red hot metal shards all around.

The Queen was hidden from sight within a cloud of dust, flame and wreckage but her screams shook the glass of windows half a mile away and made everyone flinch and reach to cover their ears. John collapsed and raised his hand to his head, groaning in pain from using the last of his reserves. There was another car still falling and he hoped it would land somewhere uninhabited. He hadn't had enough reserves to bring it onto the target. The titan raised his arm to shield his face as the debris from the explosions smashed against him.

"It's dead, right?" called Samantha from behind her tree, "I know it's a tough bitch but no way it survived that lot. It's like the ending of Halo of Doom, god I loved that flick."

"It isn't dead yet" came the deep voice of Greg. "I would know. However it won't be long. The Great Majority are already singing of our victory. Stay back a minute and let the dust clear. It will pass through the veil within that time. All of the team are well but we need to get Reg to a healer soon or he will be joining his ancestors. He is old and overexerted himself to bar the Queen from flight. I am told you have a healer with the others your team protected and guided? We should take Reg to her quickly."

"What's wrong with this lot?" asked Raoul, emerging from the river nearby. "They didn't even take a hit except the dog. Good dog," he added hurriedly when Zeeg turned a baleful gaze on him. He looked at the cloud around the Queen. "I knew that thing could bench at least six tons. Hey robot man, how much do you weigh? Want to arm wrestle later?"

"They have spent themselves to secure our victory. We owe them our lives as do all who still live. Quickly, friend Raoul, bring Reg over to us but avoid the dying beast and the discombobulated robot. Its pilot is concussed and not able to control the machine properly at this time."

"You know you still sound like a weirdo, right?" asked Raoul in his broad scouse accent, oblivious to the irony of the lilting tones coming from a bear of a man accusing anyone of sounding weird. Raoul walked to where the gravity mage had passed out and gently picked him up before moving back to the rest of them.

John was climbing to his feet as Raoul approached, rubbing at his head with his remaining hand. Once Evie was sure he was fine she immediately moved to Katie who was still groaning on the floor, she had run herself far beyond human endurance to help with the fight. She wasn't feeling the pain from running out of reserves but of spending everything she had physically and then some.

"John, revered by the Majority, are you recovered enough to send our friend to your healer? Truth, but we need some rest now," asked Greg politely.

John paused for a moment to parse the word choice into modern English. The man had no accent but framed his sentences like he was a walking Jane Austin book or something so it took John a moment to figure out what the anorexically thin and worryingly pallid man meant.

"I can port some people back, all of us in fact but Doris is too big. The thing isn't dead yet though."

As he spoke the creature finally stopped mewling and whining, going still as no more clouds were kicked up by its squirming.

"Nevermind. That's a dead dragon rat. Katie, are you OK?" he grumbled, too exhausted to modulate his tone into something like politeness.

"I'll live, John, I need to sleep for a week though. Send me and the others back to Geraldine, I'll make sure Reg gets looked at and keep an eye on Evie for you while you wait for Bob." She struggled to her feet and smiled at the one armed man

John looked her in the eyes for a moment then nodded slowly. She had saved his life *after* he had died. To say she had earned a lot of trust from him would be an understatement. He fought down his paranoia as he looked to Evie, "I'll send Katie and you back first kid, you'll dodge any assassin rats that way and I'll put you all down in the cleared area Ok? I'll be right behind you, I just want to make sure Bob is ok to pilot Doris back. Can't leave our mecha pilot all alone can we?"

Evie gave him "The Look" before rushing in to hug him, stepping back and nodding. John began blipping his friends and their new acquaintants back to where they had left the other survivors.

"So how does this teleport thing wo-" Samantha began before she vanished from the riverside.

Greg raised a hand and said "One moment John. The Majority have some questions I must ask you on their behalf. They know you have many questions of your own and will endeavour to answer them this evening. Please be patient and I will explain what I can once we are sure this threat has passed." He nodded slightly, flashed a terrifyingly skeletal grin and John, uncomfortable with the strange man, ported him back to join the others and moved towards Doris who was waving her left hand in front of her chest while her right arm spun in circles.

John approached the mecha carefully, making sure to keep a good distance away from the punch drunk machine.

"Bob, do you maybe want to step out for some fresh air, mate?" John called, standing well back and contemplating summoning his tobacco before he sighed. How was he going to roll a smoke with only one bloody hand? A moment later a pack of pre rolled cigarettes appeared, "borrowed" from the shop in town. They appeared where his right hand *would* have been had it still been attached and not abandoned... where the hell did he leave his right arm again? The pack fell to the ground and he lowered his gaze with yet another sigh. *Well this sucks,* he thought stooping to pick up the pack with his left hand and opening it with his teeth. He pulled a smoke out with his lips and dropped the pack, his lighter then appeared in his *left* hand. *Fool me once, shame on you. Fool me twice...*

He lit up as the ramp descended from Doris' chest and Bob staggered out. He had been bleeding from wounds around his head, trickles of blood criss-crossing his face where the G forces of the blows Doris had taken had smeared lines of red. Another wound showed across his chest from something in the cockpit bashing into him but the blood was drying and the wounds seemed to have largely healed up.

"Have you ever been hit by a truck, boy? I wouldn't recommend it but it is now checked off on my bucket list," he staggered as he got to the bottom of the ramp.

John smiled and reached out to steady the old man.

"That's a weird bucket list you have, mate. Also I'm 42, dude. We've been over this. Not a boy. Can you seal up Doris please? I can port us back to the others and then you can remote pilot her over when you can see straight, yeah?"

"OK lad, we did get the bitch right?"

"Yes mate, we got the bitch."

Blip. Blip.
Team report: 1 Dracorat Queen killed. 50 Essence per kill.
Essence gained 50.

Chapter 21 - Too soon?

Update:
Survivors: 578
R.O.V.S.S: 1904
Time to end of wave: 1:53:23

John and Bob appeared next to the house the other survivors had taken shelter in when the team went to face the Queen. Evie carefully hugged her dad on his left side and stood next to him as Katie, Greg, Raoul and Sam came over to greet them. Victoria and her team were spread out along the street, keeping watch to protect the other survivors.

"The conquering heroes return," said Raoul with a wild grin on his swarthy face. "I thought Greg was full of shit when he kept telling us help would come. Figured I'd end in his "Majority" while my body ended up shat out of that thing in a day or two, so thanks, to all of you. That robot is a badass machine, old man! Any chance you want to spar with me at max size? " he slapped Bob on the back, sending the old man stumbling forwards.

"Not a problem," said a wan and exhausted Katie, "I really need a break, how about we borrow the lounge of one of these open houses and talk things through without twenty odd pensioners hanging on our every word? Sparring can wait until later I think."

Some of the pensioners in question filed out of the house they'd retreated into, carrying flasks of hot tea and plates of biscuits that were handed over to the team. The pensioners smiled, thanked them and went back inside. They all gave John a wide berth and uncertain smiles. John felt extremely uncomfortable, there were a lot of new widows and widowers whose partners they hadn't saved. Did they resent him for not doing better?

The team moved a couple of houses down to a bungalow that had been left open after the tunnel rat attack. Victoria and Jennifer from the other team also joined them, the others staying outside on watch. They set themselves down on the settees and armchairs, except for John who summoned his preferred armchair from his living room into a free space *Teleportation is the best power!* He thought to himself. Zeeg sat and gave him her trademarked big brown eyes.

"What puppy? You want the other chair?" The dog shook her head. He thought for a moment. The bloody dog could use the teamchat but clearly she liked to make him guess. "You want my office chair?" a yip and unmistakable doggy smile. "Really?" A woof. He blipped over his scratty office chair that the dog seemed to love. She climbed up carefully, far bigger than she used to be, and pushed off slowly with her last leg to leave the ground. She continued spinning happily in the chair as the others got down to business. John summoned her a treat and she chewed away contentedly.

"Thank you once again for coming to our aid. I would like to provide you with as much information as the Majority has been able to give me, if that is acceptable?" said Greg in his deep voice. His eyes met Katies and she flinched slightly, her diplomatic mien temporarily unable to control her response. Greg's eyes had no iris, they were the deepest black she had ever seen and the sclera was a faint yellow with thin black lines running through it. He looked like his eyes were "terminal hangover" bloodshot, except his blood was black. It was almost inhuman.

"What is the Majority please, Greg?" asked Katie, recovering her poise. Bob was trying to dip his biscuit in his tea but was missing every other time. Concussions apparently didn't just go away with the system.

"They are those who came before. The dead, although they dislike the term. I can speak to them, when they are willing. They can advise and guide me as they see fit. Some are angry and bitter. These ones I call Howlers as they are unable to control themselves, screaming into the dark. For centuries in some cases, they are hopelessly mad," he sat down and took a breath. "The others… you could call them ghosts I suppose. They are friendly enough although usually uninterested in the affairs of the living. I suppose the best way to put it is They watch us and generally find our choices and actions… frustrating is perhaps the best word. They usually have something that stops them from going to the gods, some purpose or obsession that keeps them tethered to this realm. Many have become geniuses in the discipline they focussed on in life after centuries of thought while dead. They are all fascinated by John at the moment, as he has met the gods and come back."

"I don't think I met any gods. You say the dead speak to you? Did they speak to you before this morning? I take it this isn't a TV medium kind of speaking?" asked John, sipping his tea. Hoping desperately to avoid further discussion about his vision.

"They were as silent with me as they are with you now until I received my Essence. I volunteered to tend the graves and used to talk to them while at work. We believe the abilities the living receive are somehow shaped by our personalities and actions in life. For instance, they have told me you were essentially a hermit. Often the only person you really spoke to for days was your daughter but you worked in logistics and ended up with a very powerful movement ability. Raoul was blessed with a deep love of exercise before becoming a son of Hercules and Sam was a visual artist and special effects contractor for film and television." They both nodded, seemingly unsurprised that this strange man knew far more about them than they had told him. "I am sorry to pressure you John, but the Majority are unceasing in their requests to hear your tale from the other side. Please could you share what you remember?"

"Wait, you actually died?" asked Evie sounding shocked.

"I think so, kid. The system told me I did and then everything went weird. Katie used Rewind and then... I lost my arm instead of my head like the first time. If she hadn't grabbed me that thing would have got me for sure. I had a weird dream or I thought it was a weird dream, anyway." Evie looked at Katie who met her gaze. Evie nodded and signed *Thank You*. Katie smiled back, assuming that under the circumstances the child probably hadn't said something offensive with her hands.

"I was in this dream place. I was surrounded by mirrors that didn't reflect and doorways that lead to where I started. I ran and called out but I don't think I ever moved. After- some time, it's hard to tell how long. Time didn't work just like distance didn't work. Then suddenly a cloud of golden stuff, like fireflies, was next to me and *had always been next to me*. It called out in a voice, a voice I can't really describe, deep and light and loving and hateful all at once. Then there had always been another one of the things next to me. This one was a cloud of black spots, like regular flies I suppose. They talked about who would get to harvest me," John shivered, "and how someone like me usually survived the cull, something about a class five potential, then Katie used her power and she was yanking my head out of the way of that thing's tail," he sighed. "I am sorry but that really is all I remember." He was strangely relieved to have told his little tale and not had anyone immediately call him insane.

Greg winced and waved his arms around his head. "They are distraught, forgive me I must-" he got up and ran out into the street where he fell to his knees as though in prayer. Swirls of dark energy began to spin around him as he muttered and gestured wildly with his hands.

"Well that's new," said Sam, "he was totally unflappable, cool as a cucumber since we met him. He led us against that Queen thing and… he's been a rock. Despite only meeting him a couple of hours ago he's become- I don't know, it sounds stupid. Best let him be while he calms down the dead folks?"

"How did you lot meet up exactly?" asked Bob, having once again mastered the art of getting his biscuit to hit his tea.

"Greg brought us together and got us a few levels. I was trying to get out of the centre of town, to get somewhere open and away from the packs hunting where the people were. I'd killed a few, eye beams are- useful on the little ones," Sam shuddered. "the downside with them is you can't not see what happens to the target! I was going down by the river," she raised a hand that faded out of sight, "using this camouflage thing," her arm snapped back to its normal colour. "Greg called out from ahead of me, knew exactly where I was as he walked up and gave me a little bow. Told me we would meet up with the hulk," she smiled at Raoul, who even in human form was one of the tallest men John had ever seen and built like an Olympic weightlifter, "then led us straight to him on the edge of the marketplace. He brought us back and told us a few tricks we could use with our abilities and the system."

Raoul took up the narrative as Sam lapsed into silence, "Then the squirrely bastard said a monster was coming and we had to fight it. We were the 'last defence but help would come' and we had to hold the line. When he told me what the thing was I noped out. I'm big and strong but unlike the stereotype I'm not completely stupid. He took me aside. Told me some stuff no one should know but me. Not bad but private, alright? So I stayed. Reg turned up a bit later and Greg spoke to him as well. That was entertaining I can tell you but you'll meet Reg soon enough. Anyway, forty or so minutes after that your bunch showed up."

"John, any chance you can get something stronger than tea for me please?" asked Bob.

"Not sure this is the time to hit the bottle Bob, still a while before the rats go away and you just took a bad head wound."

"I'm not going to get drunk, boy. Just take the edge off. We could all do with a bit of a break. These guys were fighting that bitch for over half an hour before we turned up, they might need to unwind as well and a stiff drink will take the edge off."

A bottle of whiskey appeared next to Bob. "Hey, good taste lad! The islands definitely produce a superior tipple!" The top came off and he took a swig, passing it to his left to Sam. The bottle made its way round the room, when it got to Evie she gave her dad a pleading look, he fought down a smirk from showing on his face and nodded "reluctantly". She took a tiny sip and started coughing. "How can you drink that stuff? It's like industrial waste or something!"

John laughed. "When I was a little younger than you, my Dad let me have a slug of whiskey as well. I had much the same reaction when I could breathe again." He grinned at Evie and took a pull from the bottle himself, passing it to Katie who didn't indulge.

"Where did the bottle come from John?" asked Sam. "Do you have a stash of whatever it is you want at home?"

"The guy is a bit of a packrat when it comes to having a personal stash," grinned Katie. "You should have seen his garage."

"That's enough of that thank you!" said John with a smile. "I finally got round to clearing it out this morning. Teleportation is really handy when it comes to chores," he turned to Sam and continued more seriously, "I got a mod that lets me remember where something I want was the last time I saw it. As long as it's still within ten metres of where I saw it, I can blip it over."

"Speaking of you being the 'greatest gentleman thief in the world', we need to go looting this evening, matey. Doris needs some parts for repair and I want to raid the industrial estate, get my mitts on as much heavy gear as we can."

"Ha, we should call you the one armed bandit!" joked Raoul who immediately shut up under a barrage of dirty looks and the sudden silence. "Too soon?"

John looked at Raoul for a moment and then smiled. "If Dr. Richard Kimble starts hunting me, I'm telling him I worked for you."

Roaul burst into a booming laugh and everyone relaxed a little.

"Seeing as you can steal whatever you like if you've seen it, any chance you can blip me in a towel and some fresh clothes? Some of us need a shower. You more than most John, have you seen what you look like? You've got red on you," Katie said. A mirror appeared in John's left hand and he looked at himself for the first time since the wave began. The shock of the sight took his breath for a moment. His face was ruined on the right hand side. Jagged scars from the arcs of lightning Evie used to seal his stump had burned up his cheek, leaving a pattern that looked a lot like lightning falling from his eye down to his neck and chest then over his shoulder to his stump, visible through the shreds of the clothes he was wearing.

Evie's lightning had mostly missed his beard (for which he was extremely grateful) but it had taken some damage, partially burned away in places and singed short in others. His clothes on the right side were ruined, not only was his hoodie missing most of the arm and tattered at the shoulder but his blood had spattered all down his body, painting him red down most of that side. His t-shirt had partially melted into his skin but had come unstuck from the moving around he had done since. Adrenaline is a hell of a painkiller. Now he saw it he became aware of the clinging, crackling sensation when he moved as the dried blood cracked and the still wet blood stuck to him. The mirror vanished again.

"No wonder the oldies were staying clear of me before," he began in a cracked voice. His voice grew stronger as he continued, "Anyone spot where the shower is in this place? I'll port in whatever you need but I think I'll get to call dibs."

"On the right down the corridor," said Katie. "While I am dying for a shower I have to admit you need it more." She grinned as John got up, blipped the bottle into his hand for another, longer swig, eliciting a curse of surprise from Bob who had been about to take a gulp. Then he returned it to the circle and set out to scrub off the blood and sweat of the day.

Chapter 22 - Mr I'm-Not-A-Thief

John opened the door to the bathroom and a cloud of steam escaped around him. He was now wearing fresh clothes, a grey shirt with unbloodied jeans. He had summoned an electric clipper to tidy his face fungus, his beard was sadly much shorter than before and now more of a goatee than anything else. The moustache was still in one piece though so... small mercies? He had spent a frustrating 45 seconds trying to figure out how to put on a tie with only one hand and his teeth before porting it back to his wardrobe and deciding not to mention he even tried. His right sleeve swung, empty, a visible sign of what he had lost today. Once again he was less troubled emotionally than he thought he ought to be and he once again put the worry aside.
"Thought you'd fallen in," said Katie as she got up to go next.
"Fresh towels are in there and there is a pile of clothes from the shop in the bedroom next door. No idea what sizes everyone is so I just grabbed a bunch of everything I could remember from the last time I went in. If there is anything specific you want, let me know and I'll see what I can do." Katie headed out to enjoy her much anticipated shower..
"You look human again Dad," said Evie. Zeeg had grown bored with spinning around on her chair and was now sitting next to Evie on the settee, head resting on Evie's legs and enjoying ear rubs.
"Thanks Sausage. I do feel a lot better," He grinned at her and she flinched slightly, the angry scars on his face twisting as his expression changed. The right side of his mouth failed to rise as it should have done.

"Sorry Dad." Evie said. Unsure if she was apologising for flinching or causing the scars, John leant down and put his hand on her shoulder. "Thank you Evie. You're a good egg, little one, and I'm very proud of you," she smiled back tentatively as a terrible noise began issuing from the bathroom that made her scrunch her face up in horror.

"Does she know she can't sing?" asked Raoul. "That sounds like cats being fed into a woodchipper while a donkey gets chain sawed in half!"

They cycled through the bathroom one by one, no one else deciding to ruin the ambience with their "singing". Evie went last and emerged wearing the PJs and dressing gown she had asked John to bring over for her. She went back to curl up next to Zeeg on the settee, exhausted from the day's action.

Sam used a safety pin John had blipped over to secure his empty shirt sleeve and he thanked her, swinging his stump back and forth to test his movement. His balance was still off. His right side was lighter than his body thought it should be and it would take a while to adjust. In the meantime he would tend to lean to the left.

Bob and John had spent most of their time planning a route for this evening's grand larceny. Bob had convinced John that electric vehicles (for the batteries and refined metal), power tools (for cutting edges and machine parts) and bulk materials (for armour and the ever vague "you know, stuff") were the priority. While John had managed to successfully argue that food and water and the means to meet basic human needs should also be included, largely thanks to the rest of the group backing him up, Bob was strangely reluctant. He was obsessed with the loot he was sure lay in the industrial estate. They had devised a route taking them past the hardware shop by the primary school, the big supermarket on the edge of town and finally on into the industrial estate.

"It will soon be time," said Greg in his basso voice, coming back inside. "I apologise for my- indisposition. The Great Majority have been thrown into an uproar by John's revelations about those who crossover after passing the veil. They view crossing over in the same way the living view dying: no one who does it has ever reported back, so there were a lot of theories and superstitions around the idea. The debate will rage for months if not years. I do not know what they will decide to do."

"They're dead right? How much can they do anyway?" asked Raoul. Greg winced and turned his black and yellow eyes on the large man. "Please, titan-blood, show more respect. The Majority brought us together, they provided their support and guidance. Do not be so disrespectful."

Raoul looked down and coughed. "I'm sorry. Does their debate change what is coming next though?"

"Not as far as I can tell but they may be distracted and less able to assist us for some time. Now, I believe the hygiene facilities are available. I will avail myself of them. The wave will end shortly and then we should be able to truly relax. At least for a short while."

"Big guy, try not to be a dick, please. You're worse than Conan in a brothel with people sometimes," said Sam after Greg had left for the bathroom.

"Golden rule dude" chimed in Evie.

"Do unto others as you'd have them do unto you?" Raoul asked.

"No, the other golden rule. Ask my Dad sometime."

Bob sat up, taking a pull from a now nearly empty bottle of whiskey that hadn't been circling as much recently as it had at the start, then said "Aaaaannnnd… we are done. Thank god for that."

Golden writing filled all of their visions.

The first wave has been completed.

Survivors: 526
R.O.V.S.S: 1231
Average Level of human survivors: level 4
Survivors of the invading species:
Dracorat Queen: 0/1
Assassin Rat: 4/5
Star-nosed Mole-rat: 2/30
Sky Rat: 147/2300
Chittering Scavenger: 1077/10645
The Queen was successfully slain. The remaining invaders have been moved outside of the barrier and will not trouble you for the remainder of the recruitment and training process. They will however set up nests and begin breeding, becoming a pest species in the local area in the future. This process will be much delayed by the loss of the Queen.
Congratulations Recruits! You have taken the first step on a very long journey. Please attend a compulsory meeting of all survivors tomorrow morning at eleven AM local time to be held in the marketplace. A representative will be available to answer questions and advise on the next phase of your training. A modest award ceremony will also take place to acknowledge and reward the outstanding trainees in your unit. Attendance is mandatory, recruits.
The Light Shines.

"One in eight of us made it." said Sam sadly. "The graveyards aren't big enough, what the hell are we going to do with the bodies?"

"This area is clear, John moved the ones who fell earlier," Katie touched her chin in thought. "It will be a problem over the next few days though. The rat bodies as well. If we aren't careful, disease will take out most of us who made it."

Bob felt the need to change the topic of conversation. There was little they could do about the bodies of the fallen tonight.

"We can look into all that after a good night's rest and a good meal," he said firmly. "I'm going to bring Doris over now, she's a bit battered. Barely functional if I'm honest. The sword is a write off and I was really proud of that thing, copyright violations or not. She isn't going to be much use till I can patch her up and I need parts for that. She might be good to have looming outside though and her sensors are still functional? I'm worried some people might be getting ideas about looting and- with no police presence… they could get up to anything. Pretty much everyone has super powers now."

"You're planning to loot half the town Bob, you can't complain if others do the same! Still, some kind of watch through the night then? Take it in turns?" asked Raoul.

"I think so, but first: Bob mentioned a good meal. That sounds like an excellent idea to me. Let's go join up with the rest and get some food. Then you can go a-viking in the industrial estate," Katie smiled gently, "but you will get the last watch so the later you're out the less sleep you will get boys!" she finished, faux sternly. Bob and John chuckled, they'd be back by eleven at the latest all going well and both were naturally early risers. Looking at something and porting it to Doris' storage would make their thievery *very* efficient. They shared grins and nodded at each other like schoolboys planning a prank.

The team moved outside and Katie bustled off, in short order she was bringing out the other survivors to join them in the street. It was a warm autumn night with a clear sky and it was quickly decided that tables and chairs would be brought in and they would eat outside while the sun set.

"John, please meet Elizabeth" *not Liz, never Liz* she mouthed silently as she brought over an elderly lady with a very fierce gaze. "Elizabeth has some suggestions for the food this evening. I'll leave her with you," Katie smirked, safely behind Elizabeth, and beat a hasty retreat leaving John locked down by a Medusa-like glare.

"Stop slouching to the left, stand up straight boy! Well, you are a lot tidier than before but you still look disgraceful. Couldn't you have put a tie on at least? Look at the state of your hair, what there is of it! Too much to hope for one of your generation to be presentable." *What is it with people speaking to me like I'm a child today?* He schooled his face. "Don't look at me like that young man, you're ugly as sin but I've seen worse and you don't scare me! Now, we need bread, bacon, cheese and salad. And I do mean a lot of each of them! There's a lot of hungry people here and you need to make sure everyone is fat and full before you swan off on whatever juvenile madness you've got planned for later. And is that liquor I smell on your breath? Drinking at this time of day, for shame! Not another drop until I am satisfied with the arrangements, you hear?"

John was stunned. The woman was more a force of nature than a human being. He used Identify.

Level 1
Name: Elizabeth Trevelayn
Ability: Micro Management

He decided it was probably in his best interests not to fight the rising tide and knuckled down, ensuring Elizabeth had everything she demanded. When the first sandwiches and salads were brought out and set on the tables he had ported in, Elizabeth loaded him a plate and brought it over to him.

"You might look like a short, fat, one armed ogre," *hurtful,* "but you've done as you were told so maybe there is hope for you yet." *I will get Katie back for dumping this woman on me.* he silently vowed.

"John, who is this divine creature whose attention you are monopolising?" called Bob, swaggering over with a plate of sandwiches and salad clutched in one hand, a mostly empty beer can in the other. John eyed the beer with envy, spending so much time with Elizabeth had given him a thirst.

"Dear lady, it is a pleasure to make your acquaintance. I am the pilot of the mighty robot that fought so valiantly to protect you. Sergeant Robert Gillybrook, formerly of the King's Royal Hussars, please call me Bob." He saluted smartly and then gestured grandly at where he had parked Doris down the road, the mecha leaning to her left side due to the damage and looking distinctly worse for wear.

John was horrified as Elizabeth raised a hand and rearranged her coiffeur, smiling at Bob and saying, "Well, it's always a pleasure to meet such a polite man who has bravely served his country. Thank you for your *most* valiant efforts earlier." She giggled. Coquettishly. John was terrified as to what was about to happen to his friend. Based on the last hour of his life spent in Elizabeth's company Bob would be lucky to survive the verbal dismemberment that was coming. "Thank you so much for all your efforts today and keeping this ruffian in line, I'm sure without you we would have come off a lot worse. If you would like to stop by for a late supper this evening, just you and I, I would be delighted to entertain you." *Wait, ruffian? What just happened? She's like ninety and Bobs getting on but he could still be her son! What the hell is going on?*

He turned an incredulous stare on Bob who winked at him. "Perhaps another evening my dear? I'm afraid I must repair my machine and to do so I require materials. I was hoping to borrow this boy and set off shortly. He isn't much use in a scrap but his skills as a thief will enable me to get the machine back into fighting form in short order," he declared grandly.

At the mention of the word thief Elizabeth turned an icy glare on John. He was getting used to her looks so took it in stride while cursing the mechanaut in his head. She turned back to Bob with a broad smile and said "Of course, please do come by for tea whenever you get the chance."

Bob made polite noises and hustled John off towards Doris. John was shell shocked, after being on the receiving end of Elizabeth's "personality" for most of an hour somehow Bob had avoided every trap and actually *charmed* the devil in human form! He asked him what the hell had just happened and swore vengeance for being described as a thief to the harpy.

"Don't worry boy, you've just got to know how to talk to an old lady like that."

"I'm perfectly charming and I'm not a boy."

Bob gave him a side eye.

"Well, I am definitely not a boy, dude."

"We know, *dude,* we know. 'I'm forty two!'" Bob mimicked. "I think I can see why you became a hermit. C'mon lad, eat up," he grinned. "We've got a lot of shit to steal this evening, Mr I'm-Not-A-Thief." The old man rubbed his hands together gleefully.

Chapter 23 - Seeing if it improves their attitude

Bob led them over to the rest of the team who were eating a little apart from the others, only joined by Victoria, Jennifer and James. They were discussing the fight with the Queen and John was surprised to find they were approaching it as an after action report, going through what worked and what didn't and how they could synergise their abilities more effectively in future. Evie waved as Bob and John stopped next to the group.

"Feels better with a full belly right? Me and the boy," he threw a smirk at John who chose to ignore the jab, "are off to grab some goodies. Don't wait up!" Bob said with a grin.

"Before you run off looting," replied Katie, "Your watch starts at five AM, so you need to be back in time to get some sleep before that. Do you hear me?" she asked with mock severity.

Bob and John both nodded obediently and John walked over to Evie.

"Are you going to be alright kiddo? I won't be back late, promise."

"Yeah, Zeeg and I are going to sleep on the settee in the house we unwound in earlier. Can you get me Uno out of the stash? I'm gonna whip some old folks at a card game. Think I can get them to place bets?"

"Keep an eye on each other ok? I won't be long. And no gambling!" John told her as he summoned the game for his daughter.

Zeeg and Evie both nodded solemnly and John smiled. Ruffling Evie's hair as he turned to go, getting an annoyed 'DAD!' in response as she straightened her hair. He smiled and waved over his shoulder as he walked towards Bob.

"You good to go lad?"

John nodded and the pair set off, moving back past the trenches John had dug earlier. They walked in silence until they passed the site of the fight with the scavengers and then Bob began pointing out cars he wanted. John was able to teleport the cars directly into Doris' storage so as they walked they "requisitioned" rather a lot of cars.

"Get us a beer will you? Have one yourself, why not?"

John smiled and summoned a pack of beers at his feet. He passed one to Bob who opened it and passed it back to him before bending down to grab one for himself and picking up the rest of the pack. Most of the homes they were passing had been broken into by the rats. They didn't try to explore inside. The beer helped them ignore it, a little.

"You did good today, lad. And your girl's a good kid. You should be proud," Bob said as they moved onto the street leading past the primary school, heading towards the supermarket. He took a long swig from his can.

"Thanks Bob, but we would have struggled without Doris," said John raising his own can to Bob in salute. As they moved John was blipping any rat corpses they saw to the pile he had built in the school playing fields. As well as any cars Bob pointed out to Doris' storage space. More beers arrived regularly as they slowly continued down the street, committing grand theft auto on a scale that was previously inconceivable. They began chatting about their lives, past mistakes and their greatest achievements to distract themselves from the shattered doors and empty homes.

"And then," sputtered Bob, "the turd turned round and said "but what if you switch the connections"!" He rocked back and forth, smacking John on his still tender right shoulder, making him wince. John was utterly confused by Bob's punchline which seemed to bear no relation to the rest of the story at all but laughed along, nursing his stump across his chest as a warm buzz of alcohol filled his mind.

They had walked past the school and turned into the car park of the supermarket. Bob was grumbling about the delay in getting to the "good stuff", ie the very much not edible machine tools in the industrial estate. The beers were adding up and on top of the whiskey from earlier they were comfortably "in the zone". Bob had just begun telling a ribald story about what happened with three Thai prostitutes, two of his mates and an orange juicing machine when he was on a detachment with his unit in 2006 when a blast of force threw John off his feet. John assumed this wasn't from his shock at learning something he hadn't believed it was possible to do with freshly squeezed orange juice.

"You cunts should fuck off right now," came a low voice. Six young men in their late teens or early twenties stepped out from behind a parked van and spread out threateningly, partially surrounding John and Bob.

"Bob, the fuck just happened?" asked John drunkenly looking around from where he sprawled out on his back. "Did a foul mouthed gang of Teletubbies just try to pick a fight with us?"

"Looks like it, lad. Level's are shit as well! All three's bar one five. Cowards must have hidden away most of the day. Ha, tele-tubbies, nice! I geddit! Cos you can teleport them! Also, I want their van please."

"Fuck you old ma-" the youth vanished.

"Where did you shend him?" slurred Bob reaching out to offer John a hand.

"Somewhere shoft." John giggled drunkenly as Bob helped pull him to a swaying version of upright, the missing weight on his right side exacerbating his blood alcohol level's interference with his balance. John began to babble. "Oh! I had this awesome thought earlier! I didn't share it though. Would have been rude... You know that prick

Phil right? When he was being a prick when we met him, more of a prick than usual, whatever... I had this thought! It was great! I thought about dropping him into the corpse pile! Something about making a twat splat and seeing if it improves their attitude. Or altitude? It was better than that in my head. I messed up the wording... You get the idea!" he babbled happily.

The van vanished into Doris' pocket dimension.

"Bring Dave back, now!" ordered a tall young man, moving forward as crystalline blue swords grew out of his fists. "And my bloody van! This place is ours so fuck off right now!" he glowered in a manner he probably thought was threatening.

Bob roared with laughter. "Splat this twat too, lad!"

The guy vanished.

Bob waved a finger at the remaining teenagers as John swayed gently on his feet. "Now you boys need to go home and don't start fights without identifying your oppents, oppnenenents, enemies in future! Shome og dem might not be sho nishe ash ush!" he slurred.

The boys bolted past the drunken fools who then staggered towards the supermarket, leaning on each other and laughing happily.

Teamchat:
Katie Johnson: Why did two boys covered in blood just run screaming and crying past the end of the street?
Robert Gillybrook: Oh shit... forgot how close the pile was to you lot. Uh. Nothing to do with us? Don't worry about it anyway. It'll be fine I'm sure.
John Borrows: Yeah, sure it will be fine. No worries, you know?
Katie Johnson: You two... be careful. Please.
Evie Borrows: Dad, behave or I will send Zeeg to keep an eye on you.

Greg Smith: That won't be necessary. Some of the Majority are keeping an eye on them already. They are not impressed by their behaviour so far this evening, the words 'giggling imbeciles' are being bandied about. However they will alert me in advance should our friends be at any real risk. They were very amused by your response to the gang that attacked you though.
Evie Borrows: You got attacked by a gang? What the hell Dad! Do we have street gangs now? ... Can I come fight as well?
John Borrows: Just some of the ferals I think. They all ran off. Well, most of them did. The other two ran past the end of the street covered in rat blood. It was great. But we had nothing to do with that at all. Don't worry sweetie, we'll be careful.
Bob and John looked at each other, sobering up rapidly at the thought of the dead watching them act like idiots.
"You didn't drop them from high up did you? Not far enough to hurt them?" Bob asked quietly.
"Nah, six foot drop onto the pile. Enough for a bit of a splash but not enough to hurt them. Probably. They'll be fine. But... pretty freaked out I expect," He smirked at Bob who chuckled in reply.
They began going up and down the aisles of the supermarket. Long shelf life food was ported straight into Doris, tins of vegetables and meat, rice and pasta vanishing by the shelfful. John filled his fridge and chest freezer with chilled meats and then dropped a pile on the table used for tea earlier. They sent a quick message back letting the rest know to find fridge or freezer space for it. They didn't clear the place out but they took plenty of food, most of the booze, chocolate and dog treats. The latter two at the request of Evie, Katie and Zeeg. God only knew when they would get a restock from out of town so establishing a bit of a monopoly on the supply of luxury goods and food seemed like a good idea.

John cleared out *all* the tobacco and cigarettes and dumped them in Doris as well. They "broke" into the warehouse area at the back, although it's hardly breaking in when you can teleport through the little window on the door. They began moving whole pallets of stock into Doris. This was most of the food in town and while it was a bit shady to take most of it themselves, John knew they would be willing to share it out fairly. Others might not be so altruistic.

John ported a cigarette to his lips and his lighter to his hand as they stepped out of the supermarket and lit up. They began to make their way towards the industrial estate, being a bit more serious and trying to keep an eye out for trouble.

"Those things will kill you, you know?" said Bob, pointing at the cigarette.

John waggled his stump and exhaled a cloud of smoke. "Been there, done that already mate. I rubbed some dirt on it and walked it off. Let's go and clear out your old work. And I guess the showrooms? Plenty of cars there. How the hell are you going to get fuel after we clear the place out? Ah, I can port the concrete off of the top of the underground tanks at the petrol station right? Tons of the stuff in there."

Bob tapped the side of his nose and they set off. He politely chose not to mention that until the power went out he would just use the pump like a normal person.

They began clearing out the hardware store by teleporting the door into the street. John walked through and blipped pretty much everything into Doris. Sheet metal, planks and boards of various types of wood, tens of thousands of nails, bolts and strange pieces of metal intended to act as brackets joining things together or something. John wasn't an expert on this stuff. A small forest's worth of sandpaper. The power tools and heavy duty machinery in the back were the last to join the growing hoard in Doris' storage space. He left an IOU by the till. It was an independent shop, not a corporate chain, so he felt like he owed them.

John walked back onto the street, they exchanged a nod before heading into the area of town the Queen had rampaged through earlier.

They passed the old church, mercifully unscathed, and moved down Station Road. John bowed his head slightly at the graveyard as they passed on the other side of the road. Knowing that the dead were there and watching all the time… John was struggling to wrap his head around it. He used to joke that with online surveillance, back doors in operating systems and phone signal data gathering there wasn't really any privacy any more and there hadn't been for years but at least you knew MI5 or the CIA couldn't watch you take a dump. Well, they probably couldn't.

The two of them emerged from the underpass and saw that the high school was relatively undamaged with one glaring exception.

Teamchat:

John Borrows: Evie, you know when I dropped all those cars on the Queen there was one left that I didn't have the reserves to land on her?

Evie Borrows: I didn't know that because you didn't tell any of us. Might have been nice to know there was a terminal velocity car potentially whizzing down at our heads, Dad.

John Borrows: Right, sorry about that. On the plus side we've found where it landed… It demolished the reception of your school.

Evie Borrows: Awesome, thanks Dad! :) Please tell me the rest of the place is trashed as well?

John Borrows: Sorry Sausage, it looks like that was the only hit it took. Even the Queen didn't want to go near it.
Evie Borrows: Not surprised, the Queen wasn't that stupid. Maybe you could wreck up the place just a bit? I'm sure that would be OK. No one would know?
Katie Johnson: Do not "wreck up the place a bit" gentlemen.
Evie Borrows: Boo.

As John and Bob moved down the road they came to the industrial estate proper. The Queen had had no qualms at all about wrecking that place up. It looked like footage of a city shortly after western governments decided to "bring democracy" to it. Shock and Awe had clearly been in play for the Queen.

Every other building was rubble. There were no signs of people or rats. Either the smaller rats had stayed well away from the Queen or someone had cleaned up any of the corpses of the little ones already. There were patches of blackening blood here and there proving something had fought and probably died. The whole area felt eerie and surreal, like a chunk of Sarajevo from the early nineties had been teleported into a sleepy Yorkshire town that hadn't seen warfare in over three hundred years.

They stole a couple of dozen more cars on the way as Bob led them to his former employers, which fortunately was largely untouched. John went through blipping out agricultural equipment like rotovators and wood chippers as well as dozens of chainsaws, hedge trimmers, pneumatic drills, hydraulic jacks and diesel generators. Enough hand tools to equip a Soviet penal colony were also added to the stash. You name it this place had it. Now of course, Bob had it. The old man was giddy as he read through the upgrades and gadgets he could make with their haul.

"I don't think there's much point looking elsewhere lad. This was the mother lode. It'll take me days worth of reserves to make even half of what I want. Let's head back now eh? It's getting late and we need to be up early."

John glanced further up the road to the factory owned by the company he had worked for. It was a 24/7 site, churning out food every hour of every day so there would have been people working the production lines. From what he could see at least half of the buildings had been demolished. He had worked from home, only going in for occasional meetings since Covid but he knew a lot of people at the company. So far he hadn't seen the body of anyone he knew personally, or even tangentially. He supposed he had been lucky, what he didn't see he didn't have to feel quite so strongly.

He didn't think he could face investigating a place where people he had shaken hands and chatted about their kids with might be crushed in piles of rubble or left scattered in bits by the Queen's savage jaws.

"Yeah, let's head back. No point in taking the long way home."

Blip. Blip.

Chapter 24 - If I ever hear you use the terms 'meatbag' or 'flesh puppets'

They arrived back to find everyone had moved inside the houses. Greg and Raoul stood at either end of the road, already on watch. The sun had set while Bob and John had been out "requisitioning" supplies. Bob clapped John on his left shoulder and immediately bustled over to Doris, a skip in his step. When he arrived he called out to John, "any chance you can port over a comfy chair for me? My old bones and all that?" John obliged and Bob sat down beside Doris who began glowing and shifting as he started his repairs and upgrades. John walked over to Raoul and said hi.
"Seen anyone else out and about this evening?"
"Other than the two kids you dropped in a pile of rat corpses you mean?" Raoul grinned, "Evie loved that by the way, apparently one of them is a bully in year eleven at her school. The kid is a bit of a shit according to her. Otherwise it's been quiet around here. Zeeg went out for a look around earlier. There are some groups of "youths" and adults, who frankly should know better, running about in the west part of town. Some of them were fighting each other a bit but it was mostly posturing and arguing over territory. 'This is our part of the street, you owe me for that thing from years ago', that kind of crap. As if stuff like that matters anymore? A few injuries but no deaths from what Zeeg saw. There might be some problems at the get together tomorrow though. One kid lost an eye for sure. The south has been quiet and the east was- well the scavengers went through that part of town. Not many left over there."
"When the travellers to the west get a bee in their bonnet I'd expect shit to go sideways. And whatever their other flaws they get really protective of their kids, which I respect. Don't seem to give a shit

about actually raising them properly as far as I can tell, that's why Evie and I call their kids ferals. Constantly causing problems at school and in town. But we're going to have to work with them I guess. We'll all have to work together. I hope... never mind. It's a thing job we've got Katie with her maxed out diplomacy skills on hand I guess. Do you or Greg need anything before I crash out? I'll bring you some drinks or something?"

"I'm good thanks, only on till eleven so not long left and more caffeine sounds like a bad idea. You go get some rest, someone will wake you at five," he glanced at Bob who was now dancing around Doris like a shaman around a fire as he worked his mojo to improve his toy. "I don't think Bob is going to get an early night so it might just be you on watch."

"No worries. Any problems with the rest of the group?"

Raoul laughed. "Nothing major. Reg came to and is doing well, he's resting now and he'll join the team in the morning. Jen and Vic are trying to find a way to decide who gets the last spot on our team. It became a little heated at one point but Katie did her Katie thing and settled them down. I'm going to take a walk around the streets. You should go get some kip mate, it's been a rough day for everyone."

John said good night and got a "ta-ra" in reply as Raoul walked off before he headed to the house they had used earlier. Zeeg looked up as he entered the living room from where she and Evie were curled up on the settee under a blanket. She wagged her tail once, gently so as not to wake Evie, and laid her head back down across the little redhead's legs.

The bedrooms were occupied, Katie and Sam sharing a double bed for the night in one room and Reg was in the other. John went back into the lounge and blipped the coffee table over to his house. Then his mattress and covers were ported over onto the floor. He changed, opting to blip off his clothes rather than mess around with buttons one-handed again before struggling into his pyjama bottoms and curling up. He was out as soon as his head hit the pillow but his sleep was wracked by dreams of his family, scattered across the UK, and the struggles they might have been going through today.

He awoke to gentle fingers caressing his scarred cheek.

"Good morning, handsome," a sultry voice whispered in his ear. His right hand shot up to catch the hand on his face resulting in his stump sticking upright from the duvet and little else.

"You really are an early riser," the speaker was clearly smiling as she said it. Green eyes, looked down into his from a distance that felt far too intimate for John to deal with right now.

He blipped over by the door. "What are you playing at Victoria?" he hissed.

"Oh please, I just wanted to wake you up gently, didn't realise you'd freak out. I've got your bed for the rest of the night. Your shift is starting now," She stood up and began undressing without a care in the world. *Divide my own age by half and add seven… it's still a nope. Pretty sure that "rule" is not as socially acceptable as the internet claims anyway. It would mean it was fine for a one hundred year old to date a fifty seven year old if it was true and that doesn't sound right.*

He spun around as she peeled off her leggings, a blush covering his cheeks.

"You know when you blush your scars stand out?" she whispered with a chuckle, watching the jagged lines across the back of his right shoulder show white against his darkening skin.

"I've never seen someone who can blush on their shoulders before. Impressive. Go on and let me sleep. Greg is outside waiting for you. Bob didn't stop working until a couple of hours ago so he's getting a pass on the watch. Greg doesn't need so much sleep anymore, he said he'd cover for Bob."

When John turned round she had slipped beneath the duvet, his duvet, but left most of a pale and slender leg sticking out from the covers. He decided a strategic withdrawal was the best option and blipped out into the street.

"Are you going to get dressed, John?" asked Greg standing by the table they used for the meal last night, looking at him with his ghastly black and yellow eyes.

John cursed and blipped over the clothes he took off last night. He struggled into the jeans and then carefully slipped his stump into the right sleeve of his shirt before threading his left arm in and using gravity to get it to a point he could catch the bottom and pull it down.

"Bob didn't go to sleep like a good boy then?"

Greg gestured at a row of body armour, much sleeker and more refined than the set he had given Katie yesterday. Enough for everyone who had been levelling. A row of more advanced looking crossbows also lay neatly to the side. John looked over and saw Bob stretched out on the chair he had asked for, covered by a blanket and snoring like a busy sawmill.

Doris looked amazing, frankly. She was once again knelt down on one knee like a knight of old but she had grown. Her armour gleamed and was completely rebuilt. How much she had grown was hard to say with her crouched down but Bob had definitely been busy after John called it a night.

"He passed out a couple of hours ago. We will have to wait to see what he has done to his machine. Are you refreshed John? A drink perhaps?" Greg offered John a cup of coffee that he took and sipped from before putting it down on the table and summoning a smoke from his supply stashed in Doris. He lit up and breathed out before reaching for the cup to take another sip.

"I'll live, Greg, thank you for the coffee. What about you? Don't you need to sleep now?"

"The Body of Undeath has granted me many boons, among which one is that I no longer require anywhere close to the amount of sleep a normal human needs."

"Are you not human then? Anymore? Some kind of zombie?" John asked, taking in the cadaverous form and pallid skin of the man.

"I am not sure of the truth of it. My mind, I believe, remains human. Albeit warped somewhat by my association with the Majority. But I was always a little strange in the head. As to my body… I cannot say. Do I seem inhuman to you?"

"If I'm honest, I'd have to say yes. At least a little. You look like a walking skeleton. I'm half expecting you to yell 'until next time!' and run off into the distance at any moment."

Greg laughed like gravel rolling in a steel drum. "I was always slender but this transformation has exacerbated it to new heights. Some of my friends in the Majority are watching the surrounding area and will alert me if anything of note occurs. Perhaps we could take the time to get acquainted before the rigours of the day?"

John summoned chairs for them both and they sat. They drank coffee and John smoked as he listened to Greg discuss the Majority. The idea of the dead constantly watching them caused Greg to laugh when John brought it up, which once again highlighted his similarity to a certain skeletal cartoon villain from the eighties.

"In truth they are mostly indifferent to the living, John. They do not care to watch the day to day of our lives. I think for most of them it is too bittersweet. To watch young fools waste time and fail to appreciate the joys of being alive, being able to affect the world. It… perturbs a lot of them. They appreciated your little courtesy at the church last night though."

"They told you about that? I kind of felt like an idiot. I've walked past there dozens, hundreds of times and never paid it any mind," he sipped his coffee and the heat of it drove back the early morning chill. "The Majority have something of an affection for you. They were not pleased by the news you brought back from true death, to put it mildly. It has caused factions to emerge and bitter-bad arguments between them. However they know better than to shoot the messenger. Regarding the cemetery, were you a religious man before this began?"

"Not really. I wasn't practising or going to church or anything but I guess the idea of a god or the gods always seemed… I don't know, probable, I suppose? Pretty much everyone throughout history had some kind of religious belief, everyone who lived before the modern age can't have been stupid, whatever most people think nowadays of anyone born before the 50's."

"But you had no reason to believe that the dead truly *were* there, some of them at least, trapped without form yet capable of perceiving the living world around them. There is no reason to feel ashamed for not paying them more respect before, my friend. Most of them have had centuries to come to terms with the ways of the living."

"Just as a point of order: if I ever hear you use the terms 'meatbag' or 'flesh puppets' we will have a disagreement, dear sir!" John grinned as Greg laughed.

"Fear not. Speaking with the dead gives one a rare appreciation for the living. However self absorbed and bitter some of Them may be, deep down They all wish Their descendants well. They are greatly troubled by this system and the extermination of Their descendants. They wish to help as best They can. The toll taken on us here in Normanby is mirrored across the land, sadly often far worse. Many towns and villages, even cities, are devoid of the living this morning and the Majority is reeling from the losses."

John took a moment to process what Greg had said and decided it was too much for this time in the day. He made a mental note that Greg was getting information from beyond the barrier and opted to put it aside for now. He lit another cigarette and changed the topic, moving onto lighter things as the sky was tinted by dawn and the sun crawled its way into the sky.

A new day and yet another mystery from the system to be faced in this meeting they'd been summoned to. He stared upward and while they talked of inconsequential and unimportant things, John felt it deep in his bones and his blood as he watched the sky turn blue: this system was evil and he hated it.

Chapter 25 – Carnival

By half past eight the rest of the team and the survivors had emerged onto the street and John went in to make a lot of toast and a lot of coffee. As he began ferrying out plates of buttery toast the worst thing imaginable happened. Elizabeth caught him.

"Well young man, I don't approve of you keeping a fine gentleman like Robert out all night with *your filthy stealing* but I must say your attitude seems to have improved somewhat this morning. It was thoughtful of you to start on breakfast for us all." She glowered at him.

"I am sorry about that, Elizabeth. Please accept my apologies. I hope everyone likes toast? I think my team needs me for something. Please could you take over for me here? It would be best if the job was left with someone properly capable of doing it justice," he quickly passed the plate of toast to her before she could object and teleported away.

Teleporting is the best ability!

He appeared next to Katie, Evie, Zeeg and Victoria. Victoria flashed him a smile as she petted Zeeg. The dog moved over to John, demanding further attention. He no longer had to stoop down to pet her due to her rapid growth and he began administering the ear rubs she wanted.

"Morning Dad, sleep ok?" asked Evie tiredly, shovelling toast into her face.

"I did thank you, Short Stuff. How was the settee?"

"Good, the dog kept me warm. Oh wow, Doris got an upgrade!" She crammed the last of her toast into her mouth and ran off, spraying crumbs. She began moving around Doris slowly while casting a very critical eye over the changes. She was probably cataloguing everything versus various mecha animes so she could explain his mistakes at length to Bob when he woke up.

"I'm going to get some toast and coffee, I'll catch up with you later," said Victoria.

"Did she just wink at you, John? Nevermind, I don't want to know. Once Reg is up we'll invite him to the team," Katie began. "After the 'discussion' last night the girls agreed Vic would join us. Evie won the argument in the end if I'm honest. She pointed out that with Doris, Raoul and potentially you, we didn't need a dodge tank and that Jen was best off taking a central role with another team. Whereas we could use another damage dealer. 'We've got loads of weird powers but no heavy hitters other than your friendly neighbourhood storm witch' was how she summed it up. Smart kid."

"Gamers for the win. I guess," replied John thoughtfully. "How is Reg?"

"Crotchety describes him best? Or most politely. You'll see what I mean when you meet him. He'll be joining us in a minute I expect, he was getting up as we came out. Everything ok with Elizabeth?" She grinned at him.

"Fine. Thank you so much for dropping that harp- Elizabeth! Everything ok I hope?" *Please let it be ok!*

"It is fine thank you, young man. You clearly don't know how to make coffee properly but you've achieved a middling competence as far as toasting bread goes, which frankly surprises me. How that daughter of yours has survived living with you I have no idea. I have poured your *idea* of coffee down the sink and will be bringing fresh out in a few minutes."

"Thank you so much, Elizabeth!" Katie said, smiling at the woman. *Traitor* John mouthed at her while Elizabeth was looking away from him.

The geriatric force of nature, seemingly placated by Katie, bustled off to refresh the plates and remove the rest of John's subpar coffee. Katie turned to John and said "thanks for taking her off my hands last night." Victoria returned with a loaded plate that she offered around. "Are you using some kind of mind control on her? You're as bad as Bob as far as she goes. Anyway, I didn't so much 'take her off your hands' as you dumped her on me. And you really do owe me for that!" John took a piece of toast from Vic's plate as she offered it around, nodded in gratitude and began chewing.

Katie laughed, assured John that she didn't have mind control powers and she did indeed owe him one for taking the brunt of it from the overbearing old lady last night. Reg came out of the house, propping himself up on his stick and making a bee line for Katie. He was a man made of wrinkles. His wrinkles were wrinkled. John had no idea how old Reg was but he had to assume he had spent a lot of time outdoors for a lot of decades. Reg walked with the aid of a mahogany walking stick as he limped over to join them.

"Morning lassie, want to throw me an invite? I'm still willing to join yer wee club, fer now." He scowled darkly at the other people loading plates of toast over by the tables.

Katie Johnson has invited Reginald Rimmer to join Unnamed Team.
Level 4
Name: Reginald Rimmer
Ability: Gravitic Symbiote
Constitution: 100%
Reserves: 300
Guidelines:
Inertia shift: decrease your own inertia by 200%, increasing your targets by the same amount or vice versa.

Gravitic Anomaly: Boost specific gravity at a point of your chosen by 200%
Line of sight required.
Ability: Gravitic Symbiote. You are repelled by everything in the same way as gravity is attracted to everything. So now you have gravity powers.
Level 2: increases gravitic limit X2
Level 3: Increases Reserves X3
Level 4: Devourer of All
Devourer of All:
Create a small portal to the nearest black hole for 2 seconds. It will consume all within its range. Requires 80% of reserves, leaving you with one.

"Whoa. That Devourer of All ability is very scary," said Katie after a moment.

"Aye. Stupid fecked up system giving me a power I dannae dare use. I'd have done her in the middle of the Queen and finished the bish off right quick but two seconds of a black hole is nae fecking joke, ye ken? Could have fecked everything from here to Constantinople fer all I could figure. Fecking stupid system," Reg continued in his highland drawl. He looked between them and asked, with what was apparently his maximum level of charm, "So what's the plan for this morning, ye sassenach bastards?"

"Well firstly, I'd appreciate it if I could get my invite please?" said Victoria. "Seeing as we are giving them out to angry homeless old men, I'd like to get mine before you run out of stock." she finished with a grin.

"Homeless? Ye hoor of Babylon! Show some respect to yer elders ya wee strumpet! I've got warts older un you's an they're prettier too!" His walking stick was shaken firmly but briefly in Vic's face before being returned to its supporting role. Victoria was unimpressed and only smiled politely in response.

"Easy now Reg, I'm sure Vic didn't mean anything by it." Katie shot Vic an apologetic look. "We all had a rough day yesterday and must make some allowances for each other, yes? Why not go get some food Reg? We'll all be heading to the meeting the system called for this morning. A good breakfast should set us up nicely for whatever we have to deal with later."

"Aye o' course and thanks for the invite, ye bloody sassenach tossers…" his continuing insults and curses trailed away as he limped towards the toast, scowling as he went. As he drew near he began poking and prodding people with his stick to 'encourage' them to make space for him to get some food. At first he met with little success but he must have begun using his ability as people began drifting to either side of him, becoming almost attached to the people on their far side and causing confusion and a lot of apologies as they bumped into each other.

"What a lovely man, trade you him for Elizabeth?" said Katie, John shook his head as John and Vic chuckled. "Right it's your turn 'ye hoor o' Babylon'." Katie sent the invite.

Level 5
Victoria Smith
Ability: Pyrogenesis
Constitution: 100%
Reserves:300
Guidelines:
Maximum Temperature: 1000 deg. Celsius
Line of sight required.

Ability: Someone played with matches a lot when they were young? Create and shape fire. You can extinguish it as easily as you conjure it.
Level 2: Reserves X3
Level 3: Maximum temperature x2
Level 4: Fire walk with me
Level 5: Maximum Temperature X2
Fire walk with me:
You are immune to fire. When standing within a fire you can teleport to another fire within line of sight.
You have unlocked the full team buffs:
Calculating team buffs:
Evie Borrows: 1% improved reserve recovery rate
Katie Johnson: 5% improved reflexes.
Robert Gillybrook: 1% damage reduction
Zeeg Borrows: Seeing Eye Dog
John Borrows: Hide and Seek Champion 2024
Greg Smith: 5% increased endurance
Raoul Forrester: 1% improved constitution recover rate
Samantha Jones: 1% improved reserve recovery rate
Reginald Rimmer: 1% improved reserve recovery rate
Victoria Smith (no relation): 50% reduction from fire damage
You have unlocked the option to change your names in the team.
You have unlocked the option to change the team name.

There was an extremely high pitched SQUEEE from Evie followed moments late by a message.

Teamchat:
Baby Zeus: I changed all our names in the chat, you're going to love them.
Houdini: Kid, what have you done?

Houdini: Oh. Could be worse I guess. Knowing you I was expecting something ruder.
Pyro: I can live with mine :D
Pause Button: Evie, we need to have words. I can't change mine again for a week!
Baby Zeus: I almost went with an A team thing and made your name Face, so you dodged a bullet there Katie. Atlas would have been BA. Reg would be Murdoch and Bob would be Hannibal. See how nice I am?
Atlas: So why am I named after a book of maps instead of a bachelor of arts again?
Baby Zeus: Atlas is the titan that holds up the sky, dumbass. Read some mythology bro.
Atlas: Oh, really? Ok that's not so bad actually.
Corpsicle: I do not like mine and will be changing it as soon as possible. Perhaps in the future, young one, you might let us make our own choices in this regard?
Porridge Eater: What the fecking feck is going on???
Baby Zeus: Language Mr. Porridge Eater!
Porridge Eater: I'm against child abuse as a rule, but I'll make a fecking exception for you!
Houdini: If everyone could calm down please? It's only temporary.
Porridge Eater: Feck off Baldy.
Mysterio: I like mine. I think I'll keep it. Thanks Evie. Where's it from?
Baby Zeus: See? At least Sam has some taste. It's a villain from Spiderman. He uses tricks and illusions.
Mysterio: You see, now I'm not sure I'm happy with it?

Baby Zeus: It won't let me change the team name though. Stupid system.
Pause Button: Thank God.
Corpsicle: Probably for the best I feel.
Atlas: I dunno, what were you thinking for a team name?
Baby Zeus: Super Awesome Mega Team of course! Cool right?
Atlas: Yeah. Probably for the best it's not up to you.
Baby Zeus: Sod off you ungrateful gits :) Dad has to make the team name change because he started the team. We should vote. I vote for the Super Awesome Mega Team!
Shinji: What the hell happened to the team list? Why am I called Shinji now?
Baby Zeus: We talked about this yesterday Bob.
Shinji: Is this one of your animoo things? Change it back now!
Baby Zeus: Stop whining and get in the mecha Shinji! Haha , It was worth it just for that :D
Shinji: If we are maybe anywhere near done with this freakshow I suggest we begin to get organised for this morning's meeting?
Baby Zeus: Freakshow! That's a great name for the team! We're like a circus sideshow if you think about it. Dad just needs a top hat and he's a stage magician, Atlas is the strong man, Pyro is a fire swallower. Mysterio is an illusionist. Katie can be the bearded lady.
Pause Button: Enough Evie, please.
Houdini: She has a bit of a point though.
Pause Button: John!
Houdini: Not about the beard! Sorry. I meant... maybe not a freak show... more like a big top circus?
Porridge Eater: Fecking idiots.

Atlas: I kind of like the idea of being the strong man in the circus.
Corpsicle: Such wandering troupes used to go by many names. One of them was a Carnival.
Houdini has set the team name to Carnival.

Chapter 26 - Best behaviour everyone!

Doris came to her feet with booming footsteps. She drew herself up to her full height and everyone bar Bob took a step back in order to crane their necks to see her properly.
"You still want to spar with her, Muscles?" he asked Raoul.
"Um, maybe tomorrow? Feels like I might have pulled a muscle in my shoulder yesterday, you know?"
Bob snorted, "Yeah, sure," he said sarcastically.
Doris was now just over nine metres tall and weighed in at nearly eleven tons. She was all gleaming steel and smooth lines. Bob put her through her paces briefly, having her dodge and lunge in the parking area. "New trick!" Said Bob happily as chainsaws spun out and circled her feet, at waist height on a man, as well as flexible metal tentacles tipped with oscillating blades that shot out from retracting portholes in her thighs. It looked utterly terrifying to John.
"Seemed like most baddies were going to be a lot shorter than her now, so I went a bit wild with the defences on her legs," Bob explained. "She's got an upgraded sword and her left hand now has a, well, think of a taser and then scale it up to something that can melt tanks. Also a flamethrower. Because why not?"
The team stood in silence for a moment before Evie walked over to Bob and surprised him with a fierce hug. "She's so... beautiful!" she said quietly, a tear in her eye.
Bob patted her on the head awkwardly, "Yeah, she's pretty neat now but I'm still annoyed about the Shinji thing, madam."
"I'll change it to the coolest name I can think of next week, I promise"
"No, I want to pic- You know what, can you just make it Bob please?" Evie shook her head.

"I don't think Doris will be fitting through the snicket anymore. We'll have to take the long way round." Katie sighed. "How's the new Doris in terms of staying power?"

"No problem on either front, I made another adjustment as well last night. Voila!"

Doris squatted down and her shin armour split open down the middle, opening out until the edges were pointing backwards. Rows of tires emerged and she lowered her weight onto her knees, her feet rising up on tires of their own as they slotted into gaps in her lower legs. She mostly filled a two lane road but she was certainly going to be more mobile. She looked ungainly though, kneeling with her arms raised to not drag along the ground but at least she was now capable of more rapid movement.

"You *were* listening to my lecture on mechas!" said Evie happily, reaching up to clap Bob on the back.

"No, this is completely different and based entirely on my own ideas, thank you very much." He faux glowered at the red head. "She should be good up to about forty miles an hour on an even surface, give or take, a lot less if we go off road but I doubt that will be possible, she'll dig herself straight into anything other than concrete unless it's bone dry. She will also guzzle fuel and I mean a lot of fuel. John, we need to raid the petrol station urgently, mate. I've had some thoughts about rigging up some liquid storage in the 'caboose'. I cannibalised a load of the petrol tanks from the cars we grabbed last night but she'll need topping up soon. So... no more smoking in the storage ok? No idea what an explosion in the storage space would do but let's add it to the "things we don't want to find out about" list. There's seats on her thighs for nine people, or eight people and a dog I guess. Thought she could maybe double up as transport for us going forward?"

"That's a great idea Bob!" enthused Sam.

"It was my bloody idea," mumbled Evie.

"As long as it doesn't rain of course," Sam continued sweetly. "What's the weather like in Yorkshire ninety percent of the time?" Evie became conspicuously silent.

"I could maybe rig up a tarp or something. John's got loads of random shit like that in the storage. And it was Evie's idea," Bob muttered.

"Well, the weather is fine today so the Carnival will be riding in style to the meeting" said Greg, sharing his rictus grin with the team. "Now we need to make arrangements for our allies to arrive comfortably as well."

They decided to "borrow" four big cars that John and Bob had stolen the night before for the rest of the group. Reg decided to ride in a car declaring with liberal use of the word "feck" that he was definitively not a fan of the idea of riding in the open air on Doris' legs.

The elderly and other survivors were issued with crossbows which they took reluctantly. The bows were more for the look of it, after all they had one shot and then they'd be useless. The upper body strength needed to reload them was beyond most of the group and frankly the kick was likely to leave serious bruises or even break bones on the oldest of them. Bob had perhaps not thought this part through properly and had just run with it because he wanted to mass produce something.

Bob started bringing over the new armour for the teams. They looked like something a movie costume designer would come up with if they were asked to design body armour with a mediaeval/cyberpunk-samurai vibe. John took it carefully with his left hand and looked at it for a moment.

"Ah sorry John, do you want a hand with that?" asked Bob. Everyone stopped shrugging into their own armour and turned to look at him.

"Oh, ah, I mean, can I help you with that?" Evie had started laughing to herself. She quietly resolved to give Bob a *really* good nickname when the time came. Captain Inconsiderate or something.

"I've got it," said Vic, stepping in and helping John pull it over his head. "Of course if you ever do want me to give you a hand…" she winked a bright green eye and John blushed furiously, the lightning scars on his cheek glowing white. "I'm kidding! I'm sorry, I know I threw you off balance this morning! I was tired and wasn't really- anyway I'm sorry. I do think you might need to unwind a bit though," she whispered, stepping back and checking the fit. She pulled the side straps tighter till John grunted and nodded in satisfaction before stepping away. "You'll do," she declared loudly and gave him a radiant smile.

"Thank you." John swung at the waist and raised his arms. The shoulder plates came down to almost the end of what remained of his right arm but rode easily as he moved. He rapped his knuckles on his chest and received a satisfying plinking noise. It seemed like good gear. A few months ago he'd have paid a pretty penny for something like this, just to have it in the house in case of an apocalypse of some sort. And here he was getting the gear for free. Well, free if you ignored the grand larceny required to get the materials for it. That would be fine though, he was sure. He *had* got the apocalypse thrown in for free! He decided this was what winning felt like.

A short while later most of the team had been blipped onto Doris' legs and the rest had loaded up in the cars, so they set off. Punctuality is the politeness of princes after all and they had a meeting to attend, so they might as well be early. The mecha led the way, bulldozing the barricades John had made yesterday back into the trenches to make a path for the cars.

They moved slowly through the streets, silenced by the damage the first wave had done the day before. The blood spatters and signs of struggle, the busted doors and broken windows left everyone in a dark mood. These had been family homes, people coming and going and living their regular lives until yesterday. John would have preferred never to have to speak to most of the people who lived here but he found himself saddened that he'd never have the chance. Or at least that people who could put up with them would no longer have the chance.

Now the buildings were as often as not lifeless double glazed tombs. They turned onto the road leading towards town, passing the supermarket on the way. Thirty odd men and a handful of women were spread across the carpark but they ran for cover as soon as they saw Doris. The convoy took the corner and moved past the petrol station into the marketplace. They pulled over, the cars parking in a neat row and John moved the team down onto the ground. Doris raised herself off her calves with her arms and stood to resume her normal posture, armour snapping shut down her legs without a visible seam.

Elizabeth bustled over, making John's heart beat with real terror. "How about you bring over some seating for us older people? Might not bother a boy like you but some of us have conditions and can't be standing around like lemons for an hour. I for one am not going to be spending the time with my weight on a bad hip! Chairs, now, please!" The elderly had clearly left their crossbows in the cars as not one was in sight.

John nodded and blipped in a circle of settees and chairs, then brought in the table from last night and some camping gear to make tea. Thankfully, Elizabeth was happy with this and moved over to supervise the production of hot drinks as most of the rest settled themselves down to wait. Little Fred began running laps around the settee his mum was sitting in.

Doris knelt and Bob descended from his perch in her cockpit before the ramp retracted and she stood back up, towering over the impromptu and slightly sombre street party.

"How was it? On the legs I mean?" Bob asked.

"Bit windy but otherwise ok," said Raoul just as Vic said "Bloody cold, we are not doing that in winter!"

"Maybe some kind of seat warmer is in order? Electric or diesel… hmmm, could divert the exhaust from the chainsaws to run under the seats…. I'll figure something out I'm sure," Bob plonked himself down on a chair next to Sam and accepted a cup of tea from Elizabeth with a smile.

As they sat and talked quietly other people began arriving. First was the group they had passed by at the supermarket who steered well clear of the team incongruously enjoying morning tea in the car park with a bunch of pensioners. Gradually others arrived and moved into the area, forming little knots of people scattered here and there, some shooting glances at the gaggle of geriatrics and weirdos dipping biscuits in tea while they all speculated on what would happen shortly. Most of the arrivals appeared to be standard humans but a few were either keeping some sort of transformation going out of caution or had been permanently changed by their abilities. A handful of hulking forms that Raoul kept flexing at to try and intimidate them, no doubt considering an arm wrestling competition. There were a few suspiciously hairy men with bestial faces and a woman who appeared to be made out of glass that stuck out among the humdrum of humanity.

"This might be trouble," said Raoul, nodding his head slightly towards a group of men who had just arrived with some teenage boys and joined the group lurking near the road out of the town centre. Some of the boys had been in the supermarket car park last night.

"Indeed, I'm afraid the boys have not been entirely honest with their parents about the sequence of events yesterday," said Greg.

The new arrivals were talking quietly but furiously with the ones who arrived from the car park earlier and pointing in Bob and John's direction frequently.

"Pretty sure those two are the boys you dipped in the rat pile last night and their dad's keep giving us really shitty looks. Oh and here they come. Best behaviour everyone!" Raoul finished with a smirk at Reg.

"Feck off"

John summoned a smoke and lit up. He was, as has been mentioned, not a people person and angry fathers, even if their kid had been little shits and attacked him first, were not on his list of things he wanted to deal with today. The man approaching was tall with dark hair just starting to fade to grey. He strode over with half a dozen blokes who looked remarkably similar to him. A family outing, John supposed. He stopped a few metres away from where the team was sitting and pointed a finger at John.

"Cripple, come here. We need to talk about how you'll make right what you did to my boy," he said and pointed behind himself, moving away to stand and wait.

Katie stood up, "I'm not sure this is the best way to deal with this situation, maybe you'd like to come and sit-"

"Shut up bitch. If I wanted to hear you I'd have spoken to you. Cripple, get over here now."

Katie stood for a moment with her mouth opening and closing. All those years of corporate negotiations and people management failing to prepare her for this level of bad manners. Disrespect and prejudice had long since stopped being acceptable in her circles so she had had little exposure to blunt and uncompromising sexism. More subtle forms were something she could handle effectively but this was very much not subtle.

John stood up slowly and flicked his cigarette away before porting to stand behind the men.

"Nice tracksuits guys. What seems to be the problem?" he asked. *Real smooth and intimidating you pillock, you aren't working at a till for god's sake, nice tracksuits? What? And why not just say 'how can I help you today sir' if you want to sound like a waiter,* he thought to himself and grimaced. The men jumped and spun round, the man who had been speaking recovered quickly and stepped forward raising a finger.

"You attacked my boy last night," he said. The man stepped forward again, entering John's personal space and poking him in the chest, the finger bounced off John's chest plate. He was half a foot taller than John, with dark brown hair and a build that was probably intimidating before he stopped going to the gym a decade ago. Unfortunately he was clearly still strong and relatively fit, especially compared to John whose exercise regime only included walking the dog and going up and down stairs occasionally.

He glowered down at the shorter man. "He was out doing his civic duty with his mate, stopping looters like you bastards from getting into the shop and you attacked him for no reason. You owe me."

"He attacked me first, actually. If I wasn't a higher level than him, he might have killed me," John began in what he thought was a reasonable tone.

"Shut it, what do you know about levels? He and his mate were minding their own business and you jumped them. You attacked a couple of boys then you cleaned out the shop. You owe me, cripple. It's our word against yours." He raised his left hand and rubbed his thumb against his first two fingers in the universal sign for lucre.

"Excuse me, but your son and his five friends attacked my colleague-" began Katie.

The man raised an arm as he looked back and a column of fire shot towards Katie. The fire swirled off to one side, to the man's shock, as Vic collected it into a ball before throwing it into the air as it vanished. The dark haired woman smiled at this buffoon in a way that would have made John check his remaining limbs were still attached. Katie was no longer where she had been, appearing next to John as she deactivated her time stop ability.

"Attempted murder is no way to conduct any kind of negotiation, no matter how unhappy the circumstances, sir. This is a trying time and we all have to learn to deal with our new powers but violence is not the answer here."

The man and his friends snapped their heads back round at the sound of her voice suddenly coming from behind them. "I'm afraid your son has not told you the truth about last night and it's always a good idea to hear both sides of a disagreement before leaping to conclusions and causing further problems, wouldn't you agree? You aren't gangsters and can't threaten us, so please stop this silly attitude," she finished as they stared in shock at her apparent teleportation.

She gestured to the boys hiding amongst the thugs. "Your son and his friends were looting and stopping other citizens from getting to the shop last night. They attacked first and my colleague, rather than hurting or killing them, chose to scare them instead. It may have been an ill advised action to take and I am sure he regrets it," *nope* thought John, "but no lasting harm was done. So we owe you nothing and I would prefer to resolve this matter peacefully without any bad blood. Perhaps if you would-"

"Not gangsters eh? You hear that lads?" he smiled at his allies some of whom chuckled on cue. "Do you know who I am, woman? Name's

Jac Crow and I'm the King of the Romani round here. Let me make it really clear for you: it's you who don't want any 'bad blood' with me, bitch, now hand over what they took last night. Don't test me, woman. Have your pets hand it over, now." He crossed his arms as he finished.

As the rest of the Carnival looked on in bemusement at this idiot making threats he couldn't follow through on, Reg slowly drew himself to his feet, leaning on his stick. He made a vile noise as he drew something up from the deepest recesses of his lungs and spat it to the side causing everyone to look over at him. Elizabeth frowned and despite the implied, and not so implied, threats began to open her mouth to verbally eviscerate him. But Reg opened his first:

"I fecking hate gypo wankers. Bunch o' fairy shites, the lot of ye. Feck off afore ye regret ya mam litting yer da get her drunk enough to spawn ya, ye fecking poofters," he said loudly, in a voice that carried all the way across the suddenly silent marketplace.

Chapter 27 - Bigotry Olympics

Okay, thought John. That happened. In all fairness Jac was being a sexist prick but rather than de-escalate the situation Reg, the crazy bastard, decided to match Jac's sexism with racism and then raise him with homophobia like the world's weirdest poker game.

Or did he? Jac is paler than me and Reg looks like he should sleep in a wrinkly coffin, nearly as bad as Greg on the 'possibly-undead-pallid skin tone' scale... Is it racist when two white guys don't like the group they each come from? Is it racist when a Cockney hates Brummies? Or a Scouser has an aversion to Geordies? Intra-racism vs inter-racism, which is worse? I honestly don't know but both are probably pretty bad. Ok... so maybe racist? Definitely homophobic.

Or was it? Jac has a kid and the travellers aren't too welcoming to 'alternative lifestyles' from what I hear so he most likely isn't gay... Maybe Reg doesn't have a problem with gay people, he was just talking shit to push Jac's buttons, Jac probably really doesn't like gay people and so he is the real homophobe here...

Right... to recap: Jac was definitely sexist, we know that for sure, and he's possibly homophobic but we haven't confirmed that yet. Reg is perhaps a racist to certain groups of white people and possibly homophobic. How does this all balance out on the totem pole of bigotry? You see right now I wish Reddit was avail- OH SHIT!

John's rumination on the intersectional nature of the Jac vs Reg bigotry Olympics had completely distracted him from the real world but it was cut off as he suddenly realised a fist was approaching his face at what seemed to be a sizable fraction of the speed of light. He instinctively raised his right arm to block before remembering he had left it on the side of the path half a mile away. *Should probably go bag it up at some point, otherwise it will encourage rats,* was his last thought before the anticipated pain.

Which didn't arrive, much to his surprise. One moment he was about to have his lights punched out having tried to block with his stump instead of, you know, teleporting out of the way or blipping the guys arm off like a sensible person. The next moment the man swinging at him was crouched down behind Jac, face planted in Jac's left buttock and his right arm poking out between Jac's legs. This juvenile still life could not continue for long due to the momentum of the punch thrower. John belatedly identified him as a level four with the ability Boxing Prodigy before the man's momentum caused his punching arm to sweep Jac's left leg out from beneath him and dumped them both into a tangled pile on the ground.

John looked to Katie who winked at him. He nodded, genuinely grateful for being able to keep his teeth. As this was the second time she had spared him a painful impact to the head, he figured he should probably steal her something nice to say thank you. She seemed like a white wine kind of woman.

While most of them backed away, one of Jac's allies had sprouted some kind of ice armour, transforming into an seven foot tall golem made of jagged blue crystal. He raised his foot to step forward just as Zeeg leapt in front of him, growing into her latest Hound of the Baskervilles form and snarling down at him. Her jaws dropped saliva from three inch canines onto his upturned face. He brought his foot back and lowered it to the ground, raising his hands to the side, slowly. "Nice doggie, good… boy?" he said quietly. The snarl dropped half an octave and increased in volume. "Good girl, I meant good girl!"

"Jimothy Audeville Crow! What the hell are you playing at, causing trouble for these folks?" called a caustic voice from an armchair off to the side of John's team. "Jac we know what your idiot boy is like, don't think I can't see you hiding there David! Whatever that fool of yours got up to last night, you better leave these people alone, you hear? The only reason I'm still in the land of the living is this lot. Where were you and the folk while the rats tried to eat your dear Aunt Aggie and send her off to join the Majority?"

Jac had extricated himself from his friend, climbed to his feet and had been preparing to unleash some kind of attack. His arms glowed with a fiery nimbus as he raised them towards Zeeg. "Aunt Aggie? Majority?" He said in a suddenly much smaller voice. Zeeg snorted and returned to her normal size then went back to spinning in her chair.

"Aunt Agatha to you at the moment, you little squirt. I told that mother of yours that man was no good but she wanted to be Queen so she didn't listen to me. I told her it wasn't worth it. Been there, done that, got the shitty t-shirt I said. And now look at you. Stop that thing with your arms right now, you look like a fool." The aura of fire vanished, "Good boy. Now you leave these people alone, you hear? Only reason you aren't dead is cos they don't want to hurt you. If they wanted you'd be in half a dozen bits scattered from here to kingdom come right now. Idiot boy. Some of them are level eleven, you fool child." The crone levered herself out of her chair.

"Excuse me, Elizabeth dear," she began in a completely different and perfectly civil tone, "It seems I need to talk some sense into what passes for the younger generation." Elizabeth smiled at her from the next chair over and dipped a biscuit in her tea.

"Sometimes you have to take a firm hand with them, Aggie. You go sort him out."

Oh crap, now there's two of them, thought John.

Agatha hobbled over to Jac and began poking him and moving him back over to the rest of his group, taking his friends along as well. They were very deferential to the old battle axe but did shoot a few angry looks over their shoulders at John when they thought they could get away with it.

"Evie, is that you?" came a young voice from behind them. Zeeg hopped out of her chair, setting it whirling and went to sniff the newcomers over. A man and woman stood just behind a boy that John recognised as Max from Evie's class at school. They had clearly seen Zeeg's transformation and stepped carefully back.

"Max! You're OK! Hi Mr and Mrs Gawthorpe. How are you?" the girl asked her friend.

"I knew you'd make it as well! You're a gamer through and through," said Max, waving a hand at Evie. "How did you dodge the rats? Most of our street… do you know if anyone else…" The boy's eyes began to tear up and his mum stepped in to carry on for him.

"Don't worry son, come here." Max spun and clung to his mum's side as he fought to control his emotions, wrapping his arms around her as she patted his back.

"Hi John, long time no see. Looks like something got a piece of you, are you alright?" she asked gently, gesturing at his missing limb with her free hand.

"Oh, Dad shrugged that off like a champ, I think he's more annoyed he has to smoke pre rolled cigs because he can't roll his own anymore than anything else," butted in Evie. "He lost it to the assassin rat just before we took out the Queen."

John opened his mouth to correct Evie, there were many things he would miss no longer having his dominant hand for but Max's dad stepped forward, cautiously petting Zeeg who promptly lost interest having thoroughly sniffed them all so she returned to spinning in her chair. "You took out the Queen?" asked Mike, Max's father, in an incredulous tone.

"Well, it was a team effort but we put her down eventually," said Katie, joining them and offering her hand. John was quietly grateful to her for the second time in as many minutes as she once more saved him from a social situation he would likely handle badly.

"Hi, Katie Johnson, I work for- well I don't suppose that matters anymore. Nowadays I find myself wrangling this herd of cats." She waved a hand over the team. "We all sort of bumped into each other yesterday and ended up looking after this lot." She gestured at the tea party of elderly people taking place behind her, most of whom raised their glasses in salute. She smiled and continued, "We got dragged into dealing with the Queen towards the end. Our other friends did most of the work with the Queen though, we were very much Johnny come lately to that fight. Please let me introduce you to them? Do you need anything to eat or drink? Help yourselves to what's on the table, we can get more if you like."

Max had pulled himself together and sat with Evie as the adults were introduced and went to fill cups with tea and coffee.

"Why did your dad take you to fight the Queen? That's crazy dangerous! Dad wouldn't even let me downstairs until the rat things stopped coming and he'd got rid of most of the bodies."

"The little ones? Flying or not?"

"There were flying ones?"

"Yeah, the Sky Rats. Dad dealt with most of the ones of them that we saw but I got to zap a few. The little ones were Chittering Scavengers, only level ones, they were easy," she bragged with the total lack of self consciousness only children and politicians can manage to pull off.

"Get lost Evie, you're the same age as me, you didn't get powers."

"Ah well, maybe you're right? Or maybe not!" she flashed a grin. "Look at me, dude, and think: Identify."

Max must have done so as his eyes turned wide as saucers. "How the hell did you manage that… and you're level eleven? No way! Dad only got up to five and he must have killed hundreds of the little ones," he demanded in a hushed voice.

Teamchat:
Baby Zeus: Just gonna give Max powers, K? Thanks!
Houdini: Kid, wait!
Pause Button: Evie, ask his parents first!
Porridge Eater: Oh great more magic kids. This'll end reet well.

John spun to look at her but it was too late. She had offered an Essence to Max already and he had accepted.

John waited a moment and used Identify on the boy.

Level 1
Name: Max Gawthorpe
Ability: Flight

Oh crap, now there's two of them, John thought for a second time.

Max wobbled unsteadily into the air at first before beginning to make steady loops around the group, becoming more confident at an impressive rate. His mum and dad were less than happy and began barking at him to get down and explain what the hell was going on. He landed and attempted to sound apologetic as he explained what Evie had done. However he was grinning from ear to ear which kind of took the sincerity out of his words. Mike rounded on John.

"What the hell did your girl do?" he asked with a dangerous tone in his voice.

"She donated an Essence to her friend, Mike. She should have asked properly first." John shot Evie a Dad Glare™, "and I'm sorry, *as is she,* but done is done, as they say. I'm sorry, you really should've been asked before she acted but kids don't always stop and ask permission like they should, you know?"

"You could have levelled him up yesterday, then he could have helped you fight and he wouldn't be a level one noob. If you'd formed a team you'd all have got the same Essence per kill and you could have gone hunting to get stronger. That's what we did and it's why we aren't a level five nub like you," Evie said defiantly. Inside John twitched like he was in an electric chair and cursed the kid but he managed not to let it show. Fortunately Mike had focussed in on what Evie had said and was looking at her.

"How do you know my level, Evie?" he asked in a calmer voice, not rising to her attitude while John shot her further Dad Glares.

Katie stepped in with her hands raised placatingly, once more earning John's gratitude. *I'll have to steal her a really nice bottle of wine or something to say thank you* he thought.. "Look, I apologise for this misunderstanding. Maybe it would be best if we sat down and discussed things. Perhaps you'd let me explain some of the things we've learned about the system and how it works. Maybe a good place to start would be Identify…"

And so Katie gave them the basics. After a while Jennifer and her team came over and shook hands, introducing themselves. *New recruits for their team maybe? It would be good for Evie to still get some time with one of her friends, despite all that's happening,* John thought as he silently prayed that Phil wouldn't be his usual prickish self and ruin the chances of the 'merger' Katie seemed to be working towards.

As the adults talked Evie and Max snuck off to one side and began discussing their abilities in quiet voices, not wanting to draw the attention of the adults. Evie and Max ran through the events they went through yesterday and began messing about with their abilities, Max hovering and flying as Evie threw out very low powered Zaps that he had to dodge.

John sat next to Reg and lit up a smoke. "You know I've got a bunch of Essence I can't use to level. You kind of got robbed as you weren't part of the group when we killed the Queen but you did a lot of the fighting against her."

Houdini has offered to donate 26 Essence to Porridge Eater. Porridge Eater has accepted.

"That'll be fine, thank you, ye Sassenach pillock. First time an Englishman ever paid what was owed to one from the clans. Maybe ye ain't so bad after all."

"You're welcome, I think? That should get you to level seven if I got the maths right, so get your levels, it's not long till this thing starts. Speaking of which, Evie, Vic could you come over here for a minute please? Yes I know you're playing with your friend kid, just get over here please, it will only take a moment."

John quickly convinced Evie to donate twenty one Essence to Vic to allow her to get up to level seven. Vic thanked them both profusely before levelling and grinning at her new status screen. This brought the team as close to parity as possible. Reg and Vic were still lagging a little behind but they would soon catch up when they started getting Essence again. It seemed like a good idea to have everyone as strong as possible before this meeting began. After all, the system might throw them a curve ball and drop them straight into the next wave in just ten minutes.

Levelling up Reg and Vic had given John an idea. He blipped a calculator in and quickly went round the group adding up how much spare Essence everyone had. When he was done he was shocked: they had just over three hundred floating Essence. Just enough to boost him *and* Evie to level twelve or a level one all the way to level eleven with a chunk left over.

Chapter 28 - Brave, dude, but not very wise

With five minutes until the start of the meeting the last of the survivors arrived in the marketplace. John did a quick scan. There were a double handful of level eights, and one ten but almost everyone else was level two to five, mostly three or four. The only level ones were the people the Carnival had rescued and who chose not to fight. There were very few children. Besides little Fred, Evie and Max there were perhaps thirty kids who were too young to receive an essence yesterday morning still alive.

John felt his skin crawl as it sunk in. The town hadn't had a huge population but there must have been maybe a thousand under sixteens alive yesterday morning inside the barrier. His heart hardened even more against the system. Misanthrope he may be but a slaughter of the innocent like this was unforgivable and if Normanby was typical for the whole country, or even the world… a knot of hatred formed within him that he resolved to nurture for as long as it took to take revenge on this alliance that had dragged his family and his world into their war.

He blipped in a smoke and lit up to calm his nerves. He ported in a bottle of water and had to ask Evie to undo the top for him. How many times had he had to open bottles for her? Not so much recently but it had always been him helping her and now he was a cripple, as Jac had called him, all because of the system. He'd have to figure out a way. Maybe hold the bottle between his knees and very carefully open the top? He could see himself needing waterproof trousers a lot in his future.

At exactly eleven o'clock a hush descended across the murmuring crowd as a platform appeared. The platform was made of golden lines and was transparent but the figure stood atop it seemed sure footed. It was a man with scales instead of skin and a reptilian face, short snout and sharp flashing teeth, all composed of golden lines. He was mostly naked bar some kind of armoured girdle that protected his groin and lower stomach. A tail flashed side to side behind it. The thing was nearly three metres tall and on the platform it towered over everyone present bar Doris.

"Greetings recruits. I should not be surprised that so few of you remain after the first challenge, your species is pathetically weak but I still find myself disappointed. Some of you have real potential and yet you failed to protect your brothers and sisters in arms. Such a shameful showing! If you don't do better in the next round there will be so few left it won't be worth the effort of recruiting your species."

The voice boomed and carried a syrupy quality that failed to hide the disdain they were held in by the figure before them. It spoke in a lazy drawl that dripped contempt. *Conscription. This was conscription, not recruitment,* John thought fiercely to himself.

"What the hell are you and why have you done this to us?" called a voice from off to one side. *Brave, dude, but not very wise,* thought John. A flash of light was followed by the man dropping to the ground screaming in agony. The golden lizard man waited patiently for his screams to die down and for him to drag himself painfully back to his feet with the assistance of his friends. The rest of the crowd watched in silent fear.

"Thank you for volunteering to demonstrate where you untrained, unskilled monkeys stand, Recruit. Speaking out of turn, without proper etiquette will be punished. Do it twice and you die."

The eyes of the thing scanned slowly across the crowd and almost everyone dropped their gaze in submission. John met its cold eyes with a burning anger in his own; he did not flinch, although he felt the power of this thing. He used Identify and it returned nothing but a series of question marks. Its lip curled slightly in response to his gaze, perhaps in a sneer but maybe a thin smile showing rows of razor sharp teeth, before its eyes moved on.

"Today you do not get to know my name, rank or the proper form of address as you are as yet unworthy and I do not have the patience to bandy words with raw recruits. After the second test, those who remain may be given that privilege, if they perform to a satisfactory standard. Some of you snivelling monkeys have achieved 'deeds' worthy of *very limited* recognition. You will receive a modest item from the system when I depart but know that I find you wholly unworthy of such a reward. You were all blessed and yet you still failed so spectacularly."

The being moved into the centre of his stage and spun to face the crowd. He raised one arm and pointed up into the sky.

"Know that with your blessing by the Light comes responsibility. You must do your best to thrive and grow strong as someday you will be needed to defend this and other worlds from the advance of the Enemy. If you do not, you will not survive. However we are not unmerciful. The system not only grants you power but it has some bonus effects. It enhances certain positive emotional responses, your sense of belonging and camaraderie within a team. It also helps during periods of strife and danger, a mechanism has been put in place within your minds to limit your emotional responses to negative stimuli. Think of it as something similar to the battlefield drugs many of your armies use to make their soldiers "brave" and feel

less pain." Its voice somehow became even more derisive as it spoke of humanities military personnel. *If Reg has had his sense of 'camaraderie' enhanced, what the hell was he like before?* wondered John.

"It shifts your emotions to the side, shall we say, and lets you focus on the immediate needs of yourself and your team. During relative dips in stress it will gradually process emotions of grief and regret and *sadness*," sadness was said in a tone that suggested it thought such emotions were utterly beneath it. "it does this to reduce the burden when the campaign ends and the warehoused emotion is allowed to flow back into you. When this pent up emotion returns to your mind it is known as The Crash, which you will experience for the first time should you survive the third wave and be given a leave of absence from active duty."

So that's why everyone wasn't freaking out like they should have been, these fuckers have been in our heads all along! God knows what the Crash is going to look like for us, suddenly everyone will be worried about their family, most of whom are probably dead already, and dealing with having seen thousands die in a day.

"Most of you don't need to worry about the Crash though. It is unlikely you will make it that far." It sneered, an expression that seemed to come naturally to its reptilian face. "Now to the business at hand. The next phase of your training will begin at 12:00 on the seventh day from now. It is commonly known as the Siege wave. This time you will not get any advanced warning as to the nature of the enemies, which will again be chosen for you by lottery. We stop the hand holding from here on out. You are expected to work together to prepare for the siege and then fight to survive it. Additional information will be made available at the start of the wave. I do not expect very many of you, if any at all in fact, to make it through this next phase but I am legally

required to inform you that forming a chain of command is strongly advised. Any of you that survive will see me again after the second wave. I am done with you!"

And with that said the being and its platform were gone, leaving a stunned crowd to turn and look at each other in frightened silence. The silence hung in the air until a voice rang out to fill it.

"Whut a fecking arsehole," Reg declared loudly. All eyes turned to him and he spat to the side. "Whut? Why are ye pansies all looking at me like that?"

Gradually a few people chuckled quietly and it spread until most people were laughing at least a little, releasing the pent up tension. It verged on the hysterical for some of the crowd and it took a fair few minutes before the giggling began to subside.

As they regained control of themselves people began to move around. Various groups began to form as people came together. The travellers formed the largest single group with somewhere around 150 people. There were a dozen or so smaller groups, perhaps people who knew each other from the pub or work or lived on the same street. Most of them were less than twenty people strong. There was another group with about sixty people, including all the non traveller children except for the ones with John's team. They had about twenty kids ranging in age from babies through to early teenagers with twice that number of adults.

The remainder slowly gravitated towards the Carnival, greeting people they knew in other groups as they went past them but moving inexorably into the orbit of John and his friends. Katie went out to meet them as they arrived and began speaking quietly, shaking hands and introducing herself and the team.

"This is starting to look a lot like a teenager's first disco. Boys on one side, girls on the other. Who will be the poor bugger to cross the divide and kick things off by getting rejected?" asked Sam with a laugh.

"Did they have disco's back in the fifties?" asked Evie innocently.

"You know I have eye beams that melt steel right?"

"Why would you threaten an innocent child like that? Dad! Sam is bullying me!" Evie replied.

"Kid, wind your neck in please. You're both ignoring the most important issue and frankly I'm disappointed in your priorities child!"

"What?" Evie asked.

"Where is the bloody loot that the golden douchebag mentioned?" said John, "Can't believe you got distracted from loot kiddo. Shame!" He grinned at his daughter.

As if the system had been waiting for the question to be asked, boxes appeared floating in front of each of the members of the Carnival as well as the other higher levelled survivors. John reached out cautiously, he only had one hand left after all, and flipped the lid. Inside was a lozenge that glowed faintly, about the size of a grape. The box vanished as he picked it up and he used Identify on it.

Item: Enigma Core (bound item)

Description: A source of great potential. Focus on your heart's desire while looking at the device and it will make your wish a reality. Warning: while powerful this item is still limited. Desires that are too specific or beyond the scope of the core will receive a next best fit approximation of the intended result so be cautious in what you wish for.

"Well that's good, I guess?" said Raoul, staring at the core in his hand.

"We should be very careful with these. If someone steals them we're in trouble," Sam added.

"It's a bound item, no one but the person who got it can use it," said Evie confidently. "I'm going to use mine, I want to be able to fly!" she declared, staring at the core in her hand. The glow grew in intensity until it was nearly blinding before merging into her skin and disappearing.

"Evie!" cried John, panicking at seeing the glowing orb melt into his daughter.

"It's cool Dad, it gave me a bonus modification. Electromagnetic flight. Something about me being able to create a field that repels the field generated by the planet's core, yadda yadda, random science stuff, connected to all other matter in the universe, blah and boom, flight power. Check this out!"

Evie jumped to her feet and a shimmering field appeared in a disc a metre across beneath her feet. She began floating around in a circle over their heads, whooping as she went.

"It's not even that reserve intensive. I could fly for hours on a full tank!" She began to speed up and shortly Max flew up to join her and they zipped around for a short while, hollering at each other, before John and Mike called them down.

"I think these are too precious to use frivolously," said John with a lower grade Dad Glare™ sent towards his now seated daughter. "We might need a few wishes during the next wave."

"Sorry John but you aren't my dad and I have a solid plan for mine," Bob replied, focussing on his lozenge which glowed and disappeared into his palm.

"What did you ask for?" asked Sam.

"A fully equipped and automated machine shop in the stash. I'm going into mass production, baby!"

Bob hopped up from his chair, bowing slightly to Elizabeth as he passed, who smiled up at him, and disappeared into the portal of light he summoned by Doris' leg with a renewed spring in his step.

"I need armour when I use the titan form I reckon," Raoul was focussed on his lozenge which also vanished into his skin. He checked his status.

"Perfect! Now when I shift I get something called Titanic Power Armour. I'll try it out later, I don't want to impress the crowd too much right now I think. They might freak out and start worshipping me as a god or something," he grinned.

"Doubt it ye giant whatsit. Ain't no cargo cults gonna happen here lessen it's for that golden wazzock."

"Well what are you going to use yours for Reg, o master of snide?" Raoul replied.

"Dunno. Young sassenach has a point ah reckon. Might be handy to have in the back pocket fer times o' trouble, ye ken?"

A voice called out from across the marketplace in a confident tone.

"Excuse me everyone, my name is Keith Hargreaves and I think we should all come together and organise ourselves for what's coming. We seem to have sorted ourselves into groups based on a variety of affiliations, perhaps it would be easiest if each group picks one or two representatives and we hold a council to bring us all together? I'll open up the town hall and we can all sit and discuss what the best course of action will be for the coming days."

Chapter 29 - Did you just Princess Bride me?

After some pretty fierce haggling it was decided that Katie and Elizabeth would represent the Carnival at the meeting. Raoul was weirdly adamant that as the strongest he should be there to safeguard Katie but Katie demurred, thanking him for the offer and pointing out (while Elizabeth was briefly out of earshot) that bringing along one of the people who didn't fight at all and was still level one would be very good PR for the team, seeing as they included all the highest level people it wouldn't look good to throw their weight around. Evie was quietly speculating that Raoul had a crush on Katie. When the big man blushed furiously she cackled and continued teasing him.

John agreed with Katie's logic and felt a brief pang of sympathy for anyone who tried to strongarm the pair of formidable ladies.

The man who had called the meeting had approached the main door to the town hall with two followers and it had vanished as he arrived. He went inside with one of the men, the other returning to a small group. Katie and Elizabeth set off to join the flow of ones and twos from each group who headed to join the meeting.

"Well if we have to stop here until they get done, how about some food?" suggested Sam.

There was a chorus of agreement and so John began blipping in supplies and the non combatants got to work putting lunch together. Jen and James were paying court to the level ten who had joined the group gathered around the impromptu lounge John had created in the car park, trying to convince him to join their team. The man had the ability Hydromancy and was bragging about sucking the liquid out of the rats that had attacked him. It turned out he was the one who had killed the other Mole-Rat, while only level five, by flooding the creature's tunnel with sewage water from a nearby pipeline, collapsing the tunnel and eventually drowning it. He had received an Enigma Core as well and was flashing it around to everyone who asked to look at it.

"What a poser," muttered Raoul. He moved over to speak with some of the hangers on who had followed the level ten over, whose name was Oleg. Raoul began smiling, shaking hands and retelling the story of killing the Queen, rather loudly, to anyone who would listen. For some reason he kept flexing his shoulders and arms while he talked. Evie flew down to John who was sitting alone with dark thoughts written across his face as everyone else was moving around and chatting.

"You ok old man?"

"All good Sausage. I'm all good thanks. I'm just thinking." He flashed her a smile.

"You know that's bad for you right? Me and Max were going to go and say hey to the other kids that made it. Not the ferals though. We know some of the other kids from from school. Anna was one of the librarians like me."

"That's fine Sweetie but don't go out of my sight please? Also don't magic up anyone else without running it past their parents first."

"As you wish," she said with a flourishing bow.

"Did you just Princess Bride me? I'm pretty sure you used it wrong as well... It's meant to be used for unreasonable requests and I'm being *very* reasonable, you hear? Get lost scamp!" he waved his hand and grinned slightly as she flew back over to Max and they headed over to the other kids.

"Wonder if they'll set up a school or something?" said Sam, sitting down next to John.

"Evie would hate that. One of the reasons she's so chipper is that there are no more history lessons for her! Of course when it sinks in that she can't just play video games and read manga all day she might change her tune. In the old days... Ye olden days when I were a lad- ha! Back in the day a village school would have one teacher, usually a school marm, who taught all the kids at once. The older ones would be tasked with helping the younger ones understand things they had already learnt which helped reinforce the lessons for the older kids and eventually the younger ones would do the same for the next cohort of little kids. A virtuous cycle for small populations who couldn't afford to support a lot of teachers. A bog village school might have about as many kids as there are here. With so few kids left- the Department of Education will need to trim its budget a lot," he finished bitterly.

"Seems to me someone like you wouldn't mind going back to that kind of system. What's eating you? You've been sitting silently glowering at everyone and everything since golden boy vanished."

"The fucking system is what's eating me. So many- there must have been nearly a thousand kids in this town yesterday morning. Am I the only one bothered by that? Is it the system messing with all your emotions and it left me out for some reason? I'd really appreciate not feeling like I'm the only one who gives a-"

Teamchat:

Pause Button: John, Bob, please could you join us in the meeting? We are having problems with Mr. Crow. He's trying to turn this into some kind of Star Chamber over what happened last night with the kids at the shop.

Shinji: I'm busy. Building the machines to make the parts for more machines which will make new machines that will make guns. Big guns! It's going to be great! I'm going to be busy for a few days. So no.

Houdini: I'd prefer not to?
Pause Button: We need one of you and Bob's excuse is slightly better than a preference.
Houdini: I swear to Christ if Elizabeth talks to me like I'm a piece of shit in front of a load of randos I am blipping straight out of there. And possibly sending her to the pile!
Pause Button: She's going hard in your defence. I think she has this ingroup mentality. If you're in her "group" she will bully you to make the group stronger but if someone outside the group attacks you she will lock shields and fight for you.
Houdini: Fine, I'll be there in a second.
Shinji: Enjoy mate!
"Sam-"
"I'll keep an eye on Evie for you John. Have fun and don't you mind what the mean old lady says!" she finished with a laugh.
With a sigh John blipped himself over to the now missing doors to the town hall. He tried to straighten his shirt sleeve by shaking his remaining arm out but gave it up as a waste of time. He set his shoulders back, briefly admiring in a window how the armour made him look less round shouldered and marched bravely into the lion's den.
"Feeling tough today are you? Going to attack some more kids?" Asked a voice from a group standing to one side of the entrance. *Ah great, Jac left his minions guarding the door.*
"If no one attacks me first I'm usually pretty chilled out. I did keep the kid in one piece when I teleported him away. I didn't *have* to do that. Anyway, important meeting to attend, shame you lot won't be joining us." He left them on the pavement outside and walked in.
He had only been in this place a handful of times. It had been the polling station for the last general election and he had taken Evie in to

walk around a couple of craft fairs they had held in the big room downstairs. He looked into the side rooms on the lower floor but they were empty. He heard raised voices coming from the main hall upstairs so set off to find the source.

"The man attacked children, damn near killed them as well!" Jac was saying loudly as John swung open the door and walked through. "Ah, here he is. Let's see him try to justify his crimes!"

John walked over to Katie and Elizabeth. Everyone was seated in a loose circle having moved the chairs used for audiences when the hall held plays into the centre of the large, wood floored room.

Teamchat:

Pause Button: Just stay cool and be honest. I'm pretty sure Keith's friend has the ability to detect lies so this is just a formality to neutralise Jac and bring his faction into the fold. As long as you're honest.

Houdini: I'm getting the feeling he's being a bit dramatic...

"Mr Borrows, My name is Keith Hargreaves, very nice to meet you." He had greying hair and a neatly trimmed beard. John Identified him and saw he had the ability Organiser. *Probably a good choice to try to run this shit show then* he thought, *rather him than me.*

"Mr Crow has raised two complaints and refuses to let us proceed unless they are addressed. As he has a large group supporting him we must get to the bottom of this matter fairly so we can hopefully all work together going forward. To keep this brief I will summarise: last night yourself and a colleague attacked his son and his son's friend unprovoked as they attempted to stop you from looting the supermarket. Please could you explain your side of the story?"

John glanced around those seated at the table as he moved to stand behind Katie and Elizabeth. A bunch of middle aged, middle management types was his first impression. They didn't seem hostile, bar Jac of course, but he got the feeling they all had plenty of experience at keeping a straight face in contentious meetings. none of them were above level five so they hadn't done much fighting yesterday.

"Um, sure. Bob and I were out last night looking to secure supplies and parts for his mecha. That's the giant robot parked outside. When we got to the supermarket some kid hit me with an attack that knocked me off my feet. There were about six of them I think? Words were exchanged and they threatened us, saying the shop was their turf or something. I ported the first one away. The second produced some kind of magic swords and came towards us so I blipped him off to the same place as well. Then Bob gave the rest a lecture about not picking fights and told them to bugger off. Which they did. I think that about covers it."

"You lying shit! You attacked my boy unprovoked because you wanted to loot the shop, which you just admitted to, I'd like to point out. I bet it was you who cheated and made the wave harder by levelling in advance as well!"

"Sure, we were there to loot the shop. God only knows when we can get more food, I'm not seeing any lorries coming in through the barrier, are you? The thing is we know for sure that *we* will at least be willing to share and not use the food as a tool to control people. You want some food? Tell me where and I'll drop you enough to last all your people for weeks."

"So you did loot the shop?" Hargreaves asked.

"Well yeah, but if anyone wants it we'll share, no worries."

"Did you get levels before the wave began?"

"Well, yes, a few of us did." He shrugged.

"How, please?"

"We killed rats, normal rats, and pigeons. We got the Essence for killing wildlife and figuring out Identify and the team system."

"I knew it! They screwed us all over with their greed! They put us all in danger with their arrogance and greed!" crowed Mr. Crow.

"And you were attacked first?" continued Hargreaves, ignoring the outburst.

"Yep."

"This is bullshit. How can you not see what they've done, screwing us over every step of the way!" Jac exclaimed, looking around at those grey men and women seated at the table for support.

Hargreaves ignored him once more before he resumed speaking.

"Could you have hurt or killed the boy if you chose to?"

"He did hurt the boy! Dropped him on top of a pile of rat corpses that were missing their heads! He'll have nightmares for years!" shouted Jac angrily.

"If I'd wanted to hurt him I'd have just teleported his head and left the rest, like I did to a lot of those rat corpses," John replied coldly.

"I cannot be part of this agreement between us all unless this *psychopath* is properly punished. You just heard him admit what he would do!"

"Oh do shut up Jac, your boy was playing tough, likely there on your orders, and picked on the wrong man," one of the representatives from another group drawled. "At least do us the courtesy of accepting it when you've lost an argument."

"You've all seen the dragon thing's body, I take it?" demanded Jac, "This guy and his team did that. Nailed it to the turf like a fucking ten metre long bug! We cannot have people like that running around unchecked. He attacked a child for god's sake!"

"Who is hardly a child, he is what, nineteen? Your boy attacked him first after he and his friends had already begun looting the shop?"

Hargreaves paused as he leant over and whispered to his companion who replied quietly. "I believe Mr. Borrows and the representatives of the Carnival have acted in good faith but we should put it to a vote. All in favour of censuring Mr. Borrows and his team?"

Jac said "Me!" in a furious tone but he was alone.

"Motion denied then. Mr. Borrows, I trust I can hold you to sharing the supplies you acquired yesterday in an equitable manner?" John nodded

"Very well, that answers Mr. Crow's second complaint. Thank you for your time Mr. Borrows. You can go, we will have an outline of a plan to present to the people outside within half an hour. Most of it was agreed already but Mr. Crow was reluctant to commit without first addressing this issue between you. Mr. Crow, I hope we can set this unfortunate matter aside and work together to ensure we are as prepared as possible for the second wave?"

"Unfortunate? Sod off. I'm out. Bunch of cowards. You'll regret this, psycho." Jac shot him a look of hatred as he said the last part and stormed out, followed closely by his second.

John nodded to Katie and Elizabeth and blipped back to his spot on the settee in time to see Jac burst out of the town hall, yell at his faction to grab their stuff and head off back down Main Street. *Could have gone worse I suppose* he thought, *the worst they usually do is send some kids to break your windows in the night or get your kid bullied at school, neither of which poses a real threat anymore.*

As they walked away John noticed one of Evie's friends from school. He had been watching Evie and Max swirl around in the air with envy. John couldn't remember the boy's name but he knew he was one of the kids who sometimes played online with her. His parents began shepherding him away and cast a sorry look over towards John's group as they turned away to follow after Jac.

"What are you looking at that lot for dude? Bunch of losers!" Raoul slumped down into the chair next to John, clearly worn out from all his bragging about the fight against the Queen.

"One of Evie's mates from school went with that lot." John waved his hand at the backs of the group leaving, "I get the feeling this could be trouble when she finds out."

Chapter 30 - Bring out your dead

Twenty minutes later the "council" members came out and moved over to one side. John was not exactly impressed with them. If the old order had been wiped out, literally in most cases, why would they now choose to be led by people who were the minions of the old leaders? The "second raters" who couldn't climb that greasy pole quite as well before the system. They all struck John as people who got on a fast track graduate leadership program in their twenties, in a field they didn't care about and their ever growing malaise and self loathing had seeped into their bones, making them grey and low grade evil. To be fair he usually thought that about anyone in management. Maybe Evie had a point when she told him he needed to get out more?

The groups who had stayed in the marketplace moved over and formed a loose knit crowd.

"Thank you all for staying. I will reach out to Mr. Crows faction and see if we can reach some kind of entente. We must pull together, at least for the duration of the next wave but in the meantime we have a lot to ask of you. We feel it would be for the best if we could build a catalogue of the powers we have available so I will shortly ask those of you not in a team to come forward. We will invite you to a team so we can record your abilities and the bonus you provide for being in a team. Once we have this database we will try to work out the most effective ways of grouping people up. Initially we will look to form teams around people who have vital skills like earth moving and construction with others who boost their reserve regeneration rate. We intend to clear out a large area of town and construct defences. If anyone has any experience in architecture or engineering, especially military engineering, please highlight this when you come forward and we will focus on ensuring you are able to make the most of this experience to help protect us all." He paused, looked down and sighed.

"There is another issue that must be addressed urgently. This tragedy has left many of our fellow townspeople dead. I am sorry to speak so bluntly and I share your grief deeply but it is vital that we do not allow the bodies to rot where they are. We must gather them up and give them a suitable send off. There is also the issue of the bodies of the rats that attacked us yesterday. These too will fester and bring disease unless they are disposed of. We have some ideas on how to do this and once we have a catalogue of powers we will outline the plan to the people with the appropriate skills. Now, when you come forward my colleague Ms. Johnson will explain a few things about the system that her team worked out yesterday. Most of you will find the information very helpful if you are not already aware of it. I would ask you to listen to her, it will only take a few minutes, and step up to accept an invite into the teams being used for surveying abilities. There is nothing binding in joining a team, in case any of you are worried, anyone can leave a team at any time but there are many advantages to being in a full team which Ms. Johnson will cover in her talks. If you could form a queue of some sort we should be able to process everyone through fairly quickly, Ms. Johnson please could you begin?"

Teamchat:

Pause Button: You lot are fine, I've given them a breakdown of our team buffs and abilities already. John, I'm afraid you'll be in high demand for a while and it won't be a pleasant job, at least for the first bit of what we'll need you for. I'll explain properly later. Please could you ask Jen and her team as well as the others to make their way over, might as well start with some friendlies to put everyone else at ease.

Houdini: You need a Judas goat? We'll send them over.
Pause Button: Hargreaves is a good guy. I trust him.
Atlas: You only met him half an hour ago!
Pause Button: And I am an excellent judge of character. As you all already know.

John stood with a grimace, unhappy at having to do more "social stuff". Sam waved him back and went over to the rest of their group, speaking first with Jen's team and the new guy, then going round the old folks and the rest who had joined them after the golden lizard had disappeared. They began getting up and making their way over to Katie.

"John, a moment of your time please?" said Greg, standing to one side and gesturing for John to join him. John got up and walked over, Greg led him off toward the church to the east, away from everyone else.

"What's up, Greg?"

"What they are going to ask of you will be very hard. Emotionally, I mean. They are planning to send out people who are very fast, like Jen, and have them check and mark houses. They will then ask you to go round and teleport out the rat and human bodies."

"Damn. Should I yell 'bring out your dead' and drag a cart behind me as I go? My ability is great but I'm not a man with a van. Or a hearse."

"Gallows humour, though tasteless, is likely to serve you well in this task, John. However this isn't why I asked to speak to you. I told you in advance as I felt it would be best if you had some time to come to terms with what they will ask you to do. Your disagreement with the travellers has caused some of the local Majority to take an interest in Jac's plans. It doesn't bode well I'm afraid. His plans are not complex at this time, a little arson and threats to extort food while telling his people we are holding out on them. They may cause many complications for all of those still living if he successfully causes division among the survivors." Greg sighed and continued, "He also intends to arrange for you and your daughters' 'unexpected' deaths. Hargreaves is an honest man as far as the Majority can tell. He wishes to deal openly with Jac but that man will only take advantage of this and not treat us with honour. The feeling among the Majority is that Jac will play along with Hargreaves just enough to avoid open conflict while undermining the main group and seeking to manoeuvre himself into a position of supreme authority. The man is a maniac, John. His ancestors are calling for you to… send him through the veil."

"Your dead mates and his dead family members want me to kill the guy? If he is talking about killing me and Evie I'll stop him when the time comes, and thanks for the heads up, but I can't just blip over and assassinate him *preemptively*. This isn't a Philip K Dick novel where future crime is legally actionable for god's sake."

John sighed then went on. "He has people who aren't necessarily with him by choice from what I could see, but if he gets murdered, martyred, then there will be zero hope of bringing us all together for the wave. I won't do it, Greg, I can't. I'm a lot of things but I'm not a murderer."

"We know John. Believe me when I say the Majority understands you very well." *Not creepy at all,* thought John. "But it was decided that you should be made aware of the situation. Your daughter's friend, his name is Ryan by the way, and his family are indeed being held against their will, as are many others. They are afraid and are surrounded on all sides by Jac's sycophants. Only a fraction of his group has anything resembling loyalty to him, a lot simply see him as a strong man to lead them and will switch sides if they are disabused of this notion. The Majority believe that you should find a way to exploit this and bring these doubters over to the main group."

"Easy enough to say but how? In case you and the Majority haven't been paying attention, which I doubt very much based on their forensic knowledge of my private life, I am not one for big speeches and swaying a crowd. I'm not Hargreaves or Katie, Greg, it's not in me to do it and if I tried I'd cock it up."

"You have friends and allies who can cover for your weaknesses. I will approach the council with the information I have given you and offer my services as a spy of sorts. I have no doubt Hargreaves will see the benefit in my ability to speak with the Majority. Jac will not be able to plan anything without our knowledge but spur of the moment actions are ever unpredictable. Hopefully this will prevent Hargreaves goodwill from causing further problems. Let us return now and await the rest of the council's plans, my friend. Whatever will be, will be as Bob so loves to sing. I am surprised you haven't connected the dots on that one. You seem to have a lot of random knowledge tucked away in your brain but this has passed you by." Greg flashed John a skeletal grin that seemed somehow mischievous and horrific at the same time. The black and yellow eyes didn't help. They set off back to re-join their wider group, who had all gone through the assessment now, and returned to the impromptu living room in the marketplace. Evie and Max were still zooming around overhead as John got back. Greg went to sit with the old folks and began chatting with a few of them. John paused next to Agatha and said, "Excuse me Agatha-"

"Whatcha want boy? You better watch your back by the by, that nephew of mine isn't the gangster he fancies himself but he's been known to be sneaky. And mean. You keep an eye on your little girl you hear?"

"I will Agatha, I was told something similar a minute ago. This might seem strange but could you tell me who sang Que Sera Sera please?"

"Greg's a good boy. You might not understand, young people think they'll live forever but being old, knowing the end is near- well. Lot of us have a lot of respect for that man. You keep him safe you hear? That song was sung by Doris Day. I used to look like her, you know? So folks told me anyway, in my youth. I've got photo albums to prove it too! You doubt me then you come round one evening and I'll fix you and your little girl a proper meal and I can show the photos to you both, you'll see I ain't lying."

Doris. Day. Bob… did he really name his mecha after… With all that was going on John knew he should take time to appreciate the little things and he resolved to very much enjoy teasing Bob about his favourite poster girl. Smiling, John thanked Agatha and said he'd take her up on the offer of a meal if he got time. He sat back down little away from the group and lit up a smoke. He smiled his first genuine smile since yesterday morning, looking forward to teasing the old soldier about his love of a certain fifties movie star.

Someone had brought out a table and some chairs for the assessors around Hargreaves. It didn't take long until everyone had filed up and had their bonus' checked. Then Hargreaves' companion spent several minutes scanning through notes and turning pages so quickly John was impressed the pages didn't catch fire.

He had the ability Cogitator. John figured he knew what the man's ability let him do. It is by will alone I set my mind in motion. By the juice of sapho the lips acquire stains, the thoughts acquire speed, the stains become a warning he thought, remembering reading Dune as a teenager. A man to watch for sure. A mentat is going to make a huge difference to us as long he is on our side. I wonder if Hargreaves is the face for this human computer like Katie is for us? Is the Cogitator really in charge of things?

The man glanced up at John as if reading his thoughts. He leant over and spoke quietly to Hargreaves, handing him a sheaf of papers. Hargreaves stood and cleared his throat.

"Thank you all for being so helpful in this matter. With regards to the defences a colleague will circulate and approach all of you whom we feel are best able to help with the construction of a bastion of some sort. We will be drawing up the plans in the next 48 hours but will start clearing the area as soon as possible. I am happy to confirm we have access to three architects and a retired member of the Royal Engineers who will begin selecting a site and planning our fortress for the siege this afternoon. Many of you will be asked to help in this effort, we have seven days to prepare against an unknown threat but between us, with these new powers we have, we can build something to withstand any challenge, I am sure!"

He sighed and deflated slightly. He continued in a more subdued tone.

"With regards to the other urgent matter we have selected several of you whom we would ask to please help us action it. I know it is a terrible job we ask of you but we cannot allow disease to weaken us before the next wave, please could the following people come up to the table…"

He read out half a dozen names John didn't know and ended with Jennifer's and his own

John caught Jen's eye and they both set off to the table together. Most of the others named moved at inhuman speeds and arrived at the table well ahead of them.

"Mr. Borrows, if I were to ask you to provide seven cans each of red and green paint would you be able to accommodate my request?" asked the Cogitator in a flat voice.

John thought for a moment and the cans of paint appeared on the table along with seven paint brushes.

Teamchat:

Shinji: Oy! Stop nicking materials out of the stash John! I was going to use that stuff.

Houdini: Firstly it isn't yours, we stole it, remember? Secondly, Miss Day would like to say that as much as she appreciates you and your projects, we need this stuff so let it go.

Shinji: Oh ok then nevermind. Help yourself mate.

Mysterio: Miss Day?

Shinji: Never you mind! I'm busy dammit. Bob out.

Atlas: What just happened?

John smiled to himself as the Cogitator thanked him and continued in his robotic voice.

"The reason you have been selected for this job is that you are all fast. Inhumanely fast. It is a difficult request but I- we think the best way to handle this problem of the... bodies is for the movers to assess the town before we teleport the bodies to a suitable site to burn them."

"Movers? Burn them? Who put you in charge anyway?" one of the women who had been called up asked angrily.

"Movers are people whose abilities revolve around movement of course. I am developing a loose classification system for our powers. Movers, Elementalists, Shapers, Shifters and Thinkers are the broad categories I've isolated so far. I myself would be defined as a thinker. There is some crossover in certain cases, for instance, John, your Mr. Gillybrook seems to be both a Thinker and a Shaper I believe. Those of you who were named are all capable of moving very fast, one way or another, hence Movers. We propose that each of you take two tins of paint, one red and one green. You move quickly around town checking every open house and every street and alley. If there is anything to, ah, dispose of, you make a red mark pointing to it. If an area or building is clear you make a green mark. Mr. Borrows will move behind you and teleport any rat bodies to the pile he has made in the primary school playing fields and any human remains to another location nearby. Then we will ask some of the Elementalists, people who manipulate or create fire in this instance, to burn the bodies and prevent the spread of disease. In the meantime the rest of us will begin organising the work teams to clear land for the fortification."

There was general revulsion at the thought as Hargreave stood and met each of their gazes in turn. "This is a gruesome task, friends, but it must be done or many will fall sick. Please could the ones marking for John start to the east and north and come back once that area is done. John will follow behind and remove… whatever you find."

Chapter 31 - Almost a ritual

It was a dirty job but someone had to do it. John appreciated Greg giving him a heads up otherwise he might have baulked at what he was being asked to do. The speedsters sped off to the north and he followed along behind. They went through the site John's team had held yesterday at the start of the wave and it wasn't too bad. He had cleared up the worst of that area already. As the hours dragged on and John was forced to dispose of thousands of bodies, both rat and human, his mood became bleak.

Teamchat:
Baby Zeus: Hey old man, a bunch of the parents with older kids are happy for me to give out some Essences. I got permission this time. Are you cool with it too?

John thought for a moment, not about the request but about how Evie reaching out to him at this time had knocked him out of his malaise a little. His lips quirked into half a smile.

Teamchat:
Houdini: Fine by me sweetheart. You have fun ok? You might be one of the youngest but you've got a huge head start on them so if you're playing around you be careful ok? Don't zap anyone too hard :)
Baby Zeus: No worries Dad. Agatha cornered me a while ago, she's invited the whole team round for dinner tonight. When do you think you'll be done?
Houdini: I don't know, kid. There's still a lot of houses to go but shouldn't be more than another couple of hours.
Pause Button: Jac has refused to let the speedsters in to check for bodies. He says they'll take care of it themselves and we aren't

welcome in his part of town. You won't be covering anything west of the park.
Houdini: Ok. Thanks.

John hoped Jac was going to dispose of the bodies properly. If he just left them in a pile, or worse where they had fallen, there would be pests and disease running through his people in no time. He had a fire ability so he should be able to cremate them properly if he chose to. John continued with his horrible job. He was moving the human remains, usually not whole bodies, just the scattered parts that the rats had left behind when they'd broken into a home, to a separate place across the field from the rat pile. Zeeg was on site so he could lay them out neatly as much as possible. It was hard to do when all that was left was a tangle of chewed up limbs from three different people. His rage at the system had been steadily building and without Evie's message he would probably have lost it completely. He sat down on a bench on his way back from the industrial estate, lit a cigarette and summoned a beer. He hadn't seen any bodies when he passed by his old work. The factory was rubble but there wasn't anything he could dispose of. He was quietly grateful to have been spared that. He watched the birds flying in and out of the barrier across the road while he smoked and drank, wishing he could be as free.

He finished up, threw the can into a nearby bin and made his way across town to clear out as close to the traveller territory as he could. He stopped briefly as he came to the corpse of the Queen. She had curled up around the spike of stone and looked a little like a dead woodlouse. If a woodlouse was ten metres of armoured rat monster. John hated wood lice. He took a moment to admire the power of the thing's physique and wonder how on earth they had lucked into being able to deal with it. Then he blipped it to the pile in chunks before heading west.

Teamchat:

Houdini: Let Hargreaves know I'm done. I've gone as close to the travellers as I dare, there's a couple of groups following me around but not getting close or saying anything.

Pause Button: Thank you John, I know this must have been hard on you. We really appreciate it. Come back and we can discuss the next steps.

When he got back to the marketplace he found gangs of people going in and out of every building, ferrying all the stock from the shops across the square and into the town hall. They looked like they had picked clean most of the immediate area and were beginning to move onto the buildings further away.

"John, over here!" called Victoria, waving for him to come join them at the table with Hargreaves and his human computer.

The speedsters who had marked the buildings sat to one side, looking unhappy and angry. John nodded to them and got a round of subdued nods and lazy waves in response.

"Thanks John, and all of you." Hargreaves' gaze swept over the speedsters, "that can't have been easy. Miss Smith has volunteered to cremate the remains. Most people are busy clearing the buildings we are going to demolish tomorrow. My apologies, perhaps I should bring you up to speed on the plans? I have already announced the first steps to everyone else. We'll fortify the area around the town hall, using it as a temporary barracks and storage location. The plan is to construct what Bill, the ex Royal Engineer who is also a bit of a history buff, calls a star fort with a moat around it. Something about enfilading fire and covering all angles of approach. Greg assured me Bill knew what he was talking about but it might as well have been Greek as far as I was concerned!" He smiled in way that made John think of politicians and sharks.

"We will be demolishing all the buildings within half a mile to give us line of sight and deny the enemy cover then using the materials to create the walls. Bill is also planning a tunnel network beneath the town hall for medical facilities and bunkers for the children and elderly to shelter in during the attack. If you want more information, Tom here," he gestured at the Cogitator, "will be happy to provide it."

"I guess if you need earth moving that'll be my next job?" asked John flatly.

"Eventually, yes. Your ability will be very helpful for moving material quickly. We lack heavy construction vehicles so you'll be asked to pick up some of the slack on that front if you don't mind? That will be a problem for tomorrow though. First, those of us who aren't otherwise engaged need to go and pay our respects to those who passed yesterday and cremate the remains."

"Leave the kids here," said Sam, "No need for them to be there."

"I'll stay and keep an eye on them? I hate funerals anyway," offered Raoul, looking at John.

Me too, John thought. He nodded at Raoul and everyone else moved towards the school, leaving the big man behind. As they passed they picked up stragglers, the elderly and a handful of people who had stopped for a break from scavenging the shops and houses.

Around a hundred people walked out of the town centre and approached the school playing fields. John ported a section of the steel fence into Doris and they moved into the field. Zeeg came over and pressed her head into John's side before falling into step next to him. They approached the pile of rats and stood in silence for a moment. No one spoke but Hargreaves nodded and Victoria and two other flame users stepped forward and the pile erupted into white fire. The stench of burning hair was soon replaced with a disgustingly pleasant smell of roasting meat. John's stomach roiled and he felt nauseous.

They watched in silence as the pile burned down to ashes over ten minutes. Victoria's flames were so hot they flashed anything they touched into ash and gas almost instantly, turning what should have taken hours or even days into a much briefer conflagration. They moved over to the humans and repeated the process. Katie rested a hand on John's shoulder to help still his shaking. With a grim quiet hanging over them, the people turned and made their way back into town. Victoria had tears streaming down her face.

As they arrived Evie flew over and hugged her dad. "You know that girl who was a librarian at school like me? Anna? She has the Bibliophile ability! She can read super fast using her reserves and has perfect recall of anything she reads like that! Can you get her all your old books? You said you still had all your old textbooks from school and uni right? And a bunch of survivalist manuals and gardening books!"

He stuffed his misery from the cremation into a pocket in his mind and put on a more cheerful face for his daughter. "I'm not sure how much use 800 pages of biochemistry will be to her but sure kid. If she could memorise all my sci fi books I'd pay her in Essence! Just so if anything happens to them she can recite Heinlein stories to me around a campfire like a skald of old! I think audiobooks will be few and far between for a while. Maybe tomorrow I'll whizz round the library? Probably a good idea to keep all those books safe as well. Where do you want them?"

"Over by the Boss' table please?" Boxes of books blipped in where she had pointed. "Thanks Dad!" She levitated to kiss his cheek and flew off to help sort through the boxes with Anna.

"Greg's going to sit down with Hargreaves and keep him up to date on Jac's shenanigans. Come on John, let's go see what Bob's been up to. He's been very quiet in there," said Katie, catching his arm and dragging him over to the portal. John grumbled but allowed himself to be pulled along in her wake.

They went through and were shocked at what they saw and heard. The ceiling, some twenty metres up, was covered in a grid of rails running all the way across it and robot arms were shuttling back and forth, picking up and dropping crates and items according to some esoteric plan. Off to the right as they entered, the space had now been filled with a series of workshops, smelters, heavy machinery and production lines.

There was a constant clatter and clank as the arms on the ceiling moved back and forth, thumps as things were dropped into place, high pitched whines and screeches from somewhere within the tangle of manufacturing machinery as something was drilled or pressed. Bob had created an industrialist's dream in the microcosm of the storage space.

Bob was sitting in a chair, eyes closed and apparently in some sort of Zen state, his reserves clearly flowing around him in swirls of light as he enhanced and managed his machinery.

"Got any more of that steel fencing you sent me a while ago?" he asked without opening his eyes. A small box seemingly made entirely of optical lenses got to the end of a production line and four arms telescoped out from its top corners, tiny rotor blades at the ends whirred to life as it took off and flew a loop around John and Katie before parking itself neatly next to thirty identical machines off to the side.

John blipped the rest of the school's perimeter fence in and Bob nodded. "Thanks, sorry but this is taking a lot of concentration. If I keep at it a few more hours I should have it to the point where it's self regulating and I can take a break. Do you need something from me?"

"Wow Bob, this is… impressive. Yesterday Doris looked like she'd been cobbled together in a garage and now this? We just came in to see how you were doing but you are obviously keeping busy. Do you need anything?" asked Katie. A robot arm rattled overhead carrying a bottle of water, gently putting it down next to Bob.

"I'm good, thanks." He reached out, opened it and took a sip, all without opening his eyes. John was starting to feel like he was in some kind of panopticon. "I'll be out in a couple of hours I reckon. I'll need a proper night's sleep tonight!"

"Mind if we update the Cogitator and his boss about your new capabilities?" asked Katie.

"No worries, not entirely sure what the limit is at this point. Resource materials will soon be the bottleneck, I need resistors. Or non conducting materials at any rate. I'm putting together high capacity batteries with a simple enough transformer and limiter to output 240V through a three pin socket. Then if the grid does go down we can last for a few weeks at least. Lots of other things in the works as well," a bang echoed through the space as two robot arms had run into each other at speed on their tracks. "Shit, look sorry but I really need to concentrate, I'll go through what it can do tonight, ok?"

"No worries. Good work dude," said John as he and Katie made their way back outside.

At six o'clock the scavengers all came back into the marketplace and Hargreaves gave a short speech thanking everyone and asking them to come back at nine o'clock tomorrow morning. The crowd gradually dispersed and went back to their homes or moved into now empty places nearer the rest of their groups.

The Carnival and their allies said goodnight to the ones who had joined their group during the meeting, promising to meet back up tomorrow and then they made their way back to the bungalows. John ported back the furniture he had 'borrowed' earlier. Agatha caught up with John and insisted the whole team should join her for dinner that evening, it would be ready in two hours and she wouldn't accept no for an answer.

They took over two additional bungalows so they'd all have a bed to sleep in. Enough of the houses no longer had occupants that they didn't have to move anyone out to make space. John ported in their clothes and keepsakes as requested, Evie demanding her entire chest of drawers and wardrobe be brought over as well as a stack of manga she hadn't read yet. They got cleaned up and reported to Agatha's house at quarter past eight.

Agatha turned out to be a fantastic cook. The first course was French onion soup, followed by a boiled ham with vegetables and a suet pudding for dessert. John was thoroughly impressed and was feeling more like his usual self by the time she distributed crystal sherry glasses and poured them all a small glass of sickly sweet alcohol. Evie politely refused, fearing another trick like the whiskey yesterday.

Bob joined them halfway through the meal, stinking of the forge and was made to wash the dishes and himself before he was allowed to sit at the table. After the sherry they moved through into the living room and Agatha chatted away happily with them. Evie managed to nag Sam and Raoul into a game of Settlers of Catan. The collection of boardgames that John had gradually built up as a grid down form of entertainment was going to come in handy.

Agatha turned to John. "Young man, you looked like you doubted me earlier when I said I was the spitting image of Doris Day when I was a girl. Give me a moment." Bob flinched and shot a sharp look at John who tried to look innocent, but failed.

Agatha opened a cabinet and began rooting through a stack of photo albums before carefully pulling one from the bottom and bringing it to the coffee table. She began leafing through black and white photos until she found one she liked and she passed it to John. A beautiful young woman smiled at the camera, clutching the arm of a man in a sharp looking suit. She wore a floral dress and looked like she was on top of the world.

"That's my Ronald, he passed away a few years ago. Greg says he has moved on and didn't linger which is good to know. But don't you think the likeness to Doris is remarkable?"

John considered the picture and smiled. "You know I'm not too sure what Miss Day looked like, Agatha." He passed the photo to Bob sitting next to him, nursing his sherry and twitching. "What do you think Bob? Does Agatha look like Doris?"

Teamchat:

Baby Zeus: I knew you were talking crap about the Destroyer ordinance whatever!

Pause Button: Did you really name your killing machine after a 1950s actress?

Shinji: Bollocks to the lot of you!

Atlas: Bwahahaha! Anyone (other than Bob) remember how any of her songs went?

Bob took the photo and looked it over then smiled at Agatha. "You really could have been her sister, Agatha. Very pretty and your fella looked like a right dapper gentleman." He passed the photo back and Agatha preened with pride.

They talked for a while longer as the game played out, Evie claiming the win largely due to the others being new to the rules. The mood was still a little sombre despite the occasional jokes at Bob's expense. After an hour or so they excused themselves, thanked Agatha for the meal and made their way back to their beds.

Victoria had been given the third bedroom of the bungalow John and Evie were in. Evie grabbed the bathroom to brush her teeth and came out briefly before she shot into her room saying she was going to read for a while and wished them goodnight.

This struck John as odd, Evie had a process, almost a ritual for going to bed, and this was out of character for her. She didn't even ask for supper, which would normally be chocolate. John was confused but chalked it up to the stress of the last two days. John was staring after her, wondering if he should go in and speak to her to check she was ok when Victoria passed him on the way to her room. She paused at the door, halfway through and looked at him.

"John… if you need to talk, or don't want to be alone, you can just knock on my door, ok mate? I'll put the kettle on and we can sit in the living room to chat." She smiled and John was shocked by how beautiful and vulnerable she looked.

"Thanks Vic, but I'll be ok. Seriously, you go get some sleep. Goodnight."

"The offer's always there John. Goodnight." The door swung shut behind her.

"C'mon pup," said John, looking down at Zeeg, "Lets see how much of the bed you try to steal now you're twice the size you were eh?" He opened his door and went in, trying to push the image of brilliant green eyes out of his mind.

Chapter 32 - Thanks Dad, sorry Dad

Evie read in bed for a while. She had gotten the newest manga in her current series a week ago and hadn't started it yet. Now seemed as good a time as any. She listened to Vic and her dad talk and shook her head. *The dude has trust issues, he needs more friends.*

She heard her dad go through to his room and argue quietly with the dog, who apparently wanted more than her usual three quarters of the bed, before she heard his light click off and it became quiet. She turned her light off and lay staring at the ceiling. She focussed on not going to sleep. She had a Quest to do tonight and she knew her dad would stop her if he found out. She turned off the hide and seek bonus thing so he couldn't sense where she was anymore. It was honestly worse than that phone tracking thing he had her install!

She had seen Ryan being dragged off by his stupid parents earlier and she was going to go and help her friend. After what felt like forever but was only 45 minutes according to the lying alarm clock by the bed she rolled over quietly, wincing as a spring groaned beneath her and pulled out the clothes she had hidden under her bed. Dad had told her off more than once for how noisily she clomped around the house and he had shown her how to move quietly, laying each foot down gently, either flat to the ground or by rolling slowly from the heel to the toes. With practice you could walk at normal speeds nearly silently, barring dodgy floorboards. It had been more of a lecture than being shown if she was honest. Handy to know but thankfully it was not an issue on this occasion. *Thanks Dad, sorry Dad,* she thought.

She dressed quietly, standing on an electromagnetic disc floating six inches above the carpet. She floated over to the window and very slowly slid the handle up and pushed it open. Jen and the new guy had first watch tonight so she didn't need to worry about Greg and his creepy dead spies seeing what she was doing. She'd be back before they even noticed her gone anyway. She pulled up her hood and dressed head to toe in black she gently pushed the window closed behind her and sped off into the night.

She flew high to avoid being spotted, revelling in the freedom of flight. She made her way west, stopping at the park to fly a little lower and place Ryan's house. She flew back up and moved to about where she thought it would be before lowering herself slowly, watching out for any of Jac's people. She froze in mid air as she watched a group of men pass by beneath her. They were talking amongst themselves and showing off with their abilities. None of them thought to look up.

Like bloody kids, what idiots, she thought. *I've got to play this smart. I'm like a ninja, what would a ninja do? Appear in a cloud of smoke and riddle her enemy with throwing stars? Maybe I should get a feel for the defences and patrols first...*

The patrols only made her job harder but they were regular which mitigated the challenge. She couldn't fly out anyone but herself so Ryan and probably his parents, she admitted to herself reluctantly, would have to make it out on foot. She could zap any of Jac's men no problem but then this went from 'a kids silly high jinks' to a 'you're in deep shit now child' kind of situation.

She hovered silently in the sky, now sitting cross legged on her disc and trying to get a feel for the rhythm of the patrols. After half an hour she felt the time was right and she zipped down to Ryan's back garden and froze, floating in the shadows. She listened intently for any sign of alarm or shouts to indicate that she had been spotted. After five tense minutes and no sign of any reaction she floated up to Ryan's window and gently tapped on it. After a couple of minutes of persistent, gentle tapping the curtains twitched and Ryan looked out in shock. He cracked the window open and leant out.

"Evie, what the hell are you doing here? Jac will go mental if he catches any of your side creeping around in the night!" he whispered.
"That guy couldn't catch a cold, and I'm flying about, not creeping!" she said quietly. "Come on, I'm here for the rescue, get some stuff and we can sneak out. Once we're past the park I can call in reinforcements." She smiled and made 'hurry up' gestures.
"Ryan what's going on?" The bedroom door swung open and the light turned on, highlighting Evie floating outside the window.
"Dad, uh nothing Dad, I heard a noise is all."
"Would that noise have anything to do with the little girl floating outside your window by any chance?" He hissed. "You're the Borrows kid, Evie right? You know Jac is out for your dad's blood? If he catches you, you're in deep trouble. He catches you here with us then we're in serious trouble as well, he's paranoid enough already. Go on now, fly home quick." He wafted his hands at Evie.
"I'm not leaving without Ryan, I'm here to rescue you. Their patrols are crap, they're just walking in circles, we let one pass then follow behind them till we can bolt across the park. Then we're clear. Easy peasy. Why don't you get some stuff and let's go already?"
"Dammit girl, get in here and let's shut the window." He sighed and paused for a moment. "Fine. We'll grab some stuff and give it a shot. Jac is insane and I don't want Ryan and Janet to be anywhere near him."
Evie flew inside and landed gracefully on the carpet, her disc dissolving. Ryan's dad showed her downstairs and told her to wait while he got his wife and Ryan ready.
He left the lights out to hopefully not draw any more attention to the house. Ten minutes later the family came downstairs dressed and Ryan's dad was carrying a stuffed rucksack. Evie was perched peeking out of the window and whispered "They've just gone past. We give it

three minutes then we follow, head left at the street and turn left again at the end to get us to the bottom of the park, four minutes walking and we are safe."

"Hi Evie, been a while, I thought you and Ryan had fallen out? You know you're a weird kid? But thanks for coming to get us I suppose," said Ryan's mum.

"I can fry any of Jac's assholes. I'm level eleven and they're all fours and fives. If I wake my Dad with the team chat he can teleport us out easy peasy or blip in and turn them all into chum."

"Wake your dad? He doesn't know you're here?"

"Uh, he knows but he was pretty tired so he left me to it and took a nap," Evie shifted uncomfortably.

"Jesus Christ there is no back up or reinforcements is there? It's just a crazy kid trying to get herself killed! Janet, Ryan we are not going anywhere."

"Oh it's much too late to change your mind now. You're definitely going to go somewhere." The voice came from the shadows in the kitchen door. It was male yet weirdly high pitched and nasal. "But I'm afraid it's up to me to decide where that is, especially for the cripple's girl."

Evie's hands lit up as balls of lightning sprung into being and her right arm swung back to throw but the man stepped into the light and pointed a shotgun at Ryan. He was short and skinny and she discovered he had the Stalker ability at level six with a quick Identify. Sid the Stalker. *You couldn't make it up,* she thought.

"Careful now sugarplum, wouldn't want anyone to get hurt would you? Why not get rid of the sparkles? We could play my little pony later if you like. Friendship is magic after all and it would be such a shame if anything *untoward* was to happen to your friend, eh?"

*Ah shit. Dad **is** gonna kill me if this prick doesn't, she thought as she let her power fade.*

Evie and Ryan's family were shepherded out into the street at gunpoint. Evie knew she could theoretically kill Sid and the men who came around the corner to herd them along if she wanted to. She wasn't sure she'd be able to go through with something like that though. She wasn't sure she could deal with them before someone else got hurt so she chose to bide her time. She seriously considered messaging the team but they would all be asleep, Jen's group was taking care of the watch tonight.

They were led through the streets until they got a house ablaze with lights shining through the curtains. It had a handful of men standing guard outside. Evie and Ryan's family were pushed inside and they found nearly thirty people crammed into the living room, two men with shotguns standing at one end were keeping an eye on everyone. As they were shoved into the room Sid said, "Have fun now little one." He dissolved into the shadows and vanished.

Ryan's dad moved off to one side, dragging his son and wife along. They sat and started talking with some people he must have known from before, pointedly ignoring her. Ryan shot her apologetic looks in about the same number as his mum shot her angry ones. *Hardly my fault this happened*, she grumbled to herself. Jac was clearly cleaning house of people he didn't like. She sat by herself and tried to think. Dad could get her out of here no problem when he woke up but she was pretty sure Ryan and maybe even some of these other people would be in deep trouble if he did. She had thought she wouldn't care about the rest of the people but she found her recently acquired ruthlessness didn't last long when she was watching scared and defenceless people whispering to each other and shooting terrified glances at their captors.

Now she needed to figure a way out of this for herself and a way to help them all. She could use her elemental body, electrocute the guards and get everyone to run but she had a feeling that creepy git Sid was watching her from somewhere. She knew they couldn't hurt her with the guns. She became immune to physical damage when she shifted forms and mundane, old school firearms were definitely physical damage. She checked herself, her making assumptions had gotten her into a bad situation already, she couldn't afford any more mistakes. She was considering sucking the power out the house to plunge it into darkness before frying Jac's goons when she heard the front door open. *Probably for the best I didn't go through with that plan* she thought, *with the grid up I'd be draining it for hours.*

Jac walked into the living room with a grin on his face.

"Hello little girl, whatever were you doing in my part of town this evening? Not safe to be out at night on your own at your age! What kind of father would let his only daughter run around at this time?" He laughed and gestured for Sid, who appeared next to Evie as though he'd been sitting there all along, to bring her through into the kitchen with him.

"Now kid, if you play nice I promise I won't hurt you or your dad ok?" Evie knew he was lying. "But he disrespected me and he needs to learn his place. What I need from you now is some information. Where are they staying, what are their powers and how did he know my level?"

Evie looked down. I could fry him... can I kill him? I don't think I can. Time to do some lying instead.

Evie raised watery eyes and glanced at Jac before looking back down at her feet. "Bob built a gizmo to scan levels."

"Bob?"

"The guy with the mecha," Jac looked blankly at her, "the giant robot?"

"Oh, some gadget? Anyone can use it?" She nodded timidly. "That's going on the list then. Where are they?

"Northfield Close, we're staying near my house," Evie lied again. If they went in force they'd be nearby but the watch would have a chance to wake everyone.

"And finally their powers? How strong are they?"

"Really strong. Lot's of fire abilities, time and space, a good spread of offence and defence. I don't know all the details, I'm just a kid! I'm so sorry, please don't hurt me, I'm just a little girl!" She burst into tears and buried her face in her hands. *And the Oscar goes to…*

Jac stood, losing interest in her and gesturing for Sid to return her to the other room. He turned to another man, "Take the cripple a message. We've got his daughter. We'll trade her for everything he stole or we'll send her to him in bits. We'll meet outside the Old Swan at ten tomorrow morning. Maybe don't deliver it to the cripple in person? That might be bad for your health."

The man swallowed audibly, nodded and left the building. Jac followed him with a broad grin on his face. No matter how much he smiled it never reached his eyes.

Evie bunkered down in the living room with the other hostages and gradually "calmed down". She had worried she'd overdone it at the end there but Jac was apparently as dumb as he was smug. She moved over to Ryan, ignoring his scowling parents.

"You ok? What did the bastard want?" he asked.

"I'm fine!" She smiled. "That tosser is in for a world of hurt, Ryan. We just need to hang tight and not piss off these guards for a few hours," she whispered.

"What is wrong with you? You know these are all the people Jac doesn't trust, right?" hissed Ryan's dad. "He's going to kill us unless he gets what he wants. Your dad had better bend the knee or we are all screwed."

"Dad won't bend the knee. I can promise you that. That's why the prick is in for a world of hurt. Assuming Dad doesn't go mental when he finds out Jac has me. If he does then you guys are probably in trouble. I'm sure he'll try to help you but he might just go on a rampage until I'm safe if he spazzes out. I can fry these guys if things go sideways so you're probably alright, thinking about it. I'm only still here because they'll kill you if I leave and I don't want to kill them but… I guess I will if I have to. None of them can keep me here and guns won't work on me," she murmured.

Ryan's dad sat back and shook his head. "Guns don't work on you? You're mad. We're screwed. A fucking crazy child is going to get us all killed. These people are insane Evie, the powers have driven them over the edge! Your dad's just a sad old shut in for god's sake."

"Dad would probably agree with you on the last part so I won't take it personally. Up until yesterday he was anyway. Look, chin up buddy, it will all be over in a few hours and I won't tell Dad what you said about him." She grinned and continued quietly, "Yo, deadites, I know you're watching. Tell Greg to stop Dad flying off the handle when he finds out, tell him to sort it at the meeting. And tell him I'm really, *really* sorry as well please. Thank you deadies!"

"Who is Greg? What the hell are the deadites? You- you *are* insane. Stay away from us, kid," he finished in a low growl.

Evie ignored him and looked to Ryan, "It'll be fine, trust me." She winked, "I'm going to stretch out over there and try and get some sleep. You guys got a blanket in that bag I could borrow? No? Ok then, see you in the morning, it'll be an interesting day I promise!" said

Evie quietly, sharing an evil smile that did little to reassure her friend and even less to comfort his parents.

Chapter 33 - You... Don't... Threaten... My... Family

John awoke from a pleasant dream filled with emerald green eyes framed by black hair. He found Greg sat next to his bed, petting Zeeg quietly.

"Dude, I thought the whole 'my dead mates are watching you take a crap' bit was the creepiest anyone could be expected to manage but this is a whole new level. Well played. If you don't mind me asking... Why the fuck are you sat next to my bed please?" he finished harshly. Sitting up he noticed Raoul on the other side. "Et tu Raoul? Am I naked under this duvet? Do we need to have a discussion about boundaries?"

Greg began to explain the situation with Evie. As soon as he saw John's face change expression he gestured quickly to Raoul who punched John in the side of the head and knocked him out cold.

"How'd he take it?" asked Sam as Raoul walked into the living room shaking his right hand out.

"Like a champ. The guy's skull is made of steel or something. You wouldn't think it, what with him being all skinny-fat and fragile looking. You meant the Evie situation... not well, would be an understatement as to how he took it and he's going to be pissed at me for knocking him out."

"You punched him! What for?" asked Victoria.

"He can teleport. John could end up anywhere and do anything and we need to stick to Greg's plan. That's why Raoul went in with Greg in the first place, to- uh settle John down if he was going to fly off the hook," said Katie.

"It was Evie's plan, kinda. That girl is in for a bollocking later!" added Bob. Reg chuckled nastily in agreement and took a bite of toast.

"So what do we do when he wakes-"

"MOTHERFUCKER! I AM GOING TO KILL THAT SUBHUMAN SHITSTAIN!"

"I guess we'll find out."

TEAMCHAT:

Houdini: WHERE ARE YOU EVIE?

Baby Zeus: I'm fine dad. I'm in a house near the park.

Houdini: WHICH HOUSE?

Pause Button: Calm down John, please. She isn't hurt and Hargreaves has a plan to fix this. We can make it work to his advantage.

Houdini: Fuck that pricks plan, Katie and screw his advantage. Where are you, child? Why the hell can't I find you with the hide and seek champion thing?

Baby Zeus: I turned it off. You need to calm down and stick to the plan Dad, please.

Houdini: Tell me where you are. Now.

Baby Zeus: I can't. It was dark when they moved us here. I didn't see the house number or anything. Listen to Greg, the plan is good, Dad. Please, trust me?

Houdini: We will be having words Evie. A lot of words.

John appeared in the living room in his PJs and stopped when he saw everyone waiting for him.

"You all knew about this?" His eyes narrowed as he glared at them.

"They sent someone in the night to arrange an exchange. Jen woke Greg, the Majority caught him up, and he got the rest of us out of bed. Nice PJs by the way, tartan suits you. Reminds me of-" said Sam.

"But you let me sleep in while my daughter is held hostage?" he asked in a low and dangerous tone.

Katie cut in. "Look at how you're reacting, John. We couldn't let you go off like a loose cannon. Evie's not in any danger, she's only still there because she can't get everyone else out and she is worried they'll kill people if she leaves."

"He has more hostages?"

"Twenty odd. He arranged a purge to round up all the doubting Thomas' in his faction, all very night of the long knives. He took prisoner all the ones he didn't trust or didn't have leverage on according to the Majority. Late last night his thugs gathered them up and his hench-creep happened to catch Evie as she was trying to get her friend and his family out. They were on his 'unreliable' list."

"Fucks sake." He sighed. "What's this bloody plan then?" he sat down and ported in a smoke.

"Should you be smoking here?" asked Raoul.

John gave him a flat look. "Yes. And I owe you for that sucker punch." He rubbed his left temple before lighting up and blowing a cloud of smoke into the room. At that moment he didn't give a damn about how impolite it was to smoke indoors these days.

Greg ran through the details. Jac had requested John and no more than five other people come to a meeting outside the Old Swan pub at ten o' clock. John checked his phone: 45 minutes to go.

Katie took over from Greg. "We want you to take Hargreaves and some of the other leaders of the minor groups. Let them see what Jac is up to so we can keep people on side. You do the exchange, port him in a load of food or booze or whatever he asks for, we'll get it all back within a couple of hours anyway, then you get Evie and bring her home. *Then* the tribes unite and we go out with a show of force. His guys back down and there doesn't have to be any unpleasantness. It's the best way to avoid a civil war and that could cripple us. We need to focus on the next wave."

"Alright, I understand. I'm *very* not happy at being the last to know, in case it wasn't obvious. I think we can improve this plan a little bit though. Sam, you can do the active camouflage thing right?"

"You mean the blending in, mixing and merging the light? Yeah sure. Why?"

"Yeah, the Predator thing you showed us before. Show Zeeg please." Sam briefly disappeared and then returned to normal. "Can your shapeshifting do the same, girl?" John asked his dog. She cocked her head to one side and looked at Sam again before blurring out and reappearing. She looked back to John and nodded.

"Good girl. You and Sam are going to find where these shits are keeping the other hostages and set up shop nearby, just watch and stay in stealth. That prick might have some sort of system where if anything goes wrong the guards get orders to kill hostages or something. You guys will be in place to stop that."

They both nodded.

Teamchat:

Houdini: Kid, we're sending some backup in case things go sideways at the meeting. Zeeg and Sam will be on hand just in case. Better to have it and not need it, than need it and not have it. Do not tell the other hostages.

Baby Zeus: Couldn't even if I wanted to, Jac and his goons just collected me, we're going to be there early.

Houdini: I'll set off now then, no point letting him set up an ambush.

"Will your new best friend Hargreaves and his mates be ready yet?" John asked Katie coldly.

"Should be, we can set off now, we were planning to meet at the town hall in twenty minutes."

"They are already there," announced Greg in his graveyard voice.

John dressed hurriedly and the team headed into town. It was only a five minute walk and they found Hargreaves and four other councillors waiting for them by the side of the road outside the town hall.

"Mr. Borrows, I can only imagine how you must be feeling. Thank you so much for agreeing to this. I can assure you we will do all in our power to make sure your daughter is returned safely and to free the other hostages."

"Thank you," John ground out through clenched teeth. "The other side is already on the way to the meeting, we should set off now." Katie rested a hand on John's arm and gave him a reassuring smile. The others all made comforting sounds and comments, only Victoria didn't, staring at him with a grim face as he caught her eye. He nodded to her then turned away and blipped himself and the councillors twenty metres up the road from the Old Swan pub.

"What the hell?" exclaimed one of the councillors. "We were supposed to walk!" It was the man who had called Jac out at the meeting yesterday. John regretted startling him for a moment but found on balance he didn't particularly care.

"This was quicker. They'll be here soon. I'm not good at negotiating so I'm trusting you to cover that side of things, Mr. Hargreaves," John turned a frigid stare on the man.

"Of course John, we'll get your daughter back and resolve this peacefully. We'll have witnesses from outside your group who can explain what happens to everyone else."

Jac rounded the corner holding an old over and under shotgun pointed casually at Evie who was being pushed along next to him. John took a hold of himself as he felt his temper begin to spill over. Jac was followed by a dozen thugs that John quickly identified. A couple of Elementalists, one fire and one air, and the rest were bruisers and shifters of various kinds. Their abilities sounded like they had physical enhancements or they could shapeshift into combat forms. One of them had the Werewolf ability which John would have found pretty cool and spent some time asking the guy about under other circumstances.

"Early I see! Eager to give back what you stole from me are you?" called Jac. John remained silent. Jac and his associates came to a stop ten metres away from John and the councillors, spreading out into a loose half circle. Two of the lackeys had shotguns as well, both were kept pointed at Evie.

"You alright kid?" asked John, ignoring the soon to be irrelevant asshole.

"Didn't get much sleep but otherwise yeah I'm good. Before we go any further, I just want to say I'm *really* sorry Dad. I just wanted to help my friend."

"I know kid. We'll be having words later though," he said with a sad smile. "This was not your finest hour, Sausage." Evie looked down, unable to meet her fathers eyes.

"Well, isn't this touching? I'm afraid you won't be having any words ever again unless I get what I deserve."

"And what do you think you deserve?" asked one of the councillors.

It's not what he thinks but he is going to get it, thought John with a vicious glee that he hid from his face. He hoped the system messing with their emotions was why he felt no qualms about what he was planning to do.

"We want the gadget that can assess other people's levels, *all* the food he stole and reparations. I think your lot and ours aren't really meant to mix but if you lend us say half your people to work on our defences for the siege, that would be fair."

"Are you insane?" bellowed Hargreaves, "You're holding hostages and you want us to send you slaves, effectively more hostages, and all the food left in town?"

"Sounds about right." Jac grinned evilly. "Or we could let John see what his daughter's brains look like?" He gestured with the gun pointed at Evie's head. "It's really your call. I don't want to do it but if you force my hand..."

"How on earth have we forced your hand?" asked another councillor. "We did nothing but refuse to persecute someone you have a grudge against. What the hell would you have had us do anyway? Prison won't work very well with a teleporter!"

"The cripple owes me," spat Jac. "So you lot have to pay. Should have just handed him over before but no you idiots voted to fuck me over so now all of this is on you! Hand over the gadget and the food."

John looked blankly at Hargreaves who was fuming but still in control of himself. He nodded at John who then began porting in pallets of dry goods and tins of food.

"You see boys, with the right leverage you can move the world, just like I told you."

"Nice one, Dad!" replied one of the goons moving to look at the goods. *Ah, his son. That will be rough,* thought John.

"You've got what you asked for. Release the girl," Hargreaves said in a reasonable voice.

"Now why on earth would I do that?"

Teamchat:

Mysterio: We've found them. House near the top of the park. A dozen or so guys standing outside, bunch of them with shotguns.

Supa-Poopa: Should I take them down? They're bad men and scared my sister.

Baby Zeus: Aw, I'm your sister? Love you too pooper!

Houdini: No. Wait. We've got this. Kid, focus. You're meant to be scared right now.
Pause Button: Meant to be scared? What's going on over there John?
"I'm holding all the cards now! That cripple will do as I say as long as I've got his brat and none of you can move against him, he's too useful and too difficult to control. Well, I found a way to control him. Am I right?" He gripped Evie's arm tightly, making her wince. "No way am I giving up this kind of leverage. I want half of your people working for us to prepare for the siege. You know what's funny? She isn't the only hostage I've got! Show them the pictures Dave."
Jac's son, who John had dropped in the rat pile the night before last, stepped forward with a tablet and turned it around so the councillors could see. A couple of dozen people sat in a room with armed men behind them in a picture. He swiped to the side and flicked through a few pictures to reinforce the point. He sneered and tossed the tablet at John's feet.
"We didn't want you getting any ideas about attacking us when you heard my terms. See, forward planning is great, right?"
"Give me my daughter and I'll let you live." John's voice was emotionless. He spoke mechanically and sounded like a bad AI.
"Oh stop playing the big man." Jac squeezed Evies arm, "are you sure you want to cause a ruckus right now?" The shotgun was pointed straight at Evie's temple.
Teamchat:
Houdini: We're changing the plan. Evie, lightning form and stun. Don't kill any of them. That's my job.
Baby Zeus: Bout time!
Pause Button: John, what's happening?

Supa-Poopa: Dad got tired of playing nice with them. Our pack is the strongest!

Evie flashed into a being of pure energy and Jac recoiled with a yell, arcs of electricity burning his hand and arm. He pulled the trigger reflexively and the buckshot passed straight through Evie and struck one of his own men in the leg who screamed and collapsed. Evie moved like, well, lightning. She flickered through the goons, shocking them and leaving them writhing on the concrete.

"John, wait! Obey me!" called Hargreaves.

Obey me? Good fucking luck with that. John advanced a few steps and leant down to look Jac in the eyes. The man stared back in terror, seeing in John a man who, temporarily at least, knew no limits and would not be adhering to civilised behaviour.

"YOU" Jac's right arm vanished and he screamed, blood spraying out.

"DON'T" the left arm vanished just as he had moved it to clutch at the wound.

"THREATEN" Jac howled and babbled for mercy as his right leg vanished and he collapsed to the ground.

"MY" Jac looked at his last remaining limb in terror and wept as it disappeared as well.

"FAMILY" Jac's wailing face was a mask of agony. His scream was cut off as his head vanished, leaving only a bleeding torso surrounded by arcs of crimson behind.

John looked up at Jac's men who had dropped their weapons after being shocked by Evie. Most of them were slowly regaining their feet and backing away, terrified by what John had done to their leader.

"Dad!" cried Dave, Jac's son, lunging towards the remains of his father.

Evie appeared at her fathers side, turned back into her human form and reached out to catch his left hand in hers. John turned cold blue eyes on the rest of Jac's men, and the man's only son. In rapid sequence all of them vanished, one by one, leaving Jac's torso lying in the street.

Chapter 34 - An offer I can't refuse?

"Damn, Dad," muttered Evie, still clutching John's hand. "I guess the system wasn't joking about the 'this will get messy' thing."

"John, what the hell have you done? We'll never get the rest of them to join us now!" snapped Hargreaves.

"Tell them if they don't join they'll get the same as that prick." John gestured at the dismembered torso at his feet. "Sometimes a little terror works wonders. Ask Stalin. Just keep anyone who was "loyal" to Jac well away from me."

"We aren't bloody Soviet Russia you fool! How on earth-"

Teamchat:

Mysterio: The guards are moving. We heard the gunshot. You guys ok?

John borrowed Zeeg's eyes for a moment and then appeared at the end of the line of guards. He started with the man closest to him. Porting the man four and a half kilometres straight up and then worked quickly down the line. In moments the guards were all gone, the last one had just begun to turn his shotgun towards John when he vanished into the sky. John blipped to the window and removed the men watching the people in the house. *It's not the fall you need to worry about, it's the ground*, he thought. *If they hit the barrier I hope it doesn't count as me attacking it and I get melted!*

He removed most of the wall in front of him and blipped Katie and the rest of the team in, then returned to Evie and the councillors.

Teamchat:

Mysterio: Fucking hell John! What did you just do?

Houdini: I dealt with it, Sam. Katie, I'm sorry but please could you deal with getting those people back to town and away from there? I'm not in the best frame of mind at the moment.
Pause Button: That's a fucking understatement. We were all watching through Zeeg. What the hell did you do to Jac? Dammit. Yes, I'll deal with these people. You shouldn't be allowed anywhere near them. You need to speak to Hargreaves. Politely.
Supa-Poopa: Our pack is the strongest. It is as it should be.
Atlas: Oh great now the dog's Nietzsche! John, you're such a bad example! On a side note, totally unrelated, I'm reeeeaaally sorry about punching you earlier.

As John arrived back with his daughter he looked up and down the street for a moment. He blipped the supplies he had dropped for Jac back into Doris' stash.

"We should talk," he told the councillors. He removed a foot wide circle in the middle of the pub's doors, teleporting away the lock, and pushed at them. The left door was bolted top and bottom so it refused to move but the right one swung open and John went in followed by Evie and the politicians. He headed over to the bar, flicking the lights on as he went past the switches.

"Been a while since I've been on this side of a bar. Or even in a pub at all to be honest! What can I get you to drink, sirs?" he asked in a light voice.

He put ice in a glass and topped it up with lemonade before passing it to Evie who took a long drink and hopped up onto a barstool.

John pulled a pint of Guinness three quarters full and set it to the side to let it settle before topping it off. He couldn't hold the glass in the right place, lacking a second hand, so the head looked like it would take a while before he could top it up.

"I'll have the same," said the councillor who had called out Jac at the meeting yesterday, gesturing at the Guinness. John pulled another one. He was called Michael, level four and had an ability with the rather weird name of Moon Dancer. God only knows what it meant so John decided to not worry about it. Probably an MJ fan or something.
"Pass the whiskey and some glasses please," said Hargreaves with a sigh. The bottle from the top shelf and some tumblers appeared on the bar in front of him and Hargreaves poured out doubles for himself and the rest of the councillors present. The rest of the bottles on the shelves vanished into Doris. Waste not, want not. John reminded himself to clear out the cellar as well. Bob could probably rig up a system to get the beer out of the barrels.
"Teleportation is pretty handy for bar work as well it seems," said John.
"And causing a massive fucking stink, boy. We will have to play this very carefully. I will not be involving you beyond the bare minimum as I do *not* think you will stick to any plan unless it suits you. I see now why Miss Johnson always represents your group. You also need to dispose of the *bits* you left behind as soon as we are done here. Understood?" John nodded.
"That's perhaps a little unfair," said one of the other councillors, "How would you react to a lunatic holding a gun to your daughter's head? If you had the power to make the lunatic go away, forever, wouldn't you use it?" He tipped his glass at John.
"I wouldn't chop him into pieces in front of people in the process," replied Hargreaves darkly, taking a long drink from his tumbler.
Fair point. But at least they aren't all terrified of me. Dammit, Hargreaves is right about the consequences as well, John thought. Some of those bastards will have had girlfriends, wives, maybe even kids who will now be out to slip a knife between my

ribs any chance they get. If they are very stupid or just don't care they might even go after Evie. The kind of unity he wanted probably isn't possible anymore.

"I agree with you, Hargreaves and I'm sorry for the political issues I've caused. However I'm not sorry for what I did... Jac did say he would get what he deserved and I made it happen. As long as no one is holding a gun to my daughters head I can and will play nicely, like I did yesterday carting off all the bloody corpses for you. I don't mind being given very shitty jobs to do if I'm the best person to do them but threats to my family or my friends will be met with, well, what Jac and his goons got. As long as that's understood, I'll work with you to fix this as best I can."

The pints of Guinness had settled enough so John topped them up, passed the first one to Michael then took a long sip of his own.

Team Report:
18 level 4 Humans killed. 7 Essence per kill. Essence gained 126.
8 level 5 Humans Killed. 12 Essence per kill. Essence gained 96.
Total Essence gained: 222.

"Oh wow, that's awesome" said Evie.

"What is Evie?" asked Hargreaves.

Teamchat:
Pause Button: Well this just got even worse.
Houdini: Evie, do not tell Hargreaves about this. We can't let anyone know. We each got the total of their used essence. If anyone takes out one of us then their ENTIRE TEAM gets over 200 Essence each. We'd be hunted down! Hell, it would probably be the ethical thing to do to prepare for the siege! Get a load of level ones in a team, kill one of us and they're ALL level eleven. Rinse and repeat until we're all dead and there are a hundred new level elevens.
Atlas: Shit, he's probably not far off. This system sucks.

Pyro: This has to be kept quiet. John's probably being a touch paranoid because we should be able to look out for ourselves, however I can see scared people trying to get stronger, taking out someone they have a grudge with... everything would fall apart. We'd kill ourselves off without the system lifting a finger.
Mysterio: You can't "look out" for poison in your food or your throat being slit while you're asleep! John is right. Do not level! Everyone knows about Identify now and they all know the highest levelled people are at eleven, if we suddenly gain levels they'll figure it out.
Pause Button: Agreed. No one can know about this.

After a short pause Evie replied out loud "Oh, I got a lump of ice, see?" She held a lump of ice between her teeth and showed everyone. "It's been ages since I got to crunch ice! That's awesome," she finished lamely and began crunching the ice cube noisily.

Teamchat:
Houdini: Good effort child. We might still be able to use the Essence. I worked out how much free Essence we all had yesterday, it was a lot and it just became a hell of a lot. We can offer to share some of it out to level people with useful abilities up.
Supa-Poopa: We shouldn't weaken the pack Dad. We should take the power ourselves.
Atlas: Sorry Zeeg but I think it's a good idea. Not sure how I feel about using Essence taken from a human for myself or passing it off to other people, feels a bit like tricking them into cannibalism or something, but if we can use it to help everyone we should.
Corpsicle: I agree with John. This is an excellent idea. Please make the offer to Hargreaves. It would go some way to restoring

your reputation with the man as well. We will need his goodwill in the days and weeks to come.

Pause Button: Agreed. Run the numbers so we can each share two thirds or so of the essence needed for our next levels. We'll still have enough to boost our levels in the wave if we need to.

"Hargeaves, I've got an offer for you."

"An offer I can't refuse? How very cartoonish of you John," said Hargeaves, focussing on him over the top of his tumbler of amber liquid which had emptied considerably.

"What? Of course not! Look… The Carnival has a bunch of Essence we can't use. Not enough for any of us to reach the next levels, well maybe a couple of levels for us if we combine it but it's lots of levels for others. Your human computer has figured out how the level requirements increase?"

"Tom? Yes, he told me it's a Fibonacci sequence. Early levels come quickly but become exponentially more difficult to acquire as you progress."

"We've got about 300 floating Essence between us currently. I, we, were hoping to offer the spare to allow you to boost up people with useful skills to help prepare for the siege."

"Essence can be traded? Ah so that is how Evie unlocked the children's powers! We had been wondering about that. This is great news! I need to speak to Tom, he'll be able to work out how best to use it. 300? How much is that in terms of levels?"

"It is enough to push two people at level eleven to level twelve… just, or a level one to level eleven with about seventy Essence leftover. Or a *lot* of people up to level six or seven. Maybe eight if they have really good abilities and are worth the investment?"

"Hmmm, we could certainly use that kind of boost for the earthmovers and construction people." His eyes lost focus as he tried to run through how this would change his plans. He drained his glass and stood. "You *need* to tidy up the mess you left out on the street, *now*. Then we will need to adjust our plans. Please would you come and see Tom and myself once you are done?"

John used 'where did I leave my keys' to locate the remains of Jac then blipped them high enough up that it would be a hazard to low flying aircraft if there were any up there. After that he left the wind to do its job of moving the body far enough away to never be a problem again. Unless his frozen corpse lands on someone. *Crap, if I get more Essence because he lands on someone the rest of the team will not be happy!*

"Jac's remains are gone." He drained his pint and blipped everyone back into town.

"I will never get used to that," said Michael the Moon Dancer, staggering slightly. "How do you manage?"

"Meh, it's no big deal. Dad, am I ok to go and find Max please? I want me and him to meet Ryan when they get here. If his parents, who are kind of dicks by the way, are alright with it I'll give him an Essence too?"

"Looking to get out of my sight for a while so I can calm down? Yes, it's fine but you are still in trouble, madam. I'll discuss it with you later, in private. You can go find Max, kiddo."

Evie shot into the air and sped off to find her friend, glad of the temporary reprieve and praying something would come along and distract her Dad into forgetting the lecture and possible punishment he was no doubt working on in his head.

John turned to Hargreaves. "Well, what do you want me to do? Looks like people are sticking to the plan you worked out yesterday."

People were hard at work and had been for some time. They flowed like ants following pheromone trails in and out of buildings. They were now clearing the structures further away from the townhall and the ones cleared yesterday were being demolished, people throwing force beams and blasts of fire at the supports and walls as an old man directed, collapsing the buildings mostly in their own footprints.

"I need to speak to Tom and let him know about the extra Essence. We'll need to do a survey and find out if anyone else has any extra they'd be happy to donate. This will make a huge difference. We might even manage to be ready ahead of schedule! Can you go speak to Bill? The elderly gentleman who's directing the demolitions over there. He'll let you know where he wants things moving. Thanks John, I think. You've caused a major problem this morning but you've also fixed a handful of even more pressing issues. We'll chalk this up to a win overall. Just watch your back, you've made some enemies today who won't try to play fair." Hargreaves bustled off, Michael nodded at John as the other councillors set off after him, joining the rest of the leadership gathered around the Cogitator.

"Hi Bill, I'm John. Hargreaves said you could use my help over here?" said John after blipping over to the old man.

Bill turned, his wrinkled face squinting up at John. "You the teleporter? How much and how far?" he said in a broad Irish accent.

"Uh, seven and a half tons up to 45km. I can do 750kg up to four and half clicks for 0.2 reserves. I regenerate one reserve every two seconds."

Bill eyed him sceptically for a minute before breaking out into a gap toothed grin. "You just got promoted, boy! Welcome to the Normanby Engineering Corp, Lieutenant Borrows! I'm Colonel Riker, your new CO. My word should be viewed as if it came from Him on High directly, you hear? Now I need the rubble from these houses we've dropped moving over by the river. You know the car park for the Queens Head?"

"The pub? Round the back? Yes I know it."

"That's your dumping ground for now. Any chance you can take out bits of buildings still standing?" John nodded. "From a safe distance?" John nodded again. "Oh you're gonna be busy for the next few days lad! The pay's shit, there's no overtime and the bonuses are also shit so it's all fair. Now shift your arse and get this lot cleared, I'll move these now redundant people on." He gestured at the elementalists he had previously organised to demolish the building over the road. "Then we can speed this whole process up! Get cracking Lieutenant."

Chapter 35 - A wonderful opportunity

John spent eight long, dull and thankless hours pulling down buildings and teleporting rubble to a rapidly growing pile behind a pub. "Colonel" Riker was ever ready to intervene or criticise, making sure the job was done just how he wanted it doing. The man would appear as if by magic and bark instructions at John before almost disappearing. John was beginning to think he wasn't the only teleporter in town. Thankfully it kept him occupied and didn't give him time to dwell on what he'd done.

By the time he had finished he never wanted to see another brick in his life yet everywhere he looked he saw bricks! It was like he was cursed. Compared to what he was blipping about yesterday afternoon, or earlier today, it wasn't so bad though. He gazed around the marketplace and was amazed by the transformation it had undergone. Every building within a hundred metres of the town hall had been flattened and cleared. At this rate the bungalows they'd been occupying for the last few days would be taken down tomorrow and they'd need new housing.

Hargreaves had sent people round asking everyone to attend a meeting at the end of the day and a crowd gathered as their tasks were finished. Everyone seemed quite upbeat and they were chatting happily, the dramatic changes to the marketplace seemed to be giving them a sense of accomplishment and unity of purpose. John walked over and joined his friends. They were easy to spot in the crowd because Evie and Max were orbiting them three metres above their heads playing aerial tag.

He greeted them all as he arrived and received a mixed response. Katie and Sam were colder than usual, giving him polite but distant greetings. Acknowledging him and looking away quickly. Evie zipped down and kissed his cheek, explaining in a babble how Ryan had received earth magic and would be joining the building teams tomorrow. The boy in question suddenly leapt up from behind Raoul, propelled on a column of dirt and tagged Max floating three metres up, Max shot higher and began complaining loudly that Ryan had cheated.

Gravel and soil rained down on Raoul's back as Ryan's column crumbled and he grumbled, the big man shaking himself like a dog to dislodge the muck. Evie shot back off to join them and they continued to bicker noisily as they resumed their game.

Bob and Raoul seemed fine with him, exchanging warm greetings and a few jokes about his new role as earth mover extraordinaire. Bob began explaining the progress he'd made with his factory which sounded fascinating to John. The interlocking systems, each production plant making the parts for more complex plants to make the parts for the weapons, made John think of some games he used to play. Bob was planning fleets of combat drones as the next phase of production now he had the basic refining and production lines built. Zeeg came up and pressed her head against John's side before running off, likely to chase rabbits or some other small, cute and defenceless mammal.

Victoria gave him a long steady look, as though she were taking his measure before smiling warmly and winking at him, then turning to resume a jovial conversation with Sam about their roles in the demolition teams. 3000 degree fire or eye beams: which was better to take down a building? John sensed the debate might last a while judging by how strongly each of them was defending their own contribution.

Greg gave him a rictus grin and a nod as usual. Still creepy then, at least that won't change. No way to tell what he thinks, he looks like a skeleton naturally now.

Coming to terms with being a multiple murderer hadn't been something he was planning on doing this weekend but here he was. Best not to focus on it for now. He would wait till he was out of sight and Evie had gone to bed before trying to process everything. Hargreaves stood up and made his way to the front of the crowd.

"I have a couple of things to run through with you this evening before you all get to take a well earned rest. The work you have done today, as you can see if you look around you, is phenomenal and the Council is deeply grateful for all your efforts," he paused and glanced at Tom the Cogitator who nodded briefly.

"The first thing I would like to discuss is that thanks to the generosity of the Carnival and some of the other people with high levels we have been given a wonderful opportunity. As some of you, especially some of the children, already know it is possible to donate Essence. Thanks to the higher levelled people we have access to a pool of just over 350 Essence that will be donated and redistributed to enable primarily our construction teams, but also some people with abilities deemed to have high combat potential. Advancing them in levels will make them more effective in the construction of our fortress and benefit us all. Those who offered to donate Essence please could you step forward."

John and his team advanced to the front of the crowd along with the new guy in Jen's team and a handful of others. Zeeg was noticeably absent. Sharing within the "pack" seemed fine with her but she wouldn't take part in weakening their team for outsiders.

"They will donate the essence to myself, your councillors have agreed to allow me to act as an intermediary in this process. Then Tom will hand out the names of those who will be the recipients of this largesse. Miss Johnson, if you please?" He smiled warmly at Katie in a way that made John think of Toad of Toad Hall for some reason. Katie stepped up and transferred fifty essence over to Hargreaves, the rest of them followed her lead and passed some of their ill gotten gains from the morning's activities. They wanted to offer more but they knew they had to be very careful, no one, but especially the Cogitator, could be allowed to catch wind of the fact that humans could harvest Essence from each other.

The results were potentially far too dangerous at this point in time and they had privately worked out how much each would donate in order to provide just short of three hundred Essence from their team.

"Thank you all very much indeed. Tom has drawn up lists, they are now being distributed, for the people to receive boosts to their levels. Please come forward at the end if you are named and I will share the essence as outlined in the lists. We wanted to make this completely open and transparent so next to each of the names is the reasoning behind our decision. We have allowed for the keeping of a small reserve, should you feel your abilities make your advancement a benefit for *all of us* please do approach me at the end, otherwise it will be held in trust should circumstances change and we need to raise someone with a different powerset. Now on to the second matter."

He looked at John for a long moment and shook his head slightly. *Here it comes, Johnny boy gets thrown under the bus,* John braced himself internally. He began to plot where to port himself and his team should things go downhill.

"Many of you will have noticed some of those who left the main group yesterday have returned to us. I am sure you have heard their stories. Being rounded up in the night and held at threat of violence, at gunpoint." He shook his head sadly before looking up and raising a hand above his head. "Such behaviour is intolerable." His upraised hand formed a fist and slammed down into an open palm. "We were made aware of this issue in the night when an envoy from Mr. Crow's group came. He *demanded* that half of our people effectively work as their slaves in the run up to the start of the siege in return for them not harming the hostages, one of whom was Mr. Borrows' eleven year old daughter, among other children." A murmur ran through the crowd, there had been rumours but to hear it confirmed was still shocking to most of them.

"At a meeting this morning, ostensibly to exchange food and supplies for the return of the little girl you have seen flying around town, he backed out of the deal. He changed the terms and insisted we hand over all our supplies and half our people while keeping his hostages as collateral. Mr. Borrows, with the blessing of the council, dealt with this issue in a, ah, permanent fashion. Mr. Crow will no longer be a threat to us or our children thanks to the decisive actions of Mr. Borrows." He pointed at John and raised his voice.

"Mr. Borrows then went on to free the other hostages who've been joining us throughout the day. While I regret we could not resolve the situation through peaceful discourse this was the only way to ensure our safety and freedom. We all owe Mr. Borrows a great debt for freeing us from this threat. It was a tragic outcome but we will not be threatened and bullied nor will the British ever be enslaved nor tolerate such practices! It was the only way to ensure our safety going forwards." He paused and met John's eyes, nodding slightly at him. "Now, those of you on the list for advancement please form a queue over here and we will try to get through this as quickly as possible. The rest of you are free to claim anything you need from the stores, just ask the quartermasters, and I hope you all enjoy your evenings. We'll all be here bright and early tomorrow, shift leaders and coordinators should have let you know your start times already. In the morning we will begin construction of the home we will defend against whatever the system throws at us next Friday! Thank you." He moved off to the side where the line of people to get levels had started to form.

Huh, I did not expect that. Did he just paint me as a hero? Now I kind of feel worse, John wondered to himself in a daze, turning over Hargreaves speech in his mind.

As they walked back to their current abodes John was lost in thought. More than a few people approached him and thanked him or patted him on the back including almost all of the ones who had been held hostage. He was not sure how this made him feel but it was better than them trying him for multiple murders he supposed. Maybe extrajudicial killings was the right legalese?

When they got back he excused himself from the rest of the team and went to make dinner for himself and Evie. Victoria stayed back saying she'd eat with Sam and Katie but be back later. He prepared a simple pasta with a tuna and tomato sauce that had a lot of garlic in it. Evie scoffed hers in minutes. They played a round of Munchkin, which is a lot more fun with more than two people, then she quickly showered and curled up in bed with her manga. He said goodnight from the door, stressing the importance of not going out on a night time raid again, to which she nodded ashamedly and he went through into the living room with a cup of tea. He sat down, ported in a cigarette and stared at the wall in silence for nearly an hour.

The door swung open and Victoria came in. She smiled and waved at him before heading to the bathroom. She came back afterwards, wrapped in a dressing gown and produced a bottle of scotch and two glasses. "Look like you could use some company?" She said gesturing to the half full ashtray. "They don't talk much."

"Thanks. How are the rest of the team? How are they about… what I, uh, did this morning, I mean?"
"The boys are fine. Zeeg seems more proud of you than anything else. God knows what Greg really thinks, he's kind of hard to read with the skeleton face he has going on but he has said the Majority approves. Even Jac's ancestors agree apparently. Katie and Sam are a bit… scared I suppose. How are you feeling about it all?"
"I think it was the right thing to do. But the way I did it. I could have been less… cruel about it."
Vic poured two glasses half full of amber liquid and passed one to him before sitting down in the opposite chair. "It seemed pretty quick from what I saw? Poof and they were gone."
"I dropped them from four kilometres up, Vic. They weren't unconscious or dead. None of them could fly. They fell for a couple of minutes, screaming all the way if the air was thick enough, before the ground or the barrier put them out of their misery."
"Jesus, ok, that is kind of a rough way to go. And what about Jac?"
"I… took him apart. Literally piece by piece. He died screaming, his head was the last thing I took. Probably went quicker than the rest of them though. He was dead in a few seconds. Why did I punish his minions worse than I did the fuck who held a gun to Evie's head?"
Victoria swirled her glass and took a drink. She thought for a full minute before replying.
"A few years ago me and some girl friends were out in a pub in Newcastle. Some guys came over and tried to chat us up." she grinned. "We weren't interested but they wouldn't take no for an answer. They were kind of handsy. We didn't want to leave in case they followed us so we felt trapped." She took another mouthful of scotch as she organised her thoughts. "It was getting really awkward when some guy who'd been sitting at the bar reading a book on his

own got up and came over. He asked if we wanted to play a couple of games of pool. We took him up on it. The other blokes weren't happy but he'd acted like he knew us. They backed off after a while and this guy who we'd never met played some pool and bought us a round of drinks. He talked some crap, he was pretty funny in all fairness. Then once the creepy guys had left he said goodnight. I never saw him again but I'll always remember how he stepped in and helped us out." She swirled her drink and took another sip.

"I'm trying to think how I'd have reacted in your shoes. Would I have cooked them slowly? Probably not, they could still have attacked. Would I have been willing to burn them to crisp in seconds? My flames are nearly as hot as the surface of the sun according to Tom." A white flame appeared above her outstretched hand and she rolled it around her fingers. John's eyes followed its flickering dance, entranced by the beauty of it.

"Not sure why these flames don't ignite the atmosphere, they're hot enough to apparently. But they don't." The flame vanished. "If I had been in your shoes I think I'd have done the same. Protect the people you care about and the innocent, reacting in the heat of the moment the best way you could. You were like that man in the pub that night years ago. Just doing what was right, but in a much more dangerous situation. I expect you'll torment yourself over it, one of the reasons I like you is that introspective streak you have. You did the right thing John, as a father and as a man."

She put her glass down and stood, walked over and drew him to his feet. She kissed him gently and led him towards her bedroom door. As it swung shut behind them Zeeg decloaked in the corridor and snorted quietly. She walked through the door into John's room, pleased that for once she wouldn't be pushed out of her rightful place in the middle of the bed.

Chapter 36 - You have been a busy bee

John awoke to find Victoria pressed against his side, her head resting on his right shoulder and an arm flung across his chest. His stump was supporting her head and her hair was tickling his nose.

That was not how I expected last night to go, He thought in wonder, what's the right move here? Round two? Make breakfast? Try to stay still as long as possible and enjoy the moment? He glanced at the clock by the bed. Damn, better get started or the "Colonel" will make my life hell. Bloody apocalypse making things difficult.

He gently slipped what remained of his arm out from under her and rolled to the side.

"Eggs, runny yolks please," she mumbled softly, pulling the duvet up over her shoulder and snuggling down for a few more minutes. He smiled and quickly dressed then headed into the kitchen. Shortly after adding the eggs to the pan and putting the toast on Evie emerged from her room, bleary eyed.

"Up late reading last night kid?"

"Yeah, and thinking about my power. Check this out," a ball of lightning appeared and rather than float above her palm as usual it moved and flowed, forming a glove that covered her hand, she wiggled her glowing fingers and then the power winked out. "I was talking with Anna. I made her speed read your DnD manual and she suggested Shocking Grasp was a spell I should be able to learn. So I did. I'm going to try to make an entire suit out of it soon. No one will be able to grab me then!" She finished with a grin. "Pretty cool right?"

"Nice work youngling, you've already got lightning bolt and flight, now you need a chain lightning spell and you're a regular wizard!"

"It already does that doofus, the balls arc to nearby targets when they land. Thanks Dad," she took the eggs on toast and went into the living room to eat. Zeeg appeared demanding her morning treats and John obliged. Shortly after Vic came out and took a plate, giving him a swift peck on the cheek before heading through to join Evie in the living room.

Once they had eaten they met up with the rest of the team outside before heading into town. They split up and headed over to the work crews they had been assigned to. Victoria gave him a smile and a wave as she set off with Sam to join the demo team they were with. John smiled to himself and turned to Evie.

"Am I missing something?" She looked between Vic and John.

"Just… whatever. Stop smirking, it's getting annoying and it's not normal. You scowl naturally and smile weirdly old man. Ryan got some levels last night and is working today, me and Max are going to hang out with the other kids. See you later!" she waved and shot into the air.

Still smiling, although now slightly self consciously, John headed over to where the "Colonel" was berating two men he didn't know. Bob joined him and they chatted as they walked, Bob complaining about how all the "crap" being salvaged from the buildings around town was being piled up in Doris as the town hall was now full. It was starting to cause problems for his ever expanding production facilities but he was "requisitioning" a lot of materials so it was swings and roundabouts.

"Hello Colonel. Where do you need me today?" asked John as they arrived. Bill scowled and waved a hand at the two he had been yelling at a moment ago.

"Lieutenant, these parasites have demanded your services for some of the day. How I'm supposed to meet the deadline when the only effective heavy lifting gear at my disposal is being borrowed for scut work I just don't know."

"Parasites? C'mon bloke, this is vital stuff! We're building your homes for the siege! We can't just live in bloody caves mate." He had a broad Aussie accent and stuck out his hand to John and Bob. "Name's Clive, got stuck in this shithole while passing through." John waved his stump, making Clive flinch as Bob stepped in to shake his hand.

"Heavy lifting gear?" asked John. Bill looked briefly embarrassed, which John had not thought he was physically capable of, and waved his hand, wandering away. John turned back to Clive and asked "Passing through?"

"Bill's not wrong. Evie told me your middle name is Christian so you're literally a J.C.B." Bob smirked, clearly out for revenge over the Doris Day thing. John scowled at him.

The Aussie ignored them both. "Yeah mate, I was on my way to a job in Edinburgh, working at a bar, seducing the ladies with my down under charm, ya know, usual stuff. Stopped off here for the weekend and now I'm stuck." He had the ability Tunneller and was level eight, he must have been a recipient of the largesse of Essence that was handed out yesterday. "Now I've been drafted by that old prick and rather than be grateful he's bitching at me for following the plan. You reckon he was really a colonel?"

Bob laughed, "Nah, he's got senior NCO written all over him if you know what you're looking for. So you're digging tunnels?"

"Yeah mate, that weird bloke who sounds like a crappy AI when he speaks drew up the plans. This is Stu, he's an earth wizard or some shit." Stu waved a hand at them with a pained expression.

"I'll dig and he'll reinforce. You blokes apparently can make and move all the stuff needed to turn it from a dank hole into a home. Not that I'm against dank holes ya know?" he leered at them.

"How did you end up with tunnelling powers?" asked John, ignoring Clive's last remark.

"Bloody ANZACs mate, it runs in the family I reckon. My great grandad was a sapper in the Netherlands in 1916. That's my best guess anyway. I'm gonna get started, you blokes just stay around here where we can find you. Once we've got some rooms cleared out we'll give you a shout and you can do your thing."

He walked away from them until he stood about ten metres in front of the doors to the town hall on a large red cross. *Well that was helpful of Tom* , thought John.

The ground liquified beneath Clive's feet and began to flow away from him, as he descended he moved sideways, creating a sloping tunnel leading beneath the town hall. Stu stepped over, clicked on a head torch and the rock and soil began hardening into stairs descending down into the darkness.

"Waste of time. Right, I'm going back to the factory. Ping me when they need us," said Bob.

John nodded and went over to Bill. After explaining that he wasn't needed yet for the tunnels he was quickly set to work clearing rubble. Raoul was going great guns. Nearly twelve metres tall and covered in what looked like hoplite armour if the ancient Greeks had been a power 3000 years in the future, he was simply walking through buildings and stamping the rubble into a vaguely flat surface. Then earth mages came in behind him and the rubble smoothed and fused together, forming a perfectly level multicoloured glass like surface. John was set to clearing excess rubble, dumping it behind the pub. They had cleared out a dozen buildings, moving steadily to the west when Clive climbed out of the tunnel and came over.

"Stu's just finishing off the first wing, reinforcing the walls and stuff. Where's the old guy?"

John summoned Bob via Teamchat.

"He'll be here in a minute. What do you need me for?"

"Moving stuff of course. You're bugger all use for anything else mate. You've only got one arm!"

John scowled at him as he heard a buzzing behind him and he spun to see the portal to Doris' stash was open. A swarm of flying drones had emerged, some carrying spools of wire slung beneath them, some larger ones with dangling arms and grippers clutched to pieces of equipment.

A line of very creepy looking spider legged drones the size of a cow emerged and marched off towards the tunnel.

Bob walked out of the portal and headed over, left eye clouded and flickering from the drone feeds.

"Where are we starting?" he asked. "Got the capacitors and gennies ready to install plus most of the other life support gear. The little ones will run the wiring." John gawped at the swarming bots as they began to descend into the tunnel system.

Whatever one might think of Clive, and John already did, the man was clearly a hard worker. They walked down a slowly spiralling tunnel lined with stairs, following after Bob's bots that were zipping ahead and mapping out the space. After three full revolutions, as far as John could tell, the tunnel levelled out and expanded to five metres wide, illuminated by hovering drones.

"Bloody hell." he muttered, staring into the darkness that stretched out beyond the lights hovering nearby.

"Pretty sweet eh? If you gentleman will kindly follow me I'll take you to the power room. That's where we need the first deliveries. Then the drones can string lights and give us a better feel for the space. Once that's done we'll bring the rest of the stuff in and hook it up. We'll patch up any structural issues as we go once we have lights," said Stu, walking off down the corridor, head lamp shining before him. He began to lead them through winding tunnels, zig zagging back and forth and passing through occasional small rooms with staggered waist high walls stretched across them.

"Structural issues? How deep are we, exactly?" asked John as they followed Stu through the seemingly endless corridors. Dark voids came and went as they passed side passages, brief flickers of light from Stu's headlamp or a nearby drone's light showing cavernous rooms with black doorways leading further into the complex.

"Bout forty metres down, give or take" said Clive cheerfully. John looked up and imagined the tonnes of soil and stone above his head. Sometimes he really appreciated his ability to simply vanish to another place on a whim. It took the edge off his rapidly growing claustrophobia. Stu led them to a side room deep underground. It opened out into a vast space. It became clear just how large it was as Bob's drones flowed in behind them and spread out.

"The ducts are all down that wall. Generators in the middle, exhaust vents are along the ceiling, capacitors around the edges? Up there," Stu pointed at a dark circle on the ceiling some three metres above their heads, "is the duct to the mains. We'll stay on the grid as long as it stays up, this room will just be a redundancy and control centre unless it goes down but we'll route everything through here to make the change over easier if it has to happen."

"Righto John, bugger off to the stash. All the stuff I need is clearly labelled on the left hand side in there. Have a look then port back and I'll tell you what I want where."

John appeared in the stash and had to quickly duck as a robot arm carrying a low swinging crate attempted to remove his head from his shoulders.

The stash had changed. Nearly half of it was now a sprawling industrial complex of automated machines making parts and refined materials before they were fed to other machines to be put together. John watched as a drone the size of a bus lumbered into the air with no visible form of propulsion before it moved over to a marked out bay, next to two more similar machines. John could see a short, fat barrel poking out of the right side of each of them. *Well that will be handy if it's what I think it is,* he thought.

He walked over and began making his way down the neatly stencilled lines on the floor on the left of the stash. CO_2 scrubbers… O_2 producers… blast doors… capacitors… generators… water filtration systems… ventilation pumps… bio/chem/rad air filters… Bloody hell Bob. You have been a busy bee. Where the hell did you get all the materials?

He finished walking the line and blipped back to Bob.

"Righto, I reckon I'll be able to port over whatever you ask for. Have you actually slept in the last 48 hours?"

"I got some kip yesterday, it's mostly autonomous now. Runs itself and all I need to do is set specifications and issue build orders. And resolve the occasional crash. I think we will start over here…"

Bob had John port in machinery and parts as he sent tiny ant-like drones the size of mice scurrying through the ducts Clive had dug, dragging cables from the spools of hovering drones to link up with other rooms. After thirty minutes he was no longer asking for John to move things in and John checked if he was still needed, the oppressive atmosphere of being so far underground was starting to get to him.

"Nah you shoot off mate. Running the drones is a pain in the arse, too many at once. Once we get the drone hub set up Tom will get some volunteers in to take some of the strain off me. You go back to playing bulldozer. Tomorrow you'll be bringing in the furnishings and stuff for the living quarters. And the pumps for the well. After that we'll be starting to move down here en masse." He grinned at John and waved him off, distracted by running so many drones at once. John blipped back out, slightly horrified at the idea of living down there for any length of time, and went to report to the "Colonel". He was promptly put to work moving rubble again.

Chapter 37 - The uncaring stars above

Monday proceeded much as Sunday had. John spent the time moving rubble and porting in tech and machinery that Bob had built and leaving the drones to install it. By the end of the day the tunnel system had lights, a working water and waste system, air filtration and recycling and a lot of the living spaces had been filled with furniture. There were two large cafeterias, as centralising cooking had been deemed the best way to make the most of their limited supplies. The supplies themselves had been placed in various store rooms near where they would be needed.

A large pagoda-like structure was quickly built over the tunnel entrance by the earth mages to keep the traditional English weather- namely rain- from flooding the entrance to the Underground.

Almost everyone had either formed, or been assigned to, teams of ten by this point. The living areas for each team featured a large shared lounge area with comfy seating which served as the entrance to each teams housing block. A corridor stretched away opposite the main tunnel system, down which were two modest bathrooms with rows of tiny bedrooms on either side. The lack of emergency exits would have given any safety inspector from before the apocalypse conniption fits but not having numerous paths in and out was kind of the point of a fortress.

A series of blast doors were installed at important intersections so should the outer walls be taken they could fight defensively in the tunnels, retreating from one position to the next. This was played down, however, out of fear of upsetting people as they were moving into their new homes.

The plant people, by which John meant 'people with plant manipulating powers', not literal plant people were given a different task. Having said that, one of them had an equivalent to elemental body and could turn into a kind of Treant, becoming a literal plant person. They were tasked with sweeping through the underground network behind Bob's drones, leaving behind a dry, soft but sturdy covering of some kind of mutated moss on the floor and walls. The moss made temperature control a lot easier, according to Bob. It muffled the echoes from people walking and talking. It also produced some oxygen and scrubbed some CO2. An all round good idea. The plant people also left thin trails of bioluminescent fungus on the ceiling, softening the shadowy spaces between the electric lights as well as providing a pleasant starry sky effect when the lights were turned out.

If the lights went out the tunnels became utterly dark with no light at all. It had scared more than a few people into screaming terror when the lights went down due to wiring being adjusted unexpectedly and they suddenly found themselves completely blind, buried deep underground.

Tuesday was mainly focused on transferring the rest of their stores of food and textiles into the quartermasters areas deep in the bowels of the tunnel system and moving yet more rubble. They had finally begun construction of the fortress proper. The outline of a massive star was laid down around the entrance to the tunnel and the town hall, with inner walls marked out around the only entrance. John was tasked with porting in piles of stone and brick which were made to flow and fuse into the shapes the earth mages desired.

Tom the Cogitator was seemingly everywhere directing the process with "Colonel" Bill at his side more often than not. Some kind of shared managerial teleportation? *Nah, the system isn't that evil.*

Magic certainly made construction projects go a lot faster than before but it didn't prevent the overbearing site managers from breathing down everyone's necks. Clive and Stu were set to creating the moat; three metres wide and deep. In less than an hour Clive dug out a vast U shape that encircled the rapidly rising walls of the fort. The moat went around the fort but left a five metre wide gap to the south. They left the gap as a weak point with only a portcullis to drop and seal the walls off from the outside.

They dug out the moat and carved a channel back to the river from the east end to allow the overflow to return to its normal course and finally connected the west end to the river which gushed in and slowly began to fill the new obstacle. It would take a couple of days to completely fill the moat but it was expected to be ready before the wave started. Hopefully any enemies would channel themselves against the portcullis rather than try to bridge the water.

On the inside of the deliberate weak point the earth mages had constructed a series of inner walls to create a kill zone. If whatever came to attack them took the easy route and tried to exploit the weak point they would be caught in the crossfire of dozens of automated weapon emplacements Bob had cobbled together and installed, as well as finding themselves under fire from the defenders on all sides. The area had been nicknamed the Slaughterhouse.

By the end of the day everyone, including the holdouts from Jac's group, moved into their new accommodation and began trying to get used to living underground. It did not come easy to John, being shut away from the sun. Others had no problem adapting, like Evie. John was unamused and quietly hoped she got motion sickness, trusting that at some point they would have to spend time on a boat.

Wednesday saw John, Bob, Clive and Stu going walkabout. They wandered all across the area within the barrier with Clive constantly checking a map he carried. When they got to a marked location Clive and Stu would dig a five metre square tunnel straight down. Bob then had John port in drone docks to fill the hole, followed by the swarms of drones to fill them. Stu closed up the top of the tunnel before Bob had the spider drones following them install a small blast door to protect the drones and let them out when they were needed. The entire area was then reinforced by Stu before they headed off to the next site.

Bob assured John that plant mages would be following them to encourage greenery to grow over most of the sites to leave them looking as natural as possible.

John was impressed by the amount of planning and organisation that had been put into their orders. That Cogitator was definitely earning his pay, which was continuing to avoid the digestive system of a monster. Bob pointed out that the girl Anna who had the Bibliophile power, as well as Greg with encyclopaedic knowledge gifted to him by the Majority had played a big role in the planning phase as well. Greg and Katie were spending most of their time with Hargreaves and Tom while the rest of them carried out their tasks.

The last location on Clive's map was closer to the fortress but still well beyond the now half full moat. It was in the middle of a small patch of woodland, a few dozen small trees, though a couple of them were clearly hundreds of years old and towered over the rest.

They began in much the same way as they had with the drone hubs but on a much larger scale. John wasn't asked to port anything in to fill this hidey-hole.

Instead Doris, clearly newly improved stomped over. Bob would only smirk and tap his nose when asked about the latest improvements he had made to his machine,. The big mech was moving for the first time in days and settled onto her wheels before reversing down the sloped tunnel and coming to a rest a hundred metres back from the entrance. This entrance was not fitted with blast doors, the plant folks would be round to cover it with flora to hide it as much as possible. Doris was expected to take part in a counter strike early on before retreating to the fortress.

As they returned to the fortress John saw the new tower had been completed. Built next to the town hall and rising a good six metres past its three storey roof it, well, towered over everything in sight. The main walls of the fortress were now four metres tall and two and a half thick, all fused stone that looked like multicoloured obsidian, with a glassy sheen to it that caught the light of the setting sun and seemed to glow. The tower completed the look and lent the place an imposing air that had a distinctly "evil wizard" vibe in John's opinion.

John had been told that the observation platform at the tower's highest floor was to be his station for the siege. He was then taken down to "The Graveyard", a room intended for his sole use. It contained rows of 750kg obelisks, a lot of them, all shaped from the glass-like stone the earth mages produced. They were pointy and heavy, all he needed in a projectile. There were also five giant ones weighing in at just under 7.5 tonnes. This was to be his personal armoury for the fight to come. He looked them over to fix them in his system enhanced memory should he need to use them.

Thursday was filled with finishing touches. Due to metal shortages they had plant mages out growing tangles of brambles with inch long, razor sharp thorns in ragged lines to create the biological equivalent of razor wire. Everyone was told to stay inside the fortress from that point on as small man traps lined with jagged stone at the bottom were dug all across the area beyond the fused rubble that now stretched half a kilometre from the fortress, starting further away and gradually moving in towards their new fortress home.

Some of the traps were large enough to admit only a man's foot and savagely wound him whereas others were large enough that a bull could fall into them and would leave an impaled corpse resting at the bottom. They were all covered with a weave of grass and brambles across the openings and then further camouflaged by the plant and earth mages, making the dead falls as unobtrusive as possible.

As the sun began to set a meeting was called in the courtyard within the walls of their new fortress. Everyone gathered together and there was a sense of anticipation rather than fear. With all the work they had done and how they had transformed the town, which no longer looked anything close to the small, sleepy market town it had been, there was surely nothing that could truly threaten them after all their planning and hard work. Their bastion was complete.

A huge barbeque was prepared and a bar was set up outside the Slaughterhouse, prompting much grumbling from Bob who was forced, very reluctantly, to share from the vast array of booze he was "keeping safe" in the stash.

Everyone ate and drank well, with a lot of celebratory back patting between the various teams, each bragging about their own contribution good naturedly. Even the remnants of the travellers joined in and it seemed that Hargreaves' dream of uniting them all had somehow come to pass despite his own hasty actions. That man was clearly a very talented administrator and speaker. Most people chose to only enjoy a few drinks though there were some noisy exceptions who would regret it in the morning.

For instance, John was impressed by the sheer number and variety of crude innuendos Clive was able to come up with based around the concept of tunnelling that he was loudly sharing as he moved drunkenly from one group of women to the next. John wondered if this was actually the origin of his Tunneller ability, a smutty pun from the system? Clive appeared both immune and oblivious to the disapproving, sometimes angry stares he was receiving from the males in the groups he accosted, not to mention the disinterest of most of the ladies.

Finally Hargreaves appeared standing atop the inner wall that lined the slaughterhouse and called for quiet. Eventually he got his wish but he was forced to wait for a good two minutes before everyone got the message and settled down to stare up at him. Clive was loudly making a lewd joke, once again about holes, just as everyone fell silent and a lot of people turned to look at the now red faced Aussie.

Hargreaves raised both his hands and gestured around himself and called out in a clear voice, "Do you see what we have accomplished?" a ragged cheer rang out, "We have done so much and we all have a right to feel so proud of our accomplishments! This has been a hard week and make no mistake, tomorrow will be yet another challenge. Despite our preparations we cannot expect this to be easy," the crowd grumbled, he was spoiling the mood, "but we have worked wonders to give us all the best chance possible! Anything attempting to reach the walls will face waves of attacks to drive them back and this is only after they navigate their way through the little surprises we've left for them of course," a quiet chuckle ran through the crowd, even John joined in. Some of those traps were nasty, a chemist had cooked up some vile smelling stuff to coat some of the spikes.

"And even if they do make it that far, we can fall back, retreating beneath our mother Earth. We can teleport teams out to attack them while they throw themselves against our walls! Should they manage to break in we will trap them in the tunnels, bleeding them for every inch they move forward. It will not be easy but we will survive this challenge! We will conquer whatever this evil system throws at us and emerge stronger! We will make it through whatever comes at us, but we will do it as free human beings, not as slaves to this Alliance that doesn't care about us!" A real cheer erupted, people calling out and shouting their defiance at the uncaring stars above.

Eventually the crowd began to disperse and everyone made their way into the underground, heading for their team blocks to try and get some sleep for the day ahead.

Chapter 38 - Security and prosperity

Geraldine hadn't had much to do during the construction phase this last week. Since the training, or power levelling as Evie had called it, she and her team had largely gone their own way from the Carnival. They were still friendly and were barracked near each other. Evie had dragged Jen and James into a series of board games most evenings so she had been in and out of their rooms regularly, nagging Jen to come lose at Risk again.

There had been a few minor injuries from accidents that had required her attention but nothing too major. One poor fellow had had his leg crushed by some falling masonry but within a couple of hours he was back on his feet, good as new. The injury would have taken months of physical therapy to recover from before the system.

She had spent her time cataloguing and storing the range of drugs they had taken from the pharmacy and the medical centre. She wasn't familiar with some of the more esoteric drugs in their collection, she had been a duty nurse not an exotic disease consultant but she was able to put together a decent supply of antibiotics, antivirals and other essential medicines.

She was always deep in the Underground, in the new medical centre, while Jen and the rest of the team were busy with other things. The room set aside as a hospital was large and had a high ceiling giving it a light, airy feel. The walls were all white washed and the tang of whatever chemicals were used to sterilise everything hung in the air, never quite cleared out by the ventilation system.

The rows of beds with dividing screens and the permanent, faintly hospital smell felt comforting and familiar to her. She had spent the final day before the second wave making sure everything was ready for any injured and coordinating with the other former medics, now magical healers, to ensure they would triage and treat anyone sent in here in the most efficient way they could manage.

Magical healing, or superpowers or whatever the hell they had now, made a huge difference to their planning. Someone taking a serious injury that might have left them disabled for life or taken months to heal a week ago could now be patched up within hours as a rule. For all the horror she had seen, the power she now had to help people almost made up for it.

She had attended the party like everyone else and spent her time with Jen, Phil, Audrey and Oleg. Oleg was a strange man, he'd done well in the first wave, getting up to level ten while running solo, his ability was very powerful. He was also a braggart who loved to talk about himself but never talked about anything before the system. It made Geraldine suspicious of him.

The team had been enjoying a few drinks, the food was good and they were chatting away happily when Hargreaves got up to give his speech. They had listened quietly and cheered a little at the end, like most people. When the time came her team would be on the walls while she was safe in the Underground and she felt both relieved and guilty about it. Orders were orders though right? Ours is not to question why, ours is but to do or die. She didn't have much to offer in terms of combat so she was secretly grateful to not be assigned to the wall.

As Hargreaves came down from the wall of the Slaughterhouse, a place that made Geraldine shudder with its simple dedication to mayhem and murder, he approached Jen's team and made small talk for a few minutes.

"Geraldine, would you mind if I had a quiet word with you please? I want to go over a couple of things for tomorrow," he asked and gestured back inside. She excused herself from her friends and followed him as they joined Katie, Greg and the Cogitator going down through the warren of defensive tunnels before coming out into the Underground proper and heading to a conference room off from the command centre.

"Thank you for joining us. I'm sorry I haven't been able to spend more time with you and your team recently but things have been hectic the last few days. We've kind of been together from day one eh?" Katie smiled at Geraldine and offered her a seat.

"This is a sensitive topic so before we begin I trust we can count on your discretion? It would probably fall under the idea of patient confidentiality?" Hargreaves began.

"Of course, I would never break the confidence of a patient. Is one of you ill? Something the system didn't fix? I've not seen a single case of cancer or chronic disease in anyone I've examined since all this began so I thought the Constitution statistic had healed all of that?"

"No, we are all well, thank you for asking Geraldine." Hargreaves looked at her with a serious expression on his face. "This is to do with what we can expect to happen tomorrow, or rather what may happen. I take it we are as well prepared as possible to receive any injured? We've done everything we can to ensure our people will be safe up there but sadly we must anticipate some loss of life and yet more serious injuries. We have a triage process in place to prioritise the injured?"

"Of course, with healing powers..., if we can get people to the hospital quickly enough, most should be able to make full recoveries except for the most seriously wounded. We have been working on possible techniques to regrow limbs for people like John. I assume John will be helping to evacuate the injured from the walls and into our care?"

"That will be one of his primary responsibilities. It is a shame to not use him more aggressively but being able to remove anyone injured from harm's way is too valuable an ability to waste," said Greg in his gravelly voice.

Hargreaves shot a glance at Greg. The undead man gave him a skeletal grin in return but fell silent.

"What I wanted to ask was what your plans are in the *very* unlikely event of mass casualties. Will you be able to cope with more than a handful of injuries?" Hargreaves continued.

Geraldine thought for a moment and crossed her hands in her lap before answering.

"We can't use traditional triage techniques because of how much greater our survivability is due to the Constitution statistic. Most minor injuries, and even many serious injuries that receive immediate first aid to stop blood loss or handle the shock, will heal naturally in a matter of hours. If someone has a physical ability rather than a more, um, magical one the difference is even more profound.

"So we've taken triage protocols for natural disasters and adjusted things slightly. If someone looks as though they will recover naturally post first aid we will administer painkillers if they are suffering but otherwise simply monitor them. There's a series of rooms next to the hospital where we can place them to keep space free in the infirmary for the more serious cases," she paused and took a breath.

"In the event someone needs urgent care despite our improved natural healing they will be tagged, in a similar fashion to traditional triage. The most seriously injured will be treated first where possible. If we become overwhelmed the ones with the best chance of pulling through will be prioritised and we will work through them to make the best use of our resources. I hope you aren't expecting anything like this to happen? That was the whole idea of the fortress and John will be able to move people out of harm's way if he is kept in reserve."

"Of course we are confident this won't happen. We have developed a variety of plans to cover all the eventualities we can reasonably expect. But no plan survives first contact with the enemy as the military adage goes. The reason I am asking these questions is related to John. To something he discovered anyway."

Geraldine raised an eyebrow and waited for Hargreaves to gather his thoughts.

"When he murdered Jac and his cohorts he made a dangerous discovery that we have kept from the rest of the people."

"I don't approve of violence but Evie is a lovely girl, if she was my daughter I'd have done the same," Geraldine interjected firmly.

"Of course, of course, as would any loving father in this sadly lawless time. The discovery he made was that we not only gain Essence from killing monsters sent by the system. If one of us kills another person they, and their team, receive all the Essence the victim had spent on levels." Geraldine gasped and began thinking furiously.

"The Essence used to level up the construction teams? That came from Jac and his men?"

"Partially. We also had some left from the first wave we couldn't use to level up unless we pooled it. John decided to share that extra with the others to help us all," Katie said softly.

"How does this relate to your questions about triage? I don't like where I think this is going at all!"

Hargreaves raised his hands to placate her. "In the extremely unlikely event that there are seriously injured people who you are unable to help, we would like to not let their strength go to waste."

"You want me to kill the dying for their Essence? That's sick." She stood and prepared to leave, a cutting remark preparing to slip from her lips.

Hargreaves sighed and activated his ability. He didn't want to waste the Deputy slot on someone without real combat potential but he needed to be in control of this woman.

He spent his reserves lavishly, dropping by 80%. If he could manipulate someone into agreeing to become his "Deputy" as he had with Katie and Greg his ability was much more cost effective. The level of power he held over them afterwards was intoxicating.

They became more like a slave than a subordinate, unable to act against his will or what they believed his will to be. It was much easier if he tricked them into agreeing. Overcoming resistance raised the cost significantly but on this occasion he didn't have time to mess around so he had to pay the price. *Trade offs. It's always about trade offs.* After a brief struggle the healer was now reluctantly one of his closest allies and unable to work against him.

"Please, sit back down Geraldine." The woman sat, a look of horror on her face as she felt the invisible chains wrapping around her mind. "Now it would be very unfortunate if any of this information was to be revealed so you will not speak of it. Nor will you speak of myself or my other subordinates in a negative way, understood? No teamchat, no subtle hints, publicly you will have absolute confidence in me. You will be just like the rest of my friends here, loyal and trustworthy." The new orders settled into her mind like stones. She mentally reached for the teamchat but the chains in her mind stopped her before she could even begin. She could still use it but not to say what she wanted, she would only be able to act as if everything was fine and speak well of her new overlord. She was compelled to only say what was permitted.

Hargreaves continued in a self satisfied voice. "I have prepared a team of loyal men, bound to me as you are now, that will form a team with you. I will trust you to make suitable explanations to your former team? Katie will help with that. Won't you Katie?" Katie gave a shuddering nod. "We will send a replacement to your friends so they will not be disadvantaged, in fact with another combatant they will be even stronger." He smiled like a shark.

"Should there be an unfortunate," again he smiled coldly, "accident with the execution of our plans, John will be sending you rather too many people to help. Alas. Your new team will serve as, what do you call them? Orderlies? They will take any people that you flag as too hurt to save and remove them to another location to ensure that nothing of value is lost. You understand?"

Geraldine gave a jerky nod, unable to speak as she screamed in the prison of her mind.

"You must be subtle, Geraldine. No one must ever know, so do not be greedy." Geraldine shuddered in revulsion, as if she would! She had to find a way to break this control. Some kind of drug? An altered state of mind? Did they have any opiates or hallucinogens she could steal? Would she even be able to take anything if she intended to use it to break free from this hellish control? Her mind began to whirl, looking for any escape from being trapped in her own body. She'd rather die than live like this.

"You must send any unfortunates off with your new friends, they will handle the difficult part. I am truly sorry but this is the only way we can ensure any tragic losses are not made permanent. I am sure the injured would be happy to know they would continue to contribute to our," the way he said 'our' made it sound like 'my', "security and prosperity, no?"

Chapter 39 – Spectre

Victoria had come through into John's room in the night. Neither of them felt amorous or the need to talk, they just held each other in the dark, lit only by lines of faintly glowing fungus on the ceiling and thought about what was to come later that day. They took comfort in the others' silent presence.

At six o'clock John's phone vibrated. Bob had kindly installed plug sockets in all the rooms so everything was still charged. He kissed Vic gently and got up.

"I'm going to get some breakfast for the team, I'll port it back to the living room and we can all eat here and discuss… whatever we have to, so we can plan for later."

"I'll go grab a shower, before I wake everyone else up, I can't be doing with queueing for a shower this morning." She got up and kissed him as she went past, trailing a hand across his chest, on her way to the bathrooms.

He dressed quickly, as quickly as a one armed man can at any rate, and headed for the nearest cafeteria. When he got there he found the team assigned to cook for the morning had churned out eggs, bacon, toast, beans, mushrooms, fried tomatoes and even black pudding. He filled ten of the cardboard bowls they had looted from the high school cafeteria with a full English breakfast and added a wooden spork to each of them. He then blipped the food back to the broad stone table the earth mages had grown out of the rock in each of the living rooms they'd made before he blipped himself back to his new home to find Evie yelling at a bathroom door, telling the occupant to hurry up in no uncertain terms. The language she used made John wince.

"Evie, cut that out! They know you're waiting, just be patient!" She scowled but quieted down and began to do the "pee pee dance" bouncing from one foot to the other as she waited. Her ranting and banging on the door had clearly woken everyone else as they began to emerge from their rooms and head into the living room, drawn by the smell of food. They each took a bowl and sat down to begin eating.

"Did everyone sleep ok?" asked Katie. She was met by a chorus of grunts and grumbles. Clearly no one had slept very well. "Me neither," she grinned, "Still it was warm and comfy so can't complain right? Tom briefed me on our roles today, same with all the team leaders. Bob, I know you are somewhat separate. You'll be hiding in Doris and running a lot of the drones. The rest of you will be up in the tower. We're to act as a kind of reserve and cover everyone else."

Reg grunted and muttered "suits me fine lassie."

Katie continued, "Evie, Sam and Reg can blast away at any good targets, Sam throwing out illusions and decoys from safety. Vic will be busy lighting fires." The women shared a smile. "John will have a clear line of sight to take any bad guys apart," she flushed slightly and glanced down, "and he can port anyone caught in close combat out of the way or deploy Raoul to support if there is a chance to exploit a gap in the enemies' formation that a twelve metre armoured titan could do some damage in. Zeeg will be out roaming in stealth mode and feeding us info, taking any opportunity she gets to go giant doggo and take things apart. John, please pay special attention to any injured, they need to go back to the infirmary as a priority." A woof of agreement echoed from across the room as John nodded at her.

"What are we expecting in terms of monsters? And what about you and Greg?" asked Evie, slurping beans and fried mushrooms down noisily.

"We'll be in the command bunker with Hargreaves and Tom, the rest of the leadership team as well as the drone controllers. The planning has assumed we will get something like last time but we really don't know I'm afraid. We've built all this based on being outnumbered by low level enemies, Tom believes it will be in the five to nine range for the bulk of them, then with a few that are well beyond us in levels like the rat moles, assassins and the Queen were in the first wave. As it's a siege rather than a cull we expect them to work together, more like an army than the swarm we got before. They may be intelligent."

"Gonna need your help today to get the Spectres out John, they're too big to get through the portal into the stash."

"The spectres?" asked Raoul, "what are they?"

Bob grinned an evil grin, "Oh you'll see later. Guaranteed to fuck someone's day up or your money back, is all I'll say for now though." He winked at the big man and resumed scoffing his breakfast.

The team finally finished eating and donned the armour Bob had made for them a week ago. It had been a while since John had needed help to strap it on and Vic once again gave him some help with it.

"Do we have to go through that maze of tunnels and dead drops and bunkers to get to the surface again?" asked Evie.

"Those defences are there to give us a chance if whatever attacks gets past the outer wall, young lady," said Bob. "I put a lot of effort into the weapon emplacements. It's a death trap worse than the Slaughterhouse."

"It is a bit nightmare-inducing to walk through though," said Sam. "I worked on this short for some indy producer once. It was like a story about a maze and people were being chased through it by demon things. I did some great gore work in that one. Have any of you ever seen Labyrinth Hunt? It was really cool. It feels a bit like being in that film, walking out to the surface. Anyway, any chance of us skipping the real labyrinth please, John?" John nodded, pleased Sam and Katie had both seemed to have mostly gotten over their problems with what he had done to Jac.

"Sure thing, are we all ready?" He received a round of thumbs up and nods so he teleported them all to the entrance of the tunnel. People were coming out of the tunnel and being issued with helmets and armour that Bob had mass produced. They were moving with a purpose and heading to their assigned locations even though it was still three hours till the wave started.

It was a misty morning, the sun fighting to make itself felt leaving the air cold and damp. They could barely see for fifty metres.

"Typical English weather, had to be the worst it could possibly be for a day like this. Lad, you and I need to visit the stash," Bob announced, "we'll let this lot head up the tower or wherever the hell Katie needs to go and we can go prep the Spooks."

John gave Evie a hug and told her to be careful. She smiled at him from beneath her newly issued steel helmet, gave him a sloppy salute and replied "Affirmative" in response. Then she flew off to the tower to inspect the top floor. Everyone else waved and turned towards the stairs to follow them bar Katie who headed back into the underground. Victoria gave him a hug and a kiss, clanking their helmets together in the process, before following the others.

"You sly dog! When did that start?"

"A few nights ago. It just sort of happened after the whole Jac thing."

"Good catch, she's a good girl, a keeper for sure. I thought you seemed a lot more relaxed recently." He winked. "Now, to the Stash!" Bob thrust an arm into the air dramatically. John sighed and blipped them both into Doris' butt dimension. Once again John was taken aback by the changes it had undergone since he had last visited the space. The production facilities had expanded even more and where the machinery that had been used to equip the Underground had been there were now gleaming rows of death dealing drones.

"The Spectres are at the end, the big ones, but pay attention to the rest. We'll probably need to pull replacements from here during the wave as they get taken out."

They walked to the end and John admired the drones of doom Bob had designed and produced. They were four metres long, two metres high and wide. Lozenge shaped and with no obvious propulsion system they simply floated, stubby barrels sticking out on their right sides.

"What are they?"

"You know the C130's the yanks converted into flying artillery? Kind of like that, it's where I got the name from as well. Nice gear. They've only got 75mm cannons but they're railguns. Kind of. Still had to use some propellant but that was in short supply so most of the force is coming from electromagnets in the barrels. These beauties will circle the battlefield up high and rain hell on anything we don't like. While the ammo lasts. Rearming them is going to be tricky, not gonna lie."

"How do they fly? There aren't any rotors."

"Ah, one of the other tinkers, I forget his name, can transmute stuff into adjacent elements. He did a lot of work on the materials. They are basically very lightly armoured blimps. Think mini Zeppelins with cannons. They'll be slow but the solar panels on top will keep the batteries charged during the day to power the loaders and the propellers that pop out. Seeing as they'll be half a mile up they don't need much protection."

"Ok. Very, very nice. Where do you want me to move them to?"

"Now you've got a look at them, we should blip back to the tower and you can bring them out one at a time. They'll be managed by the drone controllers in the command bunker, I won't be running these ones manually."

They returned to the tower and climbed the stairs. The rest of the team were sitting in chairs around the edge of the look out floor, watching the other combat teams scurrying about like ants below to prepare for the wave. Evie had cracked out the Uno deck and was currently trying to get Sam to agree to a bet, the loser took the other's washing up duties for life. Sam didn't seem to be interested in the gamble. She was quietly convinced Evie had developed some way to cheat at this game as well.

It took over an hour for John to blip in each of the Spooks to float above the tower. The main delay was hooking the drones up to the controllers hidden below and setting them off into their orbit above everyone's heads. It took almost ten minutes each time to run through the checks and ensure the teams underground had them properly synced up. As each of the Spooks drifted up to be lost in the mist John felt a little more reassured. That was solid human military technology. Albeit made by what amounted to magic. There was something reassuring about the familiarity of the concept, however alien its form and manufacture.

Having failed to con Sam into betting on Uno, a rather heated game of Risk was now taking place behind them. Evie was accusing everyone of cheating while almost certainly trying to cheat herself. John wasn't sure how you could cheat at Risk but he was proud of his daughters adaptability. John sat and smoked while watching them play, occasionally blipping in a death blimp, and listened to the chatter of the others. Evie was excited, Sam was nervous, Reg was grumpy, Raoul was flexing. It all seemed par for the course.

He worried that his team had become complacent. Coming out of the first wave as the strongest people in town and then his brutal suppression of Jac's empire building had left a sense of authority and their heavy involvement with the construction work had only made them feel even stronger in comparison to the others. He thought about it and decided that popping that bubble would be counterproductive. Let them enjoy the false confidence, reality would disabuse them and bring them back to earth soon enough.

Members of other teams began to file up onto the lookout platform on top of the tower, mostly elementalists and people with strange powers like Disintegrator that made John's neck itch when he read them. Scary abilities. They were all polite enough, some of them slightly in awe of the Carnival, and they took seats or positions around the waist high wall that lined their roost. The mist still hadn't cleared. Even from up in the tower they could only see a couple of hundred metres, not even all the way to the end of the area the earth mages had glassed to deny cover to an approaching enemy.

A previously unnoticed tannoy system crackled and screeched. Hargreaves' voice came through a moment later.

"We will find out what we are facing very shortly. I'd like to reassure you that we haven't placed all of our eggs in one basket, each team leader has been briefed on a wide variety of plans. Depending on the enemies we will issue brief instructions over this system and your leaders will explain the details as they organise you to follow the plan we select. Please keep each other safe and work together, that way we will be assured of victory in this dark hour."

A few seconds later the wave notification arrived.

Initialising the second wave...
Normanby, population 552. Classified as a small town.
The second wave is a siege event. Survive or don't are your only options. Fight hard and get stronger, you can no longer hide. The wave will last until only one side remains.

Rolling for Wave type...
Normanby has selected: Giant Wave.
Rolling for creatures...
Normanby is now being attacked by 10 Cyclopean Monstrosities. Cyclopean Monstrosities are the inbred cousins of the true Cyclops. No one likes them, not even their own kin and they don't even like each other very much most of the time. They are large, strong and disgusting. Good luck.

Chapter 40 - Plan Giant Entity version two

Well, so much for the plan, thought John. No swarms of lowbies for our guys to level up on, just ten massive assholes who are likely so far above our level that we can't even hurt them. Great. Ten Queens to deal with at once. I wonder if Tom factored this into his computations.

TeamChat:

Pause Button: Zeeg, please locate them as soon as possible and Identify their levels.

Supa-Poopa: I will scout for you. I can smell them already, They are vile. Dad's socks smell... nice in comparison.

Houdini: If my feet are so disgusting why do you lick them any chance you get?

Supa-Poopa: Hygiene is important. If you do not then I will.

Mysterio: Gross John!

Zeeg took off from where she had been waiting below, becoming the Dog That Walks Through Walls again to pass straight through the 'mighty' defences of the fortress. *Bit of a security issue there, if these things can become incorporeal as well the walls won't do anything,* John thought. *We really should have considered that in the planning phase.*

Teamchat:

Supa-Poopa: Found them. Big. Dangerous. Dumb. I'm not going near them.

They all looked out through Zeeg's eyes and finally caught sight of their opponents for this round. After a week of heated discussion, argument and speculation about what the wave would throw at them they could now see the monsters that had come to kill them. They were gargantuan grotesqueries. The smallest of them stood at least ten metres tall, the largest over fifteen. They had grey skin and flabby bodies. Their bulk was clearly in their gut as their bellies bulged and hung down over their groins, bandy legs somehow supporting their weight. Thankfully they all wore a crude loin cloth to preserve their modesty and everyone's sanity. They had broad, flat faces and in their centre of their foreheads sat a single eye the size of a large dinner plate. Straggly white hair flapped in the breeze as they took slow steps forward, scanning the area around them in search of prey to consume. Ghastly tendrils of skin and cancerous buboes weeping pus covered much of what could be seen of their grey flesh, they looked terminally ill but were unfortunately clearly vigorous and strong.

Cyclopean Monstrosity
Level: 15

The tannoy crackled once more and Hargreaves' voice came through. "Team leaders, we are going to use plan GE version two. I repeat: plan Giant Entity version two. Hold until we confirm drone bombardment then move out through the cleared routes."

Huh, I guess Tom did cover this possibility then. That guy is scary.

TeamChat:
Pause Button: Bob, get spy drones on them fast. We need them to aim the Spectres.
Shinji: They'll be there in a second...
Shinji: Now.
Pause Button: Incoming.
Shinji: Traditionally we would say "danger close".

Barking reports echoed rapidly through the mist from above the humans arrayed on their wall. The Carnival watched through Zeeg as the barrage arrived on the creatures. Many of the rounds missed, blowing holes in the rock around the targets but when they did hit the beasts were knocked off balance and large holes a foot across were blown in the skin of their limbs as Bob's Spooks went to work.

The monstrosities raised their arms over their heads and howled in pain but none of them went down. As they were knocked back they took a firmer stance. One reached down and wrenched up a slab of the hardened rock the earth mages had made. It was two metres across and a foot thick, nowhere near enough to cover the creature's bulk completely but enough to provide it some cover. The rounds from the Spectres began to spark and ricochet off the impromptu shield when they didn't blast a chunk of the rock away.

The other giants quickly followed suit. Hunkering down beneath slabs of stone they heaved up. The wounds they had taken began to boil and bubble as new flesh grew over the damage in seconds.

Hargreaves' voice rang out again over the tannoy. "The artillery was effective." *No, it really wasn't, what the hell is he doing?* thought John. "Move your teams out and prepare to engage beyond the walls."

TeamChat:

Houdini: Why the hell are we sending people out there? The artillery did jack shit to them! Why leave the defences in the walls? Bob's built bloody cannon turrets into them!

Pause Button: Enough John, Tom's run the numbers. We stick to the plan. Evie, we need you to drop a lightning bolt on them, shift to your lightning form to recharge then drop another.

Baby Zeus: But then I'm out of the fight for a few minutes!

Pause Button: This is the plan. Stick to it. Reg, a black hole in one of their heads would make a hell of a difference as well please.

Porridge Eater: Ya fecking crazy? We could kill us all if'n I do that! And then I shot my wad as well! Won't be able to do shit for ages.

Pause Button: You won't, they are too high level, it will hurt them but it won't kill them let alone take out the whole country. STICK TO THE PLAN! Hargreaves has this covered.

As the Spectres ran out of ammunition the barrage died down and John watched as one of the monsters stood and spun with its improvised shield. It turned a full circle and then released the slab of rock in the vague direction the artillery had been coming from. Unfortunately this was from directly behind the fortress and while the slab would never get anywhere close to the machines that had tormented the beast, it would land directly on the town hall that still stood in the centre of the fortress.

Without pausing to think, John began blipping the rocky projectile away in 749 kg chunks as he saw it emerge from the mist, flying towards them. Each chunk appeared behind the head of the one that threw it. *Might as well try to take out the smart ones first.* It took four teleports to remove it all and the handful of people still on the walls screamed as they saw the rock flying towards their defences before John took action.

As the first chunk of the projectile slammed into the back of the monster's head it was knocked to the ground, the rest of the pieces came through and slammed its head *into* the ground, repeatedly. A cloud of dust was kicked up obscuring the beast and a cheer went up from the first humans to arrive at the invaders location. Then Evie's lightning fell with a thunderous boom and half the monsters twitched and danced as smoke rose from their skin. She followed up and hit the other half of the invaders, leaving them all charred and confused but now she was useless, she couldn't even start draining them for at least a minute.

TeamChat:

Pause Button: Reg now! Suicide drones will swarm them then the teams will attack.

Reg grumbled, closed one eye and used his most powerful ability, while bracing and expecting himself to be sucked into a black hole. The giant he targeted twitched and its left hand flew to its head. It struggled for a second and then half its skull and two of the three fingers on its hand were spaghettified and sucked into a point before vanishing. The creature took three stumbling steps forward and collapsed, causing yet more dust to rise and cloud their view.

TeamChat:

Pause Button: John, move Raoul in. Raoul, hit the one John took down with the rocks. Sam, send in your illusions. Vic, stand ready to burn the injured. Start with the one Reg took down.

Shinji: When do I go in with Doris? Not fair to let Raoul have all the fun!

Pause Button: Doris is being held in reserve as you damn well know. The factory is too important to us. Stick to the bloody plan Bob! Suicide drones, now please!

A whine came down from the misty sky, clearly apparent to the team through Zeeg's excellent hearing. Tiny flying bots, no bigger than a fist but covered in razor sharp blades had swarmed out of the hidden launch sites scattered around the remains of the town and now spiralled down to begin to collide with the Cyclops.

Some burst into fiery explosions, leaving shrapnel embedded in the skin where they landed, others left acid stains dripping from where they impacted, flesh dissolving as the powerful solvents they had carried began to eat into the skin and muscle of the creatures. A few were like flying buzzsaws, swiping across the beast's flesh to leave thin lines of torn skin, focusing on their eyes and hands. Once again the wounds boiled with new flesh that healed the damage in moments.

TeamChat:
Houdini: They are healing too fast. This is way beyond what we saw with the Queen. We need to keep everyone on the walls. I can't blip people out of trouble without line of sight and Zeeg can't be everywhere.
Pause Button: Trust the plan John. We anticipate some injuries but minimal deaths. This is our best shot to win this quickly.

The humans who had arrived began to attack. John blipped Raoul over next to Zeeg and watched carefully, looking out for anyone getting into trouble.

The humans seemed so small and insignificant next to the giant nightmares as they rushed in to attack the cyclops. Fire, lightning, ice, acid and god only knew what else all flew to hit the beasts at short range as physical fighters moved in under the cover of the barrage. The giants spun and stamped to drive the tiny pests away but couldn't catch them and the pests kept coming back, gradually beginning to inflict damage on the behemoths. Suddenly Raoul charged in, standing twelve metres tall, landing a solid right hook on the biggest of the beast's jaws and wrestling it to the ground. Everyone else steered well clear of their struggle, focussing on the smaller monsters and trying to bring one down while keeping the others distracted.

A column of white fire descended on the creature with only half a head as it tried to regain its feet. It howled in agony and Victoria's flame pressed it back into the ground, thick clouds of rancid smoke rising and glowing eerily as the fire at the clouds' heart continued to burn. The monster thrashed and bellowed. Even as the blazing fire burned into it more skin and muscle bubbled up to replace what was consumed. Her fire was stalemated by the monsters regeneration.

John kept teleporting people out of the way of a fist or a foot that would have turned them into paste but was otherwise an observer in this fight, all according to the plan he no longer had any trust in. He saw some teams working together in near perfect synchronisation. Ice would appear beneath a monster's left foot as an enhanced human slammed into its other leg, knocking it off balance and as it keeled over others would swarm over it, slashing and stabbing and eating away at it with their abilities before leaping away to recover and let another team move in.

Other groups seemed to have little understanding of teamwork, each member trying to grandstand or execute some 'epic' attack that inevitably failed or cancelled out a move by one of their colleagues. John spent a lot of time rescuing those fools from their own folly. Raoul and the big one had both regained their feet and again they smashed into each other. The beast got the upper hand this time and pivoted Raoul over its hip, throwing him towards two teams who were charging towards the monster Victoria had burned. John reacted as quickly as he could but was only able to move five of the twenty people away from where Raoul fell.

TeamChat:

Pause Button: John, what the hell are you playing at?

Houdini: I am trying to watch over three hundred people in a melee, Katie, through my dog's eyes. Fuck. Off. Maybe if you were over there you could have stopped time and dragged them out of the way?

Pause Button: Get better dammit John. We can't afford to take too many losses today. And I'm needed here.

Houdini: Sure you are.

John blinked away the Essence notification for Raoul landing on their fellow humans. He blinked away tears as well. Vic laid a hand on his shoulder while continuing to burn at the monsters with the flames she targetted through Zeeg's eyes. Who the hell did Katie think she was?

He wasn't god! He had to see a situation and react in time to do anything. Even with his new power, he was still just a man. He couldn't pause time and swan about moving people out of the way. It was a miracle he had snatched as many people out from beneath Raoul's fall as he had, given he had less than a second to react to it. God only knew how the big guy would take it. The first humans to die had been from him landing on them, not an attack by the enemy. That would be difficult to deal with. John wondered if he'd be able to come to terms with it at all or if it would break him. Raoul was strong in more ways than just his muscles, John decided, he'd be hurt but he'd cope.

John focussed on the battle through Zeegs eyes.

With their first losses the humans had rallied and intensified their efforts. They were spending reserves like water, then switching out with other teams to recover a little away from the fight. As he watched he saw a fist coming down on a woman surrounded with an icy nimbus who had been flinging spears of blue crystal into the face of one of the giants and he pulled her to the side so the blow crashed into the earth next to her, leaving her shocked but unharmed. She staggered back to a safer distance before the beast could focus on her again.

Evie and Reg had gotten enough reserves back to begin using their abilities again. Reg was clearly slowing the giants down as they became even more lumbering and clumsy and Evie's boost began to kick in and combine with Katies Haste, giving Raoul a slight edge in speed over the giant he was duelling.

It wasn't enough though. They had clearly hurt the beasts but even the one that had lost half its head was back on its feet and swinging dangerously at anyone who came near it. John kept blipping people out of the way of blows that would have killed or maimed them. If someone took a bad hit before he could move them, he sent them to the infirmary, deep underground where Geraldine and their limited pool of healers did what they could to stabilise them. Mostly though, if someone did get hit they were mush, no chance of saving them, as John witnessed over and over again.

The monsters were just too tough and the humans were reaching the end of their endurance. Without time to rest and regain their strength they began making more and more mistakes and John wasn't always able to save them in time.

The losses mounted up steadily. Soon nearly half of the humans who attacked had either been pulled back to the infirmary or were paste beneath the giant's feet.

Even Raoul was battered and reeling. John pulled him back as he returned to his normal size, Sam and Victoria catching him as he collapsed on the roof beside them, bloody and broken but not seriously injured. His rapid healing kicked in and his wounds began to close.

TeamChat:

Pause Button: The retreat has been called. John, pull back anyone you can still see out there within the walls, now. This has been a disaster. We will try to hold the walls with what you've left us.

Houdini: What I've left us? What the hell Katie! It wasn't my fucking plan!

Pause Button: Just focus on the job at hand. We need to use the wall defences ahead of schedule.

Baby Zeus: Katie... why are you being such a bitch?

As the team either fell back rapidly or were ported back by John they began to assemble on the walls. The confidence from earlier was gone. Replaced with a fatalistic determination. John was shocked at how few they seemed compared to before. They must have lost 40% killed or injured of the starting force but they were still willing to fight. In normal military units losses lower than 20% would break morale and result in a rout but these scattered survivors, nameless and faceless strangers to each other a week ago, stood shoulder to shoulder and prepared to face the enemy once more despite their losses.

They stood in silence for a couple of minutes, reserves gradually recovering and talking quietly among themselves, until the heavy footsteps began to echo through the mist. The Cyclops were coming. The monsters emerged from the mist slowly, gigantic shadows with no definition gradually plodding closer and closer until they were barely 500 metres away and could be seen clearly.

The turrets Bob had built into the walls spun up out of their recesses with a mechanical whine and took aim. The cyclops watched, what to them, must have looked like stone pimples emerge from the smooth wall and train stubby barrels in their direction. After a short time that felt like a moment of perfect silence as the people stopped their nervous chatter, the guns spoke.

They were the same weapons carried by the Spectres. As these were firmly seated in custom built mounts rather than bolted onto the side of what amounted to a fancy balloon they were much more accurate. Devastatingly so. The first rounds began blasting holes into the Cyclops and the monsters recoiled, shielding their faces with their arms. A barrage of ranged attacks from the people left on the walls also slammed into them.

The largest of the Cyclops crossed its arms in front of its face and began to charge. No longer lumbering along, its long legs devoured the distance to the wall rapidly. All the turrets turned and focused on it as well as the humans, reacting to this swiftly closing threat.

A series of shells exploded just under its left arm. Something had been severed and the limb swung down to hang useless at its side. Blades of razor sharp air hacked away at the connective tissue and finally severed the arm in a spray of blood. The creature screamed and stumbled to one knee. The other monsters began to charge as well, quickly catching up with their injured brother.

The beast raised its head in defiance and spat some guttural noises at the humans who had cheered as it stopped. The monster snatched up its severed limb and closed the rest of the distance despite the fire from the turrets. It began to use its own arm as a club, trying to sweep the humans from the battlements with the soggy end. John rapidly blinked anyone in the line of its attack to the halls underground. *Screw the plan, we need to rethink this.*

The turrets were not portable and were smashed to pieces as the improvised club came down. A few managed to withdraw into their recesses but the enraged cyclops began to kick and shatter the wall. It knocked holes through the three metre battlements with casual ease, sending fragments of rock flying into the buildings they had been built to protect.

Chapter 41 - I'm a mushroom too

Update:
Survivors: 403
Cyclopean Monstrosities: 10

John began moving everyone else underground as quickly as he could. Putting them safely out of harm's way, for now at least.

"We should probably head down as well," said Sam, her face grey with shock. There hadn't been much in the way of pitched battles in the first wave. Skirmishes where either the humans were overwhelmed quickly or they fought off the smaller rats had been the norm. None of them had been forced to watch a slaughter take place, or survived to talk about it if they did anyway. They had either won with minimal losses or encountered the aftermath of the many rat victories. While the remains left by the rats had been grim, John had seen more of that than most when he cleaned up the town, it had lacked the impact of this afternoon's disaster. Seeing so many people die in such a short time had shocked everyone, especially the Carnival, back to reality. Evie was subdued and clung to John's hand.

"We can still do this!" said a member from another team, the Disintegrator. He was level eight and apparently unable to read the room.

Raoul looked up from where had collapsed. His wounds had started to close but he was still seriously injured. "You won't be able to do shit, man. They're too high level. Your ability won't work on them directly. Not properly anyway."

"Bullshit. I *unmake* things!" he waved and a portion of the wall behind Raoul vanished. "I can find a way to kill these things."

Raoul looked up at Sam, "You can tell he didn't have to fight the Queen, right?" he said sadly. The man scowled and opened his mouth to reply but the tannoy crackled, drowning out whatever response he had.

"Everyone underground, now. We are sealing the blast doors in sixty seconds," echoed out over the fortress. The giants continued to destroy the walls and lunge at any humans John hadn't moved to safety yet.

The man, previously full of confidence and bluster, paled and began to bolt down the stairs, concluding he would struggle to make it inside before the doors sealed. John blipped him and the other strangers on the lookout tower to the cafeteria he had used earlier, then moved his friends down into their living room. The team collapsed into the settees spread around the large stone table. There was a strong sense of resentment at the leadership that had sent those brave people to fight up close with the giants and die rather than stay within the walls they had worked so hard to build.

TeamChat:

Shinji: John, bring me in please. Doris is safe, they're moving towards the fort, carefully, and they won't stumble across her hiding place any time soon. We might not have brought any down but we've made them cautious at least.

Pause Button: Greg will join you shortly. I'm afraid I am otherwise occupied.

John blipped in Bob, who stretched before sitting down. "They are spreading out a bit but staying in line of sight with each other. Walls are knackered, they look like a bad boxer's teeth towards the end of his career. I've got drones watching them. Tough sons of bitches, much tougher than the Queen was. The one that used the soggy end of its own arm as a club just reattached it by putting the wet end next to its shoulder. Ten queens would have been toast with what we threw at them. That was a SNAFU of the highest order. And the REMFs will blame us frontliners no doubt."

"What's a REMF, Bob?" asked Evie.

"Uh, never mind girl. Your dad will tell you when you're older."

"What Hargreaves threw at them was people. A lot of them are now dead. He thought there were enough to wear them down like Roaul, Reg, Sam and Greg did with the level fourteen?" asked Victoria.

"I'm not in the planning team, lass. I'm a mushroom too, kept in the dark and fed bullshit. So I have no idea. But it sounds possible. Bring an old man a beer, eh John?"

A can appeared in front of Bob who nodded in gratitude, cracked it open and drained it in one go. His left eye was still clouded and flickering as he monitored the drone feeds.

"Why was Katie being such a fucking bitch?" piped up a young voice. All eyes turned to focus on Evie. "She was dumping on Dad! It wasn't *his* fault what happened!"

Raoul hung his head and went to stand. Sam caught his hand and pulled him back to the seat next to her.

"I.. I'm sorry. It was so strong, it caught me and then I was flying through the air… I.. I couldn't…" Raoul buried his face in his hands. Sam put an arm across his shoulders and pulled him in for a hug as the big man wept.

"No one is blaming you Raoul. It wasn't your fault." Sam shot Evie a look over Raoul's shoulder. "I know it won't mean much now but… It wasn't your fault mate. Just take your time with it ok?"

Victoria's pretty face scowled and she said in an acid tone, "I think we need to have a very serious conversation with Katie and Hargreaves. That was world war one tactics, throwing people into the line of fire and hoping enough manage to survive to win the fight."

"Yeah, Raoul did nothing wrong, he fought the big one to a standstill, despite the level difference! We need to kick Katie in the no no zone! Really bloody hard! Screw those "Leadership" assholes!" cursed Evie, crossing her arms and scowling round the room.

"Kid, easy now, please," said John gently.

"But she took a dump on you for no reason! You were trying to fix their cock up! She made me and Reg use our big hitters right at the start and that left us out of the fight for ages!"

"It definitely felt like that, can't disagree with you there. We don't know what else was going on though."

"Don't, John," Victoria cut in, "Don't make excuses for them. We'll listen to what they have to say but they need to make their excuses, not you. And they had better be really good excuses. Evie is right, they screwed up and they need to be held accountable." Evie nodded firmly in agreement.

The door opened and Greg walked in, somehow looking grimmer than he normally did.

"What the feck happened wi' the "Plan" ye feckin' zombie bastard?" demanded Reg, surging to his feet as soon as he saw Greg.

Greg closed the door quietly and for once didn't share a skeletal grin, simply looking at them with his half undead visage. His black and yellow eyes were more sunken than usual.

"There was a… miscalculation on the part of the leadership team."

"A MISCALCULATION!" yelled Reg, "Feckin' understatement ye corpse-like wanker!"

"Reg, please. Everyone is angry. And I do mean everybody. The leadership team will be lucky to be alive this evening let alone in charge of anything and then everything will fall apart. This could turn a setback into a catastrophe we cannot recover from," said Greg, raising his bony hands in a placating gesture.

"No one could have known how much stronger than the Queen they are. There was only one level difference but they are clearly a different species."

"No shit they're a different species ye fecking deadite twat, giant one eyed bastards are obviously not the same as a fecking dragon rat! But ye sassenach wankers sent them poor assholes out to die anyway!" said a high pitched voice.

All eyes turned to Evie, who had mimicked Reg's "patois". Then they pivoted to look at Reg.

"This one I like!" declared Reg, pointing at Evie from where he had sat back down. "And she's feckin' right. No probes, no tests, just throw idiots hopped up on their new power into the fecking furnace. Worse than Bannockburn for fecks sake. Even Haig would be ashamed and that Englishman had no feckin' shame at all! As bad as that traitorous pillock Churchill!"

"There will be a memorial later and Hargreaves will lay out a more… nuanced plan. I hope you will be willing to listen to it. It will largely depend on the Carnival. The Majority are in favour of the new plan. In broad terms we will switch to ambushes using the more elite groups."

"Did the Majority approve of this afternoon's plan?" asked John.

"They approved all the plans we came up with, forty or so in total. GE version two was intended to turn the tables on small numbers of attackers by swarming and overwhelming them right at the start. No one could tell in advance that our efforts would prove to be so ineffective. It only took nine of us to put down the level fourteen Queen when we were no higher than level eleven. With hundreds we should have been able to deal with ten level fifteens. Or so we thought."

"I don't like this Greg. Are you part of the team or are you part of the leadership?" asked Sam.

"Both? Neither, if I'm truly honest."

"Neither?" asked Victoria in an icy tone.

"I am mainly acting on behalf of the Majority and the greater good. The dead want as many of us as possible to survive. It seems that perhaps They took a different view to "breaking a few eggs" in the process of ensuring the survival of the majority than the living might have done and agreed with Hargreaves' plan." The undead man twitched as he said the last part like he was fighting himself, like he wanted to say more but couldn't.

"I can see dead people not being too concerned about a few sacrifices along the way. It's just new people to talk to for them right? But why the hell would Hargreaves be ok with this?"

"He assuredly is not, I promise you that. This was not what he intended at all. I'm afraid the Majority do not have any new members today. Anyone with an Essence who crosses the veil automatically moves on to those gods John saw, for harvesting we assume. Historically most people who passed away moved straight on, but from the hundred and fifty or so who fell this afternoon there should have been a half dozen or so who refused to pass on the second time and joined the Majority. And a hundred or more from among the people who fell last Thursday. They, the Majority, have now adopted a much more conservative approach to losses and deeply regret assisting with creating plans with such a high risk of mortality. Hence the new plan, which we all hope you will agree to help with."

Evie opened her mouth to say something suitably obscene but John waved her down.

"We'll listen, that much I can promise. When's the meeting?" A flurry of hand gestures from the little girl were aimed at her Dad, making him wince at the non verbal profanity before scowling at her, she remained quietly defiant but didn't harangue the zombie-man any more.

"The leadership is worried about the malaise caused by our defeat… festering. There will be an announcement soon requesting that everyone meet in cafeteria A."

"Will we all even fit in there?" asked Sam.

Raoul looked up, red faced and angst ridden. "Those that are left will, Sam," said the big man in a small voice.

Cafeteria A was a cavernous space. It would be a vast gloomy cave if it weren't so well lit with strip lights across the ceiling. As it was it could almost have been any large cafeteria in any major organisation's workplace. The generic soullessness almost gave it a sense of mundane familiarity. If they stuck some corporate-art style posters up on the walls espousing the company "values and behaviours" it would be depressingly familiar to all the adults in the room.

All the chairs and tables had been moved to the side but a buffet of finger foods was set out down one side. Most people ignored the food but John blipped some plates back to the table in the team's living area for later. Bob had been lecturing him about army life and never missing a chance to eat or sleep was something John intended to work into his own routines.

People gradually filed in and the resentment in the air thickened. He caught a few snatches of conversation as people passed him.

"They sacrificed us…" "We were thrown at them like lemmings…" "I'm gonna kill that asshole…" "…threw us into the fire…"

Everyone was angry. Very angry. The murmur of their rage began to fill the hall.

Many approached the Carnival and thanked John and the team. There was a lot of goodwill towards them for their efforts, in particular more than a few mentioned that John had saved their lives. Raoul got a few

angry looks that made him wince but even more people thanked him which made him fidget uncomfortably. He clearly didn't know which was worse, being hated for crushing those people or thanked for keeping the big one occupied. Once everyone had arrived Hargreaves, Tom the Cogitator, the councillors and finally Katie emerged from a side room and moved up to the front. The crowd hissed and grumbled as they entered but fell silent as they stood before them.
"Today has been an unfortunate-" Hargreaves began.
"Unfortunate? Eat shit!" someone yelled from the crowd. John watched as Katie locked on the heckler, she flicked a glance to a man at the back. He began to move slowly through the crowd towards the man who called out.
"An unfortunate set back. Please! I know how you feel, we share your disappointment-"
"My husband is dead, you asshole! Your plan! Your fault!" screamed a woman who leapt forward and thrust a hand out. Swirls of air condensed around her fist and launched towards Hargreaves.
Suddenly Hargreaves and the councillors were out of the line of fire, the air blades smashing into the wall behind where they had been. The woman was also missing and it took John a moment to find her.
She was now unconscious in the arms of the man Katie had glanced at before, being dragged from the room discreetly. John's eyes flicked back to Katie, standing where she had been all along, to see her holding a blackjack carefully along her side, scanning the crowd like an owl looking for mice as a hush fell across the room.
John used Identify and saw Katie now appeared as level twelve.

Chapter 42 - I hate spatial wizards

"Sons of Arges, greatest of the Cyclops, we are the finest warband of our mighty people, hear me!" bellowed Gruthkin. To the human recording devices it just sounded like grunts and snarls but to his people it was a fine speech and it echoed out through the mist to all their ears. As the largest and strongest of the team of Cyclops the system had sent to this cursed planet he fell naturally into the leadership position. Cyclops respected many things but size and strength were preeminent in their estimation. He had stopped smashing down the fortress walls when it became clear the vern had fled elsewhere. Some he had seen go into the tunnel in the centre of their walls and he'd collapsed it to seal them in. Doubtless they had other holes to sneak out of. They seemed like a dishonourable enemy, tricks and traps and never a straight up fight would be their motif, he was sure.

The rest of the scum had simply vanished before their eyes. He was honest enough to admit he was venting his fury on the stonework in revenge for his arm being detached rather than because the little cowards had fled. The shame of being dismembered by such weaklings could threaten his standing in the troupe without a suitable show of force in revenge. His pride was wounded and that made him rage, so walls would be smashed and ground to dust.

"These vermin are as vern, weak and pathetic, we must find their hiding places and crush them between our toes! The system has cursed us to face no challenge on this final expedition but still we must slay all these cowards before we can be recalled." Suitably blustery and confident. That was a good speech by his standards. He knew some of the others were more cunning than him but he was the biggest, strongest and purest of blood so leadership fell to him whether he was worthy or not. No matter. These creatures would be wiped out soon enough and he could prove himself against a real foe once they returned home.

Fethnik strode over and sat down on a still standing section of the wall, stretching out his legs and rubbing at his head that was still bubbling as it grew back the part that had been ripped from reality by Reg's black hole. The wound had hurt, a lot, and reduced his reserves of vitality to the point that he would only survive two or three more such attacks in the near future. Given a few weeks to recuperate it would not be an issue though and now that the humans had fled there was no imminent threat.

"They have a void wizard, Gruthnik. New to his power perhaps but that one is no vern. I hunted those defenceless little creatures when I was a hafling as all our people do when I was barely taller than your codlings are now and no vern could even scratch me, even when so young. Gods that hurt!" He scratched at the wound in his skull again as his flesh and brain continued to slowly boil back into place. "They must also have a spatial wizard as well, they kept disappearing out from beneath my fists. I hate spatial wizards. They're so hard to pin down and kill."

"We have faced worse before. The planet of the fire rain? Those creatures were hellish and there was no water for months! Tartarus! Our own first wave was worse than this swarm of pathetic gnats." Gruthnik replied. "We must merely smoke them out or wait for them to starve. They will not dare to face us again, we are too mighty for them. They can barely scratch us." Sounded good? Suitably confident anyway.

"We weren't so mighty they didn't take your arm, or half of Fethnik's head. These vermin should be treated with caution despite their lack of physical prowess. Those tubes of spitting steel were painful," said a third cyclops, moving to stand just outside of the ruined fortification. Dathrik was of a lower caste but she had ideas above her station. Always ready to criticise and undermine Gruthnik. Never so pointed that she could be challenged but always chipping away at his authority. Peasants were always the same.

"No lasting harm was done to either of us, Dathrik. Such wounds are of no concern. They will not dare not stand against us in the future." He rubbed at the line of boiled flesh on his arm where it had reattached. It itched, almost as if in response to his bravado. The pain was minor, he'd had far worse wounds in his time but it pushed him to act rashly. He felt the need to make amends. Not for himself but for his son.

Dathrik gave Gruthnik the cyclops equivalent of the side eye, which with the size of their solitary eyes was not a subtle gesture. "Perhaps, warband leader. Perhaps. I for one will not rest easy against these foes. They strike me as the sneaky sort. When strength fails, rather than grow stronger and fight honourably once more, I fear they will resort to tricks."

"Let them try! We feasted aboard the Voidliner on godly fare. We need no food for months. The river will serve to slake our thirst and that paddling pool," he grabbed a lump of stone larger than a man and casually tossed it into the moat, "will serve as a latrine."

"I wonder if they draw their water for their warrens from it? That would be rich if we used it for shitting," chuckled Fethnik.

"They must have other exits than this one. We must search them all out and collapse them. Seal them in with bad air and no escape. Then we can just wait it out until they all die."

"I agree, Dathrik. Please share my plan with the rest of the band." Gruthnik grinned evilly at the smaller cyclops.

"My plan…" she muttered. "Very well wise and mighty war leader, I will do as you so nobly ask." Dathrik began to move away as Gruthnik moved over to Fethnik.

"Are you well my son? Such injuries can be hard to heal from." Gruthnik asked almost gently.

"I'm fine, father." Fethnik smiled lopsidedly as his skull continued to bubble as the skin and brain regrew. "I won't deny it hurt like nothing I've ever known before. And that hellfire! We must avoid the vern that wields that foul magic. I know you spoke for effect but we must not underestimate these creatures. Damn the system for throwing us against such mages. We have none of our own."

"Mages are for the weak. The worthy will always triumph by strength of arms. We will slay them all. You must take more care lad. We are of the pure blood. Our warband, while fine examples of our people, are not as valuable as we ourselves. You are not yet a father, it would be a shame to lose you and our line to foolish bravado on this filthy rock. The universe would be a poorer place if our lineage was to pass from it. I am too old to sire more sons, you have turned out well, my boy, and your sons will be strong as well."

"I will not cower behind lesser beings, father. That is what it means to be of the Fkrebnik. We are born to be the fire in our peoples souls. I will not hear any words to suggest I behave as less than I am. I will always take to the front and face the foe. To fail to do so would bring shame on our ancestors."

Gruthnik's heart swelled with pride. Fethnik would sire mighty sons in his time. First they must complete this bloody quest from the cursed Gods of the System. The gods had commanded these people should die and brought the warband here so it would happen. Who were they to question the gods? It would be done and then they could return home, or go to some other world to slaughter the locals. Eventually they would be sent home and could return to something like peace. It would be good to live in peace for a few decades, although peace on the cyclops home world would not be peace as these cowardly natives understand it. The tribes were constantly raiding and making war on each other but it was a natural sort of violence, not these strange worlds they had seen on their off world deployment. They would prepare their world for the invasion of the Void and could forget about this depressing arse-of-the-universe planet.

Chapter 43 - All to serve the greater good

TeamChat:
Houdini: Why have you levelled Katie? The threat of people figuring out they can get Essence from humans was too great, remember? What changed?
Pause Button: Not now John. We'll explain later. Enjoy the rest of the show.
The show? We? She's pluralising herself now?
A woman had pushed forward from the middle of the crowd and called out, "We need to stick together! We've all made mistakes today but we can't fall apart now! Look at what we achieved in just a week!" *Her words carried a strange cadence and tone. John found himself agreeing with her without thinking and his anger at the people on the stage began to ebb, a strange calmness creeping in to replace it. He used Identify. She was a level nine Performing Artist. She's plant to manipulate the crowd, he thought angrily. This is being stage managed. Katie had enough Essence left to level but no one was pushed past eight from the collection last week. They've found another source of Essence. Where the hell are they getting more Essence? The survivor total that everyone can see makes murder impossible, well not impossible but it makes it impossible to hide it.*
"Thank you, dear lady." said Hargreaves, resuming his position in front of the crowd as Katie continued watching the rabble like a bird of prey. "As tragic as it has been, we have gained valuable learnings from today's tragedy." *Learnings. I hated it when the bosses at work used to say that instead of "lessons". By trying not to be patronising they ended up being even more patronising. It was like they were in a cult with their own weird language. Like they had joined a hive mind or the borg or something.* John's burgeoning dislike of Hargreaves intensified.

"We ask that you all rest and recover for the rest of the day. Our drones are watching the enemies above and when the time is right a small force will execute an ambush on one of the beasts caught away from the rest. From now on we will aim to pick them off one by one using teams who can escape easily should something go awry. There will be no repeat of today's *unforeseeable* errors, I can assure you of that. Please everyone, we must remain strong and united in this difficult time. We will hold a remembrance service tonight, those of you who have lost loved ones may find some comfort from sharing your grief. We will all be there to offer our heartfelt condolences as well." He gestured at the other councillors behind him

TeamChat:

Pause Button: Don't go anywhere please. I think we've handled the crowd as well as we could hope for. Once they clear out we will need to speak to you all. Wait where you are.

"I'm not a bloody dog. Sit Evie, wait Evie!" the girl muttered. Zeeg looked up at her and cocked her head to one side. The dog sat down and waited. John sighed. Apparently she would only do as asked when it didn't matter.

"I'll be there tonight! I lost someone today," the plant's voice fell artfully into a facsimile of resolute sadness, "and we owe it to the fallen to act like civilised people and come together in our grief!" called the Performing Artist, using her ability once more.

Despite the efforts of the leadership there was still a lot of grumbling but the fire had gone out of the mob, at least for now. They muttered to each other but began to file out without further outbursts and with no more violence.

Once they were gone Katie waved the rest of the Carnival over and they all went into the side room Hargreaves and company had left through as they exited the makeshift stage.

They moved through the door into the kitchen. It was a wide space with clean shiny counters set in rows across it, cookers lining one wall. Katie led them to a line of four blast doors in the far wall. They were spread out, two metres between them and she approached the one on the far right and waved at a camera positioned to observe the doors.

"What are these?" asked Evie, gesturing at the doors.

"Fridges and freezers, mostly," replied Katie, as the door she stood in front of clicked and unlocked. She pulled the door open and ushered them into a dark corridor, sporadically lit in comparison to the rest of the tunnels, and closed the door behind them.

"This doesn't feel like a fridge," remarked Sam, looking down into the dimly lit tunnel sloping downwards.

"I did say mostly. Come on, it's not far from here. We'll explain the situation as best we can."

Katie led them down and the tunnel curved round to the left before it levelled out and ended in another blast door. She waved at another camera and the door hissed open. Inside was a smaller version of the main command centre, the walls were lined with unoccupied drone control points and a large table surrounded by chairs took up the centre of the room under a hanging light that threw the periphery into shadows. Partially concealed in the shadows were a half a dozen people. John identified them. They were all level twelve. *That's a lot of secret Essence... where in the hell did they get it?*

"Please take a seat," said Hargreaves from the head of the table. The rest of the councillors sat to either side of him.

"Bob, you never mentioned anything like this," said Victoria, gesturing around the room.

"I didn't know, lass. These are the replacements I made, I think. Spares in case the originals got damaged," he gestured at the drone stations. "The first drones I passed off control of were the construction and maintenance drones." His left eye flickered, dancing with light more intensely than usual. "You lot have been busy," he finished, glowering at Hargreaves.

"Apologies, this was all planned as a fall back option should things go badly on the surface and the main tunnel system was successfully invaded. It was decided that keeping it a secret was the best option. Knowing their new homes might have to be abandoned would have harmed morale for most of the people."

"Was that all just a show?" asked Sam. "Was any of it real? Was the attempt on your life faked as well? I know drama and illusion and that felt like drama and illusion."

"No, the attempt was real," Katie spoke up. "We knew there was a lot of anger and that someone would do something stupid at the meeting, putting all of us at risk. Everyone has superpowers now but they aren't necessarily wise about how they use them in the heat of the moment. Murdering the heads of the organisation would be a death knell to us all at this point in time."

"What fecking organisation?" demanded Reg.

"The rulers of the new world of course," Hargreaves smiled sadly at them all. "That sounds a lot worse than it is, trust me. Merely a bad joke, I assure you." He tried to placate them as the team's faces grew hard. "My colleagues along the walls are all level twelve and their abilities will work perfectly well against you should you behave in an untoward fashion. Please, they are only here to make sure this remains an amicable discussion and I bear you no ill will. I'm sure you will all agree that we must maintain continuity of government, of structure, organisation if you will. So we couldn't allow the rabble to run wild. We were forced to orchestrate something of a soap opera to redirect their emotions into less damaging channels. Surely you see that it was necessary?"

The team drew together as Greg walked over to stand beside Katie. His dead eyes regarded them sadly.

"We wish to work with you, we won't force your hands or try to control you. Your friend Katie has argued all along that you should have been more heavily involved in the deeper plans. We're very conscious of the flexibility of your team and your abilities. That played a big factor, as well as your place in the minds of the wider populace, making you too valuable to lose and too strong to threaten, even if we were so inclined. You could simply flee and likely survive well enough on the surface dodging the giants. However that would be detrimental to us all, as I hope to show you now. We want to help you help everyone, that's why I've brought you here. We will put everything behind you, all the resources of the survivors to use as you see fit. All we ask is that you do what you would have done anyway: find a way to defeat the beasts."

"Evie, you know you asked about REMFs? These people are REMFs," said Bob.

"I knew what it meant mate, dads collection of military Sci Fi audiobooks is pretty big and I've heard most of them. He made me read the Forever War last year, which was not fun, I was ten for god's sake!" said Evie, shooting her dad a scathing look. She turned on Hargreaves and her voice became savage. "You were messing with those people's heads. I identified that woman." John put his hand on her shoulder to calm her down.

"Evie is right," Raoul said. "What the hell happened to you lot?" Michael the Moon Dancer looked down, ashamed. "We were working together, we built this place. Where's this evil overlord thing coming from?"

"There is nothing evil here, I can promise you that. Nothing so comic book. In a position of leadership sometimes you are put in a position where dishonesty is sadly a necessity and sacrifices must occasionally be made. We are trying to keep a disparate and fractious group of people, *who just got superpowers,* united. We did this to stop infighting that would make the issue with Jac look insignificant. It was the right thing to do. All of us are trapped in these tunnels for the foreseeable future, until we find a way to deal with the threat on the surface. We cannot start killing each other," he grimaced.

"The mob is a fickle beast, Raoul. The average IQ of a crowd is the same as that of its stupidest member. It doesn't average out numerically as you would expect. We humans are still herd animals at heart and when one idiot spooks, the rest quickly follow suit. It is an extremely dangerous situation we find ourselves in.

"They love you when things go well and string you up as soon as they think you've failed. Look up what happened to Mussolini when the internet comes back online. Thanks to Tom here, we were aware of this aspect of group psychology and able to plan accordingly. With the failure of today's attack we have been forced to put… secondary options into play," Hargreaves said sadly.

"I've stopped seven assassination attempts on them so far this afternoon, guys. I didn't kill any of the attackers, just so you know, but they couldn't be allowed to succeed. It's a tinder box out there, even after Lisa's ability calmed the crowd down somewhat. If they get the smell of blood in the water they'll go wild, like sharks in a frenzy," said Katie. "It would be a massacre that keeps on growing. We'd all die. This is really the best option, between us we took down the Queen for god's sake! We'll catch one on its own, kill it, then level up and take the rest down." Katie's voice sounded passionate yet it felt insincere to John. He thought he knew her well enough to know she wouldn't support this kind of thing. Well, she'd be all for killing a lone cyclops but not manipulating people like this. The first thing she'd said to him when they met that morning a week ago had been about an honest foundation leading to a good relationship. When had she changed? "Where have you gotten the extra Essence? Going from eleven to twelve takes a lot. And I can see half a dozen new twelves watching us. I expect there are more hidden and ready to intercede should we misbehave?" asked John in a cold voice.

"We had teams discreetly killing animals for the last week, John. Inspired by Katie's and your daughter's escapades before the first wave, in fact. I know what you're talking around though. You can all see the update screen. If we were killing people to get their Essence, everyone would find out in short order."

John twitched and stared at Katie. "I told them John. This is an all or nothing situation, all our lives are on the line, including Evie and Victoria's lives. You saw the notification. Either the giants die or we do. We're trapped here until one side wins. It wasn't the siege we were expecting, ranks of armies surrounding the fort was what we planned for. We all got *that* wrong but it is a siege, nonetheless. We eventually starve underground or kill each other off *or* we find a way to kill the bastards."

"Why not use that Essence to level up combat teams? Why give it to enforcers?" asked Victoria.

Hargreaves spoke up again, "They are combat teams. Parts of teams at least. They will be keeping the other giants busy when you go to attack if you want them to. There aren't many with power sets as flexible as your team and we did not want to approach you with this until it became necessary. Katie was concerned that John's, ah, philosophical outlooks would not be welcoming to our kind of plans within plans. The idea had been to eventually provide all the extra Essence to yourselves and other highly effective teams but the reaction of the other survivors this afternoon forced our hand and we've lost that opportunity. We had to take action to maintain order."

"What will you tell the rest of the people when they start noticing all these new level twelves?" asked Bob. "Might be tricky to explain to an angry mob you were out killing that many pigeons last week."

"There are plans to cover that as well. You will all be credited with sharing more of your unused Essence, along with a number of other prominent people who are in the know. That along with the animal killing story should allay their suspicions."

"Who's gonna buy that line of shite? Why wouldn't we have just levelled up ourselves?" demanded Evie, raising a very valid question. Reg nodded in approval at her word play.

"We will have plants in the crowd when we make the announcements to help handle the response. We are confident this will be an effective play. 87% confident?" He looked at Tom who looked up and nodded back.

"Play? This isn't a game, Hargreaves! This is people's lives and you're taking away their ability to make their own decisions! Playing them like a… a guitar or something!" snarled Victoria. John sent her an approving look and smiled slightly.

"A turn of phrase, nothing more. Apologies if it offended you. The best strategy is to keep a lid on the whole situation and channel our efforts into getting a kill. From there we can snowball towards taking out the rest of the giants. We speculate that each giant is worth 75 Essence to each member of the team that takes it down. That is a lot of Essence to use to level up our best fighters, such as yourselves. This is the only way to bring some semblance of unity back to our people. This is how we will win this, by working together."

"And that coincidentally includes you not being murdered by an angry mob for accidentally getting their friends and family killed?" asked Raoul sarcastically, "How lucky for you!"

"I cannot deny it is a positive from where I'm sitting but it really is all to serve the greater good. Can't you see that? Would an angry mob murdering everyone in a position of authority really be beneficial? Now, we need to know: will you work with us and help save as many of these people as possible?"

Chapter 44 - Greg's Little Helpers

"Remember what you said when I offered you Essence after I dealt with Jac for you? Well this really feels like an "offer we can't refuse". That doesn't really support your whole "it's for the greater good" angle. More of a Tony Soprano vibe if I'm honest," John said in an bitter tone.

"Hard times call for hard measures, John. You spent years preparing for something like this did you not? I'm sure when you war gamed the collapse of civilization in your head for fun all those times you must have realised difficult choices would have to be made? What sacrifices did you make to have all your trinkets and toys and tinned food? Those resources could have been put to bettering your and Evie's lives at the time, could they not."

John glared at Katie. *She's been sharing a lot of information with these people.* He looked Hargreaves in the eyes and decided to ignore the cheap shot. "Nothing like this Hargreaves. After what happened with Jac I'd like some gestures of goodwill from you before I agree to anything."

"I knew you'd be reasonable!" Hargreaves grinned, "Name them, please."

"We haven't agreed to anything yet!" said Sam.

"In principle you have, all we need to do now is negotiate the details. And we all knew you would fight the cyclops for us anyway. It's in your own interests after all. This is how business works. We all want what is best for this community and ourselves, agreed? Well, this is the best way to help as many as possible." Hargreaves finished with a grin.

And keep your ass in charge, thought John angrily.

They demanded that the people they had helped through the first wave be moved over to accommodation next to theirs to keep their friends close, fearing abduction could once again become an issue due to the slimy approach and the unsatisfactory explanation regarding the extra Essence Hargreaves had somehow "found".

Jen's team and the elderly would all be moved to adjoining barracks and were to be considered sacrosanct by Hargreaves and his followers. The carnival agreed to take part in Hargreaves PR plans to use them as figureheads, the Queen Slayers or something catchier they would agree on later, to help unite the rest of the people in the Underground. The Carnival would also have total control of the scheme to bring down the first giant. Once they had reached an accord Katie escorted them out through a different door that opened out into one of the many store rooms filled with shelf stable food.

"I am sorry, deeply sorry, but this is the only way."

Evie's hands flashed once again and Katie smiled sadly.

"I take it that those gestures weren't complimentary? I know you feel betrayed. I only hope that someday you'll forgive me and understand that what I have done only what I had to." John thought that this time she sounded genuinely regretful, more so than he could easily explain based on what he knew of her actions.

"You shared things we agreed to keep secret without discussing it with us," said Victoria coldly.

"I didn't see any of the power levelled thugs out there earlier. Were you keeping them back deliberately? Maybe if they had been there to help I wouldn't have..." Raoul trailed off into silence and glared at Katie.

"We didn't have them then, we only got..." she twitched before continuing. "Look, it doesn't matter. You're angry and have a right to be. Just please remember I'm still your friend." Again, real feelings ran through her words.

She turned and the blast door locked closed behind her. The team made their way back to their barracks.

"John, I'm going to need a hand from you, matey. I want to get the Spectres rearmed which means they need to go back into the stash."

"I'll need to be able to see them to move them in there. Can you bring them down well away from the giants and Zeeg can go out so I can see them and then blip them in?"

"Might be best if we go ourselves, no danger anyway, you can blip us around out of harm's way and I could use some fresh air before getting stuck in the stash for another few days."

"Where are the giants now? What are they doing?" asked Sam.

"Four of them have set up camp by the entrance, they're using what's left of our walls as benches, believe it or not. All that effort… wasted. Damn and I built all those blades into Doris' legs to kill little monsters! Could have used those blades for more suicide drones! The rest of the cyclops are just wandering around aimlessly, it looks like. Looking for food or other ways into the Underground maybe? Hard to tell. Doris has recorded what seems to be them speaking to each other. 70% confidence it's speech so they aren't dumb brutes. The one that lost an arm just held it near the stump and it reattached! John is no doubt terribly jealous," he said with a chuckle, clearly still looking for payback over John discovering his love of a certain popular actress from the golden age of cinema.

"Maybe we can starve them out in the end? We didn't leave much standing above ground and all the food in town got brought below. It will last a lot longer after this afternoon," Bob said in a grim voice.

"The drones are coming down near the entrance to Doris' tunnel, we should go John."

"Isn't that risky? What if it draws them over and they find Doris?" said Raoul.

"Nah, they're way off on the other side of town and the Spooks are quiet as a ghost." he winked. "You should get some food and play quietly till the service this evening. Evie why not get Risk out again, I'm sure Sam can take you down this time." He tapped his nose and grinned. "Let's go lad, they'll be landing in a minute."

Evie ran over and hugged John. "Be careful on the surface Dad. Just- please be careful."

He patted her head and assured her he'd stay safe, he was Houdini reborn after all. He shared a brief smile with Victoria and then he and Bob were gone.

They appeared outside the entrance to Doris' hiding place as the near silent drones began to drift down from the sky. As each one floated close John ported it into the stash. When the tenth one arrived and was sent inside he whispered to Bob that he would head back to the team but Bob insisted John join him. He needed John to reload the machines. John raised an eyebrow, it made no sense that Bob wouldn't have some sort of automated facility to do the reloading but he didn't argue and moved them both into the stash.

After he blipped them both inside the pocket dimension Bob breathed out a sigh of relief. The only way John knew this was from his body language as his shoulders relaxed. The cacophony of spider drones, swinging robot arms and the still growing industrial plant made it almost impossible to hear anything in the busy factory space. Bob waved him over to a walled off section towards the far end. As they walked John saw that most of the drone bays he had seen before were now empty, the automatons they had housed having been used up against the giants in the futile attack earlier.

Bob opened a door in the walled off section and ushered John through. "Why did you-" John began but Bob held up a finger to shush him.

As the door clicked closed a blessed silence fell over them and Bob stomped over to a desk littered with terminals and things John assumed to be heavily customised keyboards. They were keyboards but not as we know them, Jim.

Bob leant down and slid open a drawer, pulling out a bottle and two glasses.

He poured them each a drink as he inspected a readout on one of the screens before turning and handing the glass to John and gesturing him into another chair.

"Sorry, can't be too careful. We're clear here, we can talk freely."

"What about Greg's Little Helpers?"

"I've got stuff in here that would make the Ghostbusters greener than Slimer with envy. Magitech is pretty versatile and I've only got the most basic stuff. I'm thinking of setting up a business after we go walkabout to find our families, assuming we make it through this and the next wave, you know? Bob's Magitech Emporium has a nice ring to it. I can confirm 100% that the only spooks in this place are the ones I built lad. Now we need to come up with a real plan. I'm sure you agree that we can't kick Katie and Greg from the team so we can have teamchat to scheme and keep it quiet from the ghosts. She'd assume it meant we were going rogue if we did and god knows what that would look like. And likewise we can't talk or slip each other notes outside because of the Majority spying for Greg. Do you think the rest of them got my meaning with the quiet as a ghost comment?"

"Are we going rogue then? It was a bit oblique but I think they are all on roughly the same page. They know what Greg's capable of."

"Rogue? Maybe. I think we work with those rear echelon pricks until they make it no longer worth our while. So, this was what I could come up with on the fly. It gives us some time to go over the plans."

"What about reloading the drones?"

"Don't worry about it, it's a fully automated process as you damn well knew." He grinned and waved a hand. One wall turned out to be a huge flatscreen in disguise and a series of flow charts and detailed explanations appeared.

"Bear in mind anything we say outside of here, anything we do, we need to assume either Greg or Katie and then Hargreaves will find out pretty fast. Right, now this is what Doris and I have come up with so far…"

Eventually Bob and John returned back to the rest of the team and they launched the Spooks remotely. The same lag occurred as each of them was picked up by Hargreaves people in the command centre. John assumed either Bob was playing silly buggers and making it hard for them to take control out of pure bloody-mindedness, possibly to leave himself the option to take back control of them, or it was a result of passing out of the stash messing with the drone's receivers. The rest of the afternoon was subdued, they met Jen's team, now including Clive and Stu, who had made the moat and the tunnel system, as well as the elderly people and welcomed them to their new homes, the barracks immediately adjacent to the Carnival's. Elizabeth and Agatha both cornered John and demanded answers as to why they had been forced to up sticks and relocate but Bob stepped in and charmed the battle axes, diverting them away from John who was struggling to keep himself under control.

Geraldine's absence was noted but as there were still so many injured it made sense she would be bunking down near the infirmary. Her having left the team caused a stir but Jen seemed happy enough with the replacement who was a powerful earth mage of some sort. He had chosen to remain with Geraldine and help her.

As the time ticked away it got to the point where the remembrance service was due to begin and all of them moved back to the cafeteria in grim silence. The space began to fill up rapidly, everyone subdued and downcast.

At the appointed time Hargreaves and his cronies, including Katie and Greg, came out of the same door as before and made their way to the front of the hall.

"Thank you all for coming. It is only right that we pay tribute to our fallen heroes and thank those who made such valiant contributions," Hargreaves began. The crowd was still antagonistic to him, judging by the quiet muttering and grumbles, but they were no longer actively hostile.

"We all lost friends and family in today's tragedy, it would only be right for those who knew them best to speak about them, share a little of what made them special to those who knew them. I know this is a difficult process, to share things openly with strangers, so I have asked Lisa, who lost her boyfriend this afternoon, to begin and she has kindly agreed. Hopefully some of you will be willing to share your own stories afterwards. Lisa, if you please?"

The woman with the voice like silk stepped up and gave a speech. She talked of her "boyfriend" and what he had meant to her. How proud she was of his sacrifice to protect the rest of the people and how they had to pull together to come through this terrible situation the system had forced on them. Her ability was laced throughout everything she said, calming them all down, redirecting their focus. It was masterfully done.

John doubted she had lost anyone at all. Now he was aware of her tricks he found himself predisposed to consider everything she said a lie. Perhaps he was being unfair, he knew nothing about the woman beyond that Hargreaves had recruited her. *People with manipulation powers are going to find life in the new world rather dangerous,* John thought. *No one will trust them after they're found out.*

When she finished, with a rousing call for unity and trust, a trickle of others began to step forward and give short speeches about their missing loved ones. Some were anecdotes, fondly remembered tales of something foolish someone did years ago. Some were short and bittersweet remembrances. Hargreaves offered his hand to each of them, hugging those who broke down in tears and, in John's estimation, did an excellent job of appearing to share the collective grief. *Am I too cynical? He seems so genuine up there, surely it can't all be a ploy?*

When the last of the people who wanted to speak had returned to the crowd Hargreaves once more took centre stage.

"Now we must turn to the future, even as we acknowledge the past. These creatures are clearly much stronger than even the Queen from the first wave so we have asked the team that put *her* down to take over planning our next attack. The Queen Slayers will become the Giant Slayers and lead us to victory! We will learn from their experience and trust in their plan. Mr Gillybrook will brief us all on what he and John had cooked up in the stash earlier.

Nicely done, Hargreaves. Pump us up and make it very clear that whatever happens it's our plan, not yours. Anything goes wrong, we catch the heat. If it all goes well you'll loudly tell everyone how great your idea to trust us was. Fucking politicians.

Chapter 45 - A melancholic grin

TeamChat:
Houdini: Greg, Katie. When we are done here please come back to our rooms. There is one other thing we haven't discussed and I'll be busy for the next couple of nights setting the trap.
Corpsicle: As you say John, I will join you.
Pause Button: Ok. I'll be there.

When they got back to their rooms, John explained what he had meant. Evie and Raoul went to their rooms, it didn't affect them. Bob asked to be teleported to the stash as he wasn't needed for this discussion either. There was a knock and Katie and Greg walked in. As the door was swinging shut John saw one of the level twelves take up position outside.

He scowled at Katie. "Bringing your boosted thugs is hardly a show of trust."

"It's not like that John. I'm a marked woman just like everyone on the Council. I didn't want to ask you to teleport us and we can't walk the tunnels safely anymore. What was it you wanted to discuss?"

"These." John pulled out his Enigma Core and rolled it around in his hand. "Maybe it's time some of us use our wishes?"

"No way John, this is bad but… Look, what if we need them for the third wave? It's gone from bad to worse so far. I'd be surprised if the system hadn't designed the second wave to counter almost all of the preparations we made! It seems highly unlikely that almost all our efforts to prepare were wasted." Sam said heatedly.

"I am thinking I might use mine now. To help take the giants down. We need all the advantages we can scrape out. Hargreaves made it very clear this one is on us. Our show. If it's a failure we are on the hook."

"It wasn't like that John! He was trying to give them all some hope. Some courage. You're too paranoid!" Katie exclaimed. Fake again John thought. Why does she switch like that? "I'm afraid this meeting isn't something I can take a position on. I already used mine."

"I also have used my wish. For what little good it has done."

"Psh, going to tell us what ye got?" asked Reg.

"Nothing that matters so no. If this is what you wanted to discuss I'll leave, I know I'm not welcome at the moment. John, you'll be busy the next few nights preparing for the attack, if I don't get to speak to you in person before the attack… good luck. And the same to the rest of you. We're all praying you'll succeed. Greg?"

The skeletal man looked around the group. He had been lonely for a long time, years spent tending graves with all his friends being the silent dead. His yellow and black gaze lingered on the living people he had briefly called friends and he felt a profound loss as their faintly hostile eyes met his. He gave them a melancholic grin and turned to follow Katie out the door.

The door swung shut and Evie emerged from her room, having been listening in. "What a bitch, am I right? So you're finally going to use your wish Dad? What are you going to aim for?"

"Language child! And I'm not sure, kid. Not sure at all." John stared at the lozenge as he rolled it around his hand with this thumb.

"I agree with Sam," said Victoria, "these are too valuable to waste. If what Katie said was true we can't even trust they'll give us the edge we want. I think we should hold them in reserve, John."

"Reg? What do you think? It kind of reminds me of the plot of Samurai Slasher, the final gamble on the unknown power. Loved that film! Did any of you see that one?" asked Sam.

"Don't matter. The only thing I want, this thing won't give me. Can't undo what happened before, ye ken?"

"What happened before, Reg?" asked Victoria gently.

"I had a wee lad, once. He were as blond as that one is fire-haired." He gestured at Evie. "So smart and the dead spit o' his ma. Nothing- Nothing to do about it then and no chance this piece of shite can change what was, so stop pestering me and feck off." He climbed to his feet and stomped away to his room, slamming the door behind him and muttering about Sassenachs.

"Damn. I thought he was just, you know, a bit crazy," said Victoria quietly. Moving to sit next to John and taking his hand.

"When did this happen? Eww! I don't need another annoying half brother!" Evie exclaimed.

"Kid, it's not- look don't worry about it ok. Try to be happy? You were nagging me to start dating for ages before this all happened. Think about what Reg just told us and then tell me this is what you should be worrying about?"

"Yeah but I didn't want to see it. Reg'll be fine. He's a tough old git. I'm going to read some manga. Call me when the," she waved a hand at John and Victoria, "*grossness* goes away or we can go kill those freaks upstairs!" She flounced off to her room leaving everyone with slightly bemused expressions on their faces.

"Was her mum… inconsistent? Emotionally I mean?" asked Raoul who had re-joined them shortly after Evie came out of her room.

"Understatement of the year there mate. She'll come around." John flashed a smile at Victoria and squeezed her hand, she looked at him with a worried expression but smiled slightly in response. "You guys want to hold on to your Cores for a rainy day which is fair enough but maybe… maybe mine might help? I want to give it a shot."

"You sure? Katie *might* have been lying but Greg didn't strike me as being dishonest. I think this split within the team has hurt him a lot and he's trying to do his best for everyone," Sam said thoughtfully.

"Maybe he is, maybe he isn't. All I can do is take the chance right?"

"What are you going to wish for? Your arm back? Or maybe… Infinite Essence? Or a car with a gun with infinite ammo?" Sam grinned at him.

"I knew I should have just thought that as soon as it left my mouth. That child is a worse gossip than... Well she's a bad gossip!" He smiled. "I'd appreciate some help crafting the wish? Maybe if we put our heads together we can word it so even if it waters down the result we still get something useful."

"What do you want? Some powerup or utility thing like Bob or Evie?" Sam queried.

"Not really, and no I'm not too worried about my arm. I've kind of gotten used to it now. Crap did someone go clear it up? I completely forgot about it!"

"Yes, it got picked up, Vic burnt it up when we cremated the people who died in the first wave," said Raoul.

John looked at Vic who shrugged. "I didn't know it was in there! So what *do* you want then?" she asked, perhaps rather more pointedly than she might have intended.

"We are all in this together. Not just us and Hargreaves faction and everyone caught in the middle but the whole damn species. I think I want to aim high, then if it can't manage what I want it can give me the second best?"

"What, like: Give me the power to save humanity? That's a big ask, chap. Maybe you're the one with the god complex? Hargreaves muscling in on your turf?" Raoul laughed.

"Hardly. I'm not the evil genius type. Far too lazy to want to take the time," laughed John. "Bob asked for a workshop and got a bloody manufactorum slash drone factory slash magitech refinery. Well, it became an industrial complex in the end anyway and god knows where he's going to take it if it gets a chance to keep growing. Evie asked for flight and got a really overpowered flight mod, it's practically free to use. They both pitched low and got more than they bargained for. Well maybe, Evie basically just got what she wanted. We don't know what Katie and Greg went for but neither seemed happy with the result. What does this tell us?"

"That it's potluck? Maybe it depends what you wish for? Maybe simple selfish things are easy and big world changing wishes get knocked down a few pegs? Raoul's' armour is pretty impressive as well and he just asked for armour right?" suggested Sam and the big man nodded.

"Maybe, maybe not. Evie being able to fly brought the whole Jac thing to a head so it got dealt with quickly. It might have been a bit of a selfish wish but if she hadn't had the ability to fly over there none of that would have happened like it did. Raoul's armour let him stand toe to toe against a level fifteen, at least for a while. I think the system screwed us on the enemies this round due to the defences we built, why wouldn't it play games like that as well?" asked Victoria.

"You're starting to sound like John there, is paranoia an STD now?" Sam smiled to make clear it was a joke, "But you might be onto something. I think we all agree the system has been playing us from the start, right?"

"I don't think so. I think it just doesn't care about us at all. It wants us to become something or die trying. We're less than lab rats. If we survive it will use us, if we die the Void whatever it is called won't be able to get us for itself," Raoul grumbled. "We can't take anything for granted about the bloody thing, that's for sure."

"Guy's, I know what I'll wish for. I'm going to roll the dice. We'll still have a few cores in reserve if it doesn't work out."

John looked down at the metallic grape in his palm and it began to glow brightly before sinking into his skin.

Enigma Core activated!
Assessing desire...
Solution found!
New Status for John Borrows.
Level: 11
Name: John Borrows
Ability: Teleportation
Constitution: 100%
Reserves: 100
Guidelines:
Maximum weight: 7500kg
Maximum Distance: 45km
Modifications:
Level 2: How about we split the difference?
Level 3: Weight limit x5
Level 4: Portion control.
Level 5: Maximum Weight X5
Level 6: Maximum Distance X3
Level 7: Reserve Regeneration rate X5 (base regen 50% per minute)
Level 8: Where did I leave my keys?
Level 9: Maximum Distance X3
Level 10: Maximum Distance X5
Level 11: Maximum Weight X3

Bonus: Third Party Logistics
Third Party Logistics: You can designate an area within the barrier and it will become a transport hub. For 80% of your reserves you can open a stable portal from anywhere in the universe back to this location which will remain active unless you choose to close it.

"How is that the solution it came up with? Damn, that… is kind of great but it's no use to us for this fight," he muttered.

"What did you wish for and what did you get?" asked Victoria.

"I wished for the best way to help humanity, as a whole, in the future. But I got a bloody town portal spell! If we survive through the third wave it will be insanely useful but right now it's tits on a bull level of helpful."

Sam laughed. "Well it was worth a shot. I guess the rest of us will keep the cores in reserve and maybe not aim so high when we get around to using them!"

"Raoul, Bob and Evie got straightforward boosts they could use straight away. This is useless unless we can get outside the barrier. And no, I can't blip through the barrier, I tried it with some stones. Didn't kill me but didn't work either, just wouldn't activate if the destination was outside."

"That was risky," said Raoul, "The barrier seems to have a zero tolerance policy on trying to pass it."

"Yeah, I wrote a note to leave for Evie if it didn't work. It was right at the end of the first day. I think I was a bit messed up."

"I think we all were by the end of that day. Then you and Bob went and got drunk and looted the town… And terrorised some yoofs as a bonus!" said Victoria.

"Well I'd already painted the town red in the literal sense, it couldn't do any harm to do it figuratively as well," he grinned at her.

"So now we just wait on Bob confirming a window to hit one of the giants and hope it all works out?"

"Not quite, Sam. Me, Clive and Stu have some very literal groundwork to do and neither of them are happy about having to spend time on the surface! Speaking of which, I'd best go find them and make a start. I'll be back later." He pecked Vic on the cheek and stood, straightened his clothes as best he could with one arm and then blipped away.

Chapter 46 - Kill it, not me!

The giants were irritatingly reluctant to do as the team wanted them to. They wandered seemingly aimlessly and twice it seemed one of them would move to where they needed it to go but then it got distracted and wandered off another way. For two days the undercurrent of tension boiled away in everyone trapped in the Underground. The leadership team were noticeably absent, taking their meals in private, presumably in their secondary tunnel system. The talk in the cafeteria and from hushed conversations as John passed people in the corridors was becoming increasingly tense and venomous. The people felt they had been trapped and tricked and that the leadership had no idea what they were doing. They had put their all into defences that proved pointless and now they were cowering like mice in the darkness. They had some hope in the Carnival's success it seemed, but not very much. How could one team take down the giants when dozens had failed so spectacularly just days ago? Early in the morning on the third day, the giant that had lost half its head to Reg's black hole attack had wandered just far enough away from the others and towards where the team needed it to be that Bob made the call. The team all examined the feeds Bob was sending through to the screen in their living area. It provided an aerial view, highlighting where each of the giants was. The giant in question had completely recovered, the missing part of its head had grown back but was layered with wrinkly red skin where it had been hurt.

TeamChat:
Shinji: *I think this is our best chance. We could wait but it might be weeks before they are as well positioned for the plan again. I vote we go.*

Mysterio: Are you sure? The others are awfully close by. It won't give us much time.
Baby Zeus: Finally! Let's rock!
Houdini: Easy kid. Got to be cool and professional with this one. But I agree with Bob.

The rest of the team chimed in, most of them wanted to take the chance.

TeamChat:
Pause Button: We'll make an announcement and gather everyone together in the cafeteria. We're putting up a big screen and we'll livestream it to the people left inside.
Shinji: No pressure eh? We won't need any other teams up top I think. I'll use drones to distract the other giants and John can drop a few rocks on any that get too close.
Pause Button: Understood. And all of you... Good luck. We will all have our fingers crossed.
Pyro: Still not going to join us?
Pause Button: Greg and myself don't have much to offer when it comes to enemies like this. We don't bring anything to help your plan either. We'll be praying you succeed.

Evie snorted and turned to her dad. "So let's do this? Time to rock and roll?"

They put on their armour just as Stu walked in. He wasn't part of the team but he needed to be where John could find him if it all worked out as they hoped, so he would be waiting in their living area for the first part of the plan to succeed.

"Ok, we've gone over it before but we need to be as quiet as possible once we get up there. I'll drop us in place, Stu, you stay in here please?" The man nodded and sat down, tension written on his face. "Ok, let's give this a shot."

John blipped them all to a bunker he and Stu had prepared in advance. It was more of a camouflaged hiding place really, there wasn't any protection, not against monsters like these. The only option with monsters like these was to run and hide. They heard distant bangs and roars of anger from the giants.

TeamChat:

Shinji: Spooks are drawing them away. I've got smaller drones harassing them as well. They aren't combat models, just maintenance bots but they're pulling the rest away. The target is still heading towards you. Raoul, you're up buddy.

The Titan Born stepped out and began to creep through the brush. The sound of the giant's heavy footsteps began to shake the ground as he drew closer. He looked up as the giant's foot came crashing down not two metres away from him and leapt into action. He was suddenly twelve metres tall, a match for this lesser example of the monsters and he lunged forward, landing a series of heavy blows to the creatures face and chest. It growled, barely hurt by the attacks and began to retaliate. It didn't fight with any finesse or skill. It threw swinging haymakers as it advanced on the now retreating Raoul.

The Titan blocked and deflected the blows as much as he could as Raoul gradually led the beast to where they needed it to be.

TeamChat:

Shinji: Some of the others are starting to lose interest in the drones. They can hear this one yelling. Zeeg, can you get eyes on the nearest two, they were above the fortress before?

Supa-Poopa: I am already there.

John looked out through her eyes and began using the smaller stones set up for him in the graveyard. He sent them far into the sky and waited to catch a glimpse of them to move them onto his targets. As they were less than 750kg each one only cost him 0.2 reserves, and while he had a lot of them at his disposal he couldn't afford to waste his reserves at this stage. The nearest giant was the biggest of them all. John watched while he waited for his projectiles to build up the momentum they needed to make a difference. The creature was somehow even more disgusting than when he'd seen it before. Strings of rotten flesh whipped about it as it moved and pus spattered the ground in its wake.

He began to bring his rocks down onto it.

The first one appeared above its head and smashed down. There was a horrific screech and the beast stumbled, falling to its knees as a cloud of rock dust, tinted red with foul smelling blood in places, swirled around it. John brought the rest of his four rocks down into the centre of that cloud, unable to see precisely where he was hitting. He knew it wasn't totally ineffective as the screeching became more intense before settling into an angry mewling.

John switched back to watching Raoul bait their chosen victim closer and closer to the trap. He had charged in and grappled, grasping the thing behind its legs and with a Herculean effort he turned and hurled it behind him. Sending it crashing through the few trees that remained and throwing up a fountain of dirt as it dug a five metre long trench through the soil.

John returned to borrowing Zeeg's eyes and watched as the dust settled around the big one he had hit. As the puppy's sight cleared his heart fell. The cyclops had a long scratch down the side of its head where the rock had stripped the flesh, leaving gleaming yellow bone and dripping blood. The rock had clearly exploded when it crashed into the things shoulder, a deep wound was leaking ichor and fragments of rock were sticking out of its neck and face on that side. The other rocks had had similar effects. Large wounds, already slowly closing, laced with glass like stone shrapnel could be seen down its back.

The thing slowly regained its feet and howled, loud enough that it must have carried for miles beyond the barrier. It raised a hand and pushed its head back into a central position and a snap echoed across the clearing. It took a halting step forward. Towards its embattled kin.

TeamChat:

Shinji: That could have been better. The others have all abandoned the drones, they're converging on the big one and he is limping towards us. We've got a couple of minutes before he gets here. Wanna drop one of the big ones on him?

Houdini: Too expensive. I need to be able to move us all out and have enough in the tank to drop a big one on beautiful over here, as well as finish the plan. I need to hang onto my reserves.

Raoul had regained his balance and charged in. Despite its lack of skill, when the giant landed a swinging fist that dented Raoul's fancy armour and left him bruised and bleeding. He was already starting to flag but he fought on, driving the creature back slowly but surely.

Evie began to hit it with drain, boosting Raoul's efforts as he got the slight buff to his reflexes, letting him block or dodge more than his battered body had been able to before. She kept the buff up but didn't take further action, she had a part to play soon. John had worried she might jump the gun and draw attention to them too early but she had what the Prussians used to call 'trigger discipline' in spades apparently.

Sam sent out her illusions to blast it with her eye beams and confuse and distract the monster, granting Raoul a slight reprieve. Her beams did little more than leave smoking lines on the skin of the beast but her attacks diverted its attention at critical moments, giving Raoul a chance to dodge or land an attack.

TeamChat:

Supa-poopa: The rest have caught up with the one we hurt. They are moving together now. They'll be there soon.

With a mighty swing of his armoured fist Raoul finally knocked the beast into position. Reg stood and with a series of relatively mild curses, for him at least, and used his black hole ability. Raoul threw himself backwards scrabbling at the ground for a grip and the rest of them grabbed onto each other and their surroundings as a maw opened that connected straight to the ravenous void itself. All the air nearby was drawn into a screaming vortex as it was pulled from the world.

The fist sized glimpse of infinity appeared half in and half out of the beast back. The beleaguered Cyclops screamed and thrashed before lunging forward. This was not in the plan at all. The black hole had been meant to pull the thing back into the pit they had dug and carefully led the thing to.

It pulled forward and with a ghastly sucking sound a huge chunk of flesh ripped away from its back, disappearing into the rip in reality caused by Reg's ability. Streams of dark blood flowed out and were swallowed up as well but the team had failed. The creature staggered forwards and went to one knee. It was injured but not where they very much needed it to be, at the bottom of a very large hole. It slowly climbed back to its feet as the black hole blinked closed.

TeamChat:

Shinji: Not gonna lie! I was kinda hoping I'd get to do this! Time for the old girl to make an Entrance!!!

Pyro: What are you doing Bob?

A rumbling began from somewhere beneath them. It grew closer rapidly. They heard a gruff voice blasting out at ear damaging volume yelling out the opening words of a song.

"Give me fuel, give me fire, give me that which I desire! Huh!" Then the riff kicked in.

From the end of her hidden tunnel Doris shot out on her wheels, legs folded beneath her. As she soared into the air her legs flipped out and jets opened up along her back, blasting fire and ash as she rocket jumped through the air to close the distance. Her sword swung around as she sliced at the neck of the badly wounded monstrosity.

Huh, he must have found some CDs and hooked a CD player up or something, thought John in shock as the robot, shorter than her opponent but fresh and fierce entered the fray with the song blasting out. I thought he was a Doris Day kind of guy? Metallica seems a bit out of his wheelhouse.

As the sword struck at the creature's neck, the robot's left arm waved at the thing's lower half as clinging fire sprayed out, hosing the beast's legs down and coating it in burning fuel that stuck and began to boil the flesh below. The sword glanced off, doing almost no damage but the shock of Doris's arrival and the damage from Reg had pushed the thing past its limits. Frantically flailing at its legs to extinguish the fire it began to keel over backwards, slowly at first.

Doris stepped in to shoulder charge the thing and her jets flared again along her back. They had to complete the first part of the ambush. As she struck, the thing was lifted briefly from its feet. It began to tumble back through the thin camouflage across the surface and into the thirty metre hole they had prepared for it. John blipped Raoul out, his part was done.

To everyone's horror, Bob's not least of all, the beast lashed out with an arm, wrapping Doris into a hug and dragging the big machine down after it. The bottom of the pit was lined with sharp spikes of rock and the sides were perfectly smooth. As the creature smashed into the bottom the sharp spikes impaled it or broke off against its tough skin, leaving it pinned in place by Doris.

TeamChat:
Shinji: Shit. Over to you John.
Houdini: You're on top of it! If I drop the big rock I'll kill you!
Shinji: Well bloody teleport me out before then! I'm not telling you to kill me for god's sake! Kill it, not me!
Pyro: That makes more sense.

John moved Bob from his cockpit to join Raoul back in their rooms. He sent Sam and Reg back to rest in the barracks as well, their parts were done. Evie and Vic both stepped up to look down over the edge. The robot was still struggling with the beast, being remote controlled by Bob from the safety of their rooms. Doris had managed to grab both the things arms and hold them in place. The left hand discharged a massive electric shock that made the thing spasm and go limp. Evie unleashed her lightning, flashed to her elemental body and did it for a second time. The red headed child and the raven haired women stood side by side, lit by the blinding light of the twinned lightning strikes, the static in the air making their hair float around their heads.

"Sorry Doris. Whatever will be, will be. You were really cool," Evie muttered as the robot flashed and sparked, finally lying still as it partially melted across the monster. Vic stepped up and poured a column of sun hot fire down on its head to keep it pinned. The creature wailed anew. It had felt this pain before.

John glanced at Stu who nodded. He had sent one of the giant obelisks, over seven tonnes of it high into the sky as Bob made his entrance. Now he brought it down with all its hellish momentum crashing into the remains of Doris' back, transfixing both her and the giant writhing beneath her to the hardened rock below.

He began porting in soil. Tonnes and tonnes of stone and rubble in 750kg batches. As he built enough of a layer, Stu held out his hand and began to harden it into the glass like multi hued obsidian that his skill produced when he fused stone, while John kept summoning more rubble on top of it. They rapidly built layer after layer and fixed it in place. The creatures' wailing had been smothered but they continued on, piling more and more hardened rock and soil to fill what they hoped would be this creature's inescapable grave.

TeamChat:

Supa-Poopa: The rest are approaching. They will be there very soon.

John and Stu could hear the pounding footsteps as the other giants drew near. They stood their ground, continuing to bury the beast. As a tree barely five metres to the side was swept away by a gargantuan arm and an evil eye locked on them in hatred, they layered the last of their rubble on. Stu hardened it quickly and John blipped them both back to the Underground, escaping just as the beast lunged towards them. The giants stomped around in circles, hollering at the sky and each other, calling for their missing kin. All that remained was a large smooth circle of impenetrable stone.

Chapter 47 - Check the update!

The crowd had been gathered in the hall for nearly half an hour. They watched from drones' eye views as the Carnival's plan unfolded.

Hargreaves had grinned internally when John's barrage had failed to take out the big one. If he could have killed them from the start they'd string me up no questions asked. He had been worried when John launched the attack but he smiled warmly at the crowd captivated by the screen. Idiots. A vast mob of useless eaters. If only I could have gotten control of more of that team, they clearly aren't useless. Katie and Greg are worth the slots but Deputising someone does have its drawbacks. Everything is always about trade offs unfortunately.

The crowd had been shocked by the violence of the repeated impacts but they cheered, thinking it dead. They had then flinched back in horror as a drone swooped in to show the beast return to its feet, battered and bleeding but not even stopped let alone killed. It had swatted at the flying camera but missed. Hargreaves had sighed quietly and resisted the urge to mop his brow.

He looked over at Katie intently watching her friends execute the planned assassination of the monster. She was by far the most useful of them. An adept speaker, pretty and likeable, and her ability… She'd been forced to save his life half a dozen times that first day of the siege as angry people had sought to punish him for their lost loved ones.

He couldn't think of anyone else who could have kept him alive. The Rewind power that had saved John's life was priceless. As a result he never let her leave his side when he was out in public or away from the level twelves he'd also Deputised. Lisa was back with the drone controllers, using her abilities to orchestrate the presentation the mob was watching. She had been easy to win over. She craved attention and influence, not knowing that they were not the same as true power. She was the definition of a useful idiot and had been swayed with little more than promises of fame in an entertainment industry that didn't exist anymore.

The drama and tension had been carefully crafted to feed into the mob's expectations courtesy of a thirty second delay from the live feed. The mildly euphoric gas that the fool alchemist had cooked up, under the mistaken assumption it was to be deployed at much higher concentrations against the Cyclops on the surface to lull them to sleep, had worked its chemical magic. Even Hargreaves could feel a mild buzz lifting his mood.

John and Stu disappeared on the screen, just as a titanic fist crashed through where they had been, the crowd gasped and recoiled. Hargreaves stood and moved to take centre stage once more. He glanced at Katie as he moved, she nodded slightly at him.

The no losses speech then. "People!" he called out, "They escaped unharmed! Our brave heroes have struck our first true blow against these vile monsters!" That gas was starting to get to him, he hadn't felt like this since he was a student leading demos. Igniting the fire in the stupid peasants' hearts to make them do his bidding. He had missed this feeling of supreme control and power. Leading his local communist party chapter on street demos and protests had been as fulfilling as he thought life could get at the time. He had never cared about the politics, only that they had an ideology which made them vulnerable to his brand of manipulation. 100 years ago he'd have been a Tory rabble rousing against the nascent labour movement. He had no true beliefs beyond that he enjoyed feeling powerful and in control. Now he had even more power and control and it had ignited a thirst for ever greater power. As he remembered those long ago times and compared them to today he began to enjoy himself.

"They have slain a beast! We've proved that with brave warriors and wise leadership we can, no, we will survive this calamity!" He waved his arms as he spoke, bringing them together with a loud clap as he finished. The crowd went wild, everyone hugging each other, shaking hands and slapping backs. For a solid five minutes there was nothing but pure joy in the room and Hargreaves stood before them, revelling in his ability to shape them to his own purpose.

"Ladies and Gentleman, we should prepare a suitable celebration to honour the brave team who have slain the first of the monsters! Who is with me? Shall we throw a party for the brave heroes in the Carnival?"

A roar of agreement echoed out in the subterranean chamber. As it died down a voice called out.

"It ain't dead!" The voice was high and shrill, a note of fear running through it. "Check the update! They haven't killed it!"

Hargreaves scowled and flicked a look at Katie. The woman who called out vanished into a side room in no time at all and Katie was back where she had been, as if she had never moved.

Update:
Survivors: 403
Cyclopean Monstrosities: 10

Damn it, cursed Hargreaves, why won't it just die? Maybe they are useless after all.

"People, it is just a matter of time!" He called out but he was too late. A susurration went through the crowd as everyone checked the update. They began to mutter that the Cyclops had in fact survived all that the Carnival had thrown at it. *I might have moved a little early on that one. Nonetheless I can salvage this.*

"The beast is buried! The others have no way to dig down through all that rock! We have killed the beast, it will simply take some time!"

"I've done some killing too." The voice that rang out unexpectedly was shredded and shrill. A woman experiencing soul breaking pain had spoken and her body shook as she tried to remain on her feet. At first only those near her turned to look and fell silent but when she repeated herself the spell spread among the crowd. There was no magic behind her words, just raw pain that anyone who heard was unable to ignore. It was Geraldine, one of the women in Jen's team who had been with them since the Carnival power levelled their new friends in the first wave. The Night Nurse, the healer.

Hargreaves frantically reached for her mind in the web of his power but found his grasp slipping away every time he tightened his grip on her mind. Something had gone terribly wrong. How had she slipped out of his control? He began to back away towards his exit.

"I've done some killing. I was meant to be in charge of the healers but there is something you all need to know." She raised her head and screamed out at the top of her lungs, "We get Essence when we kill a human! Those level twelves watching that assholes back didn't exist until I was forced to kill the injured and harvest their Essence! I'm a murderer," she sobbed, "And that monster made me do it!" she pointed at Hargreaves as she yelled the last part. "He threatened to hurt my friends so I killed yours and gave him the Essence. I'm a monster! He made me one."

Hargreaves continued backing away as the eyes of the crowd spun to focus on him.

"This is nonsense! I'm sure the good lady just needs some fresh air and to be away from so many people. The pressure of this morning-"

Geraldine produced a scalpel and slit her own throat, falling down as a crimson wave flowed out around her. The crowd backed away slowly as the blood crept toward their feet.

The drugs in the air had turned the crowd into a beast. They screamed and surged forward. Angry yells demanding explanations came through but mostly is was inchoate rage being bellowed as loud as the person could manage. Each cry drove the next to new heights of anger. The drug that had laced the air was having unexpected side effects. Drug trials take as long as they do for a reason, and even then products are often found to have dangerous effects that weren't caught in the trials. *That bloody alchemist!* cursed Hargreaves. The gas that had seeped into everyone present for half an hour had been cooked up by a half mad chemist given superpowers. It had been intended to knock giants into a deep and happy sleep but the side effects on humans were rapidly becoming apparent. The crowd could not escape the rising tide of emotions.

Hargreaves looked to Katie. She flinched and shook her head. Her ability was now on cool down after dealing with the first heckler. He raised his hands and began to back away.

"Please everyone, this is just the ramblings of a lunatic! That poor woman! Kept too long in the dark, as we all have been! But now our heroes have shown us the way to beat those things! We can return to the light! Surely you see she snapped and lost her mind?"

"Enough!" someone yelled and launched a blast of fire at Hargreaves. One of the twelves he had Deputised to ensure his control of them leapt in front of it and was thrown backwards, pinning Hargreaves beneath the man's smoking body as the crowd erupted into violence. Most of it was aimed at the leadership team, desperately fleeing for the door to their secondary tunnel system but many just turned on each other in a savage orgy of murderous desire. Hargreaves squirmed under his badly injured body guard and tried to struggle free but the man was lying across his body, pinning one arm down. He worked to get it loose and shove the body off just as a boot slammed into his face.

Something sharp tore at his right foot and he felt his leg go numb below the knee. He screamed and with a titanic effort dislodged his now dead bodyguard. Another boot slammed into his side, knocking him back down as he levered himself upright. He looked up into a sea of angry faces howling down at him. A blast of fire took his left arm off at the elbow as a man with claws and bulging muscles slashed down into his face leaving him partially blind. Another boot hit his chest. Another blast of something, this time it felt cold, made him lose sensation in his left leg as well. He blinked up with his remaining eye as the mob fought each other for the privilege of claiming his life. All his power and control came to nothing as a trickle of fear spread from his crotch and he wailed in terror as they closed in. A barrage of powers went off, lights and fires and beams of power flickering out and reaping a terrible toll on anyone unfortunate enough to be caught in the blasts.

Katie had begun to leap in to defend Hargreaves but stopped as she felt his power over her disappear. She was finally free! She began to run, she needed another twenty seconds for her power to come back so she bolted out the door, leaving the other councillors to their fate. She needed to fix things with the friends she'd had to lie to and manipulate for nearly a week. But first she needed to not die to the angry mob, some of whom had peeled off to chase after her.

Chapter 48- Her chains had ridden lightly around her neck

Katie ran for the access to the secondary tunnel system and flashed her face at the camera. The doors slid open and she dived through. The mob was still tearing apart what was left of Hargreaves and the thugs he'd enslaved and then boosted to level twelve. It had seemed so innocuous when he had offered to "Deputise" her. They had sat down in that first meeting in the townhall and he had approached her on his own. He was so polite and grateful for her team's contribution to the wave. The man had an easy charm that had put her completely at ease that day.

She had seen in him someone who was clearly willing and able to take on the responsibility of leadership for the town and when he had offered to give her access to an ability that would enhance her authority and oratory skills, or so he'd claimed and she had not seen any reason to doubt him. At first she hadn't even noticed it. She agreed with what he was doing and there was no need to compel her with the link so her chains had ridden lightly around her neck. She never detected any change in her ability to deal with people but she had always been very confident and capable in that regard so she didn't think anything of it. She had found herself unable to criticise him, even in the teamchat with her friends. She hadn't thought much of it at the time. She had agreed with Hargreaves plans and his resolution to the Jac problem. Unfortunately it had gradually grown harder and harder to pretend she was a free woman anymore.

When they all moved into the Underground it had slowly begun to change. She had tried to argue against his decisions, about minor things, and found she simply couldn't voice her thoughts aloud. She tried to reach out to her new friends and found her throat constricted or totally different words than the ones she intended spewed out of her mouth. She had sunk into despair but no one could have guessed it from her appearance and mannerisms. The compulsion that prevented her from reaching out for help also forced her to wear a mask of normalcy. She had stopped caring about her appearance or basic hygiene but she carried out the motions like a machine, forced into projecting that everything was fine.

As the blast door slid shut behind her she moved quickly towards the secondary control centre. The consoles around the edge of the room had been packed with drone controllers who had now turned on each other. A man was held down on the floor by bands of stone around his neck and limbs. He writhed as spikes of stone pushed through his body to burst out his front before sinking back into the floor beneath him. A woman, presumably having been working at the desk next to him, stood on a pillar of stone that moved slowly around him as she stretched out her hand and pulled it back slowly to summon the next spike and stab through the poor man again.

Lisa had noticed Katie staring aghast at the scenes of violence playing out across the room and she shrieked and charged across the room with a savage snarl painted across her face. She threw herself forwards, arms outstretched and fingers curled into claws aimed at Katie's eyes. Katie stopped time and fled through the mayhem. She ran past a tableau of horror as former friends and acquaintances turned on each other with a grim intent to kill and maim.

She went through the room and reached the next blast door where she un-paused time so she could trigger the recently installed facial recognition software. *24 seconds cool down* she thought as she dashed through into the next section of tunnels. She moved into one of the storage rooms where Hargreaves had hidden a sizable portion of the

Underground's supplies, taking care to dole out enough not to raise questions while ensuring he retained control of the bulk.

She moved behind a pile of pallets stacked with food and hunched as deeply into the shadows as she could. A series of bangs and crunches came from the corridor she had just left. *Earth movers. The doors won't stop them. How the fuck do I get out of this? 18 more seconds...*

Footsteps ran past the door to her hiding place, followed by a mad cackle and a blast of fire outside that set the door to her room merrily burning along the top. Smoke started to slowly build up by the ceiling. Another scream and more laughter echoed from the corridor outside. The heat became noticeable. Whatever was going on in the corridor had raised the ambient temperature a lot.

We are so fucked. I need to get to the team. Tom was deputised before me. If he makes it the others will have a much better chance with his weird prediction ability on hand. Where the hell had Tom been hidden away?

Hargreaves had kept her close to him for the Rewind skill just in case anything should happen. *Fat lot of good that did him,* she scowled. Tom had been Hargreaves' favourite pet. The man's mind went beyond what any computer could do. He could balance probabilities and cause and effect damn near perfectly. He was an organisational powerhouse. *Except when it comes to unknown side effects for an experimental drug,* she thought bitterly, *he hadn't seen that coming.*

Hargreaves had had Tom under very close protection whenever the man wasn't with him. Katie wracked her memory, desperately trying to think where the human computer might have been hidden.

Her ability had become available again and the smoke was starting to catch in her lungs so she quietly moved out of her hiding place and crept to the door. It was now or never. She grabbed a piece of wood from a pile of broken pallets and used it to push the burning door aside to run through. Outside looked like something from a nightmare.

The moss that had been grown along the stone had been burned to ash which floated in the air, gradually being drawn towards the vents providing the area with circulation. In places the stone had been heated so much it had melted and run down the walls in rivulets. The corridor was lit by the eerie glow of semi molten rock. To her left, where she had intended to go, was a man half fused into the wall, the stone had grown out around him and crushed his lower body as it dragged him in to a terminal embrace. His upper body hung, folded down over the stone encasing him and splatters of blood had run from his mouth as he coughed out his last breath.

Across from him and a little further into the complex lay a burned body, impossible to tell what sex or age, the legs were intact enough to tell it had once been human but that was it. The man entombed in the wall must have used fire to turn half the corridor to lava, the heat was making her eyes sting from several metres away. Unfortunately this meant the corridor was now impassable. Even with time stopped she would burn if she tried to go deeper into the complex, the ambient temperature in that area was simply too high for her to survive.

Reluctantly she made her way back. Creeping carefully along and listening to distant sounds of murder. The second blast door she had passed had been wrenched out of place, the stone having flowed to push the door and its fittings to one side, creating a narrow gap. She moved close and peeked through before jumping back to dry heave as quietly as she could. What was left of the people she had passed barely a minute ago had been spread across the floor. Hands of stone had ripped people apart, invisible blades of air or force had sliced and diced. Patches of stone ran with the heat left from otherworldly fires and everywhere there was blood.

She steeled herself and moved past, avoiding the splatters and parts as much as she could. When she entered the corridor back to the cafeteria she focussed all her senses as she slipped quietly closer to where she had begun. The hopelessness of her situation was not lost on her but she took a firm hold of her emotions and focussed on getting to Tom and getting him to the Carnival. The first blast door had also been removed, deformed by some great force and partially melted. She stepped gingerly past the still glowing metal and began to run. She could still hear screams and laughter but they seemed to be moving further away from her.

The cafeteria was the command centre writ large. Chunks of the ceiling had been pulled down to leave limbs sticking out of the rubble with crushed bodies beneath. All she saw was death. She moved to the door and peeked through the window into the corridor outside. She flinched back, a man with half his face burned away to the bone had been looking right at her from two feet away and as he began to howl she froze time. She ran into the Underground, no longer worrying about Tom or reaching the Carnival, she was only searching for a place to survive this insanity.

Chapter 49 - Take your reality and shove it

John and Stu appeared in the team's living room after escaping from the enraged cyclops and collapsed into empty chairs. Evie was busy moving from person to person handing out high fives until she got to Bob and became very solemn.

"Bob, Doris- Doris was awesome. She went out like a *true* legend. A queen of the silver screen. She will be missed but never forgotten. I'm so sorry. RIP in pepperoni, Doris," the little girl bowed her head.

Bob glanced up at her from where he was stretched out on a settee, recovering from being disconnected from the mecha via teleportation.

"What are you on about, child? I'll just rebuild her."

"But you lost your factory? Doris is melted around a giant freak buried under tons of hardened stone. I melted her, so I would know! Sorry about that by the way," said Evie sadly. She thought for a moment and then added, "Just to be clear though, Dad then dropped a massive rock through her back so it isn't all my fault! I know it's hard to accept but you have to face reality, old man."

"Take your reality and shove it, girl. The factory's fine. I've just re-tasked it to begin building new components for Doris MKII. Gonna go with autonomous mini drones that can combine to make a full mecha if needed."

"Like mini lion bots coming together to form a super lion bot?" asked Evie in wonder.

"Who the hell mentioned lions? They'll be autonomous units, about the size of your head but less empty."

"You, Bob, are awesome," said Evie, too excited to react to the insult. "Can we call the mark two… Doristron?"

"No we bloody can't. God, my head hurts, getting yanked out while running her directly has some serious side effects. John, that bottle in the drawer in my office… fancy bringing it over? We, all those over eighteen anyway," Evie scowled and Bob grinned, painfully, "deserve a tipple."

John reached out and found he still had access to the stash so did as Bob asked. He summoned a smoke and lit up, despite the disapproving looks he received. One of the worst things for John about being trapped underground had been the limited access to nicotine but right now he felt he deserved a smoke. The older man poured out glasses for everyone and they raised them in a quiet toast. Evie grumbled at being given orange juice but raised her glass with the rest.

"It isn't dead. How long do we think it will take to suffocate down there?" asked Sam.

"Dunno. Anywhere from two to twelve hours was the best guess Doris, may she rest in pieces, could come up with. Not exactly specific I admit but we were 98% sure the damn thing needs to breathe so it's just a matter of time." He took a long swig from his glass before it slipped from his hand and fell to the ground. "Oh shit." Bob waved his hand and the screen behind flicked from an external drone view circling the distraught giants who still couldn't find their friend to something else.

The screen showed people flinging their abilities around with wild abandon. People were blown apart, crushed beneath rocks pulled from the ceiling and punched into literal pieces before their eyes.

"What the hell is going on Bob?" asked Victoria.

"No bloody ide- shit. Hold on." A series of hisses and crashes sounded out through the walls. "Some dickhead added something to the air. I've sealed us off and got us on a separate ventilation system.

Same with the kids and oldies next door but they've been breathing in whatever that shit is for most of an hour. Do not say anything to upset them for a few hours would be my advice. It's some sort of hallucinogen from the look of what's going on in the main sections. The kids are currently watching an old Disney film for the little ones and have no idea what's going on. I've sealed them off from any other feeds and begun clearing out their air."

"Disney on magic acid? That's going to be a rough trip. I'd like to repeat the question though please. What the hell is going on?" said John, his voice rising as he saw more and more people dying.

Update:
Survivors: 273
Cyclopean Monstrosities: 10

"Christ, over a hundred people are dead!" yelled Sam.

"Damnit, look at this." A window popped out on the screen, thankfully reducing the image of the carnage in the cafeteria to a corner, and they watched as Geraldine gave her speech and took her final, desperate act.

Evie spun away from the screen and threw up. John moved to catch her hair and pat her back. He had to settle for just holding her hair back.

"That is what set them off like this?" asked Raoul, pale faced. Stu got up and ran for the nearest toilet.

Team member Pause Button wants to donate 229 Essence to you. Accept Y/N?
TeamChat:
Houdini: Katie, what the hell is going on?
Pause Button: Hargreaves is dead. Greg and I are free again. Take the Essence, I don't think I'll be able to make it out. Better to have it and not need it right?

Pyro: What's happened Katie?
Corpsicle: Katie and I were subject to one of Hargreaves abilities. It bound us to his will. He is gone and we are now free. You are aware of how he harvested those who fell on the first day of the siege courtesy of poor Geraldine.
Team member Corpsicle wants to donate 201 Essence to you. Accept Y/N?
TeamChat:
Houdini: Why are you offering me your Essence?
Pause Button: Take it. If we can escape we'll find you. It isn't likely though. I'm not sure I'm safe to be around now. I've done things in the last few minutes. And I enjoyed them.
Corpsicle: The Majority have forsaken me. They screamed in my mind but I could not respond to them as I should have. I am deep in the dark where I shall remain for now. Take the Essence John.
Houdini: Share your locations! I can port you out!
Pause Button: I did things John. Unforgivable things. The gas is getting to me. Take the fucking Essence!

John accepted the essence from each of them.

TeamChat:
Pause Button: Good choice John. No point letting it go to waste. Hargreaves put something in the air, Bob. Something a chemist cooked up to sedate the Cyclops.
Shinji: I know. I've switched us to a different system. We all got a mild dose.
Corpsicle: If I survive I hope you will forgive me.
Corpsicle has left the team.
Pause Button: Watch out for people with mind control powers guys. They are dangerous and seem to be dicks. It was fun for an

apocalypse and I'm sorry it worked out this way. Find my kids will you? Make sure they are ok. Look after them for me.
Pause Button has left the team.

The rest of them stood stunned as the screen resumed showing the slaughter as the enraged people turned on each other after killing Hargreaves and the other Councillors.

"Bob, can you lock us down? Keep them out?" asked Vic, turning to stare at Bob's ghostly pale face.

"I can slow them down but a bunch of them are earth mover types. They can dig right round the blast doors." His left eye flickered as he accessed more camera and drone feeds. "No joy anyway. Someone has been messing with my control codes. Must have had a programmer working on it in the background. Stu, can you collapse the stone in the corridor outside and reinforce it? Where the hell is Stu?"

"Can't we help any of them? Port them out somewhere?" asked Evie, wiping her mouth.

"Could send them to the surface but that isn't really a good idea. Can we send them to the stash?" asked John.

"And have them trash the factory? Fecking stupid idea," Reg chose to interject at last.

"Can't the arms grab them and restrain them until it passes? Sedate them maybe?" suggested Sam.

"They're all hopped up on whatever was in the air and they've all got magic powers. Could try but if they trash the place we are *all* buggered. I've got a secret stash in there that I didn't share and we *need* the factory."

"I don't think we need to worry about your whiskey collection right now, Bob! We need to do something!" Sam yelled.

"It ain't whiskey girl," Bob looked at Sam sadly. "Food, water, materials, some booze sure but mostly it's basic supplies for us all for a few months. John isn't the only one who learned to be a bit paranoid and keep a private reserve. Being in the army and dealing with quartermasters makes you a bit of a pack rat if you've half a brain. Duct tape is worth more than bullets most of the time."

"Shit! Is there anything we can do?" asked Raoul.

"I'm purging the tainted air. But they're killing each other so fast I don't think there'll be many left by the end."

"Why not drop the oxygen levels? Make them all pass out?" The big guy suggested.

"I'm cut out of the system, man! They're wrecking the air ducts anyway, look. Anyone who survives is probably going to suffocate."

"Any way to track Katie and Greg? We could send Zeeg and then port them out. They were slaves!" said Sam.

Bob gestured and a schematic of the tunnel system appeared. As the crowd surged through the tunnels they were destroying vital nodes, air exchangers, power hubs, and gradually more and more of the infrastructure of the Underground was going dark on his map.

"I can't track anyone specifically. I'm just watching bits of the network go offline to gauge where people are. I've got a few cameras I can still use. We need to block off access to this bit of the tunnel system. John, can you and Stu block off the corridors? Port in some of your big rocks and then Stu welds them in place? They're mostly moving away from us but some of them are coming our way."

John went and fished Stu out of the toilet where he had run to vomit. They moved outside and did as Bob suggested. Making sure the corridors allowing access to themselves and the old folks and kids were completely sealed off before heading back in.

Update:
Survivors: 136
Cyclopean Monstrosities: 10

Stu collapsed onto a settee and took a long pull of whiskey. "What the fuck is going on?" he asked faintly.

"Hargreaves thought he was a clever bastard and fucked up is what," said John coldly. He had moved to stand by Evie and rested a hand on her shoulder. Vic came up and stood next to them, a hand around John's back. They stared at the screen, unable to look away.

"They're at the barricade you built. Might need to go fight them off. Just port them back into a store room or something?" muttered Bob, "Ah nevermind, they've bounced off the stuff you piled up. They're heading back into the deeper sections. They're feral now I think, not much going on upstairs. Like angry magic zombies for god's sake. What the hell was that stuff he put in the air?"

Update:

Survivors: 83

Cyclopean Monstrosities: 10

They sat in tense silence watching the display Bob put on the screen showing the systems of the Underground being destroyed by the rampaging mob. The damage had spread out from the cafeteria in a red wave. Within ten minutes half the Underground had broken systems and failing ventilation. Any who survived the madness would be trapped and would likely suffocate by the morning, depending how large the pocket they were trapped in was.

"I'm getting back into some of the cameras. Hargreaves secretly had the whole place wired. It's pretty bad. Earth movers are pulling down walls to- catch people and then they're trapped with their former friends. They are ripping each other apart till no one is left," Bob said in a broken voice.

"Why the hell did that mad bastard do this?" asked Sam, tears streaming down her face.

"He didn't mean to. He just wanted power and it's backfired. He wanted to be king of the castle and now he's brought it all down around him," said John softly.

"We'll need to act fast if we're going to save anyone once this shit wears off. I've got the factory putting together some oxygen packs we can port in. Does Zeeg need to breathe in her ghost form?" Bob asked.

The dog woofed in a somehow negative fashion.

"How long do you think it will take? For them to come down or whatever?" asked Raoul quietly.

"Who knows? Maybe they never will. People who take too much LSD can get hung up, kind of permanently half high for the rest of their miserable lives," said Bob sadly.

"We still haven't even killed one of those things and most of us are dead," said Evie quietly. "Is this a normal siege?" She looked up at her dad.

"No kid, it's not normal. We built the walls, dug the tunnels. How were we to know we'd trapped ourselves in with the more dangerous enemy?"

Bob continued to monitor the readouts. A couple of cameras had survived in rooms where one of the people had ended up alone. They were usually surrounded by the dead bodies of the victims of their madness but Bob was monitoring for any sign the drug was losing effect and some rescue attempt could be made. After two hours none of them had stopped howling and smashing at the walls with their fists nor showed any signs of slowing down.

Update:
Survivors: 67
Cyclopean Monstrosities: 9

Team report: 1 Cyclopean Monstrosities killed. 200 essence per kill.
200 Essence gained per team member.

Even buried deep underground they heard the wails of grief as the Cyclops mourned their loss. None of them paid the monsters any attention at all.

Chapter 50 - The predators to be feared all had saurian smiles

After some debate the team decided to leave the elderly and kids next door overnight, to come down off the stuff that had been added to the air. They hadn't had as large a dose as the crowd in the cafeteria, none of whom showed any signs of returning to normal yet. Bob threw up a warning message on the screen next door when the film finished. They were told there was a temporary issue with the security systems and their door would be locked until the system could be fixed. Food and water would be teleported in and everything should be working again in the morning.

As morning came John felt a sharp pang of loss over Katie. Whatever she had done, John found he would rather not know the details so he could preserve his memories of his friend; she had been forced to act against her will. John resolved to take her final message to heart and find her kids for her. The victims of Hargreaves gas were still raging in their tiny boxes but only a handful remained alive. They would likely suffocate and soon become sluggish and lethargic before succumbing to lack of oxygen. Their own last victims would be themselves.

The team opened the door to the room with the children and old folks and went in carefully. The feed from the camera, it turned out Hargreaves had all the living accommodation bugged as well, had showed them acting normally, if a little befuddled. Elizabeth bustled over and demanded an explanation as soon as she saw John.

"Are you all feeling ok, Elizabeth?" He asked first.

"Feels like I had a night on the town yesterday, like I used to do in my youth but otherwise I'm fine, thank you. Now young man, what's going on?"

"There was a problem yesterday with the air supply."

"What sort of *problem*?" the old lady asked sharply.

"The air- there was a leak of a chemical agent. Deliberately leaked. It was meant to calm people down but everyone reacted badly. I think it might have interacted with what the system has done to our emotions? People lost their tempers very badly at the meeting yesterday."

"What happened?" she asked softly, sensing his thinly veiled misery.

"A lot of people died. I guess no one has checked the update? There… there aren't many of us left now."

Her eyes glazed over as she checked the update and the colour drained from her face.

"Who?"

"Who what, sorry?

"Who did this?"

"Hargreaves. He had the gas introduced to try and control everyone at the gathering while they watched our hit on the giant. Then they were angry it hadn't died straight away and Geraldine confessed to some things Hargreaves had made her do and everyone just… went crazy. They went for Hargreaves first but when he was dead they started killing each other."

"Jesus. I'll- I'll talk to the rest. Let them have some breakfast before we break this to them. Leave it with me. You're terrible at this kind of thing," she smiled sadly at him. "Now you've got one of the things up top, what are you going to do?"

"I'll need to talk to the team. I'm not sure we can pull off the same thing again. They might not be savvy tacticians but they are intelligent. We'll leave you be… To break it to the rest. Some of the kids who weren't orphans, well now they are. It won't be easy," he finished in a whisper, eyes on the ground.

"We'll manage, young man. I was only a little girl at the time but I survived the Blitz and that was a bad time indeed. Leave it with me," she patted his cheek like the friendly grandma he knew she wasn't and turned away to organise feeding the children.

The team beat a retreat and sat in their room, contemplating the future.

"Well this sucks. We'd just gotten a break and then it all went to shit," grumbled Raoul.

"That prick, I hope he died slowly," said Victoria with venom in her voice. "What was he thinking?"

"I've been wondering… what if the system's messing with our emotions affects some of us differently? Like, it depends on your starting frame of mind or your… I don't know personality type or something," said John.

"Are you going to start talking about a dark triad or some shit like that?" asked Raoul. "I hate those pricks on YouTube."

"No, I just don't know the right language to explain what I'm thinking! Maybe the impact is different on some of us though. Maybe Hargreaves was a psychopath from the start?" he shrugged. "I had a panic attack at the start of the first wave but you guys were all fine. I was more upset about what I did to Jac and his crew than most of you. Except Katie I guess!" he laughed sadly. "I'm not sure she was angry about what happened because it was the wrong thing to do or it was evil or whatever. I think she was mad because it made the political situation more complicated. Had Hargreaves already hacked her mind at that point do you think?"

"She started changing after that first meeting with him I think," chimed Evie. "I wish… I could have apologised for being so hard on her. At the end."

"She understood Sausage, I'm sure. Maybe… maybe that drug interacted with whatever the system is doing to our heads and it was like flipping a switch when they heard Geraldine's speech. Or it dumped all the emotions that are being kept from us or boosted the emotions it pushes to 'enhance' our survival chances. Maybe it was just angry scared people who were secretly drugged flipping out? If you know you're on something you kind of watch yourself, you know? Especially when you're in public. If you've no idea you just think it's normal and act like a lunatic."

"I hate it when you get philosophical John. You're not very good at it," said Sam, Victoria nodded. "The odds are we'll never know for sure. Whatever it was, we need to figure out what to do with those assholes." She pointed upwards. "And then try to save anyone still alive. Once the big guys, not you Raoul, are gone we can dump anyone who made it through the night on the surface and try to keep them apart."

"Ah, dealing with the big twats, that's easy lass," said Reg. "The sassenach," he waved at John, "got a load of Essence from the traitors." He received angry looks from everyone. "The folks Hargreaves took over," he corrected. "We just boost him up to level sixteen and he can chop 'em up. They can't heal if they're in fecking bits falling out o' the sky."

"That should work actually," said Bob thoughtfully. "How much Essence have you got?"

John checked his status and said "849."

"And you'd need…" Bob's left eye flickered as he consulted the computers he linked to in Doris' stash. "2351 to get to level sixteen and be able to use your ability directly on the things… 1501 Essence. Right then, let's pass the hat around shall we?" John received the Essence he needed and for the first time in a while thought *Level Up*.

You have chosen to spend 2351 Essence and advance 16. Levelling in process...

You have chosen to level Ability X5
New Status for John Borrows:
Level: 16
Name: John Borrows
Ability: Teleportation
Constitution: 100%
Reserves: 100
Ability: Teleportation.
A shut in who hates to travel. You've barely left your house for years and now you can go wherever you like at a thought. Have fun with that.
Guidelines:
Maximum weight: 45000 kg
Maximum Distance: 1650 km
Modifications:
Level 2: How about we split the difference?
Level 3: Weight limit x5
Level 4: Portion control.
Level 5: Maximum Weight X5
Level 6: Maximum Distance X3
Level 7: Reserve Regeneration rate X5 (base regen 25% per minute)
Level 8: Where did I leave my keys?
Level 9: Maximum Distance X3
Level 10: Maximum Distance X5
Level 11: Maximum Weight X3
Level 12: Maximum Weight X2
Level 13: Maximum Distance X5
Level 14: Maximum Distance X2
Level 15: Maximum Weight X3

Level 16: Maximum Distance X3
Bonus Modification:
Third Party Logistics: You can designate an area within the barrier and it will become a transport hub. For 80% of your reserves you can open a stable portal from anywhere back to this location which will remain active unless you choose to close it.

Okay. 4.5 tons going 165 km is 0.2 reserves? I've said from the start this system is insane. I guess it will be the same for everyone who makes it to this level. When everyone is crazy OP it's basically just the same as before but way more dangerous? So very much not the same. Get your head straight dude.

"Well Stu. There's no rush right now mate but I'm going to need you to build me some much bigger obelisks. In fact I think we are past "obelisk" territory and into monoliths. Is that the step beyond obelisks? I'm not sure," John said slightly giddily.

"How big are we talking?" asked Bob, no doubt calculating Doris MKIIs weight allowances.

"Max weight is 45 tons, distance is now 1650 km."

Bob whistled. "That's half of northern Europe! Or close enough. And two thirds the weight of a Challenger 3! And you can set up your town portals… I think you just put every freight haulier out of business. You could go round the world in less than a day and establish pretty much instant travel from Kyoto to New York and everywhere in between!"

"You want me to make you 45 ton rocks to drop on things? Wouldn't that look like a nuke going off?" asked Stu.

"Dammit! I wanted to be the first to get a literal nuke!" muttered Evie.

"I think when you guys catch up you'll all be equally over powered. Assuming we survive round three of course. Now I suppose I'd better go chop those giant pains-in-the-arses up into little bits and we'll do what we can to save those poor buggers trapped below who aren't dead yet. Are they, you know, calming down at all?" Bob shook his head, John sighed and left to finish the wave.

John and Zeeg appeared a short distance away from the grieving giants. Zeeg disappeared from sight. She moved away to watch and allow the team to watch through her.

The beasts had all stayed together, they seemed to be mourning their lost brother which was disturbing in its own right. The rats had clearly not been sentient, with the possible exception of the Queen but these Cyclops had demonstrated language and emotions that showed they were probably due the same respect as humans in John's mind. Were these real creatures the system dragged here from some distant corner of the universe or just simulacra that had retained the appearance of intelligence when the system created them?

John lit up a smoke and sighed. He guessed it didn't matter one way or the other. They had to die so what was left of his town could live. So he had to kill them. God, he needed a stiff drink already and it was only nine thirty. Tea would not cut it.

The nearest of them turned, saw him and then roared. The others quickly took up the cry and charged towards him. They crossed the short distance terrifyingly quickly on their long misshapen legs. As they neared him and drew back fists to crush him to powder they disappeared in chunks. Arms first, then legs, then heads and finally the torsos were gone. A hundred kilometres straight up.

He sat on the shattered trunk of a tree the giants had destroyed in their fury and continued to smoke. Zeeg reappeared next to him and he gave her a fuss, tickling behind her ears as he waited for the notification. He had smoked three cigarettes and drank half a can of beer when the message finally arrived.

Team report:

9 Cyclopean Monstrosities killed. 200 essence per kill. Essence gained 1800.
1 Harmless Seagull killed. 0.05 Essence per kill. Essence gained 0.05.
Total essence gained: 1800.05.
The second wave has been completed.

Survivors: 67
Cyclopean Monstrosities: 0
Average Level of human survivors: level 3
Congratulations! You have survived the Siege Wave. To be under siege is to be trapped with limited resources but that can take many forms as you have learned. In the future you will no doubt look back on this trial and be thankful for the strength of character you have gained from it.

"Just like Steven Segal. Where the hell did I get the seagull kill from?" John said, putting out his cigarette and patting Zeeg on the head.

"One of the frozen pieces of the Cyclops hit the bird as it fell into the sea off to the west. It was Gruthnik's, the biggest one's, left leg. You did send them most of the way into orbit when you moved them. It would have been near instant death to a human but the Cyclops are hardy beings. I thought you'd manage to keep a few more of your people alive than that but it was hardly your doing they all died. Overall a good performance. I have abused my authority a little and removed the survivors from your now collapsed Underground to the rooms you managed to seal off from the lunatics. I have calmed them somewhat so they are no longer dangerous. Although the after effects of the compound they were exposed to will linger for many weeks I'm afraid. They are all watching us now." A voice from behind him boomed. The golden reptilian was the same size as John this time round. **"The names Fasshtal, my rank is Overseer of the Waves. Well that's the short version that you have words for anyway. My kind has been in the system for a long time. The start is rough, as you've noticed, but it's good training for what's to come. Very rare for the average rank to drop after the second wave though. I'm sure when you all level up and share out the extra Essence it will jump a bit."**

"You seem far more agreeable this time. No nasty lectures or threats?" John asked in a neutral voice. John felt that being cautious with this strange creature of the system was by far the most sensible option. He wasn't scared, so he told himself, but best to err on the side of caution. Deep inside his anger at what had happened to his town threatened to bubble over but he fought it down.

"Just after the cull, the first wave, isn't the time to be gentle with recruits. The cull weeds out the stupid, the lazy and the unlucky." it shot John a glance, **"Mostly. Can't believe you actually died and came back. That's a first as far as I know and I've been around for hundreds of thousands of years. Still I suppose in a way the system worked, you must be an extremely fortunate example of your species. Were you a powerful man before the system?"**

"Just a single dad working a desk job dude. Bit of a nerd. Not special at all, except to those who cared about me I guess," he said sadly.

"Could I trouble you for one of those?" Fasshtal asked as John summoned another cancer stick. John blipped in another and passed it to the golden lizard who put the smoke in its mouth where the cigarette immediately lit itself and the being drew in a cloud of smoke that John watched swirling inside it through its translucent golden skin.

"Thank you. You have done extremely well, you and your team. More by luck than design but you have preserved a nucleus of the population, the hatchlings in particular offer you hope for the future. Many places have not been so fortunate and it is not unusual for the whole species to be left with only fighting age adults by the end of the second wave. Often the weak and the young are killed very early on in the first. However it happened you have preserved both the wisdom of your elders and the possibilities of your youth, as have some other places on this planet, although not very many I'm afraid. More than the models predicted though," Fasshtal blew out a cloud of smoke.

"What was the point of the second wave? To try to make us into monsters as well?"

"Not at all, although I can see why you might think that after the actions of some of the survivors. Your friend Katie was very wise when she gave you the warning about people with powers of mental manipulation. Sometimes they are easy to spot like that Performing Artist the Organiser used. As soon as you realised what she was doing her power lost much of its potency against you. Sometimes however a harmless name hides a multitude of sins. Enslaving powers like Mr. Hargreaves had are very rare, if that makes any difference to you, but they usually do quite well unless they run up against monsters like you and your team early on."

"We are not the monsters here," John said, a touch of anger entering his voice.

"Ah but you could be. And at some point I'm afraid you probably will be." He blew out another cloud of smoke. "My people were warlike when the system came to us. But the fighting starts when we are born. Our eggs are left in pits, guarded from predators by adults but otherwise ignored. When we hatch the first thing we do is fight to escape the pit. Many die before seeing the sun but those that survive are the strongest and the luckiest. We are not loving parents to our children. All your cultures are much more gentle than my own and I find it fascinating to watch how your various peoples have approached the situation. You are struggling with the nature of your new reality a lot more than more aggressive species do but growing much faster than usual. The cyclops got almost no Essence from their work on your allies. As your species is very weak you will level relatively quickly but you won't be able to finish off your enemies through brute force, the tyranny of rank I think you called it? I like the concept but it doesn't always apply so be warned."

"Are you actually alive or some kind of projection from the system?"

"Somewhere out in the cosmos my body fights on for the Alliance, killing worlds the Void subsumes. What you see before you is a… something like an AI avatar would make sense to you I think? All that *I* am is a recording, I suppose, of Fasshtal Ah Nafruk, taken when we were at our prime."

"So what happens next Fasshtal Ah Nafruk?"

"Ah, now the fun part begins!" The lizard threw down his cigarette and gave John a grin that activated some part of his hind brain. It made him want to climb a tree or hide in a hole and keep very still. While humans and dinosaurs had never coexisted, something in the mammalian DNA remembered a time when it was small and defenceless and the predators to be feared all had saurian smiles.

Wave 3 begins immediately.

Royal Road

This story started and continues to be released on Royal Road. Thanks very much for reading! As an independent author my work lives or dies by ratings from noble souls! If you've enjoyed the story it would mean the world to me if you would take the time to leave me a rating or a review. If you liked the story and want to read ahead most of book two is available on Royal Road for free at the moment. It will be coming to KU in August and Book three is in progress. Book three should be available on KU around December if everything goes to plan. You can check out my website: www.cjmilnes.com for updates!
Thanks again for reading!

Printed in Great Britain
by Amazon